Elizabeth Jane Oswald

By Fell and Fjord

Scenes and studies in Iceland

Elizabeth Jane Oswald

By Fell and Fjord
Scenes and studies in Iceland

ISBN/EAN: 9783337316082

Printed in Europe, USA, Canada, Australia, Japan

Cover: Foto ©Andreas Hilbeck / pixelio.de

More available books at **www.hansebooks.com**

BY FELL AND FJORD

OR

SCENES AND STUDIES
IN ICELAND

BY

E. J. OSWALD

WITH ILLUSTRATIONS

WILLIAM BLACKWOOD AND SONS
EDINBURGH AND LONDON
MDCCCLXXXII

PREFACE.

This little book is a record of travels in Iceland, of which the pleasure was greatly enhanced by the saga-lore previously acquired, and the legends gathered by the wayside. I am not aware that any other book about Iceland has taken the special line that I have attempted to follow in mine— the connection of the land with the sagas; and it may therefore assist some of the tourists who now visit the island in increasing numbers to enter more into its peculiar charm of local legend and past literature.

These journeys, made in three different years, were full of enjoyment, which increased with the knowledge of the language, and larger acquaintance with the Icelanders themselves. For much true kindness and hospitality, to which I cannot here do full justice, I take this opportunity of thanking my many friends in the island.

Some chapters relating to our first journey have already appeared in 'Good Words.' The illustrations are woodcuts, or reproductions of pen-and-ink outlines, from my water-colour sketches; and although they have lost with the colour any attractiveness the originals may possess, it is hoped that they may serve to explain the letterpress.

NOTE.

A few Icelandic words are used without translation, as—

á (pronounce as *ow* in prow), river—as Thjorsá, Thors river; Ellidá, Ellid river.

Bondí, yeoman, peasant proprietor, but often used of the head of a family even when not a landowner; hence our word husband—*i.e.*, hus-bond.

Bœ (pronounce *by*), dwelling.

Fjall, fell, mountain.

Jökull, glacier.

Prestr, priest or clergyman.

Tun, enclosed grass-land round a farm, equivalent to the Scottish *toun*.

Vellir, valley.

Icelandic is pronounced as written, with Italian vowel-sounds, besides others peculiar to itself. The consonant *Thorn*, or *th* English, and the soft modification of the *d*, which is pronounced *dh*, both represented by different characters in Icelandic, are here printed *th* and *d*, not to confuse the page.

CONTENTS.

CHAP.   PAGE

I. WHY WE GO THERE, ... 1

II. ON THE WAY THERE—FARÖE ISLANDS, . . 4

III. REYKJAVIK AND THE PONIES, ... 13

IV. GEYSIR, ... 20

V. LOCAL ORIGIN OF ICELANDIC LITERATURE—FORMS OF
SAGAS, ... 34

VI. 'LANDNÁMABÓK'—THE 'EDDAS'—STURLUNGA—WOMEN
OF THE SAGAS—SAINTS—BIOGRAPHIES—MORALITY—
MODERN LITERATURE, ... 41

VII. MOSSFELL—HVALFJORD AND ITS LEGENDS—REYKHOLT
—KALMANSTUNGA—CENTRAL LAVA—SURTSHELLIR, . 58

VIII. NORDTUNGA — BORGASYSLU — HOLTVÖRDSHEIDE — THE
NORTHERN COAST, ... 77

IX. FISHING IN ICELAND—LAXDALE AND ITS SAGAS—
KVENNA-BREKKA — BLÁSKOGÁEHEIDA — BACK TO
THINGVELLIR, ... 91

X. RECENT MISFORTUNES IN ICELAND—TRADE—NEW CON-
STITUTION—PASTORAL WEALTH—CONDITION OF THE
PEOPLE, ... 106

XI. HOUSEKEEPING — DINNERS — OUR PARTY — SOCIETY—
MANNERS—LANGUAGE, ... 114

XII. KRISUVIK—SULPHUR-MINES, ... 122

XIII. VATNSLEYSI — KIRKJUVOGR AND REYKJANES — AURORA
—HOME AGAIN—HINTS TO TRAVELLERS, . . 127

XIV. A JOURNEY IN 1878—ULFJLOTSVATN—GEYSIR, ANOTHER
ERUPTION — GULLFOSS — HUNI — THJORSÀ — STORU-
VELLIR, ... 138

XV. HECLA—NEW VOLCANOES—KIRKJUBAE—FLJOTSLID, . , 149

XVI. MARKARFLJOT RIVER — THORSMARK — FLOODS AND
FORDS, ... 157

XVII. OVER MARKARFLJOT—NJAL'S COUNTRY—FLOA—EYRA-
BAKKI—TO REYKJAVIK, ... 169

XVIII. HVALFJORD—BORGARFJORD, ... 178

XIX. EGIL AT BORGARFJORD, ... 185

XX. STAFHOLT — REYKHOLT — SNORRI STURLASON AND HIS
FATE—GILSBAKKI—PASS OF OK—BENIGHTED, . 196

XXI. THINGVELLIR IN FORMER DAYS — THE TALK OF THE
MAIDENS — SOLITUDES — BESSERSTAD — DOGS—KRISU-
VIK—HOME AGAIN, ... 206

XXII. FARÖES—TO AKUREYREI—STEINSTADR—OVER OXNADAL
HEATH — MIKLABÆ AND ITS GHOST—SORCERERS —
HIDDEN TREASURES—THE SPECTRE LOVER, . . 222

XXIII. CHURCH SERVICES—CLERGY—MAGISTRATES—DRINK IN
ICELAND AND NORWAY—TOBACCO—BEAUTY, . . 238

XXIV. TO BAKKASTADR—TO THE HUNAFJORD—THINGEYRI—
VATZDALE, ... 247

XXV. LEGENDS OF VATZDALE—INGMUNDR THE OLD—HAL-
FRED THE SKALD, ... 255

XXVI. OVER GRIMSTUNGAHEIDE TO KALMUNSTUNGA—VARMA-
LEIK—BENIGHTED—MOSSFELL, ... 264

XXVII. EXCURSION TO REYKJADAL AND EYRABAKKI, . . 276

BY FELL AND FJORD.

CHAPTER I.

VERY year a few people go now to Iceland for their summer holidays; they are generally drawn there by one of three attractions—the fishing, the geology, or the old literature. It was the literature that brought me—the vivid Sagas which set the men and women of the past before us as if we had known them ourselves, "offering the truth of them," to quote Carlyle, "as if seen in their real lineaments by some marvellous opening across the black strata of the ages." Then there is the language, a dead one now in its old Norwegian home, but the living speech in Iceland still, giving the island the sort of interest for the student of old Norse that classical scholars would feel if some lonely island could be found where the Greek of Pericles or the Latin of Augustus was still the common speech. All this had for years invested Iceland in my mind with such a halo of romance, that it is high praise of the country to say that the reality proved equal to the expectation.

A

As to the other attractions—and perhaps those who have not a good working enthusiasm for at least one of the three, should avoid Iceland—the salmon and trout fishing is sometimes very good. It is said to have fallen off of late, especially in dry seasons, though it was excellent again last year (1881). But it will soon deteriorate unless the Icelanders are roused to the necessity of preserving better, attending to close seasons, and checking the take of fish in boxes and stake-nets at the mouths of some of the rivers. There is amusing bird-shooting for those who like to go over a great deal of ground, and do not care to make big bags. There is, however, no ground game, and no large game except reindeer, which are exceedingly difficult to kill.

Now for the third attraction. Intending travellers often ask if there is fine scenery in Iceland. Yes, emphatically, for geologists; but as regards others, it is difficult to say, for in more than most cases the answer depends on taste. There will be time on the voyage to appreciate the spirit of the bold mariners who first crossed these waves, without charts or compass, guided only by their brave instincts and the midnight stars, and to realise what pluck and manhood is inferred by their choice of a home. The modern Icelanders have ratified that choice. They love their island, but it seems wonderful that they dare to stay in that volcanic waste, north of the forests, north of the corn, where only the hardy grasses clothe a fraction of the soil, —a little handful of people in constant battle with the elements. How can they face the separation of that stormy sea, the solitude of the winter, the darkness, the cruel frosts, the terrible tempests? Those first settlers who chose the land were men indeed—they feared none of these things if they had but liberty; and the stories of their voyages and wars, their home-life and conversations, show them as above all strong—*skorungr*, they are constantly styled, a word meaning stirring, dominant, or high-spirited. Defying the rude weather, the wild country, and each other, they lived their lives thoroughly, even brilliantly and gaily; they could not afford, like the people of the South, to rest and dream, and thus tend to become indolent and corrupt.

Even the passing traveller shares something of that cheery defiance of grim surroundings as he rides along the almost trackless ways that have yet been trodden by so many generations. And the scenery, though often far from beautiful, and sometimes downright ugly, is at least exciting and singular, and full of interest to geologists. There are valleys to be traversed, many miles long, all marsh-lands ; there are mountains to be crossed, destitute of any scrap of wholesome vegetation, with only occasional patches of moss of an unnaturally vivid green to accentuate the dark colours of the background; there are stretches of country, all black fissured lava, as far as the eye can see ; there are cold black bogs, and hot blue bogs, ice-laden rivers, and boiling streams. All this is not pretty, but it is stimulating. There is something more sad and pathetic in the scenery the Icelanders themselves most admire. The smooth patches of cultivated meadow-land, the little lonely houses in the wilderness of marsh-land or barren hills, the gardens where a few vegetables and hardy flowers are tenderly shielded from the storms, the sheepfolds by the farms, the stir of human life round the homesteads, the simple industries surrounded by the outside formless chaos. But the scenery is in some parts truly beautiful, in the grand blending of mountain and sea views up the fjords : and the sun, which in the South is sometimes an enemy, in the North is always a friend. All the long summer day it causes the wild landscape to pass from charm to charm ; everything rejoices in the perpetual sunshine ; the air is crystal clear, the colouring intense beyond description. No wonder that Frey was a favourite deity here in old days ; no wonder that they praised the sun in Iceland—

" Oh Frey in the North lands,
    Thou sweetest of powers,
Thy breath on the mountains
    Turns ice into flowers.
Thy smile on the meadows
    Is life to the fold,
Thy touch on the maid's hair
    Turns flaxen to gold.

Oh Frey in the South lands,
    How dread is thine ire !
Thou lord of the death-bow,
    Thine arrows are fire.
Thy light touch is madness,
    Thy warm kiss is death,
Thy smile on the marshes
    The pestilence' breath."

CHAPTER II.

EARLY in June 1875 we sailed from Leith on a Wednesday at noon, for the first time bound for Iceland. My friend and I were full of joyous anticipations as we slipped down the Firth of Forth in an oily calm. . Let those hardy mariners who are used to the " roaring forties," and know all the humours of the sea in long voyages, excuse us for writing down some of the details of our little voyage ; for, though not the most unpleasant, it was the worst we ever had. Happily ours is not a common experience on this passage.

All through the first night the calm lasted, though I did not like the look of the weather, the white light, the occasional fitful puffs that wrinkled the sea, and the thickness that gathered and grew around us.

We were ten passengers, English and Icelanders, in the little steamer, only about 250 tons burden. She has now laid her iron bones somewhere in the sea, so no one need be warned against her more. None of the ship's company had ever been to Iceland before. We especially liked the Steward, who, though he was but a shrimp of a boy, with a sweet treble voice for singing, deserves a capital letter ; for as Steward, he was a grave and sharp official, and quite up to his business. By Thursday morning we were steaming up the Pentland Firth near the red wall of cliffs, up which the foam was beginning to spring, and flash ominously. The curious swirl of water that seems generally churning there was working more than usual, scuds of rain swept from the thick weather to the east, and heavier blasts of wind drove the seas up behind us, till by the time we had cleared the Orkneys, the decks were all swimming, and very dirty weather had set in. We ought, I believe, in prudence to have stopped at Thurso, or at least run past Faröe—for all could see that a south-easterly gale was brewing; but some Danes had previously bar-gained to be landed at Suderöe in Faröe, for a fabulous bribe, so away we toiled in search of this island.

On Friday it blew worse—no observations could be taken; but after dark we came upon shoaling water, and no doubt we had reached the southern point of the island. But there was no gleam of light in the sky, nor beacon on the land. Within the lighted cabin, which was rolling about as if a giant were using it as a dice-box, I watched the officers of the ship poring over the chart with anxious faces, and the lines of Allingham's sea-song ran dismally in my mind—

> " Now bring the chart, the doleful chart;
> See where these mountains meet—
> The clouds are thick around their head,
> The mists around their feet."

The captain said at last, " Well, though we have got hold of the land, I can't tell which side of the point we are on, so I shall just put her head to the sea."

It is very disagreeable to have her head put to butt at such a sea. How she shrieked and wrestled and tossed, as hour by hour the fury of the gale increased, and with it the " deaf'ning clamours," that still do not hinder sleep, till in the middle of the night a noise beyond noises roused me ! Something broke open the cuddy-door, and tore through into my little state cabin with a rush and a roar; a great wave had come in and filled the lower berth. After the wave came the captain, saying, " No danger, ladies and gentlemen—merely a blunder in the steering."

Then came two men with swabs and buckets and a light, showing me the black water swaying about, that never left my cabin-floor again. " Well, I call this labour in vain," said one.

"You wouldn't have her water-logged?" said the other. I fell into a not cheering conversation with one sailor who came from my own county. "You see, ma'am, she was built for the trade between Kirkcaldy and London, and you know what that is : she was never meant for these seas." And these words recurred in the grim grey early dawn, when I thought that the port-hole which opened into my berth ought surely to have had a dead-light ; it went under water at every roll for quite an appreciable time, leaving me in darkness, to which succeeded an awful view of grey mountain waves, with foam like a drifting snowstorm whizzing past—and this, too, in a deck cabin. It became too dreary, so I contrived to jump over the water in the cabin, and make a hasty toilet in the empty saloon. On looking out at the door, it seemed as if the waist of the ship was a river, rushing alternately to starboard and port, and foaming against the masts and hatchways. In front a tall grey wave rose above the bridge, and the steamer climbed straining up, and then rushed down into a shadowed valley on the other side. I turned away remarking, "And she was built for the trade between Kirkcaldy and London!" "And I wish we were trading there," said a sailor. However, the captain told me she was holding her own—which was something to know, whatever was her own. But it was sad to think that all this time we were going, if at all, the wrong way. They got a sort of observation out of a brighter spot in the clouds, as it seemed to me, and found we were sixty miles out of our course already ; but we could not put about, and were thankful for sea-room.

At night, when we did put about, we were duly warned, and yet, in spite of all precautions, I was jerked off the sofa on the transom, where I had taken refuge from my flooded cabin. But when we had a course our spirits rose, and all seemed pleasant ; we admired the great rollers, called here Spanish waves, and contrived to laugh at our numerous discomforts, except on that fatal day when the salt water leapt into both the tea and the soup. Our meals were like games at ball ; for in spite of guards and fiddles, everything was flying. The swinging tray swung things off. Soup or tea had not a chance except in the hand ;

bottles were only safe in the pocket; and meat slipped off the dishes.

There were occasional rifts of blue in the stormy clouds when we sighted to the south-east the gaunt blue precipices of the southern Faröes. The islands rose in stupendous cliffs, their steadfast lines contrasting grandly with the changing undulating billows which broke high on their sides. We advanced between two mountain-chains, separated by a stormy gulf, where rose the two great rocks called Store and Lille Dimon. Store Dimon is a great resort of puffins—about 5000 are taken there annually. They say a basket of eggs can be let down straight from the top to the sea, 1500 feet below; and yet there are inhabitants, and a clergyman visits them once a-year. His flock pull him up by ropes, the only mode of access. On Lille Dimon there are only four-legged sheep.

The Faröese cliffs, though smooth below, are often fantastic above, broken into what the natives call *troll kona fingers* (troll wife's fingers) which our sailors call devil's thumbs. One such appeared at first like a gigantic black monk, with arms stretched out as if in blessing; but as we advanced he lost grace, and became huge, uncouth, and threatening—a good emblem of the Dominican order, which began with theological learning, and developed the Inquisition.

When we swung round the point into Hvalbae Bay on Suderöe, we were in the so-called garden of the Faröes. There was a little wooden village dotted irregularly over the steep shore, whence the mountain rose abruptly in grassy slopes to the basaltic cliffs above. There were waterfalls and little streams, and a few fields of rye. Here are coal-fields also, which our Danish passenger meant to work; but they lie inconveniently high up the hillside, unless, indeed, the coal could be lowered down the cliff straight to the sea. There were several fishing-smacks in the offing; and kindly-looking brown-clad inhabitants came down to welcome us. It all looked sweet and peaceful to us storm-tossed mariners, especially when lighted by a gleam of sun. We met some Kentish fishermen, however, who evidently did not admire the country. "Look at the apples and pears!" they said; "see the crops!" and then with sudden pathos, "Oh, ma'am, can you tell us, are the cherries ripe yet at home?" The captain allowed us one hour ashore; and an amiable man, who knew a little English, came forward, took us to his house, gave us coffee and Muscat wine and biscuits, showed us the tidy church and well-furnished store, and did the honours with a simple courtesy that quite

pleased us. This island is not without old romantic legends, many of which cluster round Sigmundur Brettisson, a real hero, a converted sea-king, who imposed Christianity on the islanders at the sword's point. After many adventures he was assaulted by some traitors in his castle, on an island about four miles out to sea; but he escaped through the sea caverns and swam all the way to this island, where, unluckily, he was found resting on the sea-weed by some thralls, who slew him for his golden bracelets. His story has lately been retold in a poem, written in a kind of modern Icelandic or archaic Danish which some Norwegians are trying to revive; a useless effort—for one may as well try to stop the current of a river as of a language.

It was very rough still when we steamed away to sea; but as we sat on the now dried quarter-deck, holding by a rope looped to the mast, we thoroughly enjoyed the sailing and the view of the islands till they sank behind the stormy horizon.

All went pleasantly on the following day; and the day after that, when I came on deck in the early morning, I found the sun was shining: the sea, though still high, was bright blue, and before us rose Iceland. There was a peculiar effect of largeness in the

view,—the sky was so transparent, and the land on such a big
scale that the whole scene was sublime in its simplicity, and
in the contrast between the driving Atlantic billows in the foreground, and the repose of the huge mountain-masses of 'eternal
ice and snow beyond. These mountains rose in long rounded
forms and shone with the glitter of ice: they formed part of
the great glacier system of
the Vatna and Oraefja Jökull.
As we drew nearer, the blue
shadow below the ice resolved
itself into high black cliffs half
veiled by the leaping foam of
the sea, while here and there
we could perceive the opening
of a dark-green valley leading
inland, and straight before us a

Faröe.

huge square rock called Ingolf's Head stood conspicuously outside a narrow bay. We were a good deal to the eastward of the
point usually first made, which was, however, very satisfactory to
those who had read the Sagas. *Ingolfshöfdi,* or Ingolf's Head,
was the first point of land sighted by Ingolf, the earliest settler
in the island, and it was there also that the gallant Kári, the
avenger of Burnt Njal, was wrecked close by the home of·Flosi
the Burner. Kári went up to his house, uncertain as to his recep-
tion; but although they had been for years occupied in killing
each other's relations, the claims of hospitality were paramount,
and from that day they became the best of friends.

The weather was clear and bright, and it was most enjoyable
coasting along the shore, past the great wastes of the Vatna
Jökull which even then were being ascended by the only persons
who have ever explored them—Mr Watts, a member of the
Alpine Club, and six Icelanders ; past the great arched rocks of
Dyrholar or Portland, and the cliffs under the Ejarfjall Jökull,
where we could see the waterfalls connecting the upper snows
with dark-green valleys, scattered here and there with mounds
like mole-hills, which we were told were houses. Towards

evening we passed the low lands where the Markerfljot river runs by several foaming channels into the sea—the scene of the Saga of Burnt Njal. On the other side the Westmanna Islands rose in huge square cliffs out of the sea, and beyond them whales were spouting. Meanwhile, as night drew on, the sky was again breaking into windy flaws; more water than usual came on deck, and the coast and the islands were lost in drift. The strong current that runs round Iceland met the sea and roused it into foam, and then the south-easter tore down upon us again.

It was like the Pastoral Symphony, — peasants dance, and shepherds pipe sweet music, till a few chords break it with threatening significance, then suddenly the storm-music rolls up terrible and overwhelming. The sea seemed to me quite unnatural, sloping slightly upwards on one side and downwards on the other till lost in scud; it was all tilted to one side rather than wavy, a slope that foamed like boiling water. We knew the point of Reykjanes headed us, and that beyond the fairway round it, a terrible line of reefs ran twenty miles out to sea—but we could see nothing. No sailor on board had ever been there before, and there are no lights on the coast, though if there had been, I believe we could not have seen them two miles off. We could, however, only go on as we were; we tried to lay to, but made very bad weather of that.

There was a little shelter from the projection of the quarter-deck at the cuddy-door, and there, clinging to an iron railing, it was interesting to watch the furious sea, and the sea-birds that wheeled screaming over our deck. As they came driving into sudden lamp-light out of the darkness, one excused them for not respecting our deck; for it was almost like the outer sea, black water broken into foam, the stinging foam that drenched us all. Depressing things began to occur. The little steward bustled up, apparently in command of two or three seamen, and carried off the cabin mattresses forward. "Is there water in the engine-room?" I asked despondingly. "Oh no, ma'am, only a little coming down the fore-hatchway." There was water in the hold, as we afterwards found when we unpacked our trunks. Then a

ship's officer whispered to one of the gentlemen something beginning with, " Don't tell the ladies," and of course the ladies
instantly wished to know everything; but it was only what was
plain enough, that we *had* to drive on, and *had* to hit the right
channel, and did not know exactly where it was.   Happily the
little steamer behaved bravely, and did not break her screw-
propeller *till* the next voyage; but the motion was excessive,
and at last the swinging cabin-lamp, the last breakable thing,
smashed to pieces and left the cabin in darkness; and the captain
actually wished to shut up the ladies in that darkness !   But we
felt ourselves better off where we were, and would not go ; and
indeed, though the tension of nerves was great, it was not wholly
disagreeable.   I can still see, in the first glimmer of morning,
or rather of lighter weather, for there was no night, the face of
a young Icelandic girl, fair against the darkness, with floating
golden hair, as tranquil as the figure-head of a ship, or as any
of her sea-roving ancestors.   And at last an Icelandic gentleman,
who had been all night on the look-out with the captain, swung
down from the bridge, and ran up to tell us, with a voice of
joyous congratulation, that he had seen the land close by—had
recognised a landmark, and knew how to steer.   By 3 A.M. all
anxiety was over—wind and sea abated as the tide went down ;
and moreover we saw, blessed sight, a schooner before us in the
fairway—the first ship since Faröe.   I went into the engine-
house to dry myself, and condole with a weary engineer, who
wanted to know if we were near a port, and began again to
suggest we ought to have been coasting between Kirkcaldy and
London ; but I would hear no more of that.   We tumbled thank-
fully into wet berths, and slept till late morning, when we woke
near Reykjavik, just a week out from Leith.   We were rolling
still in the swell, but in an arm of the sea running up to the
left under fine mountains.   The morning was brilliant, and the
colouring of sea and land was intensely vivid.

Reykjavik lay to the right.   It was like a small Norwegian
town, a cluster of black wooden houses scattered irregularly
along the shore and up a rising bank.   Behind it lay a black

flat, bounded by a fine range of distant volcanic hills—the sulphur-mountains of Krisuvik. To the left the purple mountains trended westward, till sixty miles away the snows of the last of the range, Snæfell Jökull, glimmered like a daylit moon.

There is no pier or inner harbour at Reykjavik, only some wooden jetties, but usually there is a fair amount of shipping in the fine roadstead. We were soon surrounded by small boats, and people glad to welcome us in safety; for there had been a gale in Iceland heavier than any that had been experienced since midwinter—most unwonted weather for June. Bad passages are, however, like bad dreams when one awakes, they are forgotten on arrival, or, at least, not remembered so as to deter people from going to sea again. We landed,—and I may mention as characteristic, that as our boatman had to carry our numerous packages a long way up to our lodging, I paid the boy what seemed to me about enough; but meeting the man a few days later, he insisted on returning to me one-third of the fee, as it was too much. The next agreeable trait which met us was the hospitality. We were asked everywhere to coffee, to dinner, to tea, both by people to whom we had introductions and others, and we were never a day on our own resources all the first week we spent at Reykjavik. But such things belong to pre-guidebook days, and will vanish before the advance of the tourist.

13

CHAPTER III.

REYKJAVIK AND THE PONIES.

THERE are three streets in Reykjavik parallel to the shore, and one leading up inland at each extremity of the town; these are nicely gravelled, and neatly kept. There is also a square, with grass in the centre, in the middle of which stands a fine statue of Thorwaldsen, the only ornament of the town. The rest of it is all irregular, houses dotted about by twos and threes over a considerable space of country. The public buildings consist of an ugly salmon-coloured church they call the cathedral—a plain whitewashed house for the governor—and a larger one, salmon-coloured again, for the college. Most of the houses are of timber painted black, picked out with white; many stand in gardens among hardy flowers, or, with a complete disregard for appearances, turnips and potatoes. How I longed often to do a little gardening, and *square things up!* for the Icelanders have no ideas about out-of-doors amenity. The houses are, however, generally neat inside, and some of them are daintily pretty; and they are usually ornamented by roses, carnations, and geraniums, blooming in the windows—tender favourites, which are rarely exposed to the open air. There are a few old turf-houses, which are among the worst and smallest specimens of the genuine Icelandic *bœ* or dwelling; and of late many new substantial houses of grey whinstone have been built. The red Danish flag flutters from many a roof, and the whole place has a thriving air, and an increasing trade and population.

The two or three stores—which are like our Highland "general merchants" shops, places where you can buy everything rather dear—are crowded in summer. There are stacks of fish on the shore which are built up in rain, and spread out to dry in sunshine. The dried fish is *made* indeed, just as we make hay, by busy women, while numbers of men are employed in plying with boat-loads of fish to the ships in the roadstead. The women all wear a pretty black cap, like a small Greek cap, with the same sort of tassel falling over one shoulder; and it sets them off not a little. They have smartly fitting dark jackets and skirts, and gaily coloured handkerchiefs and aprons; and they wear Scotch plaids over their heads in cold weather. The men have no especial costume, except that their brown suits look very loose and clumsy; and in cold weather they pile clothes on above and below till they have the figures of bears. The richer sort are dressed like people elsewhere, only constant riding inclines them towards wearing clothes to suit, and high boots.

There was no inn when we were there first—only a public-house; but though the town now boasts of a humble hotel, it is better for ladies to lodge, as we did, in a private house. They told us we could dine at the hospital. This sounded rather melancholy; but it proved to be a jovial sort of hospital—where dinner-parties and balls were given, and where an excellent cook provided dinners for many strangers. There were only four patients there at that time, and when there are any infectious cases, they are sent to a lonely house across the bay. An English gentleman I met at our hospital told me he disliked towns in general, but he liked Reykjavik certainly better than any other town; perhaps because it is as little of a town as a town can be. It has the advantage of a very pleasant little society, simple in externals, yet refined, and withal rather ceremonious.

Excellent bridle-roads run in every direction for a few miles over country which, but for the distant views, is ugly. The soil is disintegrated lava, and hardly to be distinguished from ploughed fields at a little distance; the cultivated grass meadows near the town are edged by this brown waste, and, for some miles, the natural grass only grows in a few sheltered places. But in fine weather the views are beautiful. There is a pretty walk by a little lake which bounds the town to the south; but the best views are westward, near a headland where we often strolled to see the sunsets blazing away behind Snæfell Jökull. There are grand mountains to the north-west; a lower coast with strange volcanic formations, trends away south, as far as the eye can see. There in the spring-time the inhabitants watch day by day for the first streak of the smoke of the steamer which returns from the outer world after an interval of four months. The men watch the sky with their glasses, and the boys are always waiting ready to rush to the town with the good news of the arrival of the mail.

The first ride in Iceland was memorable to us. We started in the broad sunshine of ten o'clock at night in June, and rode a few miles to a lonely sea inlet, where there was a drove of 250 ponies destined for our steamer. A bevy of wild lads and girls on barebacked ponies, with bits of stick and reins of string, careered about; there was also our supercargo, mounted on the pick of the drove, a most dainty high-stepping pony—too good, as they phrase it, for himself; there was our engineer, too, suffering great things, holding on to an animal that "wouldn't steer;" and our guide the Icelander, Oddur Gislason, who seemed in command,—and we all proceeded to drive the herd of ponies to Reykjavik.

A splendid sunset lighted the Faxafjord and surrounding hills, and the brown stony waste over which we cantered, chasing and driving the ponies, who, with their tumbling hog-manes and wild heads, neighing, kicking, and scouring here and there, were wonderfully picturesque. Then by our watches rather than the sky, we realised for the first time in the north that it was mid-night, broad "daylight," but hushed and still; the little islets in the neighbouring sea were covered with ducks, asleep on their nests; nothing stirred though all was bright. The red clouds of the sunset still lingered in the north-west, and close by was the clear pale-yellow light of dawn, marking the place where the sun would soon rise again over the mountains. And when he rose, although there had been no intervening darkness, in some subtle way the freshness of a new day succeeded to the weariness of the night.

People sometimes complain of the restlessness induced by the constant daylight in high latitudes. I cannot say I ever suffered from it myself, though less sleep than usual seems required; and, on the other hand, it is said that men and women tend to hibernate like other animals during the long winter darkness.

These ponies are so important to the traveller, that I shall say something more about them here, especially as it was to us a delightful novelty to see for the first time thorough equine happiness, or ponies running free together by the hundred. In this herd there were many shabby-looking little beasts, with tufts of winter hair still hanging about them, and many ugly ones in proportion to those that were handsome, but all had good legs; and there was not, I think, a marked knee among them.

All preconceived ideas of horse's manners and powers must here be laid aside. One of the remarkable things about Reykjavik is that you come across groups of shabby-looking ponies about 12 hands high, lounging together, unfastened and untended, some burdened, others free. Their good qualities are hidden under masses of rough hair and a most phlegmatic demeanour. When you see a man of fifteen stone or so, jump on one of these ponies and dart off at a gallop or a run, you long for the Society against Cruelty to Animals. But a little observation shows that the pony moves with ease. The rider, too, goes easily; never rising in the saddle, he sits close and glides through the air with the still speed of a swallow-flight. The riding-ponies which are trained to the quick amble, when both legs move together on the *same* side, are technically called *thiedh* or *skeid*, in contradistinction to the *hastur* or trotting, and *klá* or burden, horses. Whatever objection may at first be made to the unaccustomed pace, it proves the best for pony and rider too in the literal long-run. They are the easiest animals to ride that can be imagined. Their small size and smooth amble makes riding them seem like acquiring four active indefatigable legs of your own. So docile and intelligent are the good ones, that you become quite unaware of guiding, but go with a mere wish where you will. I always rode without my third pummel in Iceland, as it is more convenient for jumping on and off, and for lounging on the saddle at times during a long day's journey; and no Iceland pony wishes to throw a comfortable rider. Among the very many I have ridden and come across, I have only found one vicious, and that was rather negative obstinacy than positive malice. Some, no doubt, are lazy, and most go better in company than alone. Even the trotting ponies are generally smoother than ours, and keep their easy speed up over wonderfully rough ground; and they are very surefooted and intelligent in finding their way over lava, or bogs, or in the night. I never presume to guide a willing pony in such places in detail, only giving him the *route*, and allowing him to carry it out as he thinks best; and it is probably owing to this that my ponies kept fresh, when sometimes their companions, who had been more interfered with, were exhausted. Such ponies need no riding in the technical sense; all that is needed is the sympathy between horse and rider—the comprehension of equine feelings that even unpractised people may attain to. Yet I have heard and seen tourists abuse ponies which I have found on trial quite willing and easy-paced. Some tourists even tumble off such ponies, but for this they have small excuse.

So far, I have been speaking of fair average riding-ponies, such as may be hired by the traveller for from one and a half to three *krone* a-day. But there are others which are seldom exported, because they command a price in Iceland that could hardly be got for them in England, owing to their small size—say £18 to £25. These generally belong to farmers or gentlemen, who take pride in them, feed them well during the winter, and do not hire them out. They are often very well shaped, and fine movers, with high crests and large quick eyes; the neck and chest much developed and broad; the legs fine, flat, and clean. Every movement is alert, every nerve quivering with spirit. It is difficult to exaggerate the merits of those little animals when in their exhilarating native air, and fed on the peculiar strong grasses of the country. Such will go over ground, that would seem elsewhere almost too bad for any horse at a foot-pace, with a gay snort at a hand-gallop. As a rule, they wish to go fast wherever the road will permit it; and unless indulged in a rattling gallop now and then, can be decidedly skittish, especially if they suspect another horse of a design of going before them. Many such ponies have been lent me by their owners; and I know no greater pleasure in its way, than rushing along over greensward through the pure air, mounted on one of these horses, small yet vigorous, and so intelligent that his short ears prick at every sound of his rider's voice. Domestic as a dog, he follows you when you are not riding, and rubs his wise head confidingly on your shoulder; for he is accustomed to run loose by his master's side when he is riding another horse, and when off duty to lounge about the farm as he pleases, grazing at leisure, instead of being handed over to a groom and the dulness of a stable.

Mr Slimon of Leith has imported several thousands of these ponies during the last few years,—an excellent trade, which has brought much specie into the country, and taken away in autumn the surplus of the large young horse population which Iceland is admirably fitted to maintain during the summer. Formerly, before winter they had to destroy many horses and foals—now, by selling some, they can buy more food for the others. Ponies have in consequence risen in price, and the Danish monopoly in this branch of trade, at least, is completely destroyed.

There are no sights in Reykjavik; we realised this with calm pleasure—it was such a contrast to one's usual toil in a foreign town. There is a small collection of old curiosities, then kept in the roof of the church, but the choice antiquities of Iceland have long ago been carried off by the Danes: there is hardly even a valuable MS. left in the country which produced so many.

The only fine art which flourishes is decorative metal-work. From the earliest times the Icelanders were clever iron and silver smiths : the old designs are very good, and the modern work well executed. Many of the women are skilled in working the beautiful embroideries in gold and silver which are worn on the full-dress national costume.

The men are often very fair wood-carvers, and while away the long winter nights by decorating bowls and boxes and chests with the same style of ornamentation which we find on Runic stones and crosses. The design on the cover of this book has been drawn after one of these boxes in my possession, evidently a very old one. We have no means of fixing the date, but it may well be two or three hundred years old. Most of these things are carved in the driftwood which comes ashore in quantities all round the south-west coasts.

CHAPTER IV.

GEYSIR.

ONE lovely summer day we started from Reykjavik bound for the Geysir,[1] which every one goes to see, as it is only seventy miles from the town, so that the trip may be made during the stay of the post-ship; but as Geysir does not always "receive," it may prove a disappointing expedition. We were fortunate in our guide, Mr Oddur V. Gislason, a theological candidate; and the success of our journey was greatly owing to his unfailing good-humour, energy, and kindly care. He brought with him his comfortable little marquee-tent, with divisions; we took—besides a tiny *batterie de cuisine*—some provisions, cork mattresses, plaids, and waterproofs,—so that, with the addition of a folding bath, we had good furnished apartments wherever we went. As we did not mean to hurry, we took only nine ponies this time, which gave us four to ride, three for baggage, and two relays; the fourth rider being Skuli, a youth who drove for us. And so on the 2d of July we started gaily over the brown desert bordering Reykjavik. It has no beauty except the distant views over sea and mountains, this day exquisite in tint. The salmon river, four miles off, was of the deepest blue; not less intense in hue were two lakes we

---

[1] The name Geysir, which properly belongs to the largest of the hot springs in the valley of Haukadal, is derived from the verb *geysa*, to rush furiously; and *geysi*, the adjective, is used commonly in the sense of violent, enormous, or gushing. Some trace of the word lingers in Scotland, where the Icelandic *geysi kaldur* would be well rendered by "*gey cauld.*"

passed further on ; but for the extraordinary vividness of colour, the landscape reminded me of our Hebrides.

The glory of Iceland is its colouring. With considerable experience of the finest scenery in Europe, I could not but feel that even Switzerland, unless, perhaps, above the constant snow-line, is not so clear and glittering ; Italy, with a stronger light, has not its peculiar purity ; and Scotland, after it, seems toned down with a damp sponge. The forms of Icelandic scenery are, however, more curious than beautiful, though they had for me a weird fascination. There is often great width of contour ; the hills are in long hummocked masses, with perhaps a volcanic cone suddenly breaking the outline ; there is a sort of disconnected uncombined effect about the landscape, easy to perceive but difficult to describe. Trees would not suit it ; and its wistful melancholy grandeur is partly, no doubt, owing to the absence everywhere of enclosures, square fields, roads—all lines, indeed, save those curves which nature never draws amiss. The road, when there is one, is generally a mere product of the hoofs of a hundred generations of ponies, sometimes worn into a deep ditch or hollow way, sometimes branching into a dozen little tracks, just large enough for their small feet ; and it needs some practice to choose the best line. It is merry riding in the pure light air : the loose ponies rattle on before ; constantly one or another strays off after some fancy of its own, and has to be chased back by the drivers, who, dashing up and down, cracking their whips and shouting, adjuring the ponies by name to keep the path or beware of the dogs, make the cavalcade lively ; and the way must be bad indeed to reduce it to a walking-pace, which always causes the loose ponies to stray more. We usually rode at a steady trot, but with many little halts, now to adjust a box, now to mend a rope, or perhaps to bait our little steeds on some choice bit of grass.

We had gone about thirty miles, and the evening had grown cloudy, when we suddenly came to a deep cleft and rough rocky steps leading downwards ; this was the well-known Allmanna *gjá*, or rift, a long split between two lava precipices. We came out by a side opening into the solitary grassy valley below, the celebrated Thingvellir, all unchanged since the days of the old commonwealth; it seemed still ready for the booths of the freemen who flocked here of old from all parts of the island for their annual parliament. The only buildings are the little timber church across the river, and the low turf-house of its parson close by. We hurried to the church, eager for coffee and supper, after our seven hours' ride. It may seem at first some-, what sacrilegious to sup in a pew and sleep in a church; but when my friend and I had shaken down our cork mattresses and plaids on each side of the altar-rails, we thought it looked fairly comfortable, and could not but approve of the custom of giving the best buildings in the land everywhere to the church, which in its turn lends them to strangers like ourselves.

The weather was unsettled, so we lingered all next day at Thingvellir: rain came on in the evening, and continued till noon the following day, when we started up the mountain-track, and thence in three hours descended into the green valley of Laugardalr. We rode close under wild impending mountains, where black crags and red corries contrasted with tracks of most wonderfully green moss; on our other hand a lake lay in a wide plain, far-off rivers shining in the distance below a range of misty hills. We had been riding among the mountains again for an hour or two before we reached a wide river swelled by the recent rains, the Bruar-à, or Bridge River—bridges being very rare in Iceland. Midway across this stream its broken waters fall foaming into a deep cleft in its rocky bed, and over this a few wet planks were fixed, the ponies marching over them unhesitatingly midway in the deep ford. The turbulent river, with its clear flashing waters rolling down among the dark lonely hills, delighted me; had it been a little later in the season we would have camped there and tried the fishing; but as it was, we rode on to the church of Utlith, which we reached in the clear twilight of 11 P.M. The church was as small as it could be, and half full of wool already; but we took the rest of it, and some courteous damsels soon served us with coffee, good even for Iceland, and there we slept hardly less quietly than the dead folk just outside.

It rained in the morning, except when it was blowing very hard indeed; so, after breakfast, we went over to the neighbouring *bær*, or farmhouse, and into a cavern called the *eldhus*, or kitchen, where, with patience, a person who can stand steadily on one foot may dry the other over the few sticks that, crackling between two rough stones, count as the kitchen-fire. Nice people were there, who made much of us, and gave us excellent cream. About one it cleared up, and we cantered off merrily, sometimes over sound turf, but sometimes plashing through bogs, which had drunk so much rain that I feared they would swallow us down as something solid. At length we came out from the hills on a sloping plain, which, except where one snowy peak showed beyond it, melted into misty distance. Near us it was dotted here and there with clouds of steam rising from the ground. We rode over the soil blasted by sulphureous vapours to the farthest and biggest of these clouds; and this was Geysir, and here we dismounted on a bit of greensward, and prepared to pitch our tent. This may not read as if the place were pretty, nor was it—it looked odd, and perhaps a little mean; but then the day was overcast, the lamps were not lighted. Soon we found much that was curious. Hunger impelled us to the accredited kitchen, Blezi, which is a pool like a wide, deep *crevasse* in a blue glacier: the boiling water is so exquisitely pure that the silica rocks below become bright blue through its medium. To Blezi we confided a joint of lamb, a tin of preserved fowl, and a fish, tying them in strings and lowering them. I regret to say he swallowed our fish; the string breaking, we beheld it deep blue in the depths, and no doubt it is now a petrifaction. Round the margin of this pool ran a charming fretwork of petrified leaves, chiefly silver-weed; many we took away, but, like fairy-money, when we unpacked them they were dust.

The crater of Geysir is a mound of siliceous rock, which has been aptly compared to an inverted oyster-shell. The pool is about sixty-five by fifty-five feet in diameter, and there the transparent water simmered quietly, looking perfectly incapable of any such frisky proceeding as springing into the air. Strokr, or the Churn, another hot spring that boils and tosses angrily some way down a deep pit about eight feet across, looks far more violent and flighty, and some of the other smaller springs also boil furiously close to the surface. Others only make a perpetual, dull, thudding noise below, as if the dwarfs were forging metals at the subterranean fires: others, again, look quite quiet and limpid, and lie in little fairy arches or caves of greenish moss, where bright flowers and little delicate ferns nestle in a southern climate. About twenty of those hot springs are scattered over a space of a few acres; and there seems to be such a waste of heat and energy, that we longed to give the water-sprites some useful work to do. The water is not quite suitable for baths, for it has a petrifying quality—and we discovered, with consternation, that our hands began, after washing in it, to shrivel and harden like parrots' claws. Still it might do some work. Hothouses perhaps might be made here, and grapes and vegetables grown to supply the island. As it is, the farmer who owns the land and charges a trifle for the tent-stance, finds it not worth while to put up a hut in the wilderness for the few travellers, who must therefore bring a tent, or wander about all night. Three such homeless beings rather disturbed our first night in the tent; they were Icelanders, two girls and a youth, who beguiled the time by singing and talking, and causing Strokr to explode at the dead of night, with thundering, hissing, and roaring. I was lazily glad to hear it was only Strokr, whose explosions excite little interest, as they can be produced at any time by choking the funnel with turf. We could have an eruption whenever we wished, so there was no need to turn out.

Next day the weather was lovely, the lamps were lit, and all was transfigured. The distant snow-mountain gleamed with opal lights, the ferruginous soil and dark colouring of the near hills were glowing reds and rich purples, and the boiling water-jets seemed like handfuls of diamonds tossed into the sunny air. We now had the desert all to ourselves. We strolled about as far as the river would let us; we bathed, and dried all that was wet, and cooked an excellent dinner. Moreover, we cut a pile of turf and flung it into Strokr, and in about twenty minutes the fountain hurled up to a great height, I suppose from fifty to eighty feet; again and again it leapt into the sky, flinging down mud and pebbles, and our turf thoroughly boiled. After nearly an hour, when we thought it was all over, we were startled by the most beautiful jet of all, because the purest, the water having partly cleansed itself from the mud.

About six o'clock P.M., a low subterranean thunder made the ground shudder, and Geysir rose a little in the centre in a pure white jet glittering in the sunshine, in size and form like a veiled white woman, reminding one of Fouqué's "Undine" rising from the fountain. It gently subsided, and the water brimmed over the basin and ran down the rocks. That evening, one of the loveliest sunsets I ever saw made the whole sky blaze with splendid hues, which were variously reflected in the strange water-springs. Even when we lay down in our plaids about midnight, we could not persuade ourselves to close up the tent, so warm was the daylight night, so brilliant the sky. Gislason stood on the edge of the crater, and invoked Geysir by all sorts of adjurations, ancient and modern, from Odin onwards, to appear. Finally he threw in a silver coin as a bribe, and counselled us to be on the alert. So twice in the night, when the underground thundering roused us, we all ran out only to see the wan white figure rise and fall again, but we remarked it had grown taller. It was morning when the warning cannon went off again, and this time, after the eight-foot rise, the fountain did not subside. With a booming roar, not a mere central jet, but the whole of the water to the very edge of the crater, rose majestically in a great massive dome higher and higher, till it was lost in steam in the sky. The height was said to be about a hundred feet, but what with the noise and the steaming, the wind swaying the column to leeward, and the torrents of hot water that were pouring down, one did not know where next, I was thankful to be unscientific, and to confine myself to looking and running out of the way. The water sank and rose again five or six times, the later eruptions being lower, and the whole commotion subsiding by degrees, till at last all was calm, and there was not a drop of water left in the crater. When it was cool enough to walk on, we went to the brink of the well in the centre, and could only just see the boiling water tossing far below.

The weather had now become cold and rainy, so we lounged in the crater, enjoying the sort of comfort that can be derived from sitting on a hot oven under a cold shower-bath. Moreover, Gislason found the blackened piece of silver, which, from its position, had evidently been erupted; and now it decorates my watch-chain as a memorial that, like some other Icelanders, Geysir, refuses all payment from travellers. The water gradually filled up the crater, which by evening was brimming over, and the ground began to shiver again, just like the lid of a kettle of boiling water. The crust above the springs is in some places only an inch or two thick, and feels hardly safe; but, as it has lasted through stronger explosions than now occur, we may expect it to serve our time. Judging from the accounts of early travellers, these springs are evidently less active now than formerly; indeed on the day we first arrived they were simmering low, and there was little to be seen but puffs of steam. But now, as if fresh fuel had been piled on the furnace, boiling jets and spurts of foam rose and sank in every direction. A fountain, called the Little Geysir, pulsated up at short intervals ten or twelve feet in the air; all the springs seemed in mad commotion—in fact, it was a general boil over.

The wind howled, the rain-storm slashed against our little tent, where we reclined on our mattresses by the boxes which served as tables, while every now and then the ground trembled beneath us as the underground thunder rolled up and shuddered away into the depths again. We made ourselves as comfortable as circumstances would allow; we brewed strong tea and weak toddy with the boiling water of the Geysir, and as we had no light literature we made it for ourselves,—verses among other things,—when it appeared that Miss Menzies had quaffed most deeply of the ethereal cup of Bragi, if not of sulphureous Geysir tea; for her verses were the best, and I give them here, as they seemed to me at the time to give a graphic description of the place.

"Where the caldron of the North
Spouts its boiling waters forth,
From the caverns far beneath,
Where they ever lie and seethe,
And with steam, and hiss, and boom,
Send a tremor through the gloom,
Till, above, the solid ground
Vibrates with a dull rebound,—
    In that place I stood, and saw
    Things that filled my soul with awe.

Where the sunset of the North
Sends its radiant colours forth,
Turns the sulphur rocks to blood,
Glows upon the steaming flood,
Paints the pools with ruddy light,
Turns to brighter day the night,—
    In that place I stood and gazed
    Till my spirit was amazed.

Where the boiling torrent flies
Upward to the morning skies,
Shakes itself through air around
With a wild and hissing sound,
Wears a robe of mist to hide
All the angry rising tide;
Till above the mist it parts,
And to earth repentant darts,
In her bosom to assuage
All the madness of its rage,—
    In that place I stood, and found
    That it was enchanted ground.

Where the vessel it has left,
Of its presence all bereft,
Feels itself exposed and bare
To the unwonted summer air,
Deems it yet akin to death
To be cooled by such a breath;
And with fierce and fervent heat
Scorches men's invading feet,—
    In that place I witnessed how
    Still the caldron seethed below.

Quivering with thwarted pride,
Wild to spend its seething tide;
Still for ever bubbling up
Towards the margin of its cup,

> And with utmost speed and strain
> Boiling to its brim again ;
> Quiet then awhile to lie,
> Till the secret sorcery
> All its former rage restore,
> Bid it rise with hiss and roar,—
> This I saw when to the North
> Valiantly I sallied forth."

A tent is delightful in fine weather ; but now, when the least touch on the canvas was followed by a drip—when in spite of trenching the ground inside was growing wet, and one had to lie stiff and straight to avoid rolling into a puddle,—now one could realise the value of everyday comforts, such as a mere house, a commonplace bed, as never before. Twice the Geysir rose pretty high in the night, and seemed to me nothing better than a witch of the worst kind, as I waded through lukewarm water under the heavy rain to see her ; but we did not like to miss the chance of seeing another grand eruption. The rain continued in the morning. The tent was now so saturated that it was diffi-cult to pack, and a very heavy load. We tried to provoke Strokr again by choking it with turf, but—a circumstance which I have never seen noticed before—no eruption followed ; perhaps because the Geysir was still greatly agitated, boiling over at short intervals, and jetting up high in the centre. All we had was wet, and nothing could be dried, so we started under slash-ing rain to ride back to Thingvellir. The floods were out ; sometimes we rode through wet morasses, sometimes along stony tracks deep in mud, consoled by the reflection that we probably owed the grand eruption we had seen to the bad weather. The day cleared up at last, but the sunshine was still watery, and had no drying power ; if it had been as warm as it often is in Iceland, it would have saved me from the chill which I certainly caught this day, for I had long been wet through and now began to shiver. This was the only time I felt at all ill in Iceland, owing probably to the want of a complete change of warm clothing.

It was pleasant riding when we reached the green valley by Laugevatn, where we were joined by a rural dean on his visita-

tion tour, mounted on a very clever pony. At the neighbouring
farm, where we halted to rest, we were told that the road further
on had become almost impassable from the rain. Nevertheless

The Lake from the Hill of Laws.

we pushed on, diverging from the usual track to visit a very
curious extinct crater called Tintron. The black pit of unknown
depth is arched over by reddish-coloured lava of the most grotesque forms, and it lies isolated in an ashen plain near a range
of cinder-crags. The road, when we reached it, was a mere
ditch of yellow water rising to the stirrups, flooding lava-boulders
about the size and shape of bolsters ; but the ponies felt through
the thick water for the lava with their little feet, and seemed
never at fault. Rain again before we reached Thingvellir after a
ride of nearly forty miles, at half-past ten ; the people had gone
to bed, and I thought the church-key would never come as we
stood at the door, battered by wind and wet like outcast spirits.
But here it is at last, and coffee, never more welcome.

The sun shone brilliantly during the three days which we
now passed at Thingvellir, with which we were charmed. Seldom

indeed does a place visited for its historic interest so fulfil all
expectations. For nothing here is changed. Names and places
are all unaltered, and the old sagas are living realities, and our
best guides about these solitudes, which seem waiting for the
return of the ancient heroes. The grassy valley lies between
two long cliffs of lava: the one to the west is split up again
into a deep rift, forming a green fairy valley only a few yards
across, but more than a mile long; and at one point the great
Ox River flings itself over the western crag in one broad fall,
and, after a short course in the rift, breaks out into the broader
valley, and flows gently down half a mile to the lake. This lake,
about twelve miles long by ten broad, with a fine mountain-
barrier, is strangely lonely. No sail animates its surface, no
houses dot its solitary shores; it is left to the swans and wild
ducks, and at this time to ourselves, to enjoy alone. Parallel to
the great rift, another long chasm has split up the opposite lava-
cliff, leaving a wall of rock running up the centre. This central
rock is the place whence the laws were promulgated of old, the
Lögberg. Here, as you sit on the long grass facing the lake,
with mountains all round, you have on either hand a straight
cliff, down which you look thirty or forty feet into dark deep
water, reflecting the overhanging rocks with their lichened greys
and greenery, and flowing, like Dante's Lethe—

> " With a brown, brown current,
> Under the shade perpetual which never
> Ray of the sun lets in, nor of the moon."

These chasms, into which the river flows by a subterranean
inlet, quite isolate the Hill of Laws except at one narrow neck
of land. At one point only the rocky walls approach within
eighteen feet of each other; and here, according to ancient
tradition, Flosi, the burner of Njal, being hotly pursued by his
enemies, leapt over the chasm—and Lord Dufferin, not to be out-
done by an Icelander, wished to imitate the exploit. Looked
at in cold blood, there is a most awkward, narrow rocky shelf to
alight on; but Flosi perhaps had the advantage of being in a

fright. Old lava lies for miles round Thingvellir; it is all split into fissures and chasms, but is full of pretty details from the luxuriant growth of bog-myrtle, crowberries, blaeberries, wild thyme, and flowers; here and there a cleft or pool of pure deep water opens in the rocks. The variety of the place is one of its many charms. It seemed wonderful that we should have it all to ourselves—wonderful that there should be no house for miles

Kitchen, Thingvellir Parsonage.

and miles round, but the tiny parsonage. There are many stone foundations left of the booths, that used formerly to be built by the people who flocked here for the annual *alting* or parliament; and in front of the church is an old stone marked with the standard measures, and supposed to date from the tenth century.

The sun was very hot during our stay, but there was always a pleasant crispness in the pure air; and each night a splendid sunset lit the sky, the lake, the cataract, and the snowy and purple hills, with a blaze of changing colouring.

It was with quite a wrench that we tore ourselves away from the valley on the 12th of July, bound for Reykjavik by a longer and more interesting route than the one we had come by. The weather continued beautiful. The riding was good, and much of it over sound turf. We halted in a green pastoral valley near a pretty little rocky lake. In the evening we reached the parsonage of Rennyvellir, and found the bachelor-parson who received us, so occupied with his outside farming that he could not attend to the inside of the house, which suggested the hole of an untidy rabbit, much magnified. Yet he had a large household, and was draining his fine pasture-land scientifically into the pretty river which runs through the valley. We improved the guest-room by taking out the whole window, frame and all, as it was not made to open; and we longed further to improve it by turning in the stream. Our host enjoyed the reputation of being a very good scholar, and this was confirmed by the collection of books in Latin, Danish, English, German, and Spanish.

Next day a strange little mounted funeral procession came up through the lonely grassy valley to the church,—some seafaring men bringing for burial the bodies of two sailors who had been drowned in the adjacent stormy Hvalfjord, in coffins balanced on the backs of ponies. First the people sang in the church, the clergyman in his ruff and gown standing by the altar; then they dug the graves, and then followed a service in the churchyard, much resembling the Anglican funeral service, especially I recognised the burial ritual of "Earth to earth." We began by feeling respectful and interested at this funeral; but as hour after hour actually went by, and we went and came to find them still at it, it became like a nightmare. Our *quasi* clerical guide was in the thick of it, singing in the interminable hymns, blind and deaf to our signals of impatience; and indeed it would not have been considered quite respectful to go till it was over. I had caught a feverish chill in the bad weather, and this was the fourth day that I had lived on air and water, happily both of the best, and consequently, perhaps, I got well very soon; but this day I began to feel, though not tired, very dreamy and incoherent. Would these men never be buried? And when could the guests venture to hope for the funeral ale? Nearly four hours went by and still the proceedings were not over; so we ordered our ponies and rode off with Skuli about four o'clock, leaving Oddur to follow at his leisure. During the season of the long summer nights, people seem to care little when they begin a so-called day's journey. We cantered up a wild valley between bare, scarped hills, and thence over a bright green bog, filling up another dark valley. I have always stood in awe of bogs, and there was a size, depth, and brilliancy about this one which seemed to me almost sublime; but I had not then ridden over Myra (or mire) Sysslu. Following our guide closely, we did pretty well, but a straying baggage-pony stuck fast for some time, kept only by his boxes from sinking altogether. We halted for a while under a pass over a spur of the mountain Eysja; below rushed a great river, heavy with melted snow; the dark mountains on either side had a good deal of lingering snow in their black ravines; there was no touch of vegetation, except some vivid green moss; and all looked very savage and arctic. The pass, though short, was a steep zigzag, and from the top a wide expanse of hill and sea was seen, with strangely-shaped rocks in the foreground. Down we rattled, careless of the steepness of the way; indeed for the last few hours we rode at a good canter or hand-gallop, sweeping the loose ponies before us, nothing loath as they were going home, all the way to Reykjavik, where we arrived at 10.30 P.M., glad for a few days at least to return to the comforts of civilised life.

C

CHAPTER V.

As the Icelandic literature influenced many of my impressions of the country, it is time, before going on with the story of our journey, to give a slight sketch of its nature and history,—a sketch which, however inadequate, shall not be a mere list of books, as I shall dwell chiefly on those works which I have read in the original, and am, therefore, best able to appreciate. For the old Icelandic will not translate without losing quality; it is the expression of a different form of life and state of society from all that exists now, and its strong individuality makes its spirit hard to render in a modern tongue. And Iceland is chiefly curious and interesting, because this language, stamped with the forms of ancient days, is still there the current coin. It is no mere dead language of the past, but living and flourishing now; and any enthusiastic student who wishes to follow Sir W. Hamilton's advice, and learn, not for mere utility, but for the love of knowledge itself, cannot do better than study it. Laing says in the introduction to Snorri's 'History of the Kings of Norway:' "During the five centuries in which the Northmen were riding over the seas, and conquering wherever they landed, the literature of the people they overcame was locked up in a dead language, and within the walls of monasteries. But the Northmen had a literature of their own, though a rude one." What, then, was the character of this literature, and what its relation to the national life of the Icelanders?

Iceland, as every one knows, was first peopled, not by savages,

but by a race already advanced in civilisation, and not as most
colonies, by the mere overflow of the population of the mother
country, but by the most able and spirited of the Northmen, who
would not endure the feudal innovations of Harald Fair-hair, the
first king over all Norway. About A.D. 870, Iceland was an
uninhabited desert. By the middle of the next century the
emigration was over, the good land occupied, and the population probably not much below its present number—about 70,000
people. This is a very small population for 38,000 square miles ;
but it is estimated that only a ninth. part of the land has ever
been permanently inhabited. Those colonists fled from feudalism ;
they clung to the *alodial* land law, and introduced it into Iceland,
where it is in force to this day. This *odal* land tenure did not
flow from a sovereign ; land was no gift of a master ; it was held
by no written title, no payment of service ; every right was included ; the children were all equal heirs, and their rights inalien-
able, and though they might and often did sell these rights, by
repayment in full they might reclaim them. To this day the
title of a purchaser of land in Norway is for a given date of a
somewhat precarious nature,—a person *odal born* to the land may
return, prove his title, pay the price, and recover from any other
holder.

The Icelandic colonists, in order to avoid too large an accumulation in one hand of even the barren lands of Iceland, made a
law that each new-comer should only claim the land he could
circle by fire—*i. e.*, cause a man to ride round with a lighted
torch—in a day. The chiefs, however, often appropriated a good
deal more than that, and settled their crews round them. Each
chief consecrated a *hof* or temple near his own house, and exer-
cised some authority as its priest over the district. The later
arrivals were compelled to buy land from others, for then, as now,
the habitable lands were small in proportion to · the wastes.
There were no castles, nor villages ; each *bondé* or landowner
made his dwelling independent of the rest, had his cultivated
tun and his out-fields. Several farms constituted then a *hérad* or
hundred. There were various local *things*, where the business of

the commonalty was despatched, besides the *althing* which met
at Thingvellir and settled the government, and decided the law
cases for the whole country. Every *bondé* had an equal voice
with all the rest at the *althing*. In Norway the king himself
appeared there like any other *odal* proprietor, and had to sway
the assembly by his own eloquence, or, as sometimes happened,
to see his plans defeated by the free speech of some unknown
peasant. How far such a system of *odal* land tenure could be
made to work in a dense modern population is a question, but
it is certain that it bred up a race of independent, free, and happy
people in these old days; happy, indeed, if we contrast their
lives with those of the people in the rest of Europe in the early
middle ages. Elsewhere we find a very small free class, the
barons and free lords, and below them the villeins and the serfs,
with their dreary portion of bondage and want, and the peasant
hordes living in a condition of servility and deprivation that
was only rendered endurable through the mitigations afforded
by the benevolence of the seigneurs, and by the protecting power
of the Church.

The literature of Iceland, from the years 1000 to 1300 inclu-
sive, is the product of this free individuality of the Northmen,
and quite unlike everything else in Europe. It tells us of the
life of the farmer, the shepherd, and the sailor, as well as of the
exploits of the warrior and the prince. All who go to Iceland
should really know something of it; for it gives the strange little
country, even in modern days, a peculiar interest to the English
traveller, explaining, above all, the true character of our Scandinavian ancestors who have made Great Britain what it is. For
from them we inherit our political freedom; like them we excel
in literature; and we are the true heirs of their empire of the
sea.

The outburst of literary activity which followed the introduction of writing into Iceland (*circa* 1100) has hardly a parallel
in history; but we can, perhaps, trace some of the causes in the
situation of these colonists. The Norsemen of that day already
equalled, if they did not excel, the contemporary nations in many

arts, as well as in arms. They were the best shipbuilders then known, which infers skilled work in several trades; they were choice and graceful artificers in silver and gold, as their weapons and ornaments are still here to prove; they were beyond their age in geography, the knowledge of stars, the flow of tides, and all wave and weather lore; and they were a law-abiding people at home. Far more internal order seemed to prevail in this strong race than among the Saxons, Franks, and Frisians, whom they plundered. They were the terror of our coasts, and were bracketed in our litanies with fire and famine; but they have left behind them poems, histories, and biographies, which show them in quite a different light from that in which they naturally appear in our monkish Latin chronicles. In fact, the Norse lion, unlike his prototype in the fable, has painted his own picture. Most of the old Norse books were, however, written in Iceland, or at least by Icelanders; and various causes, no doubt, contributed to foster literary activity in that branch of the race.

The Norse chieftain found his position somewhat altered when he settled in Iceland. There was no wood to build the Longship (or war-ship) in which he was wont to go before on Viking cruises. The ship he bought abroad was necessarily a ship of burden, because meal and wood had to be imported. He had wide lands, and plenty of liberty and elbow-room; but both the cattle and the fishing, on which his welfare depended, needed industry and attention during the summer. Then the winter was long and restful. He had time to meditate on the deeds of the national heroes and of his own ancestors,—time to turn some of his intense energy into the form of poems and histories, and to repeat them to others, who learnt them by heart from his lips. His son very likely went to Norway; half a warrior half a poet, he lived awhile in the king's court, had his strong imagination yet further excited by change and wanderings, and returned to Iceland—which then, as now, had for her sons an irresistible attraction—able to tell a better story, and chant a finer poem, than before. And so the light was kindled and spread from homestead to homestead, and a class of men rose up, the poets or Skalds, who

could repeat the sagas word for word for hours together. It is
mentioned of one Skald, but not as anything very extraordinary,
that he knew 250 long poems by heart, besides short ones and
sagas. The Icelanders still have excellent memories, if they
cannot quite rival their ancestors in that respect : and it is quite
credible that the histories generally first written down at the
close of the twelfth or the thirteenth century had been handed
down very correctly through one or two previous centuries. The
excellent and very detailed legal code was thus transmitted ; and
it was the duty of the "Speaker of laws," the president of the
althing, to know the whole of the code by heart.

The Icelandic family histories are unique in medieval literature, indeed there is nothing of any date quite like them. They
are often too diffuse as works of art. Besides the more stirring
adventures, they give us with the utmost detail, accounts of lawsuits, little household wrangles, boundary quarrels, stories about
lost horses, and pet lambs not properly marked, and such homely
matters, which all have a kind of value from their graphic truth-
fulness and antiquity. Some of them are at times rather dull, till
the reader has acquired that sort of taste which enjoys a certain
odd literary flavour—that degree of knowledge which delights
in a little more gossip about an old acquaintance.

They certainly make us better acquainted with the Icelanders
and Norwegians of seven or eight centuries ago, than we are
with any other people of the middle ages.

In one respect the sagas differ much from the early literature
of the rest of Europe—they are singularly pure, remarkably free
from grossness or coarseness of all kinds. Their authors seem to
take no pleasure in a bad story ; the morality is high, save on
the two points of manslaying and drink. A hero was expected to
be able to drink deep without bad consequences, and to go night
after night *vel drukken*—*i.e.*, well drunk—to bed. And the ladies
served the ale—nay, they sat over the mead also—but happily
not so long as their lords ; like us, they went away after dessert.

No doubt a few of the songs of the Skalds are coarse enough.
The Skald who could compose a poem in honour of a friend,

would also deliberately use his power of song to vilify an enemy. Scurrilous verses are to this day not unknown in Iceland. But such verses are wrapped up, like riddles, in language which makes them almost unintelligible; and they lie about in the literature like uncracked nuts among fruit, without imparting any taint of their flavour to the rest.

The later Skaldic poems, whether good or bad, are all alike in being difficult to understand. The words are tossed about at random, with no regard to anything but alliteration and measure; and the periphrases are so far-fetched and bewildering, that only a good knowledge of the *skaldskap* or Skald's art, as given in the ' Younger Edda,' will help the reader through their intricacies. Icelandic prose is, on the contrary, easy to understand. Of that it has been well said, that "in terse, picturesque, and crystal-clear expression, it vies with Latin; while it equals Greek in distinctness and combination of words.

We have a long list of historical sagas, biographies, and also romances and law-books, dating, in the form in which we have them, from the first introduction of writing into Iceland. The saga literature may roughly be said to have passed through three phases: first, the sagas were said; next, they were written down as said—and many have come to us in that second form; these are more bald and archaic in style than the next group, or those of the third phase, to which the finest sagas belong—such as Njala, Laxdæla, Egil's Saga, and others. They have been edited and made more artistic by authors in the thirteenth century. We feel ourselves in the presence of fine writers dealing with times and stories already two centuries distant from themselves, and viewed through a halo of romance.

It is to those well-told essentially true stories that we may ascribe the interest we take in the scenes of their events, similar to that interest which has been conferred on Scotland by Sir Walter Scott. In most countries the tide of modern life has rolled over the past, obliterating all save its ruins. But here few things change. Farms and names and manners remain much the same; the people know about the histories of their fore-

fathers, and love to recall them. They point out the fords and
hillsides where the champions fought; the site of the halls
where they feasted, and the graves where they are buried; and
such associations with vigorous life, lend a charm to the wild
landscape, making one feel how, in spite of bleak surroundings—

> " Man is man, and master of his fate."   .

Like Scotland formerly, Iceland is still for practical purposes
divided into districts, consisting of the fertile lands by the side
of a river or fjord, which originally were settled by some
chieftain, who drew friends and dependants round him, and
founded a sort of local magistracy. The sagas also are strongly
localised in districts. Thus the great legal " Saga of Njal " is
chiefly concerned with the wide flat land between Hecla and the
sea. " Floamanna Saga " is a history of the early settlers in the
Floa, or delta of the Thjorsá, in the south, and of their voyages
to Greenland. To the softer "Dales" of the west belong the
memories of the "Egil Saga," and the "Laxdæla" and "Gunlang Saga"—stories in which true love is mingled with hard
fighting—and various others.

In the north a whole group of sagas tell of the lives of the
men of Vatzdale or Waterdale, a valley which runs inland from
Skagafjord; and other shorter and wilder narratives tell of the
people of the far north, such as the story of "Gisli the Outlaw,"
translated by Dasent, "Grettir the Strong," and the Saga of
Viga Glum, also translated, and others. The east of Iceland has
been far less fertile in literary work than the other quarters.

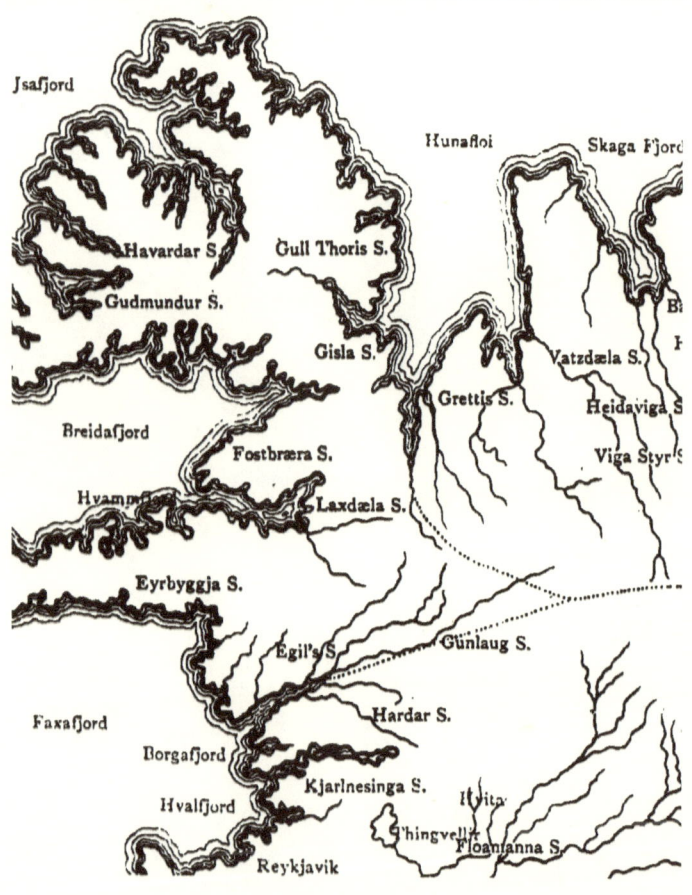

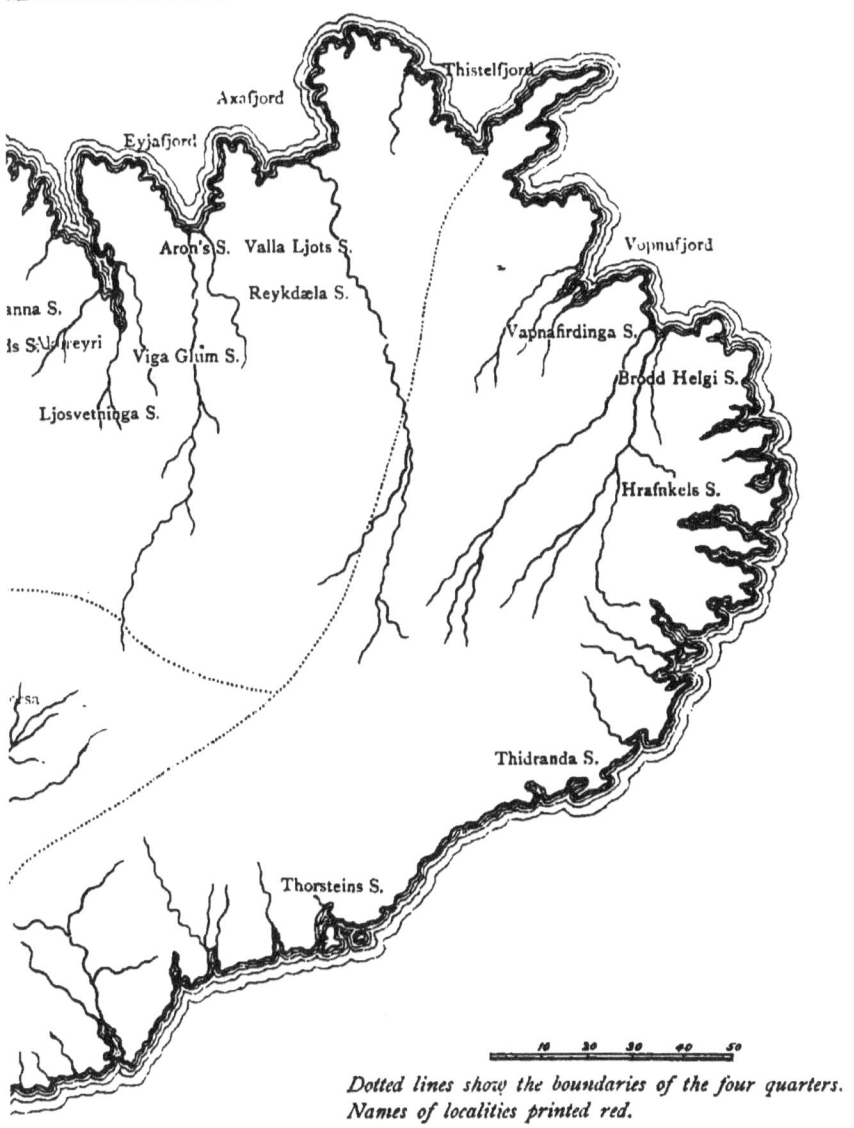

Dotted lines show the boundaries of the four quarters.
Names of localities printed red.

CHAPTER VI.

'LANDNÁMABÓK'—THE 'EDDAS'—STURLUNGA—WOMEN OF THE SAGAS
—SAINTS—BIOGRAPHIES—MORALITY—MODERN LITERATURE.

So far we have been dealing with anonymous literature exist-
ing as tradition, and written down, not by the authors, but by
clerks and compilers, one or two centuries after their date, who
could write what had originally been spoken.

'Landnámabók,' or the Book of the Settlement of the Land,
is the first book we have written down in Icelandic by a known
author, Ari, called the Historian, who died in 1148, aged eighty-
two. He had great opportunities of collecting historical facts.
He was the great-grandson of Gudrun, the heroine of the "Laxdale Saga," and descended also from Hall of the Side, who
figures largely in the "Njal Saga," with whom he lived in his
youth for fourteen years. Hall was a clever man, who lived to
extreme old age; he remembered the introduction of Christianity
into Iceland, and was well acquainted with St Olaf. Ari wrote
two other histories besides 'Landnámabók,'—'Islendingabók,'
which is partly lost, and the 'Book of the Kings,' which served
as a guide to Snorri Sturlason in his history. G. Vigfusson says
of him :[1] " The true father of Icelandic letters, as well as the first
prose writer and the first historian, Ari's influence and example
kindled the flame which burns with no uncertain light in many
a noble story, and shines fairest and brightest in the works of his
true spiritual sons, the Sturlunga."

[1] Prolegomena—"Sturlunga Saga," 5 : Vigfusson.

'Landnámabók,' written before 1140 A.D., treats of the whole
island, and might be a sort of guide-book to the traveller. It
is a fascinating record, telling of the pedigrees and exploits of
the first settlers, of the lands they found, and their adventures,
and letting in many a curious side-light on life as it was then.
Four thousand names are chronicled, one-third of these being
women, who, we may observe, took a prominent part in old
Norse history.

The outline of the story of the first settlement of Iceland has
been often told, but a slight sketch of it is almost necessary to
connect it with some other less known incidents that I shall give
out of 'Landnámabók.'

The time is the middle of the ninth century. First come the
discoverers. Gardarr the Swede is first named. He was driven
out of the Pentland Firth far to the north and west till he sighted
land. He sailed all round and found it was an island. He spent
a winter by a fjord, called from that first house he built on its
shores *Husavik*—good fishing quarters to this day. "And much
he praised the land." Then came Nadd-Oddur the Viking, who
dwelt alone on Faröe because he had made all other lands too
hot to hold him. He was steering for home when he was driven
out of his course by the waves—*sæhafi* is the one word which
describes it—to a fjord in the east, where he landed, and climbed
the highest mountain near, but saw no smoke nor any signs of
man. But the snow fell, and he called the land Snjóland—and
praised it much. Next came Flóki the Viking, who was the first
to sail in search of this much-praised Snjóland. He let three
consecrated ravens fly, after a time, to show him the way, "as
the loadstone was not then known," says the author, apologeti-
cally. The first raven flew back to the mast, the second flew
high in the sky, but returned again, but the third raven flew
far away, and Flóki followed and found the land. With him
were Thorolfr, and Herjolfr, and Faxi from the Hebrides. They
stayed the winter, but found so much fishing that they neglected
to make hay in time—found no grass lived through the winter,
and thus lost their cattle. "The winter was rather cold. Flóki

went up a high mountain, and saw a fjord to the north, full of icebergs, and he named the land Iceland. The following year they returned to Norway, and Flóki said evil of the land. Herjolfr said the whole truth, good and bad, and Thorolfr said butter dripped from every blade of grass."

Now came the first actual settlers—two foster-brothers from Norway, who had got into manslaying troubles, Leif and Ingolf. Of Leif it is briefly said that "he warred in Ireland, and found there a great earth-house"—a tomb, or perhaps a Pict's house. "He went in, and it was dark till he saw the glitter of the weapon that the earth-dweller held. Leif killed the man"— who had already been killed once before—"and took the sword, and much property besides, and afterwards he was called Hjorleif, or Sword Leif." He married Ingolf's niece Helga, who sailed with him, and he brought besides ten thralls from Ireland. Ingolf sacrificed much to the gods, but Hjorleif would never sacrifice. Together they went to Iceland, and first settled the land A.D. 874. They settled in different places on the south coast. Hjorleif was murdered by his Irish thralls, who fled to the islands called after them ever since, the Westmanna Islands. Ingolf followed them there and killed them all.

Ingolf himself considered it a duty to settle where the wooden pillars of his temple, which he had thrown overboard as guides, should drift ashore. They drifted up in barren Reykjavik, much to the displeasure of some of his followers. One—Karli—remarked, "Ill we did in passing by the good lands to settle on this *út nes*" (promontory). And he went back to the Olfus river. Many people have since echoed that remark, but destiny has been too strong for reason, and Reykjavik remains the capital of Iceland to this day. There Ingolf lived and prospered, much deploring at first the fate of Hjorleif—"That good fellow who was vilely slain by slaves; thus, I see," he moralises, "what happens to those who will never sacrifice."

Three religious types were already found in these early days: the man who trusts to himself and ignores all power above him, the man who sacrifices much according to the forms of the day, and the man who penetrates through that form to the ideal in all religions—the pure life consecrated to the All Father. Of Ingolf's grandson, Thorkell Máni, it is, said: "He was a heathen man who lived as purely as the excellent Christian men of after-times. When he was dying he told them to bear him into the sunshine, and gave himself to the hands of that God who had created the sun."

Many such vivid sketches of character are given in a few brief words in 'Landnámabók.' I shall quote a very few more. "Hallr the godless was the name of a man, he was the son of Helgi the godless. Father and son would never sacrifice, and trusted only in their own might."

The next settler is quite a variety. Orlygr was fostered in the faith of Bishop Patrick, in the Southern Isles, and he took out with him wood to build a church and bells, and consecrated earth to put under the corner pillar of the church. The bishop described the lie of the land where he was to settle, and through storm and tempest he sought it, wintering in the fjord he called after the bishop, Patrick's Fjord. At last he settled at Esjuberg, under Kjarlaness, and founded the church still there, which he dedicated to St Columba.

Another early Christian, called Asolfr, came out, who wished not to eat with heathen men. Wherever he went he had good fishing, thus exciting the not surprising envy of the neighbours, who had no sport. They drove him from place to place, but always with the same results,—his brook or waterfall swarmed with fish, which disappeared, or at least were not caught, when he was gone. However, he settled at last at Holmi, where the church now stands, and was considered a holy if much-tried sportsman. These were, I think, the only recorded Christian settlers, except, indeed, the Lady Aud, the Deeply Wealthy, who came round by Ireland and Orkney, bringing with her many Christian traditions and a cross, which she set up, but which after her death was desecrated.

Thorolf Mostraskegg, on the other hand, was a devout follower

of Thor, to whom he consecrated a shrine on the promontory running out beyond Breidafjord, where all was held most sacred.
Here he set up a Thor's stone, where men were broken in sacrifice, and a doom-ring, which men held when giving judgments,
and a place where the quarter *thing* was held.   Both in heathen
and Christian times Church and State were well knit together in
Iceland.

Another settlement with a dash of legendary sorcery about it
is thus described.   Grimur, who had come to the place hence
called Steingrimsfjord in the North, was out fishing one day with
his men.   His son, Thorir, lay at the stern with a sealskin bag
drawn over his head, which in those days was connected with
magic, perhaps as protecting wizards from evil spirits.   "Grimur
drew up in the net a sea-monster or merman, and as he came up
the captor asked him to give him a forecast as to where he should
settle."   The obliging monster answered that he could say nothing about Grimur; "but as to your son, who lies in the seal bag,
he shall take land where Skálm your mare lies down under the
cliff."

They got no more out of the merman; and "later in the winter,
when the son was ashore, Grimur and all his men were lost at
sea.   Thorir and his wife followed the mare Skálm up and down
the land for long, until she lay down under a cliff, south, near
Borgarfjord; and here, at Raudamel, he settled and became a
great chief.   In time the mare Skálm died, and was buried by
the spring still called Skálmarkeldu.   "Thorir lived to be old
and blind, when one evening late he came out and perceived
[how?] that an ill-looking big man rowed over Kaldarós, went up
to the farm of Hrifi, and dug there by the wall-side, and at night
the earth-fire came up there, and the great Borgar lava was spread
over the farms that now are all hidden."

This family legend has a touch of Southern folk-lore about it
which reminds us that many of the colonists, like the Lady Aud,
the Deeply Wealthy, came round by Orkney or Ireland, bringing
with them Erse names and traditions; bringing also, it is more
than likely, an infusion of the poetic Celtic temperament to blend

with the realistic Teuton mind. For the earliest Icelandic poetry is full of that magic charm of expression which, as Matthew Arnold truly says, is the missing quality in the verses of the purest Teutonic races.

The compilation of ancient poems called the 'Elder Edda,' has been associated with the name of Sæmund the learned (born 1056): although first written down in Iceland, they are older than its settlement, and the property of the whole Scandinavian race. They are full of untranslatable beauty. The concise force and fire of the language, where all sentence-formation is subservient to the idea, makes that idea wonderfully luminous; while the inflections render the meaning clear whatever may be the position of the words. Good poets have in vain tried to translate them, proving that though the sense may be rendered, the aroma, the poetic fire, is lost.

Vigfusson[1] is of opinion that these poems originated chiefly among the Norse settlers in Ireland, Scotland, and the Western Isles ; that they were chiefly composed about the time of Alfred, in the very high tide of the Viking expeditions, and first recited at the feasts or night-watches by sea or land of these wandering warriors. He brings various philological reasons forward in proof of this, and at least shows a connection between some of the songs and Celtic lands. For instance, birds of the British Isles are mentioned, and Scottish river names ; and there are Celtic turns of expression. Even socially there is a description of the thrall as an ugly person—a creature of a different race from the *karl* or freeman. This points to a society in which the thrall was of the captive Celtic race, a different race from the Northern conqueror, and does not apply to either Iceland or Norway. Wherever these poems were composed—and some date from Greenland—there is no doubt the ancient Norse rovers were their authors, and they form a fair poet's garland for any nation. Certainly these Norsemen excelled the Saxons as much in song as in arms : and one can easily imagine the spirit kindled by the Skalds who chanted these songs of the heroes to the Vikings by the

[1] Prolegomena—"Sturlunga Saga."

inland camp fires, or on the crowded decks when the wind was good and the men were idle.

The 'Elder Edda' may then be considered a fragmentary collection of the poetry of the Norsemen, unwritten when Iceland was colonised, but known there as in Norway, chanted at the meetings of the dividers of the land, and over the cradles of the next generation, and written down by Sæmund or some other Icelander two centuries later. Some of the poems, as Voluspa, tell of the old mythology, or, as Morris puts it—

"Tales of the framing of all things, and the entering in of time
From the halls of the outer heaven; so near they knew the door;
Wherefore uprose a sea-king, and his hands that loved the oar
Now dealt with the rippling harp-gold, and he sang of the shaping of earth,
And how the stars were lighted, and where the winds had birth." [1]

Many lays tell stories about the Asa or gods, and through the veil of the fairy tale a hidden meaning of deep significance can often be traced. They are not always respectful in tone towards the Asa; indeed some of them are full of jests at their expense. Words of wisdom and counsel are the subject of other lays; and others, the most beautiful of all, are stories of the heroes, and of the proud and faithful ladies who were their queens and companions. Such are the lays of Sigurd, the fragmentary remains of the oldest form of the *Nibelungen Lied*, the 'Lays of Helgi,' and several more. It is worth while learning Icelandic, if merely to read these fine poems, as only they can be read, in the original. The women are there represented as brave and true, and as willing to lay down their lives in a just cause as the men. Vindictive and merciless to their foes, yet intensely affectionate and true to their friends, they were worthy of the high respect in which they were held, and of the love of the heroes. In the 'Lay of Helgi' for instance, it is related how Helgi had slain the father of Sigrun his wife, to rescue her from an abhorred marriage; but in due time her brother was forced to avenge the father by slaying Helgi, and tells her regretfully of the deed. She breaks into a terrible denunciation. A few lines will show something of the

[1] 'Sigurd the Volsing,' Book I., by W. Morris.

concise force produced by the negative form of the verb—the
suffixed *t* which reverses the action, *e.g.*, making *renna* (may it
run) into *rennat* (may it not run)—

"Skridat that skip	May that ship not sweep onwards
er und thér skrida	That ought to sweep on with thee,
Thott oskabyrr	Though the wished-for wind
Eptir leggast.	Blows straight behind it.
Rennat sá marr	May that horse not run
er und thér renni	That ought to run for thee,
Thottu fjandr thina	Though from thy foes
fordask eigir.	Thou hast need to fly.
Bitiat that sverd	May that sword not bite
er thú bregdir	That thou shalt draw,
Nema sjálfum thèr	Except against thine own self.
Syngir um höfdi," &c.	It sings round the head, &c.

Then one of Sigrun's maidens tells her how she has seen a
great sight near Helgi's mound—a company of horsemen—of
men who had departed; was it the twilight of the gods already?
or had the dead heroes leave to revisit their homes? Sigrun
after this stayed always by the mound haunted by Helgi, who
said that all his grief was owing to the cruel tears wept by his
true wife; "every tear falls on the breast of thy lord, cold-wet
and bitter-sharp, heavy with sorrow." But Sigrun's plaint goes
on, "Now the night has come, and the earnes sit on the ash-
boughs, and all the folk drift to the Thing of dreams," and yet
Helgi comes not." And so she dies beside him, assured that, as
he said, they should yet be happy together, though they had lost
both lands and life; "for now are brides abiding in the mound,
king's daughters sit beside us."

The 'Younger Edda,' was written by Snorri Sturlason, perhaps
the greatest writer Iceland ever produced—born A.D. 1178—died
1248. It is a sort of handbook of the old mythology, written in
his own beautiful prose, with many fragments of the old lays interspersed. He gives, besides, a kind of dictionary of the expres-
sions and periphrases used by the Skalds, with examples from
their poems. From this book we derive almost all the knowledge
we possess of the Northern myths, and the inner meaning of the
Northern poetry. Snorri wrote, besides, the great history of

Norway called the 'Heimskringla,' elsewhere spoken of. Several other histories and many historical biographies were written about this date ; of which the 'Orkneyan Saga' is especially interesting to us ; and the brilliant era of the ancient literature was closed by the history written by Snorri's nephew Sturla, hence called the 'Sturlunga Saga.'

One notable point on this whole literature is the light it throws on the position of women in the North. Originally, here as elsewhere, the woman was the ward of her father or husband or brother. The daughter was indeed the property of her father, often his most precious possession, but there is no trace of purchase of the woman from her father by the bridegroom, as in most early societies. It is evident, from the very meaning of the word for marriage, *Brudlaup* — *i.e.*, *bride-run*, that there was a time when the bride was carried off by force from her home ; and many marriage customs point to such an origin. But in historical times, marriages were carefully arranged with the consent of the heads of both the families concerned ; and the greatest sensitiveness was shown in the matter of honourable courtship, though the youths and maidens were allowed to meet each other freely. The bride brought her dower with her, sometimes a rich one, as she shared with her brothers. And in case of widowhood or divorce, she reclaimed all the property she brought with her, though, if divorced, she had to leave behind her the property settled on her by her husband, called the morning gift. Divorce had to be taken into consideration, for it was very easy in heathen times. A few angry words, or a slap on the cheek, were grounds enough —the wife could in such a case call witnesses, declare herself divorced, and go away with her dowry. The wife, it is said, often threatened to divorce her husband, if he would not act according to her wishes ; for it was not difficult to find a pretext, although divorces were not, after all, nearly so frequent as one might have supposed from their facility—a certain discredit was attached to them. If a man wore a woman's dress, or *vice versa*, it was ground for a divorce ; the same if a woman wore her hair cut straight across the brow like a man. Such a law might

D

liberate a good many couples in this country now. Even in present days the Icelanders are at liberty, like other Lutherans, to divorce each other, for what seem to us small causes, such as mere incompatibility of temper, but they have to give notice of their intention two or three years before the law can take effect; and meanwhile both the clergyman and the magistrate have to be called in to adjust matters if possible: and often before the required time has elapsed, the couple have made friends again, and live together happily ever after.

To return to the days of the sagas. After a woman had been once married, whether she was a widow or divorced, she became a free agent. The married woman was, from the earliest times, the true household leader, the queen or companion of her lord. The sagas tell of the same freedom of the wife in her own sphere, and association with her husband's life and pursuits, which is the ideal of wedded life now in this country. She was not, like the Greek wife, doomed to a narrow life in her own side of the house apart from the interests of the men; still less was she like the plaything of the Eastern harem; and old age did not deprive her of her influence, while it added to her dignity. Her words were often then held sacred, her influence grew paramount, as one to whom the gods had imparted a more than human wisdom. The wise women of the North were old; they did not need to enhance their power by the young beauty of Pallas Athene. A glance at the respective mythologies will show us the contrast between the stories of Frigga, pure and strong, the ideal of the married women, Iduna, the tender goddess of youth and spring, and Freyja, the honourable northern type of Aphrodite, and the impure legends that have gathered round the names of the divinities honoured by ancient Greece and Rome.

The power of the Asa[1] or Summer Gods, satisfactorily summed up, I am bound to think, in the name Asvaldr or Oswald, is almost always in Norse mythology on the side of right and justice. But that power is limited and foredoomed to an overthrow, when

---

[1] Ös = Ásvaldr, meaning power of the Summer Gods, was much used by the Teutons as a name of dedication, and especially popular in Northumbria.

the giants, or the blind natural forces, and Loki and his children, or the evil forces, unite, and all is crushed into ruin in the "twilight of the gods." Hope lives on indeed, like a streak of morning dawn in the horizon, the hope of some brighter and calmer existence beyond that darkness; but all that is definite in the thought of the Norseman about life and futurity may be summed up in the ideas of combat, and of all-conquering fate. This fighting ideal no doubt reacted on the character of the Norsemen; it naturally fostered their cruel propensities, and also, as they were used to consider the combat in its essence as an almost hopeless struggle against blind fate, that idea blunted their conscience with regard to treachery, their greatest and deepest defect. May it not be allowable to take any advantage that can be snatched, when, in the long-run, one is sure to be so terribly overmatched? Luck and ill-luck were tremendous factors in all actions; and the lucky man might steal the horse, while the unlucky man was bullied for looking over the hedge. The gods themselves were not incapable of availing themselves of rather unfair stratagems; and Loki, who exhibited the very acme of treachery, was more laughed at than reprobated by the more respectable inhabitants of Valhall. There was, however, a great deal of redeeming humour about Loki, some of which has no doubt been passed on to the devil of Norse and Scottish popular stories, who is in some respects a personification of mischief rather than of evil. And in spite of the many fine qualities of the Northern race, their qualities of cruelty and treachery in due time bore their own bitter fruit. The fierce warriors who owned the "White Christ" as their master, but imported into his service the wrath of Odin and the delight in battle of Valhall, destroyed each other by their own ferocity, and in time affected the national character in the manner they would least have liked, exhausting its energies, so that the spirit of gallantry and enterprise seems to have died away with the warlike instincts which were once so powerful.

The beginning of the end is to be seen in the 'Sturlunga Saga,'—a history of Iceland from *circa* 1100 to 1263, by

Sturla,—told chiefly as centred in the great Sturla family. The
style is so vivid that the events seem to pass under our eyes ;
but they show a terrible condition of public affairs. One chieftain rivalled another, maintaining a court of followers who knew
no law but his word. Law cases were indeed decided at the
annual *things;* but the criminals constantly received the protection of some chief, who by favouring reckless outlaws hoped to
add to the number of his lawless followers. ·And so it went on,
till the best men, weary of the hopeless state of affairs, flung
their free republic into the arms of Norway,—and Iceland fell,
never to revive. It is an interesting study of the result of too
weak an executive,—the political freedom was absolute, but the
State too weak to defend individual freedom.

The bad times may have been partly produced by the cessation of the Viking expeditions, which cessation certainly brought
dire confusion into Norway. There was no European outlet for
the warlike chiefs, little provided for by the *odal* laws of the
division of land ; and they worried each other like wild beasts in
a cage. The division of the landed estates among all the children
of the owner, which worked well in a small population, and with
resources beyond seas, showed its weakness in other circumstances. It has probably prevented Norway from ever developing into a great nation, and may be one of the causes of something there is disappointing in the otherwise excellent modern
Norwegian national character. There is in it a low level of tolerable contentment, but a want of dash and enterprise—of briskness
—a want, indeed, of men who can show the way ; perhaps to be
summed up in the want of an upper class, or of leaders. And the
Icelanders may have suffered in the same way. The habitable
lands were getting narrow for the inhabitants in Sturla's time ;
yet we read of parties of six or seven hundred armed men riding
together. It is difficult to understand how they could have been
fed by their leaders. No doubt, before Newfoundland stock-fish
and southern whales, not to say gas, were in the market, Icelandic produce, such as dried fish and oil, was far more valuable
than now. In the numerous petty wars not many men were

killed, but numbers were kept unsettled and idle ; and the best were killed—there was no survival of the fittest in the struggle for existence. To do the leaders justice, the men who made the quarrels were the foremost in the fight : the old families were mostly stamped out, and Iceland began to deserve the reproach of a Norse lord in the ninth century, who said he would never settle in a mere fishing station.

Before the heroes were all gone, it fortunately occurred to some excellent contemporary authors to write their biographies. These lives of the great men and bishops, written in the thirteenth and fourteenth centuries, are somewhat realistic narratives, evidently aiming before all things at truth ; but they often show great dramatic power, bringing out the character as well as the history of the men they tell of, reminding one rather of Plutarch than of any medieval writers. We become well acquainted with such persons as Aron the brilliant warrior, Gudmundur Dyra the fierce chieftain, Hrafn the man of many accomplishments. Hrafn, for instance, "was mighty in metal and timber work, as Volundur the smith, poet, lawyer, and the best of doctors ; learned in all wisdom, elegant and winning, a great bowman, and the best of spear-throwers ; a tall man and strong, with straight fair features and dark hair, kind, and of noble disposition." Who would not wish to read the checkered life of such a hero ?

Among the most salient characters set before us in the biographies is the blessed Gudmundur the Bishop. The country abounds in local legends connected with him : the churches are still shown that he consecrated, the wells that he hallowed. Bishop Gudmundur just missed being canonised,—he never passed the examination at Rome for full saintship. And indeed no wonder,—the devil's advocate might have easily held a brief against him ; he remained, therefore, in the lower rank of *Blessed*. He flourished in the thirteenth century, and first took the priest-hood owing to a shipwreck in which he met with an accident which made him a hopeless cripple. All the same he was a most stirring personage, and he left his mark on the land. He attracted to him a company of devoted followers, especially wild

young men. He lavished the money of the see upon troops of
idle vagabonds, who followed his fortunes wherever he went;
he only just did not fight himself, but was the cause of many
a fight between the secular chiefs and his followers, in which,
however justice might be divided, pluck and self-devotion were
never wanting to the bishop's men. One of his last retreats,
the lonely island of Grimsay, far to the north of the northern
coast, was the scene of a most exciting fight between the
bishop's men, who held the island, and the Sturlinga, who
assaulted it by sea. The bishop's party were overpowered, and
he himself was carried off a prisoner; for his person was always
respected, though his followers were slaughtered by his fierce
enemies.

Iceland boasts of two full saints, Bishop Jón and Bishop Thor-
leikr, who were duly canonised. They were, however, comparatively tame characters. There was far more enthusiasm for the
memory of St Olaf, or even our own Orkneyan St Magnus, whose
life in Icelandic is a good specimen of a later form of literature
which succeeded the spirited biographies of the thirteenth century. The influence of the Church and the cloister now began to
be felt, and the life of St Magnus is in style a curious mixture of
the saga and the "Golden Legend."

We are told that "Magnus the Saint, Earl of Orkney, was a
great warrior, and successful in war, handsome, just, and valiant,
and so popular that his cousin, the rival Earl of Orkney, who had
equal *odal* rights, murdered him out of pure jealousy, A.D. 1115."
The saint may have been rather provoking, as when he was
quite a young man, cruising in English waters with his cousin,
Magnus Barefoot, King of Norway, and a fight began between
the Northmen and Hugh, Earl of Chester, Magnus spoke up,
and said nothing would induce him to fight against people with
whom he had no quarrel. "Go down below, then," said the irate
king, "and do not lie about among the feet of the men who will
fight, if you dare not fight yourself, for I do not believe that
religion has anything to do with this affair." Magnus, however,
sat where he was, "took up a psalter, and sung psalms all

through the battle, not guarding himself at all. The battle was both hard and long, and for a while undecided, but at last Earl Hugh was slain, and King Magnus conquered. This was a fair miracle, for all might see how, in the midst of the heavy onslaught, when armed fighters were falling all round him, he remained unhurt."

We are told how, long afterwards, " this knight of heaven went to his death as if to a festival," encouraging the reluctant executioner, only directing him that he should strike him on the head with his battle-axe ; " for so should princes die, not hit on the neck like common men." Perhaps the Viking spirit needed some such valiant protest against it as that of the psalm-singing St Magnus, who seems, indeed, to have been an excellent man. Twenty years after his death, his murderer, Hakon, laid the foundations of the fair cathedral St Magnus in Kirkwall, which still preserves his memory fresh in Orkney.

It would take too much space if I were to follow the history of this literature beyond the point where it lost its unique character and became similar to the contemporary literature of the rest of Europe. There were always good writers in Iceland, if they ceased to be so original as their predecessors. But the lamp of literature has never gone out, it has been handed down through the darkest times, and now burns again clear and steady. The beautiful religious poem of the " Lily " was written in the monkish days that first succeeded the enthralment of Iceland : then the ballads were made, and many religious books were written. About two centuries ago some of the old literature was examined, rescued, and printed. In spite of the poverty into which the land had fallen, the establishment of two printing presses caused a great revival of literature.

Henderson, in 1812, speaks, indeed, of good writers toiling hard for their living in the hay-fields ; of clever MSS. that never saw the light owing to the poverty of the authors.

Brighter days have now dawned, and good writers, both in prose and verse, are to be found in large proportion to the population. Above all, the grand old literature is more and more attracting the attention both of landsmen and foreigners. Icelandic has been placed in the curriculum of the Norwegian universities, and the language has even been named as an alternate subject in the examinations offered by the London University.

It is a constant pleasure, while travelling in Iceland, to hear the old inflected language on every side. Every peasant knows the grammar, and runs through the complicated inflections of the nouns and pronouns with unfailing accuracy. Our experience is, however, that very little of the language can be picked up during a summer tour; but although it requires hard study, it also rewards it. Within the last ten years some books have been published that make it not difficult to acquire enough Icelandic to enable a tourist to understand a good deal, and make good progress when in the country. Chief among these is the 'Icelandic Prose Reader,' by Vigfusson and Powell, Clarendon Press, which every tourist should possess. For more advanced work, there is the excellent 'Icelandic-English Lexicon,' Cleasby and Vigfusson, and a fine new edition of the 'Sturlunga Saga,' both Clarendon Press. In illustration of the low estimation in which Icelandic has long been held by the Danes, I may mention that a leading bookseller at Bergen, at whose house I dined, informed me that his grandmother, who was daughter to the then Governor of Iceland, was forbidden by her parents to learn the "peasant dialect of the country," meaning the classic Norse, from which Danish has been derived and has declined. He was greatly surprised on being shown the above-mentioned works. There is, however, an old Norse Society in Norway, which encourages the writing of books in an archaic dialect, verging on Icelandic. It may be more to the point, perhaps, for scholars to promote the study of the classical language itself, and to preserve it from the foreign admixtures and Germanisms which have injured the Danish language. Three newspapers are published in Iceland, which are useful to the traveller, as they contain plenty of modern words which are not to be found in the sagas.

The modern books are more difficult to the foreigner than the sagas ; and many recent books are translations, which, of course, do not count as literature. The translation of Milton's ' Paradise Lost ' is, however, said to be remarkably fine, and quite like an original work. There are one or two novels, rather wordy and German in style; but the one said to be the best, ' Piltur og Stulka,' I have not read. There are several modern poets and good song - writers, such as Bjarni Thorarensen, Steingrimur Thorsteinson, and Mattias Jochmundsen, the last a living writer.

Modern editions of several of the sagas can be procured at Reykjavik ; and the ' Heimskringla,' or History of Norway, by Snorri Sturlason, and the ' Eddas,' can be purchased at Copenhagen.

A learned society, the *Islenzka Bókmentafèlag*, has existed in Iceland since the year 1852, which issues three or four books annually, including generally, besides a *résumé* of the news of the year and other official pamphlets, an edition of some old book, often printed for the first time from the original manuscript.

CHAPTER VII.

MOSSFELL—HVALFJORD AND ITS LEGENDS—REYKHOLT—KALMAN-
STUNGA—CENTRAL LAVA—SURTSHELLIR.

WE left Reykjavik for Akureyrei, the chief northern port of the
island, on the 22d of July, expecting to meet there the Scottish
steamer. As it happened, neither we nor the steamer ever
reached that port, as she broke down at sea, and had to be towed
ignominiously home ; and we in consequence had to return to
Reykjavik, and put off our departure for six weeks. But we saw
all the more of the country ; and our journey back by another
route left us nothing to regret. The start was a prolonged
amusement of two hours : our twelve ponies collecting at the
door with much stamping and bustle ; friends inviting us to
farewell coffee-parties in their houses ; everything we wanted
appearing too late ; our guide's pretty wife running down with
her little children to see her husband off ;—in short, we had intended to go at six in the evening, and rode off at eight, and we
considered ourselves punctual—so demoralised as to time-keeping
had we by this time become. But what matters time, when no
one.is kept waiting, and there are no trains to catch, and it is
light all night ? Besides, here no one really knows what o'clock
it is. Those who like to feel that they are punctual, may make
it whatever time they like, as at sea, and regulate all matters by
their own watches. It is much more important to keep temper
than time, as fussy tourists will soon discover. A genuine Icelander will not be hurried, and resents any incivility, probably

making no reply, but letting things quietly go all wrong with
an air of imperturbable innocence.

One is sometimes inclined to envy the frankness with which
the Americans describe their friends in print, but without ventur-
ing to rival them, we may say of our guide, that he proved on
better acquaintance to be quite a character. He was so versa-
tile : there was the clerical side—for he had completed his theological course, though he had hovered for years outside the
clerical profession ; then he was a keen sportsman and clever
shark-fisher ; he spoke idiomatic English, and had translated
the 'Pilgrim's Progress' into Icelandic ; his cod-liver oil had
gained a prize at the French Exhibition ; he was a hard rider,
and often shod the ponies himself ; he knew botany, and was so
medically inclined, that the old women used to run up from all
sides to consult him and receive his homœopathic medicines ;—in
short, he was a host in himself, and an excellent guide, as he not
only knew the country well, but, it appeared to us, every one in
it. At eight in the evening he called for us, with Skuli and all
the cavalcade ready at last ; we were at a final entertainment at
a friend's house, and rode away, followed by the farewell greetings of all the company.

The way to Mossfell, whither we were bound, is a pretty ride
to the north-east, and may be recommended to any one staying
at Reykjavik. Where the path skirts the sea-shore we passed
some fishermen dividing their newly caught grilse and herring
into shares, after the old fashion called *kjosa og deila* (choice
and deal)—one man dividing, and another with his back turned
assigning the lots. We bought some herring as a change from the
usual salmon, and rode on to Mossfell church, which we reached
exactly at midnight.

There is something rather eerie in this kind of arrival till you
are used to it. No inn appears with kindly lights and welcom-
ing voices, but you grope up to the churchyard gate, and dismount among the graves like Leonore and her spectre lover, and
a silent little black church receives you and offers you for all
entertainment a floor. But the "missionary mattresses," as our

cork pallets are called, and the good Scottish plaids, soon make
the floor comfortable; and we rested well, till a lovely morning
lured us out into the sunshine.

Mossfell church and parsonage are prettily situated on the first
slopes of the mountain-chain of Eysja, among steep meadows.
We breakfasted under the shade of the haycocks; for all the hill-
slope was astir with haymaking. These grassy hills rise above
into bare precipices of pink or white marl and clay, reminding one in appearance of some of the Apennines. Indeed both
the colouring and the temperature recalled the mountain-lands
of central Italy. The day was so hot, and the pastor and his
family so pleasant, that we lingered till 1 P.M., and then rode off
in a blaze of sunshine. We crossed the pass over Eysja, the mountain which is conspicuous from Reykjavik, and enjoyed a beautiful
view before descending into the valley of the great bog which had
seemed so formidable on our way from Rennyvellir; but it was a
trifle in this dry weather. We then went over a second mountain-
ridge, under lava-crags,—wreathed masses of wrenched, distorted
stuff, which looked as if, when liquid and boiling high, it had suddenly been turned into stone. Presently a fine view opens of the
beautiful Hvalfjord—or whale firth, which is well worth visiting.
It looked like a bit of the evening sky lying among the high purple
crags which enclosed it. When we reached the shore about ten
at night, we had to wait some time for the tide to go down, to
enable us to take a short cut to the other side, through the head-
waters of the fjord. The scene was exquisitely beautiful. On
one side stretched the fjord, narrow between the hills, and lighted
up in bars of red and gold by the sunset; on the other side a
good-sized river fell in an unbroken sheet of foam between two
grand, dark, square, basalt cliffs, and a distant pink-tinted snowy
hill showed over the black rocks of the foreground. Thence we
scrambled on towards the head of the longest branch of the fjord,
and when the tide was low, turned into the sea and rode through
the shallows for more than a mile to the opposite mountain.
The night was only a stiller and more mysterious day. Hundreds
of sea-birds slept on the dim water, but as we roused them, they

rose with shrill clamours, and broke it into long lines of silver. Then a clear yellow light began to peer over a mountain, it looked like a fire at first, but there appeared at last the very brightest moon I ever saw—too bright by far, said our guide, as it foreboded wind, which was already making the riding less pleasant. On we cantered over rough tracks, the morning brightening over the night sky, which was never at all dark, and the wind growing furious, screaming in our ears, and blowing up our sleeves. I had reached that dreamy state when the

mind refuses all fresh ideas, and I seemed to have been riding for a time beyond reckoning on a cream - coloured pony, in pursuit of a clattering drove of loose ponies, dreamily shifting before me, when at half-past one we stopped at what looked like a grassy mound, which was the farm of Hrabnarburg. After long knocking, a tall man doubled himself up sufficiently to get out at a very low door and helped to raise the tent, a matter of no small difficulty. They brought us hot coffee ; and in spite of straining ropes and storm and cold, we slept comfortably till morning.

This day's ride was really beautiful in the summer weather, but in this odd climate a change of wind to the north, such as had now occurred, brings sudden winter. It froze in the night outside our tent, and the gale continuing in the morning, made our further journey impossible. You could lean quite comfortably back on the wind. Everything not tethered was flying : my handkerchief went away into space. Washing in the little inlet which lay among the rocks could best be managed by tying a long string to a big sponge, and throwing it out beyond the froth to fetch water. We piled turf high round our tent, but still feared that it might take to flight ; and Miss Menzies was rather inclined to take shelter in the house at night, until it was clearly ascertained that this meant either sleeping in the *badstofa*—a room like a ship's cabin, with a double row of berths, the sleeping-place of the whole household—or on the kitchen-floor, which was of earth, and sloped away ominously into darkness and the unknown. This *badstofa* was just like a *cubiculum* in a Roman catacomb, and might have confirmed the views of a party whom I had met in much the same sort of room in the Catacomb of St Calixtus. They had evidently just landed in Italy, and when the guide explained that in this cemetery the holy Pope Damasus and other martyrs were interred, the family all turned with eager questions to the young lady of the party who obviously had learned Italian, and was their trusted interpreter. But her mind evidently still ran on the recent voyage, and with some gentle hesitation she explained, pointing to the largest grave, that, "Early Christians once lived here, and *that*," she faltered, "is the berth of the papa." "To be sure," said another, with fine faith ; "and the little ones had the smaller berths. Poor things, how crowded they must have been ! "

And crowded the folk of Hrabnarburg must have been ; but though their house was so poor, they had several horses and cows, and they were not poverty-stricken. Ulfheldur, the hostess, made signs of great amity ; but we could hardly talk together then. Four years later, when we passed that way, she told us she had always thought us charming people, and longed for our return,—perhaps the more, as she had only once had visitors since. On our last day's journey we had met no one but the postman with his three horses, although this route is considered to be frequented.

The scenery was grand. Two mountain cliffs stood opposite each other like huge threatening castles—one called the Eagle Rock (*Arnafjall*), the other Raven - burg (*Hrabna-burg*); grass slopes descended steeply from them to the basalt cliffs of the shore. In these cliffs were deep crannies where the wind could

Hvalfjord.

not disturb us, though it flattened the water before us, tearing the foam up into the air, which was salt with sea-drift. A place of tempests this from the earliest recorded times. The first settler here—a thousand years ago—a man called Kalman, from the Soder Isles, or South Hebrides, lost two sons in a storm in the fjord, and then moving inland gave his name to Kalman-stunga, whither we were bound. Drowning, however, seemed to run in his family, and who can escape his fate? He was drowned in the ford of Hvità, a river which we were soon to cross. The sailors whose funeral we had attended the other day at Rennyvellir were already not the last of Hvalfjord's victims, for on this day another boat was lost.

Opposite lay the large rocky island, inhabited in the heroic times by Hord and Geir, the chiefs of a stirring party of out-laws, with their wives and families, whose adventures are told at length in the *Holmveryja* or Island Defence Saga. It is an old story of heathen times, and gives a graphic picture of the manners and customs of Vikings at home.

Hord and Geir were foster-brothers. Hord was of good family; but his father, who was already an old widower when he married his mother, the proud Signy of Hvalfjord, was never much loved by her. Signy possessed two treasures which she valued beyond all else—her horse Svartfaxi (dark-mane), and a certain necklace. Svartfaxi, on the journey to her wedding, fell over a cliff and was killed, and Signy wished much, therefore, to turn back, but was overruled by Torfi, her brother. Afterwards, when her son Hord was three years old—a fine child, but slow in walking—as she sat in the middle of the room in her best attire, prepared to attend a sacrifice, he tottered for the first time alone across the floor, grasped her necklace and fell, breaking it in three places. So angry was the father, that he sent Hord to be brought up by Geir's parents, who were peasants. Signy later went to visit her brother Torfi, and there she died after giving birth to a daughter. This child was therefore hated by Torfi, who desired that it should be exposed to perish; but it was so pretty that his servant spared it, and Torfi discovered, to his great wrath, some months afterwards, that it was alive. It had also been named Thurida, and water had been poured over it; and as it would have been counted murder to kill it as he wished *after* these ceremonies, he packed it on the back of a beggar-man, and sent it to its father. However, Thurida grew up into a fair woman, and in due time she married Illugi, who lived on the shore of this fjord. Hord[1] and Geir became great warriors, and were

---

[1] Hord is not the most dignified form of this name, but it, or rather *Hördr* is the nominative form, *Hardar* being genitive, *Herdi* dative, and *Hörd* accusative; and it seems incomplete and unfamiliar without its declensions.

liegemen of Harald Greyskin, King of Norway, and friends of Hroar, Earl of Gautland. Hord married fair Helga, his daughter, and she sailed with the champions; and they won fame and property on all the seas. Then comes the beginning of the end—a chapter ominously headed "Drink." Very likely this was the first cause of Hord's misfortunes, if not exactly as related in the saga, which now goes on to tell, with considerable force, one of the stock heroic achievements.

On the first night of Yule they were all drinking hard in the earl's hall, when Hord stood up and vowed on the pillar of the high seat, "Here I swear that before next Yule I shall have broken up the burial-mound of Soti the Viking." The earl said, "A mighty vow, and not easy to keep; for Soti was a great troll while living, and is one half more so since his death."

Hord's friends, however, swore to follow him, and the saga tells how, in a thick wood, they found a great mound; but only after five days of digging did they reach the timber burial-chamber and break open the door. Hord bade all beware of the evil odour that would come out, and he waited behind the door till it dispersed; but two careless people died of it. Down then went Hord, lowered by ropes, into the darkness; he found a second door, and then came an earthquake, and all the lights went out. Geir now came down also, and brought wax and fire, while those above held the ropes; and then they broke open the door and found themselves in a ship. Soti sat by the mast in the midst of his treasures, and was fearful (*ógoliger*) to behold. Hord now began to collect the gold, when Soti sprang on him. Hord called from under him to Geir to kindle the wax-light. "Bring light," he shouted, "and let Soti see how lovely he is!" and whenever the light shone on him the vampire slid downwards. And Hord got much gold and a splendid sword and helmet; also a ring sure to bring ill-luck to the wearer unless it were a woman. "No longer shalt thou enjoy the gold of the sea, thou over-old wretch" (*skaud af gömul*), said Hord, as he came out of the tomb to find that some of the people outside had gone mad with

E

horror, and were struggling with their braver comrades, who wished to prevent them from running away.

Hord now returned to his hereditary estate here at the head of Hvalfjord, but nothing went well with him. His household were too rich and too powerful not to excite jealousies. The neighbours quarrelled with them about horses, about games, about everything, and banded against them, including even Illugi, his brother-in-law, till they were fain to retire to the island, where they lived by plunder. There were always from eighty to a hundred people on the island, and they held it long against all comers. But there was one foe with whom they could not cope—Thorbjorg Katla, an old sorceress. When she waved her staff over her head darkness and wild weather was wont to follow, and confusion fell on her foes. One might well suppose Katla still dwelt, a *skaud af gömul*, by Hvalfjord, so strange are the caprices of the storm here. Years went by and Geir at last was caught by treachery, and Hord next day was lured to the land by a false friend, Thorstein Gold-clasp, suspecting nothing till he beheld drifting on the low skerries the corpse of Geir. It only remained to sell his life dearly, and all his men were also slain or dispersed.

The women now come to the front. Helga stood on the island and saw her husband's betrayal and fall, but she would not fall into the foeman's hands. A Roman matron would have killed herself, but the Northern spirit never despairs till, as the proverb says, all the refuges are choked with snow. She cast herself to swim off to the land at night, and carried with her her four-year-old son Bjorn. She landed him and returned to meet her eight-year-old son Grimkell, who was sinking exhausted in the sea, and brought him in. Carrying one boy and leading the other, she walked far to the house of Illugi, where she sat down under the *tun* wall, and sent in little Grimkell to ask his aunt Thurida for protection. "When she saw Helga she could not speak, it was so much to her. She led her and the children into the out-bower (*uti-bur*), and in the evening home came Illugi and many men with him ; and they all talked joyfully of the death of Hord, and how Thorstein Gold-clasp had slain him. In the night Thurida came with a short sword and aimed it at her husband as he lay in bed ; and his hands were much wounded by grasping the blade. She said: 'All is past between us, yet if thou wilt have peace between us again, bring me the head of Thorstein Gold-clasp.' And Illugi consented. Next day he fought with Thorstein, and brought the head to his wife, who loftily remarked that she cared nothing for it now it was off his shoulders. 'But further,' she continued, 'you must be a friend to Helga and her sons if ever I am to love you again.' He replied that doubtless they were drowned, as they were not on the island, and had no boat ; 'but willingly will I promise thee this, as nothing need be done about it.' Then Thurida brought them forth. 'I have said too much,' said Illugi, 'but my words must hold.' All thought Thurida had shown herself great-minded."

Next day we rode over the low mountain-pass which separates the Hvalfjord from the Borgarfjord district, the pass over which poor Helga had toiled with her children. The wind was still furious, but we faced it, which would not have been possible the day before. The valleys on the other side were all covered with fine grass. Several lakes lie among them, lashed this day into waves of steely blue—the last one, Skoradalvatn, was edged by welcome birch-trees, and recalled a Scotch Highland loch. Not so the pretty valley of Reykholt, which we reached towards evening,—it could only have been in Iceland. The sun shone out and showed puffs of smoke and jets of steam, or leaping fountains of boiling water, glittering here and there all the way up the broad grassy valley. Several farms were visible on the slopes, and haymakers were at work near them. Cattle and horses grazed about ; and fiery little bulls galloped up to inspect us, and had to be driven off by a firm countenance and cracking whips. The abundant river ran in loops and curves all along the valley, while we rode quite straight, and forded it thirteen times. The hot springs which we passed were various, and quite unlike each other. One rose in an intermitting column of steam from a kind of boiling bog ; another burst in a beautiful fountain of hot

water out of a rock in the middle of the ice-cold river. It was
also slightly intermittent, sometimes bubbling low, and then
again leaping six feet high for a few beats. Another was a kind
of double spring with two jets, which worked alternately. I
wished that invalids could come here and enjoy the sweet air of
this lonely valley, and the hidden and unknown virtues of these
doubtless healing mineral springs; but it is a long way to Reykholt, and there is no inn to receive such patients as might chance
to survive the journey.

We were received by the *profastur* or dean at Reykholt, who
lives by the church ten or twelve miles up the valley—a fine-looking cheery man, but reminding one of a jovial skipper rather
than of a clergyman. He gave us the guest-room, where my
companion at once nestled under the eider-down *duvet* to warm
herself; for it was cold, and there are only two means of warming
yourself indoors in the summer-time—to put on eider-down or to
cook. I chose cooking, and must apologise for saying something

about it; for I should convey
little idea of our wandering,
if I did not mention a matter
which was of such great importance to us, and the first
excitement wherever we arrived. Anything hot we had,
except coffee, was almost
always cooked by ourselves
with varying success. Be-
sides the methylated spirit
can which cooked the soup,
and the kettle, we had a frying-pan with tripod, which was
my special pride, bought at Silver's, Cornhill—a shop, by the
way, that makes one long to rush to some wilderness to try its
gipsy luxuries. It only cost 5s., and all shut up into the size of
a small soup-plate, and was supposed to cook mutton-chops and
steaks, &c., with only newspapers and rubbish for fuel. I had
made what might have almost been called a sacrilegious attempt

to fry trout in Thingvellir Church, which had consumed at a
blow all our packing-paper and the rubbish wedged in our boxes,
and with the poorest gastronomic results. This morning we
had game, and once more the pan was started, with bits of
peat and sticks for fuel. There rose a great smoke and a strong
smell of burning; all the inhabitants, headed by the *profastur*,
rushed to see what was the matter—to witness our failure, a
cold, smoked, singed bird, which Oddur carried off with others to
simmer in the hot spring. But hot-spring cookery certainly
destroys the flavour of wild ducks and plovers ; besides the sodden
effect, a certain suspicion of sulphur can be detected   For the
benefit of other travellers, I may add, that after giving up the
newspaper-fuel idea—which is not likely to be successful, as
there are probably no newspapers in a camp—I succeeded in
frying well in the pan, by cutting up the game, adding French
mustard and seasoning, and cooking briskly over the spirit-lamp ;
at least the dish used to taste delicious in a tent after a long
day's ride.

Reykholt was the home of the historian, Snorri Sturluson, in
the thirteenth century. His history of Norway is generally
allowed to be the best chronicle written in the middle ages ; and
indeed for animation and interest it is unsurpassed in the whole
range of historical literature. He wrote also the ' Younger Edda,'
a book to which we owe all our systematic knowledge of the
myths and religion of the old Scandinavians. Close by is the
church on the site of one he built consecrated to SS. Mary, Peter,
and Barbara. Some Runic stones in the churchyard are said to
be of his date ; the church bells above the lych-gate are old ; but
the chief relic of his time is a circular bath which he is known
to have built, and the excellent masonry of the thirteenth century
is still in complete repair. It is about sixteen feet in diameter,
and water-burdock and dock leaves droop over the brimming hot
water. If used as a bath, it is necessary to stop up the inlet
for a while, to let the water cool ; but there is a conduit, originally
intended for cold water, which is now choked up. Why is there
but one good bath in Iceland, and that one six hundred years

old? Yet it is known to have been otherwise in former times, and the chief bedroom of a house is still called the *badstofa* or bath-room. Now it may in some cases pass as a grisly sort of vapour-bath, owing to damp and crowded humanity.

Once upon a time, many hundred years ago, there lived a Norse Viking and hero called Ulf Usvo, which means the Un-washed Wolf. He was killed in a sea-fight, but apparently left a numerous race,—so numerous, that to this day it is to be feared his *sobriquet* would be no great distinction up the country in Iceland. It is no doubt difficult to keep an earth-house clean. Washing would only produce mud, and the deposit of peat-smoke within is warm, and gives a fine bit of colour; but the other fact, the personal dirt, in presence of plenty of fresh cold water, and often of hot water, laid on by Nature herself, is inexplicable, and really the worst drawback of Iceland. Still there is improvement here as elsewhere; cleanliness is more insisted on in the schools: and the houses of the better sort of people, to whom what I have said does not apply, are often beautifully kept; but I have been told by several ladies that it is achieved by dint of a hard struggle, with servants brought up in the dirt, and apt to feel chilly and uncomfortable when required to clean and be clean.

We were now travelling inland towards the icy hills, which loomed larger and larger before us; passing sometimes over stony wastes, sometimes over old lava pleasantly covered with birch copse six feet high. We forded the wide and rapid Hvità, whose white waters told of the neighbouring glaciers, and came pretty late to a grassy knoll, encircled by a rivulet, where stood the farm of Kalmanstunga.

It was too late to pitch the tent, so we decided on sleeping in the farm, and made our way into a dingy guest-room, with two beds and a box in it, and a low beam across it, which caught your head with a good rap every time you passed under without remembering to stoop. A good deal of roughing and fatigue are no doubt involved in Icelandic travel, but they are generally easily borne, owing to the pure wholesome air, which soon puts the traveller into first-rate condition. It was most pleasant to wake in the tent to its morning freshness, and the scent of grass and thyme; and the churches, too, are at least airy: but in an average farm like Kalmanstunga, the little window of the guest-room will not open, and the air has to pass through low winding passages among ever-increasing odours, before it reaches the bed-room door. We sometimes broke the window and paid for the accident; but this place was too far inland, and glass too precious for that resource. The guest-room was not, however, as bad as it looked: it was not peopled by small pests; and the depressing closeness of the night made the icy freshness of the morning air outside the more delicious.

The interior of Iceland, as is generally known, is a great un-inhabited grassless desert, for the population is mostly confined to the sea-shores and neighbouring valleys. In travelling from coast to coast this desert must be crossed; it edges the inhabited land, as the sea surrounds it on the other side, and gives it a strange charm—for us who suffer from over-population. We were now on the borders of this region, crossing a great valley or plain of old lava, with a background of snow-capped moun-tains. The lava was like a very rent and *crevassed* glacier, but all black, the sombre colouring being only relieved by the patches of grey and yellow lichen. Right in the middle rose the isolated conical hill, Erich's Jökull, with dark crags below, and perpetual snow and ice above. The Bald and Lang Jökulls, chains of ice-crowned hills, stretched away to the west—a great glacier-system; and a high yellowish table-land, with purple hills beyond, rose to the north.

The formless, unsubdued, terrible element of Nature was here in its unshaken majesty. All round was a repose which hinted of fearful activities. The icy domes rest on rocks whose configu-ration tells of the fires tossing not far below. The lava is full of cavernous hollows, where a whole river has lost its way and wanders unseen, till it rushes into daylight where a misty foam a few miles off marks a waterfall. Certainly this is a land of the giants still unsubdued by Thor, though he has made some not-able conquests in Iceland. Of such places as this the Skalds thought when they sang how Thor left the Asa at their heavenly feasts, to go out into the waste lands to assail the giants in their fortresses—Thor, who represents the ordered force that makes the rude world fit for man, the patron of the pioneer and peasant. Even on that sunny day the scene conveyed the strongest impression of vast, weird, remote desolation; and while we cantered over the last bits of grass that lay by the lava, we might well recall the Eddaic tale of Geirod the frost-giant, and his fire-palace, —for we were bound for the lava-cavern of Surtshellir—*i.e.*, the cave of Surtr, the fire-demon, who leads the van of the unchained forces of destruction in the twilight of the gods.

Some critics think the "Lay of Geirod" is a kind of parable about the fires of Iceland: it seems probable that the recently explored volcanic island was in the mind of the Skald who first sang it. "Loki, the beguiler, flew off one day in quest of adventures in Frigga's falcon dress. He flew from curiosity to a huge castle over the seas. There he saw a great hall, alighted, and looked in at the window. Geirod saw him, and ordered them to catch that bird. The messenger climbed with difficulty up the wall, it was so high. Loki liked to see the trouble he was put to, and resolved not to fly up till he had led him all the bad way. As the man caught at him, he spread his wings and spurned away: but he was too late; his feet were caught, and he was brought to Geirod the giant, who, when he looked in his eyes, suspected he was human, and bade him answer, but Loki was silent."

Loki could only regain his liberty by promising that he would lure Asa Thor to the fastness without his hammer, when Geirod made sure he could destroy him. Thor was easily beguiled into accepting Geirod's invitation, and started unarmed; but luckily a friendly and powerful giantess, called Gridr or Grace, in whose house he lodged for the night, lent him her staff and iron gloves. Then it is told how Thor waded the sea, and though opposed by Geirod's daughter Gjálf[1] or Yelp, who flung the waves at him, he pitched a rock at her, and he never missed what he cast at; and

[1] *Gjalfr* means the din or roar of the sea.

so by the help of the borrowed staff he won his way to land. Here he grasped a friendly rowan - tree, and got safe ashore. (The rowan is the only tree that attains any size in Iceland, and ever since has been sacred to Thor.) Having won his way into the fire-castle, the Asa was invited to take a seat. No sooner had he done so than it flew up to the roof of the hall, where Thor would have been crushed had he not, with the giantess's staff planted against the roof, pressed downwards so effectually that he was the death of the two raging water-storm daughters of Geirod, who had tried thus to blow him up. If they were the Geysirs, the next foes were the Volcanoes; for Geirod now challenged him to fight in the hall, which was all lined with fire. Thor caught the red-hot weapons in the iron gloves of the wise woman, and hurled them back on Geirod, who in vain crouched under an iron pillar to defend himself; for Thor crushed the demon of underground fire into black rock—into lava, in fact—and flung the fire-caverns open to the day. And when the demon is crushed small enough, the triumph of Thor is complete; for there is no better soil than thoroughly disintegrated lava. So runs the old fairy tale, but underneath its extravagances lies the true idea of a never-ending struggle between the lower destructive forces and the higher vital and intelligent powers.

We left the beautiful grass which edges the lava, the product of its crumbled dust, and rode over the black rock till we reached a yawning cavern leading underground, where we dismounted. The cave had a floor of pure transparent ice, covered with some inches of water. We drew fishing-stockings over our boots and waded in. Fishing-stockings thus worn, are, by the way, an excellent protection for ladies who have to ride through deep fords. We often kept our feet dry and warm by wearing them, though the struggles we went through in our efforts to take them off when well wet and clinging tight over heavy boots, may be imagined. The last sight of daylight, looking back to the mouth of the cavern, reminded me of the blue grotto at Capri; for the ice below gave a perfect reflection in blue of the over-arching rocks. We lit candles, and slid down a sloping floor of ice, under beautiful archways which seemed all set with diamonds, from the frozen water which had percolated through. Tall spires of ice touched it from the floor; while down in the clear depths below we could see the black shapes of the lava, as Dante saw the traitors, like flies in amber, in the ice of his frozen Inferno. All these caverns, which are said to run two miles underground, must once have been great gas-bubbles in the boiling lava, and the fantastic boulders scattered about in them flung from some furious volcano. Then came the frost-giants and made the place . their summer palace. We lit a torch where the cavern was highest, and the ice rises in tall columns all round, and huge fantastic icicles depend from the roof,—the whole place flashed back prismatic colours with a blaze of light which made our two little candles seem very dim when it was out. At the far end of this cave, in a hollow rock, we found seals, and coins, and carved names left by former travellers, some of them dating from early in the century. We added our names, as we were the first ladies who had been in the caverns,—not that there is any special difficulty about going there, but that hardly any ladies do travel in Iceland. We went about a quarter of a mile underground, perhaps further; but I am diffident about giving distances where there is no map to measure—time, not length, being the measure of distances in this country. We were certainly a good while scrambling through the caves, and decided that the outlaws who once inhabited them must soon have become the most rheumatic of men.

We returned to Kalmanstunga for coffee, and started thence again at 5 P.M., nothing loath—for though the situation is beautiful the house is not, and the inhabitants are rather like the Swiss, without their cleanliness. Our way lay along a hillside, down which Oddur rattled with a complete disregard of any track, which was sometimes his style of riding. On such occasions, when we had picked out our way more slowly down loose stones, over lava, or through bogs, as the case might be, he would ask with sarcastic interest if the ponies were lazy, as if a round trot or hand-gallop were the usual way of descending a rough hillside, or crossing a bog up to the knees. We crossed the valley below of mingled grass and lava; we should have kept to it, but we went up the opposite hill instead, and the ponies dispersed over a shaking morass — as disagreeable a bit of riding as I can remember. There are no worse bogs than on the high table-lands, always to be avoided if possible. On rushed Oddur, sinking, splashing, now finding a passage, now failing and trying another place. I was not near enough to profit by his lead, for my pony was timid in bogs, and kept refusing to advance, smell-ing the ground, and neighing wildly to his companions, who were scattered far and wide. Glad were we when we had succeeded in scrambling over to the priest's house at Gilsbakki, where we were introduced into a clean timber room, and presented in form to a humorous-looking old parson. Presently entered a pretty but very little woman, who gave us coffee and then retired into the corner of the room. I took her for the youngest daughter; but the old priest, nodding towards her, said, "*Kona min*" (my wife). She was a very retiring third wife, and we tried in vain to bring her into the lively conversation. The priest was making game of the ecclesiastical intentions of our guide, who indeed has since been ordained. "A first-rate lad for riding; but for preaching—save us!" While Oddur explained that his view of parochial work was not so much standing in a pulpit preaching as going about the parish, knowing every one, and being ready to help when wanted. "Running about! *that* you will do," said the old parson, who further cordially pressed us to stay the night, but we were anxious to get on.

Our plans were altered, for we had met a postman who said our steamer was certainly to touch at Bordeyrei on the Hruta-fjord, in the north-west, instead of Akureyrei, and that she was already due there. We had now settled to wait for the next steamer six weeks later; but it was necessary to send letters home by this one, and needed hard riding to meet it, so we turned out into the chill evening air.

Our way grew very desolate over stony plains, between shape-less hills, swept by the keen north wind, which blew up our

sleeves and sought out weak places in our wraps as if it were
an enemy armed with a dagger. A brown desert strewed with
stones often succeeds a plain of rich grass in Iceland with as
sharp a difference as a ploughed field borders a meadow, and we
passed several such alternations this day. Latterly the country
improved. Fine-shaped hills appeared in the west. We forded
the Nordrà salmon-river, and were glad, after ten hours of
travel, to halt at the farm and chapel of Nordtunga. They
opened the cold little church and lit the altar candles—the first
day (26th July) we had needed lights, even at midnight; and we
wrote our letters while Oddur prepared for a further journey of
twelve hours. He set out at midnight driving a relay pony
before him, while we in the church nestled into our plaids to
sleep. Next day the weather was miserable, with a dull unchanging pewter-grey sky above, and a never-ceasing blast,
flowing rather than blowing, from the north-east, like the strong
current of an icy river. My friend and I asked each other if this
was July, and why we came to Iceland. The cold drove her at
night to sleep in the house; but I, having her plaids (which I
borrowed) besides my own, remained in the church.

CHAPTER VIII.

NORDTUNGA—BORGASYSLU—HOLTVÖRDSHEIDE—THE
NORTHERN COAST.

HE wind died away in the night, and
when I woke a bright sunshine
poured through the little square
windows on either side of the humble altar, which, however, was duly
railed off from the rest of the building. The church was about forty
feet long by fifteen wide, built of
single overlapping planks like a
shed, and it was very cold, as the
damp of the piled-up churchyard outside had rotted the lower boards.
But it was ecclesiastical in plan,
with pews to the west, and a pulpit
in front of the chancel. The hinges
and bolts of the door, of well-wrought
iron, were the only handsome things in it, and probably they
had descended from the richer days when the islanders gathered
wealth on the high seas.

I have often been asked how the day goes when the inn is a
church, so I shall give fuller details than usual from my journal
of this day's history from dawn till midnight. I spring up
dressed—for we do not undress in a church, though we change

clothes for the night — and with some difficulty open the massive bolt and pass through the dewy churchyard, over the wall, and down a steep bank to the salmon-river that swirls past in a glitter of sunbeams. Here, in a secluded creek, I have a bath; the pure cold water is most invigorating, and fortified against all cold, I regain the chapel and put on my habit. By this time Miss Menzies appears, and with her the farmer's wife, bearing hot coffee and cream. So far good; but of farinaceous food there remains only some shortbread, which did not go well with our plover-stew the night before, and some biscuit-crumbs, reduced by shaking on horseback to the finest powder. The sugar in another box is quite a geological study; it has assumed the forms of river-shingle, and has a uniform brown tint, which we look at with much suspicion, till we remember that it is all that remains of some chocolate-cakes once packed with it. There is no bread at all at the farm, and rice will take long to cook, so we stir up our biscuit-powder with cream, and resolve to go to-day where sea-biscuits are said to be—to the Scotch salmon-fishery on Borgarfjord, about eighteen miles to the south.

Nordtunga stands in a wide strath, through which winds the Nordrà salmon-river, which has worn down a channel with low steep banks, in the alluvial soil of the valley. All round is a circle of more or less distant mountains; for to the north the rocky spurs edge the flat about a couple of miles off, while to the south the serrated blue range beyond the Borgarfjord is more than twenty miles away, clearly as every indentation shows through the transparent air. The strath, where stony tracks lie among grass-lands and great sweeps of emerald-green bog, is good for riding, but nowhere pleasant for walking, all is so rocky or so miry.

A dozen people or so are tossing hay in the *tun:* they all sleep at the little farm whose low out-buildings face the main house. It is like a ripple of mole-hills magnified, with its grass roof and sides, and bulging walls, some six feet high, rising to fifteen feet at the three gables. To enter, you must stoop low in the doorway, nor must you walk rashly upright in the dark

passage within, or you will soon hit your head against a rafter
spanning the cave. The floor is of trodden earth, the walls of
untrimmed turf, and you grope your way through the darkness
into a higher cavern, the *eldhus* or kitchen, where a stick-fire
burns amid stones, and some of the smoke wanders out through
a hole in the roof. Clothes, stockings, fish, all that is wet and
needs to be dried, indeed, hangs suspended on the smoky rafters;
a big pot boils rice and milk on the fire. There are no chairs, but
you may sit on an inverted tub and warm yourself, and admire
the rich brown shadows and blue smoky lights, which set off the
clear complexions of the children who lounge about, while the
mistress prepares the dried fish, which is the substitute for bread:
and a very aged party, a poor relation, who in this busy hay-time
is her only indoor assistant, and has become, like some insects,
just the colour of the smoke and earth she lives in, potters about,
almost indistinguishable in the dim light. To the right the
passage leads to the family room, where on one of several box-
beds some one is always sleeping; for they seem to rest in turns
as on board ship. Fish-bones ornament the floor. By a ladder
you reach the loft where the *bondé* and his wife live; by a door
the wainscoted guest-room, Miss Menzies's abode, where a good
bed, some chests, a table, and four battered chairs, which look as if
they had walked here in the rain, make up a very tolerable room,
if the window would open, and if the air were not the mere leav-
ings of the family den. This is hardly an average farm. And
as regards our host, I shall only mention the trait we most liked
in him, his careful attention to his delicate but kindly wife.

It was good practice for us to have to make our own arrangements in very broken Icelandic, in the absence of Oddur Gislason.
We contrived to make Skuli and the *bondé* understand us, and
soon started with the latter and his wife for Borgarfjord. She
rode a neat chestnut pony, on a saddle like an arm-chair with
rich brass mountings: a gaily coloured cloth was first laid over
the saddle, and then wrapped round her knees like a railway
rug. No wonder ambling ponies are so esteemed here for women;
trotting with such a saddle would be most uncomfortable.

The air was so fresh and light that we felt twice ourselves
in strength and spirit; it seemed a joy to breathe—far more
to ride across the trackless plain, cantering over unenclosed
reaches of fine turf, splashing again and again through the river,
or feeling our way carefully over the bogs,—for they are appalling, miles long and miles wide of alternate tussocks of bog
vegetation, pools of dark water, and shaking quagmire. Leirljos,
my pony too, good in all other difficulties, is nervous about them.
First he stops, then smells, then tries one foot, withdraws it and
tries the other. At last, with a despairing neigh, he perceives
the rest are far ahead, and stimulated by his rider's hunting-whip,
plunges on a little further, when the whole begins *da capo*. I
feel afraid we shall vanish altogether, and that I shall be preserved for a few hundred years as a very bad specimen of the
costume of the nineteenth century. However, on good ground
Leirljos can make up for lost time. This is Myra—or Mire
Syslu, and is worthy of its name. The Mire men and Mire
horses have proper local instincts, but for the rest of the world
it is pleasanter to have land and water separate, instead of mixed
in equal parts. There is a farmhouse every six miles or so,—a
large population for Iceland;—and at every farm our *bondé* liter-
ally runs to earth, for they are turf-houses. First comes a good
deal of the usual kissing, regardless of age, sex, and appearance
—then comes coffee, and then brandy; the people admire my
big knife and our little watches, and read aloud the newspaper
we bring; and then we are off again towards the southern hills,
which now rise high before us.

At last we drew rein at what Scotch ballads would call "a
wan water,"—the turbid white waves of the Hvità or white
river, rolling down in a broad current, heavy with melted snow.
Skallagrim and his followers who first settled this part of the
country A.D. 878, gave the river that name, "as they had never
seen before waters which fell from ice-mountains, and thought
the river marvellous," says Egil's Saga. We who knew Swiss
rivers yet thought it rather marvellous to ride through this long
ford, the only one for many miles, as advantage can be taken of

two sandbanks in the middle. So we crossed successively four streams of cold rushing water, about as deep as the ponies could manage without swimming, and so rapid that it was needful to look at the bank or leading horses to avoid giddiness.

Trotting over meadow-land, and splashing through another brighter river, the Grimsà, we arrived finally at an iron house with two large rooms one over the other, where a Scottish merchant often spends the summer superintending the salmon-fisheries, living, like an otter, just where the salt water begins to touch the fresh. The workmen, including one Scotsman, received us kindly. The two gentlemen were from home, but it did not matter. Those who have read the legend of little Silverhair and the three bears, can imagine what we did,—we ate their dinner, and sat in their arm-chairs, and read their books; and as there was no third bear with especially choice and brittle possessions, we did no particular harm. Then we climbed up among the tumbled grey rocks which overhung the clear waters of the river, and gave a fine fram-  ing to the noble view of the hills and sea-reach of Borgarfjord. Far-off puffs of vapour marked the hot-spring valley of Reykholt : the view all round was exquisitely clear, and glittered in the western sunshine. The bondé and his wife had gone on to see some friends, rather to our relief; two chatty Icelandic girls strolled about the rocks with us, till we returned to the house for tea. Evening was now drawing on, and with eighteen miles or more between us and home, we began to wonder what had become of our guide ; without him we could not have ventured over these bogs and fords, and in him we had little trust, though more in his wife. As we sat at our tea above, we heard, through

F

the open boards of the floor, the men below at *their* tea, dis-
cussing him,—the foreboding questions of the Scotsman, and the
canny reply of the Icelander.

However, he came back, and we carried off as a gift a good
deal of biscuit and some salmon, feeling rather like Vikings
"acquiring property," as their mode of helping themselves without paying is delicately put in the sagas. This was after seven
o'clock on as sweet an evening as I have ever seen. We rode
alongside of Grimsà, whose waters lay like another sky on the
dark ground, reflecting the celestial tints. The nearer mountains
were deep blue in colour; there was a bright red gleam on the
glacier hills, and on the cone of Baula; the lower sky of tenderest
green was varied by rose and topaz clouds; and at last, when
the sun was gone, a glow of crimson light and a gloom of alternate purple shadows spread over all the heavens in ever changing darkening beauty. We rode fast, except where the dark
morasses hampered us. The *bondé* got again into every farm,
but, with the help of his wife, we tore him from his friends, and
cantered away again into the rising wind, which was increasing
to a gale from the north. Every wrap went on and was insuf-
ficient; and glad were we to get to our own farm at 11 P.M.,
where, after a cup of hot coffee together, my friend and I said
good-night, and I returned to the lonely chapel.

Now we had slept contentedly in churches before, but till last
night we had been together, and our guides in the gallery, and
it had never struck me it was an eerie thing to do till to-day,
when the Scotsman had remarked that nothing would induce *him*
to sleep alone in that chapel. And now when the heavy key
turned with a resounding clang, it felt lonely indeed. A round-
headed white gravestone seemed by the light of the candles
within to be peering in from the darkness through the little
window, reminding one how all the company of dead folk lay
between one and the living. Moreover, as I walked up the aisle,
heavy footsteps seemed always to follow me; it was only the
wind, but never till that night did I know what pranks a gale
of wind could play in the way of mysterious noises,—howling,

stamping, shrieking in the rafters, and shaking every creaking plank of the little wooden building. I arranged my cork mattress on our boxes so as to get my head into the comparative shelter of the pulpit floor, and slowly shook out the plaids to postpone the bad moment of having to extinguish the candle, which flared in the chilly draught. At last I lay down to try if my couch was firm, and flapped the end of my plaid accidentally into the candle, which went out, and I had quite forgotten where I had put the matches. But with the darkness, and after a short sleep, came a new sensation,—an indescribable sense of utter loneliness, combined with a suspicion of some presence beyond the roaring blast and creaking timbers. Of old the vampires— the wicked corpses with some hideous half-animation—were said here to " walk the roofs : " was not the stamping overhead just such a noise? The cairn of Glaumr, a vampire of fearful fame, was not so many miles away over the desert waste to the north, —he of whom the proverb goes, if any one looks scared or frightened, " he has seen Glaumr's eyes." Why, also, would Sir Walter Scott's really unpleasant ballads come into my head? What had possessed me to learn them, or at least to know them by heart? " The Baron of Smaylho'me " was bad enough ; but " Frederick leaves the land of France " was so much worse, that I quite dreaded thinking to the end of it, which, however, I was irresistibly impelled to do :—

> " Weary, wet, and spent with toil,
> Where his head shall Frederick hide ?
> Where, but in yon ruined aisle "—

just my chapel.

> " Thundering voices from within
> Mixed with peals of laughter rose."

So they did, quite distinctly.

> " High their meagre arms they wave,
> Wild their notes of welcome swell ;
> ' Welcome, traitor, to the grave !
> Perjured, bid the light farewell ! ' "

Worse and worse—and no possibility of changing the subject. And there are surely footsteps approaching. I can see nothing for the pulpit. *It* is coming round though, and soon Its eyes will meet mine. I make a movement, and there is a sudden startling clang. Curiously enough that culminating crash seemed to restore me to myself. I guessed with truth that I had knocked over the brass candlestick—went comfortably to sleep; and I spent the following night alone in this church, with no sensations of nervousness; but I took care to have the matches within reach, for in such cases light makes might.

The next morning we were much surprised to find that our guide had not returned; however, we had our ponies driven up and loaded, and were just starting when he arrived, bringing with him no bread and no jam, to our great disappointment. The steamer, which had been hourly expected at Bordeyrei for the last week, had never arrived, and he had waited as long as he could in vain. He had made one interesting purchase, a nice little iron-grey mare with a white tail, which I bought from him for my own riding, as she was very smooth-paced and gentle. We returned with him as far as Hvamr, a parsonage situated in a pretty narrow grassy valley about eight miles off, where the clergyman and his young wife received us cordially. We slept in the church, I in my favourite place in the pulpit, but I was woke by the plash of rain on my face; it was pouring, and the roof leaking so much that I dragged my mattress forlornly up and down for long in search of a dry spot. It rained hard all day, and everything was wet, including the house, which received you with a deep puddle just inside the outer door. But it was clean further " ben," and the mistress of the house showed us stores of old and handsome jewellery stowed in a curious ancient coffer. She dressed one of the girls in her own Sunday costume of green cloth and velvet, who looked in it like a stately heroine of a saga, and I recognised a resemblance to the costume of recumbent figures on old tombs of Normandy. The helmet-like cap was bound across the brow with a fillet or coronet of wrought silver-gilt; the green cloth bodice was embroidered richly in gold down the front and round the sleeves; the skirt was similarly embroidered up to the knees. A belt of beautifully wrought silver-gilt went round the waist, and fell in a pendant below the knees, like a medieval girdle. The costume was finished by a cloak of green velvet, fastened (by large silver-gilt clasps and chains) across the shoulders. A long lace veil softened the glitter of this charmingly picturesque costume, which perhaps looked rather incongruous in the shabby little room. Probably, in this fashion, the dresses of our ancestors were far more beautified than their ordinary living - rooms. Now we have pretty  rooms and plain or too often ugly clothes.

Next day we started in mist and rain; but when we got out of the valley, as our guide had prophesied, this ceased, and we found the weather pleasant though cloudy. The path was very picturesque, rising above a tumultuous river, leading over a dizzy ridge called the Cat's Back, and gaining a solitary high table-land—Holtvördsheide, the waste land between the Western Dales and the northern shore. During the whole day we passed only one dismal little house : there lived a woman, earth-red in colour, strange in manner, a sort of mountain-gnome. She examined our hands and ears, in search, she said, of gold. In Italy one would have suspected bandit relatives lying in wait further on, but in Iceland it was mere feminine curiosity—the only womanly trait visible in the gnome. She brought us into her cavern, and after a while produced good coffee and sugar-candy. Still I can see the dim room, the little window looking down the waste we had ridden over, where whirled the fantastic mists that seemed this day to be always pursuing us as we rode on into clear weather, and the queer old woman with wild eyes, like Norna of the Fitful Head, staring at us fixedly, while Oddur, very much of the present and the ordinary world, was making himself agreeable to her after his usual *débonnaire* fashion. As a rule, Oddur kissed all the hostesses, as in duty bound, but I am not sure if he rose to the situation this time.

We met nobody all day, and there was hardly any track. We plodded as best we could across the table-land, over bog, or rock, or stones. Snow had fallen there during the late northerly storm, which Oddur had encountered in full fury the night he had left Nordtunga, and he had had some trouble in forcing the loose ponies against it. Most dreary must this way be in bad weather, though this day it was not without its own wild charm, especially when, from the upland ridge, we sighted the long narrow Hrutafjord, which opens into the Arctic Ocean. Thence the ride by a river with many waterfalls was less dreary than above, though the wide red channel, worn or rather torn by the river, would have certainly looked more cheerful had there been a little vegetation on the bare soil. In our latitude this would have been a beautiful *den;* here it was a good study for a geologist.

We stopped at a large tidy farm in the valley, at the head of the Hrutafjord, called Melar; such a usual halting-place for travellers that it is almost an inn.

The charges, usually so moderate, were here high enough to make us criticise our accommodation; for there was no "gift horse" in the question, and the *bondé*, a rich fellow who saun-tered about with a perpetual pipe in his mouth, watching every one else hard at work in the hay, has not fairly grasped the traveller's side of the innkeeper's trade.

The 1st of August, Sunday, was a lovely day; and in the afternoon I rode with Oddur the ten miles to Bordeyrei in an

hour, taking our swiftest ponies, which hardly slackened the pace
over sea-weed and rocks and shallows in the sea. The ancient
port of Bordeyrei, which is printed in large letters on the map,
consists merely of a big store, a merchant's house, and a flag-
staff. The merchant, who has lost a leg, and who has a special
regard for Scottish people from grateful memories of the late
Professor Syme, asked me in to luncheon with the ladies of the
family. Being then on very short commons, I enjoyed it as
we people of the comfortable classes rarely have the chance
of enjoying a refection. It seemed strange to see fashionable
wall-papers and white-and-gold shutters in this remote corner
of the world.

The ride back to Melar that sunny evening was delightful.
The path overhung the narrow sea, so lonely as regards humanity, but all alive with birds—eider-ducks, sea-gulls, wild duck,
and swans. The great northern diver laughed, the lesser diver
wailed, and every discharge of the gun woke on all sides a startling clamour. Oddur shot a few wild ducks, which were not
easy to pick up. Skuli gallantly swam his pony right out into
the sea to retrieve one bird; for in this hungry land one can ill
afford to lose any addition to the dinner.

We rode through the head waters of the fjord to where a herd
of three hundred ponies was grazing, waiting, like us, for the
steamer. They were of all colours and qualities; and tossing
their bushy manes as they chased each other over the grass, or
standing reflected in the river in the intense sunshine, they
made a charming picture with the background of hills and rock-
bound sea.

Next day was oppressively hot, and we rode to a neighbouring river, where it was very pleasant fishing down in the deep
clefts of the rocks. When we came back, the post had arrived.
The postman had tucked himself up in the bed supposed to belong to our men; and the bags and a crowd of people—all the
neighbourhood, in fact—were settled, unbidden guests, in the
other room, for which we had at least paid. The *bondé* was
slowly reading out addresses and papers to his audience,—

spectacled, composed, not to be hurried. After waiting some time and seeing no chance of recovering our room, we went off next door, only ten miles, to Bordeyrei to dine, returning at midnight, though not in the dark, to our room at Melar, which had now ceased to be a post-office.

No steamer appeared, for indeed she had broken her screw-propeller off the Faröe Islands, so on the third day we continued our journey to the north, up the Hrutafjord. We were accompanied a good way by a calm-minded eagle, for Oddur shot him on the wing as he slowly sailed by, and we saw he was touched by the feathers that fell; but the gun was loaded with very small shot, and he seemed to despise us too much even to avoid us, continually perching near us, a little out of range, and keeping in sight of us for miles. Two more eagles came close to us this day, and the birds on the heath above seemed remarkably tame.

Then we turned west over waste lands and quaking morasses, commanding latterly fine views of the Breidafjord. It was a grand though gloomy journey; for the day was cloudy, and the landscape, vast in scale, seemed utterly desolate. Towards evening the sky lighted up behind the mountain-chain to the west, showing range beyond range of the wild hills which defy the Atlantic waves in the north-west promontory of Iceland. The country seemed to us like the end of the world, and yet it was once the centre of much intellectual life. Out yonder in Breidafjord, among many other islands, is Flatey, once the site of a monastery, where many learned men lived, and some valuable manuscripts were preserved. Among the fjords which intersect those piled-up mountains, lie the scenes of the "History of Gisli the Outlaw," a man of noble disposition, whose hard fate made him an avenger of blood and an outlaw for many years: his faithful wife shared all his perils, and fought by his side at the last. One of his fatal quarrels rose out of a game at ball on the ice, evidently a sort of hockey on skates, in which the people then delighted. Much is also told of this district in the authentic biography of Gudmundur of Dyrafjord, a stirring chieftain of the twelfth century. The saga begins with a lawsuit, which rose out of a ghost-story.

Teitr and Oddkatla were a young married pair, rich, handsome, and much attached to each other, when Teitr went away on his first voyage beyond seas. On a day of early spring Oddkatla was giving an entertainment to her father and various relations. The tables were set, the board spread, and with the other women she was entering the hall, where the men were already placed on the benches. Suddenly she stopped, turned pale, and refused to go further. There, she said, among the other chiefs, she saw Teitr her husband, but even as she looked he vanished away, and she knew he was dead beyond seas. She declared herself separated from him, and requested her father to take her, with her dowry, back to her old home again. All were surprised, as the husband and wife were known to be much attached to each other; but she said, gladly would she return to him if ever he came back. In the summer a ship came from Norway with the tidings that Teitr had died that spring day of the festival, and the lawsuit followed about his property, of which, however, Oddkatla had already secured her own share.

As some of the finest scenery in Iceland is to be found up Isafjord, it seems a great omission not to have seen it; and we longed to ride over the peninsula, but there were good reasons against it. There is no straight track over the inland waste of stones and ice-mountains; the pathways all follow the lines of the converging fjords, for only along their shores is inhabited land to be found, so it is best to visit them by sea. The bogs also were very difficult on the narrow neck of land where we were; and last, not least, we had not been able to reprovision ourselves at Bordeyrei, and it is hardly safe to depend too much on birds or fish taken by the way. So we turned regretfully south, looking wistfully at the mountains, with an unappeased craving to explore them.

Ponies in Waiting—Hjardarholt.

CHAPTER IX.

FISHING IN ICELAND—LAXDALE AND ITS SAGAS—KVENNA-
BREKKA—BLÀSKOGÀEHEIDA—BACK TO THINGVELLIR.

SHALL not follow my diary closely for the next ten days. The reader, should such a being exist, has probably had enough of it; for there is great sameness in the record of a very varied life. Fishing looms large in it, and so does poetry. We wandered about to visit good pools and scenes of the Laxdale Saga; towards evening we pitched our little tent, and made a home of the homeless wild. We were contented with little to eat and coffee to drink, and pitied travellers who go from inn to inn.

Something should be said about fishing in Iceland, even by a lady who only aims at trout. I have to confess to a great liking for fly-fishing, and am ready to defend the sport as suited to the quietest ladies,—those who are the reverse of sportswomen; though how any lady can look a bird or beast in the face and then kill it, unless merely to put it out of pain, I cannot understand. But with fish it is quite different. In their relations to

us they are evidently made to be eaten, more emphatically so
than poultry, cattle, sheep, or game, for which we sometimes
contract most inconvenient friendships. Fish are outside our
circle altogether; and we may have the further satisfaction of
thinking, that though they seem to live particularly careless
jolly lives, they all end in being eaten, either by us or by each
other, unless they meet with great ill-luck, such as chemical
waste in rivers, and are poisoned. Now, for every big fish we
kill, and it is these we aim at, a number of merry little fishes
have longer lives; so we anglers are really benevolent institu-
tions from a purely fishy point of view. Real fish, too, as distinguished from whales and seals, have no attachment to each
other—they are only rivals; witness the fighting for bait in a
shoal—witness the withered old carp wrestling with each other in
ancient palace waters; therefore, in catching a fish you make no
home desolate, you bereave no fond creature of a friend. Cool,
calm, and selfish, the fish goes on his glittering way like a
regular man of the world; he misses nobody out of his water
home, and when he ends an easy life by an easy death, nobody
misses him.

Then there is the pleasantness of fishing—evidently generally
felt, as is proved by the many delightful books about it; and yet it
is hard to say why it should be so very enjoyable. Perhaps it is
because no out-of-door pursuit lets the spirit of nature so imbue
and saturate the mind as the gentle craft. Gardening, compared
to it, is too active in its continuous work; sketching is a struggle;
the scene is changed too rapidly in travel; a book, of course,
brings its own thoughts; and doing nothing brings a kind of rusty
retribution; but while lingering beside still or rushing waters,
occupied but not absorbed, the whole power of the scene and the
season seems to sink into our very heart. Thus, though the
angler may enjoy good sport, we find he or she is generally content to do without it; the spaces when nothing happens are so
pleasant, that a rush of fish becomes sometimes even rather a
trouble, and were it continuous, would spoil the delicate flavour
of the sport. It is whispered that on some of the upper waters

of beautiful Highland salmon-rivers, when a fish *is* killed after many blank days, the bells are rung, and bonfires lit, and the gillies are all treated. And if that is not exactly true, something like it is, proving that the pleasures of the higher and more skilful sort of fishing are independent of "good sport." We are of opinion that fishing from the bank is much pleasanter than from a boat, though, of course, a lady, as she does not wade, is more likely to take a large fish from a boat. But there is a touch of monotony in rowing to and fro over much the same sort of water, perhaps getting chilled, and having little to do but look out for a rise ; while wandering by the river-side from pool to shallow, from shallow to run, is most fascinating, even if it infers wet feet, possible falls, and more trouble in securing the fish. But why do I speak of fish, when so often it is rather

" The water-spirits are singing
Their melodies unto me "

while loitering on a sweet June day by one of those beautiful streams, whose ripple flows through one's summer dreams like delicate music? Yes, believe me, you people who glance with incredulous contempt at the literature of the gentle craft, the sweetest fancies haunt the still or running waters, the fairest imaginations people the solitude. Let it be a solitude—angling is no social sport. You may have a friend within call—probably you will forget whether you have or not ; but a friend beside you is likely to be a disturbance or a rival.

Nowhere is fishing pleasanter than in the Scotch Highlands ; but it must be owned, though you pay for it in privations and discomforts, as well as in money, that sport is better in Scandinavia. In Norway, for instance,—land of streams, paradise of fishermen, though almost in scale beyond the powers of fisherwomen,— the rivers are so huge, so turbulent, and roll down to the sea with such a rush of water, bearing with them such enormous fish that they call for heavy rods and tackle, and mighty men to wield them, and deftly-managed boats to cross the heavy currents—that is, as far as they are salmon-rivers, for, owing to the steepness of the mountains, they average shorter than our

Scottish streams.   Soon you come on most of them to a thundering waterfall which no salmon can mount.   In the upper waters
the ladies' sport may fairly begin ; there trout abound and many
excellent fish.   And trolling for sea-trout in the inland reaches
of one of the grand fjords is not to be despised.   Magnificent
mountains enclose you where eternal snow rests above, and the
birch-trees clothe the lower slopes, and seem to have descended
in a graceful fantastic dance down the grey cliffs whose base is
washed by the salt sea-water and lapped in amber-coloured sea-
weed.   It is very pleasant to fish there, even from a leaky boat,
with your feet on the thwarts, and some one constantly baling—
a not uncommon state of affairs in Norway, where familiarity with
the deep sea about the doors has certainly induced some contempt
of its dangers.   The fishing in these fjords is very miscellaneous,
—our hopes may range over such wide possibilities of fresh and
salt-water fish that they need never flag—indeed, we are pretty
sure to catch something.

There are many good rivers in Iceland, but one seemed to me
quite ideal, yet it is a river with a name—a name known in
legend and chronicle for many hundred years.   It runs through
a fair far lonely land, and falls into the sea, no matter where.
At its mouth the salmon linger in shoals, and the seals swim
about with wistful, solemn eyes, as if they were poets rather than
the poachers that they are.   Some way up the river is a pretty
little waterfall, where you can watch the salmon mounting.   They
leap first to a back-water half-way up to rest, and thence either
gain the top by a desperate dart or fall back into the foaming
pool below.   I have seen ten or fifteen leaping at once at this
fall, and often failing to get up.   Many fish do surmount it,
however, and till a second higher fall a good many miles off
there is fine fishing along the solitary shore.   No houses, no
people, no cultivation to be seen, only the glittering water,
gliding or rushing between grey rocky banks, clad with bog-
myrtle and low birchwood.   Only a great blue mountain above,
with a greater snow one peering over its shoulder, till you come
to the ravine in the black basalt, where the river rushes in a

mass of foam from the upper falls, which no salmon can stem. I shall say no more, for as the simple grandeur of the scenery almost spoils one for other landscapes, so does the sport spoil one for other fishing, and the recollection for other memories. For we who know where it is and how to get there, even we can hardly hope to find the river we left—the ideal is seldom twice attained; the weather will be less fine, some one else may have found the place; at any rate, we ourselves shall have grown older, perhaps lazier. All the more do we treasure the memory of that river. And as it may be said that, in speaking of fishing for ladies, I have spoken chiefly not of fishing but of its accessories, let me add this last touch to the sketch of my ideal river, that we do not loiter there for mere idle sport; we are probably very hungry, and fishing anxiously for dinner. After all, none know what fishing really can be except those who kill for food, and will get less or worse food if they fail to kill.

It is curious how seldom the Icelanders fish with the rod. They take the salmon in boxes in the most wholesale unsportsmanlike manner. I have seen from forty to fifty fine grilse and salmon taken at one time out of a little box—the accumulation of twenty-four hours. In very hot weather we have seen the men lower little hand-nets under the rocks in the salmon-rivers, and then scare with stones and shouts the salmon, which generally thereupon enter the nets by twos and threes,—I could not clearly understand on what principle. It has also struck me that what we consider good fishing weather is comparatively rare in Iceland; if cloudy, the weather is apt to be too cold—if fine, too bright, for good fly-fishing. But sometimes there is splendid sport—lively sea-trout, and large salmon-trout, rising freely and rushing about in the swift currents in the most exciting way. The absence of all trees gives one a great advantage in securing fish.

The fishing here goes with the land, and leave should be obtained from the farmer or parson who owns it. Some rivers, as Ellidà, near Reykjavik, are closely preserved; and it would be better for the fishing in the long-run if more were. There are great complaints of the falling off of the takes in the upper waters. No wonder, considering the number of salmon netted at the mouths of the rivers. But there are trout-streams everywhere, and, far from all habitation, there seems no reason against fishing them freely. The Grimsà, the Nordrà, the Western Laxà, and the tributaries of the Hvità, are all good for trout as well as salmon. The salmon, as far as my experience goes, average smaller than our Scottish fish; whereas the trout and char, both in the rivers and the lochs, are very large and heavy. They are extraordinarily bright in colour—rose-pink and deep yellow. The sea-trout are simply first-rate. There are very few places where tolerable lodgings can be found near rivers, so that the sportsman should be prepared to rough it in a tent, and say farewell to luxuries, even more emphatically than in Norway.

We were now in the district called The Dales, among soft pastoral valleys and rounded grassy hills. We descended on the Hvammfjord, a branch of the Breidafjord, which runs far inland between high mountain promontories that melt in the distance to the west. How peaceful and remote all must have seemed to the early settlers! how far away from the harassing wars of ambitious kings and their rivals! In winter the inhabitants would have all these fertile valleys, from the seas to the waste lands, to themselves; the ships would be drawn ashore and turfed up till the path of the sea opened again in summer, connecting them with the south and its wealth. One can understand the attraction of Iceland in those days when the trouble of life was, not that there were many wars, but that there was never thorough peace, except in such solitary places as these remote valleys.

This district round Hvammfjord was first settled by a woman, Aud the Deeply Wealthy, whose stately figure has been handed down to us in a lifelike word-picture. She was the daughter, the wife, and the mother of sea-kings, and used to sailing in ships. She came from Norway with her husband Olaf the White, who warred in the *west viking*, took Dublin and much of Ireland, till at last he was killed there. Aud lived for a while with their son Thorstein the Red, who ruled Katanesi (Caithness), Sutherland, Ross, and Merrhafi (Moray), till he too fell in battle in

Katanesi. She then built a cutter, and sailed to the Orkneys with many followers and a large party of grandchildren. One granddaughter she married in Orkney, and one in Shetland, coming finally to Iceland and choosing land for herself. She is said to have landed on the promontory yonder in Hvammfjord, where she dropped her comb, and hence it is called Kambness. She took all the land hereabouts, assigning estates to her followers and grandchildren. She married them all off as they grew up. At the wedding of Olaf, her youngest and favourite grandson, she made a great feast for all the country, to last for several days. She had now grown large and heavy and "weary with age;" but she came into the hall, stately as ever, to receive her guests. She bade them not wait for her to begin the carousal another day, nor shorten the feast which might perhaps serve both for the wedding and for the drinking of her funeral ale. Next day the old chieftainess was found, richly clad, sitting upright in her bed, as she had died all alone. She had said she would not lie in unconsecrated ground, and therefore had ordered that she should be buried within the flood-mark, that the sea might come and go over her grave. Did some idea of consecration belong to the sea, or was it only that the old sea-king's wife loved to think that the stir of the waves should still visit her last resting-place?

Hoskuld, her grandson, bought a lovely slave in Norway, a Viking's captive. He paid little for her, because she was said to be dumb. But some years afterwards he overheard her talking by the brook to her little son Olaf, telling him what her sad pride had revealed to no one else, that she was the King of Ireland's daughter, a royal lady who never condescended to speak to her captors. Then matters mended for her, and when her handsome son Olaf—surnamed *Pá*, or the Peacock—grew up, he went to visit her old parents in Ireland. It is told how he took his mother's old nurse on his knee and showed her the knife and jewelled belt she had put on her fosterling long ago. He offered to take her to Iceland, but she was too old to venture on the long voyage. Olaf's son was Kjartan, the handsomest and plea-

G

santest man in all the North—the hero of Morris's charming
poem " The Lovers of Gudrun," which is a versified expansion of
an episode of the Laxdale Saga, full of love and passion.

These histories, so long past yet so living still, haunted me as
we rode down to the shores of the Hvammfjord, just " where Lax
river joins the Western Sea," and went along the bay. The evening was splendid, and most impressive was that lonely sea rolling
in heavy breakers on the lonely shore. A dark-purple mountain
rose on one side, and it was shrouded above in a cloud blazing
with those celestial colours that one can only remember dimly
and never describe. Little islands showed in dusky purple where
the fjord opened into the wider Breidafjord, and the far mountain-
peaks of the north-west peninsula rose beyond. To the south-
west, the fine mountain-range ending in the consecrated Helgafjall
closed the prospect. Many swans were sporting on the sea, and
gulls wheeled and dipped all round; otherwise with all this extent and beauty we saw no signs of life. The bright waves broke
with strange effect upon black instead of yellow sands, consisting (as is often the case here) of comminuted lavas. Sometimes
the scenery reminds one of our Highlands, of Shetland, or of
Norway; and then, again, comes the difference, that sort of weird
element of *diablerie*, which it owes to the volcanic forces.

The fair Gudrun, the heroine of the Laxdale Saga, lived at
Laugerstadr, not far from this sea; and her lover Kjartan's
Hjärdarholt is a farm about eight miles distant and three inland
on a bleak hillside, but commanding a fine view of the fjord and
hills beyond. We were hospitably received by the priest who
lives there, and who was very busy making hay in the pretty
grassy valley below the church. Opposite, across the river, is
Hoskuldstadr, where I stood by the burn that runs below the *tun*,
where Hoskuld first heard his supposed dumb slave speak, eight
centuries ago—but the centuries make few changes here. Fortunately they have laid the vampires, or *walkers-again*, as ghosts
are called here. A very bad one lived hereabouts, Hrapp. He
was most unpleasant in life, and when he died his family were
weak enough to fulfil his desire that he should be buried " head

upwards at the kitchen-door, that he might still be able to take a look round." And a pretty life he led them, frightening the maids, chasing the men, and making the byres and outhouses a terror with his hauntings, till the body was dug up and burnt. A horrible but homely ghost, and not without a dash of humour in his pranks.

All the people were making hay in the fine August weather. The *tun* hay was mostly garnered and thatched with turf, and the out-hay was being brought in: towards evening long files of laden ponies were to be seen converging towards every farm. However it may be at other seasons, there seemed at this time a want of hands rather than of labour or pay; good wages (about 2s. 2d. a-day for a man, less in proportion for a woman) were within reach of all: and at some farms we only found a very old woman at home, past all work, but watching the big pot, in which rice and milk boiled for the haymakers. The day we left Hjärdarholt on our way back to Reykjavik, we reached towards evening the last valley farm close under the hills we had to cross. The weather was splendid, and all the folk were up on the hillsides haymaking, except the usual old woman, and a rather tipsy man, who gave us a maudlin welcome. We had to dine here on our own provisions and their coffee; but afterwards when we were about to start, the man appeared mounted, and what we call " roarin' fu'," swaying about on his pony all over the place, charging the baggage-ponies, and insisting with a kind of friendly fury on escorting us over the pass. We told our guide nothing would induce us to consort with such company; but the man was proof against Gislason's mild representations: he swore he would go. So our guide detained him talking by the wayside while we rode past, and with Skuli driving the ponies in front, we ambled easily up a beautiful glen. Cascades fell straight down the square black basalt cliffs. The way grew steep—the cloudless sky widened as we rose out of the valley; and by a slightly traced zigzag we reached the table-land at the summit of the pass of Kvenna-brekka—a waste of stone, over which the track was marked by little stone-cairns, called from their appearance *kerling*, or old wives. The view was magnificent, owing to the extraordinary splendour of the sunset. One side of every block of stone seemed golden, the other blue. All round us were mountain-tops, pointed, jagged, or square; some turned a deep pink, others purple, in the evening sky, which changed from ruddy gold to deep crimson, and cooled into ambers and yellow-green as evening stole on. At one point the light glittered on a glimpse of sea. All was utterly barren, for the vegetation was hidden in the valleys, which were mere clefts of purple shadow from above; and all that stirred were the ravens croaking over some horse-bones, and an eagle, which sailed about as if it were lord of the land. We had to dismount to scramble down into the valley below, which seemed dark and dim after the blaze of light on the hill-top. We puzzled our way among a confusion of horse-tracks over a river, and wondered where our guide was. It was past ten o'clock, and Skuli, who had never been there before, was not so sure that we had not got into the wrong valley. Of course we had met no one to ask the way, but I did imagine that through the dim light I could make out horses; and away I cantered through the river, and reached horses indeed, but no riders—mares and foals, which were living here alone. They made the solitude of the desolate valley more emphatic. On one side rose the conical mountain Baula in strange white tints. It consists chiefly of a peculiar whitish basalt, and is a geological curiosity.

Till lately no one had ascended Baula, which was formerly considered one of the gates of fairyland: and it is still whispered that those who go up the right way, and in the right frame of mind, may meet the elf-folk. Anything seemed possible, as we picked our way after dark over the rocks, guided chiefly by the glitter of the little river. And indeed it is not surprising that the old superstitions should still linger in these solitudes where man is so insignificant and nature so powerful.

It was quite dark when the clatter of horses' feet announced our guide's return—our tipsy friend, he said, had insisted on riding up the pass with him, and asked also a ransom for the coffee we had had from him. As accusations of drunkenness are some-

times brought against the Icelanders, I may say here, this was
the only time we came in contact with anything unpleasant of
the sort; but the standard of public opinion on this matter is not
high in any part of Scandinavia.

We pitched the tent near the first farm beyond the pass,
rousing the good-natured inhabitants, who made coffee for us,
though morning was hinting its approach in the sky. Next day
was Sunday. We had had twelve hours of travel the day before,

Baula from Hvassburg.

and Hvassburg, our camping-ground, was very pretty, so we
lingered till 5 P.M. The farm, though small, turned out several
well-dressed and well-mounted men and girls, who rode off to the
distant parish church. We pursued our way in the evening
across some low rocky picturesque hills, past pretty lakes, down
to the salmon-river, our old friend the Nordrà; fording it, we
went to another Hjärdarholt, the residence of the magistrate for

the west. Here we were received with warm hospitality, taken
to a pretty drawing-room by pretty ladies, and joined the party
at supper—to us a feast. I am afraid we looked like vagrants
indeed, in spite of all efforts to tidy ourselves up; and I know
that a closed bedroom with a curtained down bed, was far too
luxurious for me to sleep in well, for I had not been in a real bed
for a fortnight or more. And how little it matters! how much
pity is wasted on tramps which might be bestowed on sleepless
people in feather-beds!

The next day we forded Hvità at the long ford where we had
previously crossed it from Nordtunga. The current was very
heavy, and the water as deep as we could well manage without
getting it over the saddle. All day we rode among bogs, and at
one place, with a plunging struggle and a snort, my pony subsided
altogether. I sprang off on the shaking morass, and still remember the despairing expression of the hill-pony's face as his chin
rested on the soil. The lowland ponies mind much less being
stuck in a bog; and I have seen them coolly eating all round
while waiting for help. If you have to leave a bogged pony to
get help, it is well to leave a cloak or something beside him as
a pledge of your return, and then the sagacious beast expects
you to come back, and will not struggle. Luckily some peasants
were passing, and soon hauled out my cream-colour none the
worse, except in colour.

We refreshed ourselves at the farm of Varmaleik, and then
pressed on through the grassy valley watered by the Grimsà,
and camped by the farm of *Eingland—i.e.*, meadow-land. There
is good fishing in Grimsà. We made a long day's journey from
here to Thingvellir, from 1 P.M. to nearly midnight,—a beautiful
mountain-ride, first by the upper waters of the Grimsà which
leapt in many cascades down the rocky valley that divided two
hills. Further on the view opened to the glacier hills—Lang
Jökull, Bald Jökull, and Ok; glittering white mountains with airy
pink and blue and ice-green shadows, the colours below them deep-
ening from the pale gold of the distant wastes, to the stronger
browns and greens of the foreground, where the ponies grazed

among the crowberry and juniper bushes. Most remarkable was the delicate alluring colouring of ground which we knew might be called a hideous waste ; but Nature will not be baffled in her contrivances for beauty,—she can make the wilderness as lovely as the rose, and only with our help succeeds in attaining ugliness —as, for instance, in a stretch of good flat arable land highly farmed and cropped in " roots." We had some scrambling riding across country, latterly by preference down the bed of a little river, till we emerged on a trodden horse-track, which, by comparison with what went before it, quite deserved its name of the People's highway to the North. Before attaining the lava-valley of Thingvellir, there is a lake called Sandkletteir-vatn which had then receded quite into one corner of its basin, though sometimes its waters fill the whole of the sandy bed, over which we rode as fast as the most tired of our ponies could go, for night was coming on. The lava-crags on each side close in at the head of this lake, leaving a narrow cleft between. It seems as if you could in passing almost touch the cliffs on each side ; and all is black, unrelieved by any other tint, grim and sombre to a degree. For a while a pleasant riding-path among low birch-trees runs alongside of the lava that fills the valley into which the defile opens ; but soon it becomes necessary to turn on to the lava, which, after nightfall as now, is very difficult riding, as it is full of cracks and fissures, often masked by willow and birch and luxuriant blaeberry-bushes. Happily horses see much better than human beings, or we should never have reached Thingvellir church, as we did just before midnight, without the least accident, —our surefooted little animals, that seemed sometimes to smell out their way, not having made even a serious stumble.

It rained in the night, and in the morning I went to wash in a deep shady pool of Oxerà. The sponge fell in and settled on a point of lava-rock far below. Being a swimmer, and having a bathing costume, I rather rashly jumped down into the water, which was far beyond my depth, to rescue it—but never had I imagined any water not ice could be so cold. I scrambled out as quickly as possible ; and as I was warmed by the bath for the rest of that cold day, I recommend it to other travellers—perhaps it was the rain that made it so very exciting. We rode back to Reykjavik on the twenty-second day of this expedition. We had only calculated on about ten days of travel, as we had meant to sail from a northern port. And our appearance was now very suggestive of wear and tear; we were battered by rain, and burnt by sun. Moreover, straps and ropes had almost ceased to exist— we could only just manage to cord our baggage on to the ponies. Gislason had contributed to this his last saddle-girth, and kept his saddle on by the stirrups, firing, too, occasionally from his pony's back, which always then swerved violently; strange to say, he never quite slipped off. My bridle had become so short that I could hardly get hold of its knotted remains. Of food, we had had coffee, black bread, and curds for breakfast that day; and for dinner there was a little bit of cheese, and some very old black bread which, judging by the flavour, had been kept in a tobacco-jar,—and yet we were well and flourishing, and I never felt stronger in my life. Each long day's ride only gave the pleasurable fatigue that brought sound sleep at night, however hard the couch; and the good air and good appetite made any-thing palatable that we could get to eat. At least we had always had good coffee. Never in the East, whence, like so many other good things, coffee first came, nor in France, where all things gastronomic reach their full perfection,—never have I tasted better coffee than in many a primitive, lonely, Iceland *bœ*, far from all the luxuries of high civilisation. The art of making coffee is thoroughly understood in Iceland, and no doubt the excellent cream counts for much in the final result.

The ponies, knowing the journey was nearly done, ran gaily and willingly till we reached the Artun, a cottage about four miles from Reykjavik, where we had calculated on our evening coffee. But there were sounds of music and dancing, and a large tent was erected in front of the little house—some people of Reyk-javik were entertaining the officers of the Danish war-ship, and we felt far too travel-worn to join the party; but with a shyness for which we were afterwards much reproached by the hospitable

entertainers, we retired to another farm, where we reposed ourselves on the grass, enjoying coffee and biscuits, which tasted
delicious on that austere day, and watched the revellers riding
home along the road not far off. A picnic and a dance is rather
a favourite summer amusement at Reykjavik, and seems to create
great hilarity, ending with a gallop home in the evening, and
sometimes, as now, the entertaining spectacle of sailors on horseback. We were glad in the evening to find ourselves comfortably
at home in the house of our guide and his wife. Below is a
sketch of Eysja mountain and the roadstead, from one of the
windows of our pleasant apartments.

106

CHAPTER X.

RECENT MISFORTUNES IN ICELAND—TRADE—NEW CONSTITUTION
—PASTORAL WEALTH—CONDITION OF THE PEOPLE.

REYKJAVIK, where we spent at different intervals as much as a
month, was unusually lively that year, owing to the sitting of
the first *Allthing* or Parliament of Iceland, since the recent grant
of a constitution. Till the other day the Danes, though their
own government is constitutional, were despotic in Iceland, not
from right of conquest, or any other right—for when they acquired
the island by treaty they were pledged to uphold its old laws
—but simply because they were stronger. Indeed the history
of the connection between Iceland and Denmark was, till quite
lately, a mere history of wrongs. When, with Norway, the island
passed by treaty under their power, there was a thriving population, much wealth in cattle, and a trade in woollen cloth, fish,
and oil, which brought a good return in specie. It should be
remembered that besides the Danes there were at least two other
causes of decadence—the destructive volcanoes, and the decrease
in value of Icelandic exports. This was owing to the discovery
of the Newfoundland fisheries, and to rival cloth-manufactories
elsewhere. But if early travellers are to be believed, the Danes
are responsible for a series of acts of tyranny and oppression
that would indeed, if they had been perpetrated in some less
out-of-the-way district, have roused the indignation of Europe.

About the end of the fifteenth century the Danes first checked
the brisk trade between Iceland and England, forbidding its

ports to all English vessels, and allowing a most oppressive trade
monopoly to the Hanseatic Towns. A country dependent on
trade for all its corn, for the very necessaries of life, especially
requires free trade; but in the seventeenth century the Danes
imposed on Iceland a commercial bondage almost incredible in
its injustice. The Government sold to certain Danish merchants,
at a high price, the absolute monopoly of the Icelandic trade;
no Icelander was allowed to trade with any but a Dane, not even
with a countryman. He could not legally sell a fish at sea to
another ship. The Danes imposed their own prices on exports
and imports; what these were we may judge from an instance.
The *skippund* (a certain weight of fish) was in 1782 worth from
thirty to forty dollars in the outer markets, but in Iceland it had
to be sold to the Danes at seven dollars. No wonder that the
population diminished, that lands were deserted, enterprise lan-
guished, and the deep-sea fishing fell entirely into the hands of
foreigners, where it remains, to a great extent, to this day. The
wonder seems, not that the country retrograded, but that it existed,—that the love of it was strong enough to enable the people
to fight the battle at all against such a severe climate and such
disastrous laws. The year after this monopoly was first imposed, it is on record that three hundred people died of famine.
But when, more than a century later, the misfortunes of the
great volcanic eruptions of 1783 were added to the other burdens,
and nine thousand people perished from want, at last the Danes
consented to relax their code so far as to make trade legal with
all Danish subjects, an enactment which had an immediate good
effect.

"Previously the natives," says Henderson,[1] "were in a state of
absolute slavery to foreign merchants. They were prohibited,
under pain of whipping and slavery, from repairing to any other
mercantile station than that in the district to which they belonged, and if they chanced to come there after the ship had
completed her cargo, they were compelled to sell their goods for
a mere trifle. Chiefly to these circumstances we ascribe the com-

[1] Henderson's Two Years in Iceland: 1812.

parative want of spirit and poverty which characterise the present
race of Icelanders under the iron yoke of oppression. All spirit
of enterprise is damped."

.When, in the wars of Napoleon, our ships swept the Danes
from the seas, the Icelanders were in real danger of starvation.
Both warlike and peaceful efforts to relieve them were made by
the English, not, by all accounts, encouraged by the Danes.

The few Englishmen who visited Iceland early in this century
speak in strong terms of the misery and squalor they found
there. Mr William Hooker, F.L.S., who was there in 1809,
when the island was suffering from the famine caused by the
war, and things were at their very worst, tells us that the starving inhabitants were prohibited from buying provisions from
English ships then lying in the harbour, under pain of death.
Of all the valuable cargo offered for purchase by the supercargo
of an English ship, then at Reykjavik, only salt and grain were
to be had elsewhere, and these, being entirely monopolised by
the Government, were only to be purchased at considerably more
than twice the price asked by the British traders, yet no one
dared to buy at the cheaper market. Such things as these
brought about a little bloodless revolution. He says that although
assistance was given by an English privateer, it was virtually
accomplished by twelve men; not a drop of blood was shed,
not a gun fired, nor a sabre unsheathed, but the inhabitants
seemed satisfied with the change. A certain Jorgensen (a Dane)
was proclaimed protector, and the chief object of this mild revolution was to upset the Danish Government and have free trade
with England. Unfortunately Jorgensen's position was considered contrary to the law.of nations by the commander of a
British war-ship—he was brought back a prisoner to England,
and the Danish governor was restored. However, public attention was turned to the starving Icelanders, and Sir Joseph
Banks succeeded in getting leave from the British Ministry to
open a trade between Iceland and England, and also an order to
permit ships of other countries to trade there freely. For a time
these measures gave great relief.

Hooker speaks in 1809 of people wandering from farm to farm to beg for a little food. Our experience is that we have never once seen a beggar, nor have we met with any one who asked for charity in any form. He says that people in good position, and priests, were so reduced by famine in bad winters, that they not unfrequently died of sheer starvation. The population was rapidly diminishing. Barderstrand Syslu in the year 1749 contained 3000 inhabitants, and nine years later 2175. Heavy as were the taxes, there were no hospitals : "the sick and lame are seen crawling about in almost every part of the island, presenting most pitiable objects of distress and misery." "In former days wrestling and various feats of strength used to occupy their attention. Chess was much practised ; cards, music, and dancing diversified their leisure hours ; but all these are now scarcely heard of." Hooker has mentioned the usual amusements of the Icelanders at the present day, which shows that the country has revived like a flower from the old root. He, however, sees no good future for Iceland except in a union with Great Britain. The English merchants from this time till 1815 did carry on some sort of trade, underselling the Danes. But after the peace this beneficial trade was once more stamped out by the Danes, who required from foreign merchants a prohibitive licence. The Icelanders had now, however, acquired wider views, and they extorted from the Government some relaxations of the trading code ; and in 1830 the *Allthing* was re-established, though at first only as a powerless council. Irreparable mischief had indeed been done. The Danes always bartered their goods ; and by paying no specie into the country, they made trade with other countries very difficult at first, and entangled the people in meshes of debt. The cloth-manufacture had been almost destroyed long before by the monopolists, who found they got a better price by exporting the fine wool, bought much under its value, and importing manufactured, cheap, and inferior cloth. The English travellers speak of misappropriation of the confiscated church property, and also assert that a large collection, which was made in Denmark and other countries for the relief of the starving population, after the volcanic eruptions of 1783, was detained in Copenhagen, and only doled out by dribblets to the people for whom it was intended. But such statements must be received with caution, as we were then at war with Denmark.

Happily these bad times are past. The trade restrictions have been gradually removed, and since 1854 trade has been free. In 1874 the present King of Denmark, who is very popular, restored in great measure the legislative power of the *Allthing*, and Iceland enjoys home rule. The population, in spite of a good deal of emigration, is steadily on the increase : the revenue is good, and the country thrives.

Now that it forms so large a part of the territory of the reduced Danish monarchy, it is to be hoped that the Danish Government will in all ways foster and develop the island instead of actually preying upon its resources. Perhaps it is only fair to the Danes that we should remember that they were hardly worse than some of their neighbours in their misgovernment of their provinces. The Icelanders would perhaps have fared as badly had they, as some of them wished, been subject in early days to Great Britain—witness the history of Orkney and Shetland. At least the Icelanders were only plundered, they were not harassed and enslaved like our northern islanders. There was never there an Earl Robert Stewart to make a capital offence of a journey in the country without his passport ; never an Earl Patrick to torture innocent people into confessions of impossible crimes, that he might murder them with forms of law, and seize their goods.

The contrast between the story of the free national life of Orkney and Shetland, as told in the Norse " Orkneyinga Saga," [1] and the misery and slavery of the inhabitants in the sixteenth and seventeenth centuries, is as striking as in the corresponding history of the decline of Iceland.

For the last forty years the Icelanders have demanded the privileges of self-government from the Danes ; and this is now in a great measure granted. The *Allthing*, which now legislates

[1] Written before A.D. 1230.

for the country, is divided into two chambers,—an upper one of six nominees of the king, and six deputies from the lower chamber, which latter consists of thirty members, elected by the people. The king, however, appoints a Governor, a Secretary of State for Iceland at Copenhagen, and most of the officials; and it does not appear on the surface what means the *Allthing* has for giving effect to its decisions. As long as the Executive works with it, of course all may go smoothly; and the restoration of a public assembly of the people is in itself a great benefit.

No country can be expected, however, to recover at once from centuries of dependence on an alien government, and old habits of restricted trade. There is steady progress, no doubt; and in each of my visits I have observed many signs of advance, many improvements; but there is still a good deal of sluggish adherence to old ways, and a great deal to be done. The real wealth of the country is in live-stock. The grass in the inhabited parts is beautiful, and in many places would support far more sheep and cattle than it does in summer; but the winter keep, depending now entirely on hay, is the difficulty. Round each farm is a well-manured *tun*, or infield, yielding a heavy crop of hay; beyond are the unmanured fields, where inferior wild hay, called *out-hay*, is gathered : and there is generally, besides, a great range of summer hill-pasture. In this farming, the hay crop, always so dependent on weather, is too important: there should be two strings to every bow, and that second string might surely be found in the turnip. It grows well in patches about Reykjavik, and would only need ploughs, which are very rare, and sustained labour, which is also not common, to succeed in many places. The summer, though warm, is too short; and the frost is too long in the ground for any sort of corn, even fast-ripening rye, to be a safe crop; but a store of turnips to help the live-stock through the winter would be invaluable. Lately, many thousands of the small Icelandic sheep, which make first-rate mutton, have been brought to Leith in the autumn—an excellent trade, which will cause the sheep-farming to become much more profitable.

There is a good deal of annual emigration to the New Iceland, in America, from the more remote districts of the country; but the Icelander, unless quite young, is not well calculated to succeed as a woodsman and corn-grower. Some have much regretted that they ever left the old island, which has its advantages over the remote shores of Lake Winnipeg. It is always well that the door of emigration should be open to restless spirits, especially in a country without corn; but there is a want of hands rather than of labour in Iceland in summer. We came upon none of those signs of over-population too common here in our own country. Wages are good, at least in summer, and steady work would probably be as well rewarded there as in the locust-haunted plains of the far west of America. Only within the last few years has Iceland had a chance of retrieving itself from the distress produced by the burdens on trade. Farms which were known before these burdens were imposed to keep forty cows, now keep six or seven; but they might keep forty again, it is said, if people worked hard in summer to provide their winter food. The fisheries, also, are not half worked. There is a great deal of inshore fishing, and a good trade in salt fish with France and Spain, bringing, among other things, good cheap wine to Reykjavik; but the very profitable deep-sea fishing is virtually in the hands of the French. This is chiefly for want of large fishing-vessels, and in these the Icelanders dare not invest till some safe means of insurance[1] are provided. There is no bank on the island; and the *bondés* are said to be rather attached to the unprofitable form of stocking-heel and teapot investments. A better style of house-building in the country is the most needed improvement, but of course the scarcity of fuel and timber makes that difficult to attain; though the coasting steamer, which has begun to ply regularly, and can bring materials more within reach of the farmers, will be a great convenience.

Improvements—all we who write of Iceland seem ready with

[1] An insurance company now exists, and the number of Icelandic decked fishing-boats is largely increased, and they pay very well. There is also a thriving herring-fishery lately established.

...ch fish for themselves, and do not trade with the Danes. The Spanish do trade for Iceland fish, but e Danes.

our suggestions of improvements, but are we sure, after all, on which side the balance really weighs? It would be a dull world indeed if we were all improved to the same point. On landing again in Scotland, it certainly struck us that the people looked clean—and unhappy. As refreshing as the uncontaminated air, is the absence of that money-winning, money-loving care which weighs upon our people. An Icelander may be a sharp hand at a bargain, but he is soon content with his position; if he have enough to put him beyond the fear of want, he neither covets, nor esteems, nor requires wealth. The *bondé*, however poor in money, is generally well of in the essentials of life; his farm gives him good meat and dairy produce, good clothing and wool for trade. He is owner of wide lands, and has the independent dignity of the lord of the soil. He has his fishing and shooting, and his long pleasant rides, not over dull highways, but across the free country "beloved of horses." His servants, if independent in their ways, are educated companions; their indolence may hamper him, but on their honesty and kindliness he may rely. Crime, stealing, and violence are almost unknown; gay and easy tempers are the rule.

We saw no abject poverty, no one even insufficiently clad; those who are not well off themselves, seem at least to have well-to-do and helpful cousins, for the people are within reach of each other and know each other. The country can never be rich or support a large population; all the more refreshing is it to be able here to realise the advantages of the earlier simpler forms of life,—the real pastoral age, when wealth meant sheep and cattle, and people felt to each other as friendly neighbours, not as competing rivals. So let us hope that Iceland may improve by developing, not by changing, and that our feverish civilisation may never destroy the charm of this rough and simple land.

H

CHAPTER XI.

HOUSEKEEPING—DINNERS—OUR PARTY—SOCIETY—MANNERS— LANGUAGE.

WE were invited to various entertainments during our stay at Reykjavik, and something may now be said of them, and of what I gathered about social matters, not only then, but in my two other visits.

The day always begins with fragrant coffee; and it could not do better. We British are accused of being morose and ill-humoured, but compared to the Latin races and the Icelanders, we have not a fair start in the morning. They would never think of beginning the day's troubles unfortified by the most reviving, inspiriting, and sustaining of all drinks. Early tea, with a heavy breakfast following soon afterwards, may be a nerve-destroying luxury, but coffee before a late breakfast is a wholesome working stimulant. Biscuits come with the coffee, or sometimes delightful little rolled-up pancakes. Second breakfast at about 11 was a serious meal; frequently we had, when travelling, nothing more, except a stray cup of milk or coffee, till about 9 or 10 P.M., when *skjer* and fish, or perhaps meat, formed our supper. At Reykjavik we dined at about five, and had a good meat tea in the evening. The Scandinavians certainly do not eat so much as the English, or, more emphatically, the Germans, and, as a race, they are more slim and spare. The women are sometimes stout, perhaps because they stay so much more indoors. The ladies do the housekeeping—at least all are expected to understand it. There is sometimes in a good family a working housekeeper, often a relation, who lives with the family as an equal; and young girls frèquently make a stay at friends' houses to be trained in house-wifely duties. The servants in the town are generally young lasses, well-mannered, and treated almost as equals, but usually quite untrained to service, and apt to go home or marry as soon as they become valuable. They are generally trimly dressed in the costume, and look very nice. At Reykjavik the ladies dined with us, but almost everywhere up'the country they served the dinner, and only the women who were guests sat down with the men. This old Scandinavian custom goes much against the grain of courteous Englishmen, who sometimes quite fidget the society by springing up to prevent some fair Enid from fetching and carrying the dishes for them. But I am bound to say the ladies do not wait *respectfully*—they join in the conversation, and give their orders, and are considered the givers of the feast. As soon as it is ended, every one rises and shakes hands with the mistress of the house, saying, "Thanks for the meal," to which she answers, "May it do you good;" and then there is often hand-shaking all round, like the last figure in the lancers. At a formal dinner the gentleman who takes a lady in to dinner also takes her out again, even when he returns later to the wine, which did not occur often when I was present. Then we used to have talk, and sometimes good music, just as at home.

The soup is often sweet soup, made with sago, claret, and cinnamon. I acquired a taste for it, and much more easily a taste for the national dish *skyr*, a sort of sour curd, like the *laboun* of the East, but very superior in that it is eaten with plenty of rich cream. When well made it is very good and also nourish-ing, and is a staple dish at every dairy farm.

Fish and mutton, both excellent, are the standing dishes. Many little condiments, or appetite-whetters, are about on the table to amuse the intervals, such as thin slices of raw salmon, sausage, caviare, odd pickles, cheese, and even whale; and there are plates of bread in slices, alternately black and white. A quantity of butter is consumed, even by children, as it is good heat-producing food. A dinner generally concludes with a large crisp cake, new out of the oven, which is made by one of the ladies and placed with some ceremony on the table with the dessert wine.

Dinner-parties are too like each other all the world over for these to call for any special remark, unless that the people we met were many of them very agreeable. The hospitable bishop and his pleasant family were especially kind to us, and also the sub-governor and his graceful wife. All the English praise the genial old Doctor Hjaltalin, who loves our nation,— a handsome old gentleman, whose youthful freshness and brilliancy of complexion has survived more than seventy years of work and wear. He and others entertained us well, but our own small attempt at a return entertainment to our friends was much more out of the common. It was meant to be a kind of garden-party in the meadow rented by our guide, which commanded a beautiful view. We had pitched the tent over the cakes and tea-kettles, when, at the very last moment, down came the rain. We had all to run a long way too, between the tent and the house, to save the good things; and finally, we carried them, cakes and coffee, biscuits and champagne, tea and shortbread, up into my bedroom, as the only resource. This was luckily a good room with four windows; and its only bedroom feature, the little camp-bed, was hastily smothered in a plaid and made to do duty as a sofa. But the access was quaint, being up spiral steps, which only one person could mount at a time. That person, unannounced of course (for there are no door-bells in Reykjavik) emerged like a spectre up a trap-door in a melodrama. It is difficult to receive society which comes straight up like that; you are not always sure till the shoulders appear who it is, and if you bow too soon the rising guest cannot respond gracefully. However, we had, thanks to our visitors, a most cheerful afternoon. These included some pleasant French naval officers from the frigate in the bay—Normans and Bretons of the fine type of the French gentlemen of the past rather than the present.

We did not expect any countryman of our own, but much
éclat was given to our party by the unexpected arrival of one—
Mr Watts the explorer, the greatest lion then in Iceland. And
if anything could have added to the interest with which he was
regarded, it was that rumour had once said he was lost; and
again, that though he was alive, he was detained in the north,
utterly shattered and unable to move. This had appeared in
print, so with all the more distinction he rose upon us, a little
lame from a frost-bite, but otherwise sound and strong—a regular
athlete. Mr Watts had crossed the Vatna Jökull, and had thus
drawn a line over a district of absolutely unexplored glacier 230
square miles in extent. Two years he had been baffled, but this
third time he had succeeded, though he had suffered great things
in the remarkable storm which we had encountered at sea, and
which detained the party for several days in a hole under a
snow-drift. His success had delighted every one, the more
as only Icelanders had accompanied him; and he certainly had
the power, valuable for an explorer, of inspiring his guides, or
rather followers, with a personal enthusiasm which would have
made them dare anything for him. Those who wish to know
about these explorations will find his book, 'Across the Vatna
Jökull,' good reading.

Mr Watts was also one of the very few who had explored the
district where some new volcanoes had appeared. There had
been an alarming eruption in the spring of this year, chiefly of
ashes, pumice-stone, and hot water. The ashes had destroyed the
grass of six farms in the east ; but just when a terrible calamity
was expected, the disturbance moved westward into the deserts of
Odada Hrann or " terrible lava," which was already nothing but
volcanic *débris*, and could not be much worse. A succession of
new craters erupted one beyond another in this district : we
had seen the vapour from the far distance when we were in
the centre of the country. Mr Watts had camped near these
new volcanoes, which were then glowing, steaming, and smoking,
throwing up showers of boiling water and ashes, accompanied
by strange sounds and horrid smells. It may be imagined how

anxious every one was to hear his views as to whether the disturbance was increasing or subsiding; for though the volcanic
fires to a certain point are beneficial to the soil and climate,
it is a matter of great anxiety when the natural furnaces begin
to glow,—for who can tell what destruction they may not work
before their terrible energies are spent?

After many lively evenings, with no lack of laughter, and
persiflage, and interesting conversation, we were surprised to
read in some books of travel that the Icelanders, whose society
we had found so pleasant, were a gloomy, melancholy race, who
could not understand a joke. Captain Burton, for instance, whose
book came out shortly after our return home, informed us that
" chaff is unknown in Iceland, and gives terrible offence." However, on the next leaf, he names a certain well-known Icelandic
gentleman, oddly enough in connection with the following remark: " He first showed me the popular habit of making unpleasant and antipathetic, if not rude, remarks; this mordant
tone is still a mania in Iceland." This looks as if the natives
had ventured to chaff the author; and it is the more likely,
as there is no doubt that the Icelander alluded to could hold his
own in any conflict of wits all the world over. However that
may be, such broad assertions, based on small premisses, are too
common in books about Iceland, perhaps because so few foreigners
understand the language,—and without at least some knowledge
of that, it is impossible to judge of the social character of the
people. This would seem too obvious to be worth mentioning,
but for the remarks sometimes published by hasty tourists, who
scamper through the country for a few weeks or days, and talk of
the people as if they knew all about them without understanding
a word they say. The Icelanders, as a race, have the complexity
of an old civilisation, and differ widely from each other, as we do.
Some are brilliant, others are dull; some unite with a sad brow
no small share of what we are wont to call Scottish humour.
As far as my experience goes, I have found them at least prompt
to enjoy a joke, though not always an English one, especially
when they do not understand the language, and a good deal

inclined to good-humoured raillery. Indeed they are sometimes irreverent enough to amuse each other at the expense of that august being, the Great British Tourist himself.

Danish, English, and French are much understood at Reykjavik; but all, even the first, are of little use up the country. Often the people there, who at first seemed indifferent and reserved, when they heard our Icelandic, which was no doubt enough to make them laugh, at once became kindly and interested. They would compliment our lame efforts, and teach us more; and we used to have plenty of lively talk.

Having now spent six months in the country, and made some progress in talking and reading Icelandic, I must still own to finding it a very difficult language. The nouns are of three genders, without rule or reason apparent to foreigners, and have many declensions; the dative and accusative are carefully distinguished; everything is declined, even some of the numerals, and all proper names, as in Latin; and the root-vowels often change with the cases. The definite article, or whatever the new grammars call it, is suffixed to the noun, and modifies its declension. The pronouns are the worst of all: *sá*, "that," *odrŭm*, "other," and many more, have twenty forms or modifications, according to case, number, and gender; and so have many adjectives; and to add to the difficulty, everybody but the puzzled foreigner speaks good grammar. There is no low Icelandic, though there is a slight difference of pronunciation in different districts. The general tone of voice is soft and refined. The language, at a distance, sounds like well-spoken but rather slurred English; while many old words still used in Scotland, which have dropped out of modern English, strike familiarly on the Scottish ear. People who are intimate say thee and thou, as in Shetland. Acquaintances who wish to become intimate, "drink thou" to each other, and are then considered sworn friends. Icelandic is very rich in all but modern scientific terms, which, however, can easily be supplied by the formation of compound words. In the old language words are found that require a paraphrase to translate them; and it has great force and musical expression when properly declaimed in a speech, though it must be owned that too often in common conversation it is slurred and murmured in the back of the throat in a manner that is disagreeable to foreigners.

Education is universal in Iceland. It is part of the business of the clergy to see that every one is taught at least to read and write. And parents are bound either to teach their children themselves, or to send them to school in the winter, should there be one near enough. Regular schools are becoming much more numerous, and in them Danish is always taught besides Icelandic. Judging by the results, good manners are also taught; though, perhaps, it may be partly owing to race that the people are so free from boorishness. Even the children are not rude, but respond prettily when spoken to; and are always ready with thanks and a little hand, if not a proffered kiss, in return for a sugar-plum. Bad manners, when they do exist, take the passive form of a heavy, stony stare, which, especially if united to great *nonchalance* about ascertaining your wishes, is sometimes rather provoking. We once met at a farm a very composed boy, who seemed indeed to be the master of the house. His father was dead, and his mother subservient. He questioned and patronised us, and then gazed at us with such a long, steady stare, that we all—four English people—agreed to try to look him out of countenance, but we quite failed. Then our guide asked him how old he was. "Twelve," he answered. "And how old are you?" The guide being no longer quite young, the boy had the best of it.

To conclude, Iceland and Norway are the two countries where, as far as my experience goes, the stranger feels most at home, and most thoroughly protected. Everywhere there is complete safety—nothing to fear in the way of rudeness or dishonesty from the inhabitants. Doors are left unlocked at night; valuables may be left about without fear of loss,—indeed it is difficult to get rid of anything; and old rubbish, as well as articles of value, that may be left behind in a journey, pursue you relentlessly all over the country. The people are honest in their dealings also, though, of course, as elsewhere, bargains should be arranged and well understood on both sides. The charges in Iceland are generally very moderate. The traditional habit of the people is to entertain strangers freely for a night; but, except where the means are evidently ample, I do not think it fair of tourists to avail themselves of a custom which is a good one only when there is a prospect of the hospitality being returned. We met with much real hospitality, and with kindness that could not be paid for, even when we gave money. Often in good houses they took nothing; but generally we gave a fair equivalent for food and trouble. Twice or thrice there was an attempted overcharge. Travellers would do well to ascertain the fair prices, so as not to be either mean or lavish when no definite charge is made; and yet something is expected by people too poor to give away the provisions which, through long transport, become pretty expensive.

I have said that the people are well-mannered; but there is, both in Iceland and Norway, a strong feeling of equality—the employer is not considered privileged to treat the employed as an inferior. But a courteous traveller in Scandinavia need not be on the defensive; he will probably meet with true friendliness and warm hospitality, and can confidently rely on the honesty and kindly disposition of the people.

CHAPTER XII.

THE range of purple hills at Krisuvik rises about twenty miles to the south of Reykjavik, in pleasant contrast to the dark flats which intervene. We longed to see the hills nearer; and so, with no small satisfaction, one fine morning we started with nine ponies on a three days' excursion to their recesses. First, by an excellent bridle-road, we reached Hafnarfjord, a village seven miles distant, prettily situated on a sea inlet, which is so much safer for shipping than the more open roadstead of Reykjavik that it has been suggested to transplant the capital to its shores. There are many wooden houses and stores dotted along the edge of the sea; but the lava-rock, over which some of the road is carried on causeways, crops out everywhere, and gives little room for building. There are some small houses built into this lava, which is very dry, but so hard to work that the inhabitants must just accept its natural fantastic shape if they make use of it.

Beyond this little fjord, with its bustle, shipping, and neat houses, we came out on the great lava-stream which spreads over most of the south-west promontory of Reykjanes, and our ponies had to pick their way up and down rocks, and over perpetually recurring rifts and crevices. I had formerly stood on the edge of the red lava-streams on the side of Vesuvius during an eruption, and thus I could easily imagine the scene when all this enormous extent of lava was liquid fire and glowing red. The rocks often lay in

round swirling ripples, and circular bubbles, and twisted spires
—to all appearance suddenly petrified while boiling high. In
places they are forced into strange contortions, where some
fresher fire-fall has crushed the half-cooled masses; sometimes
a series of cracks, made in cooling, will stretch, widening across,
till they enlarge into gaping caverns, where delicate ferns and
yellow cistus nestle, while above nothing grows but the melancholy grey lichen, planting a seal of long ago on the lava which,
with all these signs of violent motion, is now so changeless and
still.

We found ourselves about mid-day reclining on a green slope,
an oasis in the desert. Grass and crowberries grew around,
and we gazed as we sat there at the magnificent prospect before
us. Looking back to the north-west, the great tract of lava,
variegated here and there with pale yellowish-green moss, was
in the foreground; then came the sea, which was quite calm and
a deep blue, and beyond it the long mountain-range which skirts
the Faxafjord, with the Snæfell Jökull towering above all in its
snow-capped splendour. All this, with the contorted black rocks
across which we had ridden, presented a contrast of vivid colours
never to be forgotten. These large masses of lava appear often
in grotesque and distorted forms, which suggest to the imagination demons or wizards; they seem to triumph over the waste
places of the earth, devoured by fire, and their fertility stamped
out for ever.

All those wild shapes were black—and the Krisuvik hills, so
softly purple in the distance, now we neared them, resolved themselves into gigantic cinders, still smoking in places. They looked
as if they were the ashy remains of fires lit by the giants of the
Edda. We crossed them where a cone had evidently fallen in
and formed a caldron-shaped valley or crater called the "Kettle."
On the other side steaming yellow streamlets with red mud banks
ran down black gullies, shapeless blocks of lava strewed the
valley, jets of steam and trailing folds of mist confused the dreary
scene. There was a forlorn horror about this burnt-out place,
which looked like a lunar landscape in a telescope; and the

Danish proverb, "God made the world, but the devil made Iceland," which had seemed such a libel among the soft valleys in the
west or the fine hills in the north, we felt at last was in a degree
accounted for. A rain-storm added to the mess; but we splashed
through a dismal marsh, which, being green, seemed comparatively
cheerful, to the little farm of Krisuvik, beneath a startling hill
which rears right up in a cone in front of it. Here we took
refuge in a tiny chapel where service is held once in six weeks.
M'Kenzie says it is eighteen feet by eight, and he is probably
right. Viewed ecclesiastically, it seems calculated for one hermit
only; but it reminded us rather of an old-clothes shop from
the garments hanging from the beams. We shut the shutters,
lit the candles, unpacked the bread and ham, while hot coffee
and *skyr* came from the farm, and we thought ourselves most
comfortable, reading aloud from a saga till bedtime, when my
friend spread her cork bed on a bag of beans, and I poised mine
on the top of the family chest, while the wind and the rain
battered outside, and before long lulled us to sleep.

News of a fine day came with the lassie who brought the
morning coffee, and we were soon afoot looking at the then un-
worked mines, and very curious they were. A valley and hillside of hot white clay were traversed by a little yellowish streamlet, above were black rocks, and red mud banks sloped down
to the white mud below. Bright-coloured varieties of stones and
clay were strewn about, formed no doubt by the play of sulphur
and ferric compounds; and the whole place was dotted with puffs
of vapour, in which some of the sulphur was escaping into the
air, in combination, to judge by the smell, with hydrogen—but
a good deal was deposited in powder or crystals round each little
crater, and more no doubt might be condensed. In the wide
valley below lay a little lake of as intense a blue-green as any
in Switzerland; great boulders strewed in verdureless shores,
and cinder-like hills trended away northward, glowing red and
purple in the brilliant atmosphere. Following carefully in our
guide's footsteps over the white clay and the red mud, we
climbed to the top of the little hill. The ground was every-

where hot and treacherous; sometimes we sank in deeper than
was pleasant, in spite of little planks with which we bridged the
worst places; and we hardly knew whether it was singeing or
scalding that was to be dreaded—our boots suffered from both.
We gathered some specimens of the mineral called here *krisuvik*,
copper carbonates, and pretty crystals of sulphur; and we also
cooked a nice hot little dinner just below the surface,—it was
slightly flavoured with sulphur, but we hoped only the more
wholesome for that.

These mines were not worked at that time, though the sulphur
is plentiful[1] and of excellent quality. The difficulty of transport
on horseback over the bad lava was a serious drawback. Circumstances had, however, altered; the neighbouring lake of Kleyfirvatn has been obliging enough of late years to sink so much in
its bed as to leave a good route round by its shore—a far easier
way to Hafnarfjord than over the lava, which was formerly the
only one. The mines have been profitably worked of late by Mr
Paterson, a Scotsman, who puts his own shoulder to the wheel;
and so much sulphur has been found that a company has just
been formed called the "Icelandic Sulphur and Copper Company,"
which is likely to prove very remunerative as soon as the first
expense of laying down a tramway about twelve miles to Hafnarfjord has been surmounted.

Next day we returned to Reykjavik, by the shores of the clear
green lake of Kleyfirvatn; and it was a very pretty ride on that
lovely day, though nothing could be gloomier than the scarred
barren mountains all round where no grass grew. Beyond
the lake we stopped on the grassy slopes, lit an aromatic fire
of bog-myrtle and juniper, and dined there, reclining luxurious-
ly in the enjoyment of a beautiful view, a good appetite, and
food that seemed excellent under the circumstances. Thence
we cantered gaily over sound grass between low lava - cliffs,
accompanied by some unbroken colts that frolicked alongside,

---

[1] Professor Geikie, who inspected the mines last year (1881), estimates
the total quantity of ore in sight as 250,000 tons—roughly equal, according
to the average quality of the ore, to 120,000 tons of commercially pure
sulphur.

till we reached the flat country and stopped by the edge of the Kallirå or Cold water—a mysterious river which, after a brawling course, disappears suddenly into a cleft in the lava-crust, and finds some unknown way to the distant sea. The people of a neighbouring little farm brought out fragrant coffee and cream, and set the tray before us on the grass, and we loitered there till the twilight warned us to go on to Hafnarfjord. There it became quite dark, but as the road was excellent it did not matter. Fireworks disputed the empire of the sky with the Northern Lights—the former the farewell salute of the departing French frigate, the latter the first greeting of winter, for August was nearly gone. As we rode by an inland creek, the rockets and the merry dancers looked beautiful reflected in the water, and cheered all the dark way to Reykjavik.

CHAPTER XIII.

SEPTEMBER had come, and the days were shortening fast; but at night the stars were wonderfully lustrous and glittering, and the Northern Lights were beginning to hold high festival in the autumnal skies. One night the display was magnificent—a great curtain of light seemed suspended from the zenith, waving towards the earth. It was not stretched straight, but seemed gathered in deep folds, changing, but not rapidly, as if it were indeed a texture woven in delicate colours shot with silver, and swaying with the wind. The night sky looked the blacker from the contrast with these exquisite veils of many-coloured light. Then suddenly all the drapery was gone—it had flashed into a thousand spires and sheaves of light that darted upwards and downwards all over the heavens. What matter if the night be long that is spent in the excitement of such glorious caprices !

The night had indeed come, "and the longer night was near." It was time to consider how to return home. The uncomfortable little post-steamer was known to be so crowded with Danes flying from the winter solitude that we, with Mr Watts, had almost settled to sail for home in a small Scottish schooner, commanded by a master well known as a dashing seaman. Fortunately the Queen steamer arrived, with three or four tourists, to fetch away a last cargo of ponies, and we all resolved to return with her. Meanwhile, not to lose time at Reykjavik, we started with Mr

Watts, and one of the newly arrived gentlemen, to explore the promontory of Reykjanes to the south-west. It has been the scene of recent, as well as ancient, volcanic agitation, there having been a great disturbance here in the year 1831, at which time a new island appeared, and one of the Garefowl skerries tumbled into the sea.

As usual, when the time came for starting, some of the ponies had run away. Ponies from the country dislike the barren environs of Reykjavik, and are very apt to scamper off a hundred miles more or less back to their native farms. So we were delayed; and when we were about seven miles beyond Hafnar-fjord down the coast, the gathering twilight warned us to stop at a place called Vatnsleysi, where two good farms stood by the sea. We were a large party, for Mr Watts's head guide, Pàl Pàlson, a merry young fellow, was with us, besides Oddur Gisla-son and another man. The people at the farms seemed delighted to have us, and could not make enough of us, especially "Vatna Jökull," as Mr Watts was called, from the scene of his exploits. Miss Menzies and I were considered very adventurous also, for ladies. And here, as elsewhere, I often received a little gift as a keepsake from some Sigurd or Gudrun I had never seen before, and probably will never see again—kindly little memorials of warm-hearted people—a horn-spoon, a carved wooden bowl, a curious stone, a silver button, or an ornamented box. I have gone over a good part of the European playgrounds without ever getting a present from any one, except a bouquet from some wealthy landlord after the bill was paid. Soon perhaps progress will bring about the same results in Iceland. Yet I wrong Italy. Once, near Amalfi, two of us were so tired of being begged of, that we agreed to beg ourselves from the very first passers-by. Three ragged girls came by, and we tapped our mouths with the usual remark. How were we overwhelmed with confusion when the girls gave us oranges and a blessing, and passed on!

From Vatnsleysi we followed next day the line of coast over dull unpicturesque lava, disintegrated into a stony flat, and bearing the same relation in interest to the lavas at Krisuvik that a moraine does to a glacier.

The track was like a furrow of yellow mud drawn over piles of loose stones, wearisome in the extreme; for while it was not bad enough for the smallest excitement, it was generally too bad for fast riding. This ought to have been most dreary; but even this dull district was transfigured by so pure an atmosphere that the smallest details of the distant mountain-range were quite interesting from their clearness, and so bright a sunshine that the browns and greys of the rocky waste showed in vivid colouring against the deep blue sea. The grass, the usual wealth of Iceland, only grew here in scanty patches, for the country is ill off for water; yet we passed several farms by the sea, more tidy and thriving than any I had hitherto seen in the south. The wealth of this district is the fishing; and numbers of people come every spring from the inland parts of the country to earn a share in the cod-fishing, which is generally exceedingly productive. Six-oared open boats with sails are chiefly used. They seem but small craft to go out on the wild Atlantic waves that thunder down all the coast; but they often do sail out till they sink the land.

The shark-fishing, which requires some adroitness and daring, is especially popular; and the sharks, when taken, yield better cod-liver oil than the cod: an interesting fact for invalids, who are often, when they least know it, feasting on the fierce shark instead of the mild cod. We had a refreshing little scamper over the sands and shallows to Holmbud, a pretty farm, where we stopped for our afternoon coffee. It was situated on a creek, where two or three small decked vessels were beached, their brown sides heeled over in the bright sea-weed. A high rocky headland sheltered the inlet from the breakers of the open sea to the south. Towards evening we got on grass, and went racing over the turf with much satisfaction till we stopped at the hospitable doors of Kirkjuvogr.

Here, as is often the case in Norway, we found several farms clustered together for company : three large timber farmhouses, each with its own out-buildings, and a good-sized, well-kept, black-

I

and-white church. Everything looked neat and thriving. The
turf-walls were trimmed to the utmost straightness, the houses
were clean, the wind, even after it had blown over the farms,
was deliciously fresh, and laden, doubtless, with ozone ; for close
by the Atlantic waves were riding grandly in from the west,
and dissolving on the low red rocks in clouds of foam which
sprinkled the houses and dimmed the windows looking seaward,
while the air was filled with the concussion of the sea. Two
sweet little piebald lambs, white with brown tippets, sat on either
side of the front door ; geese strayed over the grass, mingled
with flights of long-winged sea-gulls ; people bustled to and fro,
and the owners of the farms received us with a hearty welcome.
Three brothers had lately occupied these farms : one, Vilhjalm,
had lately died, but his widow, who was our guide's mother-in-
law, received us most kindly, while the rest of our party were
put up at the other farms. The *bondés* were fine powerful-
looking men, great fishers of shark and cod, and bold sailors ;
on the walls hung medals and testimonials for the lives they
had saved in shipwrecks. We all had a merry supper in the
widow's house, and played at whist till bedtime. Morning
dawned grey and threatening, but I took heart and bathed in a
creek of the roughening sea, and, thoroughly warmed up, started
after breakfast to ride with the gentlemen to the point of Reykjanes. We galloped over the grass-land to a desolate region
of lava-rocks. Paul called on us to admire the finest church in
Iceland, and I was quite taken in for a moment by a huge architectural-looking pile, very like Winchester Cathedral, rising in
the misty distance. It was, however, really a hill. Near it rose
a pyramid so geometrical that it was hard to believe that it was
no hand of man but the wild volcanic forces that had piled it up.
Meanwhile the ground had changed from rock to sand of a deep
purple brown, like gunpowder ; it made an effective background
for the one break in its unity, a long pale-green grass, growing
so sparsely that the single blades knotted themselves in graceful curves loosely over the dark sand. It would have been an
excellent pattern for furniture cretonne.

Deeper among the overhanging lava-crags we rode. Far and wide all was a mountainous desolation, till at last the air grew warm, the ground smoking and treacherous, and the ravine opened on a green hillside, sloping towards the cone of a recent volcano, where abundant clouds of steam rolled up in various places. Here we dismounted among all sorts of queer surroundings. There was a crater or caldron, some fifty feet in diameter, of boiling bluish mud, bubbling and wreathing up in circular ripples. The overhanging sides were jagged, and the ground above was rotten—a regular boiling bog, in which you sank through cohesive hot mud, into thinner, more scalding stuff, and might easily sink too deep to be pleasant. Gislason being tenant of the place, and having at one time worked a quarry here, knew his ground as far as so shifting an affair could be known, and we followed him carefully; but we were all more or less in the hot mud. Little craters opened here and there, going deep into the ground, and in another great caldron red mud boiled instead of blue. In the middle of all this steam a great rock stood out: above it was brilliantly white, and of some very light stuff; lower down it was pink and white, layers of hydrated silica, mixed with some iron, friable above but growing harder as you dug deeper. Perhaps a fine porcelain-clay may be found here, and Iceland may some day produce her own choice china. We saw a pretty piece of chemical action going on where the red vapour was rolling out of some mud which impinged on the lava-rock. The men broke the earth off the rock with their pickaxes, pulling a little rapidly down though it was almost too hot to touch. Then as the vapour rose and condensed rapidly in the cold air, we saw the lava-rock glance over, apparently in the very act of being silver-plated. This was, I think, owing to the iron in the vapour being, through contact with the air, precipitated and deposited on the lava, silvering it over while we watched. Some of the plating rubbed quickly off, but I have other specimens which still glitter.

On remounting we went towards the point of Reykjanes, so well remembered as a peril of the sea in our late stormy voyage,

of iron, probably something connected

and those weird rocks like giant buildings, which had been in sight all this time. But the grey weather was changing for the worse : a sea-fog rolled up, thick rain set in, and it was of no use to go any further ; we could have seen nothing, and the trackless solitude we had crossed would have been bad riding after dark, so we turned reluctantly homewards. We made a halt to collect the company by the last of the daylight, and I thought we did not look like a party it would be pleasant to meet on so dark a night as this threatened to be. We were armed with pick-axes and hammers ; we were dripping and dirty, smeared with red and blue mud, with lank waterproofs, and rain streaming off the brims of our hats—one especially, who wore an Icelandic knitted cap of many colours, whose face was now streaked with all the tints of the soaked wool, and whose clothes hinted of long sojourn in the mountains, presented an appearance which would have been scorned by a civilised scarecrow. One gentle-man alone, who had only been five days in Iceland, retained the ordinary form of the point-device traveller, and gave far too high a standard by which to measure the rest of us wanderers for long in the wilds. We rode hard in the twilight, my pony springing over the obstacles I could not see, till none too soon we hit on a real track—for then, though it was dark, we could still canter over grass full tilt for the lights of Kirkjuvogr. The rain and the wind and the bleak night seemed the bleaker from the con-trast of the light which streamed from the friendly shelter. It was half-past eight, and I had had nothing since an early break-fast, so coffee was welcome, while I dressed and substituted borrowed Icelandic shoes for my boots, which had been utterly wrecked by the boiling mud. These shoes are green—made of soft sheepskin—pointed, without soles, and tied on by thongs bound round the ankle. They rather resemble moccasins, and I have seen them used in Shetland. The wearers must, I suppose, resign themselves to wet feet. That rainy night, as the supper was spread in another farm, I had to be carried over the worst places on my way there, as my green shoes were no protection. Kettil gave us the feast that night. We sat down to a great

spread in a comfortable dark-wainscoted room in his house, the
dash of the sea outside, and the rattle of the wind and hail at the
casements, only adding zest to the mirth within, though the
weather made us rather anxious about our plan of returning to
Reykjavik by sea on the morrow. Oddur Gislason acted as host,
while Kettil sat apart looking with quiet satisfaction at the noble
justice we were doing to our excellent fare. He once got up
and pointedly removed our own wine which we had placed on
the table, substituting some excellent Bordeaux of his own, also
cherry - brandy and other liqueurs. It was not till half-past
eleven that the idea of a six o'clock start next morning made us
break up the entertainment with hand-shaking all round, and
grope through the black rainy night in search of our own
quarters, guided partly by the dimly discerned foam of the roaring breakers.

By morning, however, the wind had abated, and the sun shone
brightly on the wet fields and subsiding sea. We went to look
at the church, which was far too neat and ecclesiastical within
for any one to venture to use it as a bedroom. We returned to
a great breakfast, concluding with prolonged adieus to a number
of people—toasts, songs, speeches in English and Icelandic, and
clinking of glasses all round. So far good; but we were rather
surprised to hear that we had to drink farewell at Kettil's farm
too, whither we adjourned, to find more company, more wine,
and more food. I contrived by means of keeping my mind
on the future, like Dugald Dalgetty, to partake of some excellent pancakes, and drink a *hesta skál*, or stirrup-cup; and so we
cantered off, though some of the party remained to take leave
at the third farm also. We rode in two hours to Njardvik,
almost a village, by a creek, where our boat waited for us. In
going to it we passed some hideous sharks not yet cut up, about
six or seven feet long—a most evil type of animal life. The
boat was a large open one with two masts, with a crew of six.
One of these men we could have declared was Irish, but he was
a born Icelander. He had the short round face, regular features,
black hair, and blue eyes with long black lashes, which form the

most accepted type of Irish good looks. Oddur Gislason took
the helm; we cleared the land with oars; the men took off their
hats for a minute of silent prayer, according to custom; we
hoisted sail, and were soon making good way over the tumbling
blue waves. We discussed our last bottle of champagne; a song
was called for—many songs, till intense sleepiness reminded me
I had been up since five in the morning, and I only woke up
among the shoals and skerries near Reykjavik, after a very quick
run of five hours.

This was our last expedition that year; for directly after, on
the afternoon of the 7th September, all the half-dozen English
people in Reykjavik embarked on board the Queen steamer,
accompanied by many Icelandic friends. We pledged each other
in a parting *skál*, their boats pushed off, and before they had
reached the jetty we were gliding away from Reykjavik. How
different it looked to my eyes in the afternoon glow from the place
I first saw in the chill early morning! Then it seemed small,
remote, and cold — now it appeared an important town, and
favoured by a delightful climate. The real balance may be
struck between those two opinions, but it is the last which
remains my own as regards the climate. The wonderful benefit
my health received from its influence, in spite of some fatigue,
hard living, and exposure, proves that this is no mere fancy of
mine, but that there is some truth in the graduated scale of
the value of fine air which places the Engadine at the foot of the
list, Sweden next, and Iceland as superlative—best where all
are good.

The night we sailed the aurora again lit up the sky and
dimmed the stars; besides the splendour, it was so fantastic and
surprising that it kept all the wondering passengers on deck till
long after midnight. The captain, however, did not share our
delight. "I don't like it so high in the sky," he said. Next
day we were battling with an equinoctial gale, which, though it
did not much interfere with the comfort of the small and pleasant
party of passengers, kept us out two days over our time, and
cost us the lives of forty of our cargo of ponies. The poor little

beasts had not sufficient space, and chiefly in consequence of that, I think, could not stand the rolling of our most lively steamer; but the transport of ponies is now better understood, and they are usually landed quite safely and in fair condition. The .sea was nothing like so high as on our outward passage, and my own pony, which was favoured with much notice and occasional tit-bits, was none the worse for the voyage.

The communication with Iceland is now more frequent and regular than in the year 1875. Slimon's steamer the Camoens begins at the end of June to run about every three weeks, from Granton to Iceland, till the beginning of September. The Danish mail-steamer runs from March to November about once a month between Copenhagen and Iceland, calling at Leith on her way. Last year a midwinter mail-steamer was sent, but it may be discontinued, as the Phönix s.s. was lost on the voyage out on the 31st of January last, in the Faxa Floa, through sheer stress of weather. A furious gale and snowstorm prevented her from making the port of Reykjavik, and the snow and sea-water freezing on the deck canted the steamer over so much to one side that she became unmanageable, and ran on the skerries outside the coast of Snæfellness, where the crew contrived to get ashore, but the vessel soon went to pieces. This sharp warning against the winter seas, which were never faced in old times by Viking or merchantman, may induce the Icelanders to submit again to their usual deprivation for the four winter months of all communication with the outer world.

HINTS TO TRAVELLERS.

I have been asked to give a few practical hints to intending travellers, especially ladies; and remembering how puzzled we were what to take on our first journey, and how much experience has taught us, I believe they may be found useful.

A lady should bring her own saddle. It should be a light one, and can hardly be too much padded, to suit small ponies. It is well to bring a

single rein also ; but the ponies go best with the Icelandic bit. Little
preparation is needed for the expedition to the Geysir, which is all
arranged for, and for which a tent can be hired ; but people who go
further, especially ladies, should take their own tent—one of Edgington's
smallest-sized marquees we have found excellent, and much better than
any bell-tent in bad weather. A very light mattress of ribbed cork
makes a good enough bed, especially in a War Office valise—a delightful
invention I used on my last journey, which has waterproof sides lacing
up, so as to give great protection on damp earth or windy floors. This,
with a Scotch plaid and a waterproof sheet, is very comfortable, and it
serves as a packing-case by day. Very little luggage can be taken across
country, so woollen clothes are to be preferred. A short habit that will
easily loop up to a walking length, and a woollen gown as a change, are
needed ; and a good gown for Reykjavik. The habit should have a
warm outer jacket ready to slip on, for the change of climate from even
the sunny to the windy side of a hill is very great, and in a day's ride
the glass may vary nearly forty degrees. Strong walking boots and soft
leather gaiters are needed ; fishing-stockings to go over all are a great
protection if the route leads over many rivers. Some tins of preserved
meat or soup should be taken, as there is very little choice at Reykjavik.

As to expenses, it is difficult to make an estimate, as, except for the
excursion to the Geysirs, for which there is a regular tariff, so much
depends on the number of the party, the route they follow, and the
degree to which they are prepared to rough it. Two or three persons
pay more in proportion than a larger party, but are more comfortable,
and more sure of finding pasture for their ponies.

We two sometimes travelled with fourteen ponies, which is as many
as can be comfortably disposed of at night on some farms. At other
times, for short distances, we had only seven or eight ponies, thus greatly
reducing the expenses. The hire of the ponies is from one and a half to
three *krone* a-day, a *krone* being equal to 1s. 1½d. They may be bought
from 100 to 200 *krone*—more for a fancy pony ; and it is well to buy at
least one, if any stay be made in the country. There are not many very
competent guides. Some student will always be found who will be glad
to accompany a traveller as interpreter ; but very possibly he may not
know much of the country, and be obliged to hire a local guide at every
turn, or chance finding the way. We once met a party travelling with
a guide who asked ours a thousand questions ; he knew nothing of the
route, but with admirable presence of mind never allowed his party to
guess his uncertainties. The best guides are generally young men of
good position and education, and are excellent companions. An under-
man or driver is needed besides, if there are many ponies. Our guide
the first year was familiar with all the ways, but he is no longer avail-

able, having become a clergyman. Mr T. Gudmundsen, who accompanied us on all our other journeys, knows the island far and wide, and has the real enjoyment of travel, which makes him suit this profession admirably.

Though a short excursion may be done pretty cheaply, extensive travelling in Iceland is a good deal dearer than most foreign travel, though not dearer than travelling on horseback elsewhere, which is always an expensive if a very pleasant way of exploring a country. The life is wholesome and strengthening, though perhaps it might be rather a heroic remedy to recommend to a really delicate person. Such little comforts as a folding india-rubber bath and a railway travelling lamp should not be forgotten : a *puggery* is useful for the sunshine ; for the rain an umbrella is useless ; and a good macintosh ulster, though it is heavy to walk in, resists the weather much better than the lighter waterproofs.

CHAPTER XIV.

A JOURNEY IN 1878—ULFLJOTSVATN—GEYSIR, ANOTHER ERUPTION—
GULLFOSS—HUNI—THJORSÀ—STORUVELLIR.

IT had long been my wish to visit the south of Iceland, the chief
scene of the Njal Saga. This fascinating story has been well
translated by Sir G. Dasent; but to be thoroughly appreciated,
should be read in Icelandic. It was written about 600 years ago,
and is a model of prose-writing, vivid and idiomatic—throwing
great light on the character of the North, showing, not only what
people really were in the eleventh century, but what the author
thought they ought to be. Gunnar, the hero, is the ideal character; his bad beautiful wife works him all evil but that of leading him to act wrongly himself. Njal, his best friend, the man
of wisdom and peace, is also surrounded by relations who are the
cause of his downfall—fierce sons, who are wrought upon by
Mord, the evil genius of the story, to deeds of violence and injustice. The death of Njal and the innocent women and children,
brought about by Flosi, a man also of noble nature, on whom the
obligation of a blood-feud had come with a heavy weight, is
grandly tragic. The whole is a reliable history of some families
who inhabited this district from about A.D. 950 to 1010, condensed
and heightened into a sort of prose poem by an unknown author
circa 1250, and it should be read by all travellers to Iceland.

The journey to this district was achieved in the summer of
1878 in spite of weather; and it was fortunate that the lady who
joined me for the expedition, the Honourable Emily Cathcart,

was not to be easily daunted by climate, for it seemed as if we had offended the guardian water-spirits, so persistently were we persecuted by the rain. First, while the island was basking in sunshine, our steamer was groping about in quest of it in a dense fog; then when at last we had arrived, we came with the long-absent clouds. After waiting during several days for the threatening weather to pass off, on the 18th of July we took heart at the sight of some blue in the sky, and left Reykjavik. We engaged Thorgrimur Gudmundsen as our guide, and Haldor as our driver. We had fourteen ponies in all—each two to ride, and the rest for relays and luggage. I took my little marquee tent, which could hold two people comfortably, and two more in the outer porches if required, and we set off, bound for Ulfljots Lake and the Geysirs; thence we meant to go to Hecla, where there had been a recent eruption; and then to the south-east coast and the scenes of the Njal Saga.

The ladies at Reykjavik shook their heads, and spoke of the wild rivers we had to cross; people were drowned in them every year. They had indeed been very low in the past dry weather; but if it rained we would see what they could be—and it did rain, and we saw what was meant. But the gentlemen at Reykjavik cheered us up. The people drowned every year were generally tipsy; we, seeing it was not creditable, determined certainly not to be drowned. Moreover, they said we had in Thorgrimur one of the best of guides, cautious as well as daring—and that also turned out to be true.

As to possible dangers in riding across Iceland, Henderson, whose book, though somewhat out of date, gives more real information than all the others I have seen put together, is on this point an alarmist; mountain perils were more dreaded then than in our days of Alpine clubs and rough travel. Still he was never deterred from going where he wished, though by his own showing often in a mortal fright; he threw his heart over the rivers as the hunters say, and duly followed with his ponies. Captain Burton, who did not succeed in his explorations, goes to the other extreme, laughing, not always without reason, at the perils

imagined by former travellers, and talking contemptuously of the
hills of Iceland, because they are not the Andes or Himalayas.
But if you do fall over a precipice, it does not matter much how
far, to a few thousand feet. It is enough, as Mercutio says ; and a
mountain-land without roads worth mentioning does require careful riding sometimes, but of course in perilous places every one
takes care not to fall.

The rivers are sometimes dangerous, and cause a certain annual
loss of life. Captain Burton, who travelled in an exceptionally
cold and dry summer, makes light of them also, saying that they
are crossed by ferry-boats when more than three feet deep. Of
course that means in the fords, from which a small deviation may
plunge you into very deep water ; and a ford even three feet deep
in a very heavy current is quite enough for a little pony. Many
rivers are too swift for ferrying, and often there are no boats ;
and if they cannot be forded the traveller has to wait till they
subside, for they vary much on different days, and even at
different times of the day. The sudden mists which sometimes
descend from the mountains may also make travelling unsafe
unless with an experienced guide. The country is very solitary.
Often there are no tracks at all, and the compass is of little use
owing to magnetic disturbances. The ponies are often the best
guides in a mist ; and indeed, unless they are biassed by a wish
to return to a wrong farm, are very reliable for finding the way,
either in a fog or in the dark.

A sunny morning wiled us away from Reykjavik on the way
to the lower end of the Ulfljot Lake, but wild rain overtook us
on a stony plain which lies beneath the volcanic hills we had to
cross. The rain and hail cleared off when we reached the hills,
but the sky was grey, and grey too, the shale and rock over which
we clambered into small circular valleys, apparently old craters
surrounded by contorted hills. On every side forms like slender
spires, or wedges, or round towers, rose black into the clouds.
One could imagine that hooded figures, or deformed dwarfs with
outstretched arms, had been turned to black stone, so strange
were the weird shapes of that region of spent volcanoes. The

ponies clambered down impossible places, so steep that I almost
lost sight of the neck of the one I was riding; but the rough lava
rock gives good footing, and is not so bad as it looks. When
we emerged into flat land under more reasonable hills, we rode
long before reaching the lake called Ulfljotsvatn, and a little
farm beneath a grassy mound, which was crowned by a black-
and-white wooden church. There we took up our quarters. I
cooked some soup, and we shook down our plaids and mattresses
on the floor. The men found room at the farm, the ponies on the
tun; and so we rested till morning came in storm and rain. The

farm is a poor one. The *bondé* was from home, and his wife had
added a baby to the household the day before, so we were rather
left to our own resources.

One of these was the river Sög, which tore down into the lake
not far off, to which I crossed in a leaky boat. There was no
lack of fish, but it was not easy fishing for a lady—the grass was
so long, the banks so broken; the water, too, was very strong
and swift, and the wind and rain importunate. But a heavy
sea-trout was soon on my fly—he was not mere sport, he was
dinner, and the moment was proportionately agonising when, as
I gave him line, there was a check, a spring of the rod, and he

was gone. That reel had not been looked through since our Norway fishing days of the previous year, and there was a tangle. Deeply repentant, I sat down on a wet stone and sorted it. The fish had fortunately only carried off the fly, and soon I secured

Thurida.

another, which showed much sport, and proved to be nearly three pounds in weight, and enough; and as I was now very wet, I came home and crept into the farm kitchen, the entrance to which was just three feet high. Here I sat on an inverted tub and sketched, while several inhabitants and two dogs also contrived to squeeze in, and we whiled away the time with stories, reading, and talk. The Icelanders are so superior to their surroundings that their culture constantly takes one by surprise. But of course to appreciate this, one must at least understand something of their language.

The next day the weather was even worse. It needed some patience to put up with the clammy church, or the other alternative—the stuffy farm; but outside the air seemed about as wet as the lake. We were not, however, so out of the world after all —we actually received a morning call. A being entered the church clad in a macintosh, once white, and possibly elegant, but now all stained and frayed into fringes and holes, and girded with a rope. With a Parisian air he took off a very bad hat and introduced himself as an American gentleman, Major M——; and a very pleasant gentleman he proved to be in spite of his articulation, which had been affected by a wound in the mouth received in the American war, and his attire, which, however, was only the natural result of two months' travel in Iceland, and which *then* contrasted unfavourably with our fresh apparel, but would have been no contrast a fortnight later.

The next morning was our first lovely day. The hills were purple, the lake Mediterranean blue: grass and buildings glittered in the sunshine. We crossed the lake in the boat; the ponies had to swim the river Sög[1] lower down, but we found them when we landed grooming themselves by rolling in the bog-myrtle and juniper, and away we rode over the untracked heath towards the richly coloured hills above Langavatn, the lake on the road from Thingvellir to Geysir. The ride was delightful. We lunched on the grassy slopes above the lake near some caverns, and then went on again by the usual road to Geysir. Haldor had gone back to fetch something we had forgotten, so we did not quite see our way to camping at Geysir; for it takes two men to put up the tent, and I was not sure if the united strength of two ladies was equal to another man. The people of Utlith cordially invited us to stop there as I had done before; but though a few stars began to show themselves, the ponies were fresh, the riding good, and we pushed briskly forward. It was a time of keen enjoyment. Grand hills were round us, their lower slopes pleasantly clothed with birch and juniper-bushes; far white mountains shone in the sky; there was nothing but the plaintive cry of the bittern or the plover to break the silence—nothing to contaminate the delicious breeze, which was scented with the fragrance of aromatic plants drawn out by the heat of the past day.

Now the white steam rolls up from Haukadale, the open land before us, and plunging through bog and river, we ride up to the hot springs at about 11 o'clock at night, finding there not absolute solitude. A little tent like a dog-kennel was pitched near the Great Geysir, and out of it crawled, on all-fours, what seemed like a polar bear, but proved to be our friend the Major.

[1] I observed this day what I had been told before, that but for the drown-ing rain I could not have fished in the Sög. The "fly" was out in swarms, in clouds, in atmospheres. I thought, as they do not sting, they would be contemptible—and so they are, meanly contemptible, and yet more than a match for man and horse. They are large and lazy, and walk in dozens into your eyes and nose and ears, or they cover your veil and blind you. They make no effort to escape; their long legs come off at a touch, and you can kill any number, but merely add corpses to the crowds jostling for a place. Though they are without the malignant power of the mosquito, and very local, so that you can step out of them easily, if they are on the river, there is no help for it—you must go away.

A stroke of good luck for us, as otherwise we could hardly have pitched the tent, which he helped Thorgrimur to raise, and then we soon nestled into our plaids, and slept well after forty-five miles on horseback.

How different would my impressions of Geysir have been had this been my only visit! Honest souls who tell the truth are as misleading as the idealists who try to see what they expect. And that may be nearer the truth, after all, than the prosy facts which happen at the moment to be before them. Perhaps there is something ridiculous in the very position of waiting in humble attendance on a fountain in hopes of an explosion, never daring to go half a mile away for fear of missing the sight, and having only the comforts of a tinker to fall back upon. Besides, not only did it rain next day, but other tramps came with their pots and kettles,—first an English party of sportsmen, and then some Danes. Probably they were just as good as we were, and I own they had as good a right to be there, but from our point of view they were quite *de trop*. Had we come out into a desert and camped on an explosive hot-water bog to be haunted by the ordinary shooting-coats and small-talk of society? The Great Geysir also did not show, though at night it gave various false alarms, booming and boiling over, and inducing people to emerge · from the supposed shelter of the tents into the chill wind and rain. Strokr of course exploded to order; but who that has seen the Geysir cares for Strokr?

But on the third morning, when the Englishmen and the Danes were gone, and we were packing our traps,—after a preliminary underground roar, and ● swirl all round the crater, up went Geysir in a great blue-black sloping wave, high into the sky— seventy or eighty feet up—dissolving into foam and steam, and descending all in whiteness. The explosion, which repeated itself several times, was certainly less beautiful than the one I had seen before, when the water rose like a dome before break- ing. But it gave a very impressive hint of the hidden powers that are seething and struggling below the thin earth-crust. Meanwhile the Little Geysir, half a mile off, played with great regularity in a pretty jet of about fifteen feet, and the other springs were all in agitation. So we left them, sending Haldor with our luggage and spare ponies to Huni, while we ladies, with Thorgrimur and Major M——, took a circuit by Gullfoss, which I should recommend to all travellers. We first crossed a bad bog which stretched far and wide, having to scramble from tussock to mound of grass, plunging through deep pools, and trusting much to the ponies. We rode through a deep ford on Arbrandsà, where the water rose over my saddle, and on over trackless desolate places, till the roar of water was in our ears, and grew and grew. At last we dismounted in the long wet grass, and scrambled on

foot to the edge of the swollen Hvità, or white river, which here hurls itself down in the Gullfoss (pronounced Gudelfoss), or Golden Fall.

Few will cross the marshy desert to visit these grand falls, but these few, especially after rain, are well rewarded. The river is very wide, like the Tay at Perth, but far more rapid. Against the horizon it comes down in a broad short fall, then swirls away in broken water, sweeping in a magnificent curve to the great

K

main plunge of the whole river, quite even and unbroken, down
into a mist of foam veiling an unseen abyss. It is golden in
colour—a tawny gold; it reappears again raging between the
basalt walls, tearing an angry way out of the deep prison, and
speeding off from the barren wilderness above to the solitudes
below, for here the Hvitá flows through quite uninhabited land.

With some difficulty we scrambled down to the edge of the
furious river some way below the fall, and there, though splashed
and deafened, I was delighted with the grandeur of this, in some
respects, the finest waterfall I have ever seen, and among those
may be included the grandest both in Norway and Switzerland.
We had a rough ride of some hours, always in rain, till we halted
at a ford by the farm of Tungafelli, on the other side of the
Hvitá. A frail leaky little boat put across for us, and we
achieved a haphazard sort of passage, albeit carried far down,
spun in the current, obliged to bale out water, but arriving—
which is, after all, the main point in a voyage—without having
to swim like the ponies. Tungafelli—associated in my mind with
a wise man who figures in the Njal Saga, Asgrim Elligrimson—is
the only habitation in the neighbourhood, and the only place for
many miles round where the Hvitá is more or less fordable,—*less*
sometimes, for many accidents have happened here. Thence we
went over prettily diversified country among rocks and meadow-
land to the parsonage of Huni. Here its owner, Sira Jöhannes
Briem, received us hospitably; he spoke English well. Two
guest-rooms were prepared, and a real supper on a table, prettily
served, and real beds, did feel very pleasant after several rough
nights.

Next day, the 24th, we took a wet walk in the morning on the
pretty grassy hills near, and starting on horseback at twelve, we
rode by thriving farms through a pleasant land; but our usual
companion, the rain, did not desert us, coming in showers and
scuds and increasing the river-floods. A farmer lent me a choice
pony, as swift as sure, which carried me gaily over the rough
ground, till towards evening we reached the Thjorsà, Thor's
river, our Thurso. We sat down on the bank and watched the

somewhat anxious process of getting our ponies across. Their
loads were placed in a scrap of a boat, and they were expected
to swim this great rapid river. "He rode over Thjorsà" is an
ever-recurring sentence in the sagas; for whether encountered
high up, as here, or near its mouth, the Thjorsà, in the absence
of all bridges, or even of fixed ferries, divides Southern Iceland
into two parts. People meet easily or not, according as they
live on the same or opposite sides of Thjorsà.

Again and again our ponies refused to face the yellow waves,

Ferry on Thjorsà.

while our men, aided by some volunteers from the nearest farm,
made a ring round them, cracked whips, flung stones, and at
length succeeded in launching the whole fourteen. Two cream-
colours, brothers, well known for cunning, laziness, and strength,
soon turned and swam back; the other twelve by degrees won
their way across, their little heads sometimes quite disappearing
among the waves, which carried them more or less down the

river. One known as the weak piebald, in spite of a rest on a sandbank, was carried a mile down, and we were very anxious about him; but at last all were safely landed and collected on the opposite side. We fastened the refractory creams to the stern of the little boat which had returned for us, and pushed off. But the brothers made a good fight,—working together like one, they dragged us ashore again several times. Helped by allies on the shore, we at length conquered, and dragged them out into mid-stream. Thorgrimur let go their halters when it was easier for them to go on than to turn back. They snorted and rolled their eyes and splashed, but as they really could swim as well as the rest, at last we were all safe across. The evening grew bright, and the ride was merry, now over a great mountain-bordered plain, Storuvellir, or the big valley. We came to a large comfortable parsonage, the abode of Sira Asmundur, well known to all travellers to Hecla. He gave us good quarters, and with his daughter I took a pleasant stroll in the sunshine late at night.

CHAPTER XV.

HECLA—NEW VOLCANOES—KIRKJUBAE—FLJOTSLID.

Now we were under the snowy cone of Hecla, for the snows, which later in the year dissolve in the hot ashes, lay still in thick rounded forms above the black volcanic rocks. Hecla, which in the old geography lessons of one's childhood meant Iceland, was rather disappointing as being only one of so many volcanoes, and neither among the finest in appearance nor the most active in work; even the volcanic action of this year was fully eight miles from Hecla, nearer Kratatinkr to the north. Hecla has the advantage of appearing the first advanced-guard of the various mountains which rise in this district of hidden fires. To-day she generally (for she is feminine in Icelandic) wore the cloud-cloak, *Hecla*, whence her name is derived. The eruption which had occurred three months before our visit, had first startled the nearest inhabitants, who were about twenty miles off, by a blaze in the sky, which had not continued long, but a stream of lava, from ten to twenty feet thick, had been erupted, that had filled up much of a waste valley among the cinder-hills. There is always alarm in Iceland when the ash-showers and earth-fires show themselves, — the terrible weather, which takes its origin, not in the heavens above but in the earth beneath. This time the fire-forces had expended themselves in the desert land which stretches north of Hecla for 200 miles, and which cannot be worse, indeed might be the better, for the slow-consuming fires and the feeding volcanic ash.

At noon our party, including Major M——, started to explore
the new volcanoes. We took a little food, some wraps, and my tent,
and the cream-coloured brothers to carry the baggage. The way
led first through a birch-wood four or five feet high, and thus to
the last farm, where we were regaled with chocolate, and picked
up the *bondé* who was to guide us—one of two or three men who
knew the way. Then we went over a great ashy plain; on one
side thundered the Thjorsà, sometimes in noteworthy rapids, on
the other Western Rangá ran. Above it rose Hecla's black
buttresses and icy cone, on the other side rose Gullfjall, a great
wedge of a mountain, utterly bare and the colour of old gold—
awful in the sunshine. In front, trackless dark sands swept
towards the blue and snowy hills in the northern horizon. The
rain had, happily for us, hardened the sands which often rise
here in dust-storms. They sang Grimur Tomsen's riding-song
as we cantered gaily forward—

> " *Ridum ok ridum, reykjum yfir sandum,*" &c.

The beginning may be roughly translated—

> "Ride we and ride we, dash across the wide sand,
> Low sinks the sun, now west by Arnafell,
> Strange things uncanny out about the wild lands,
> Haunt the desert ice-hills—ride we swift and well.
> On with you, ponies, keeping up the speed;
> Nothing evil overtakes the fast-running steed," &c.

We turned to the north about four miles beyond the last spur of
Hecla, as if to go round the mountain, and reached, about 7 P.M.,
a last little knoll of verdure. Here we took the burdens off the
cream brothers, and tied each one's head to the other one's tail,
and so left them. These brothers were so attached by affection
also, that if either missed the other he even lost his natural
laziness and would rush in wild pursuit; but together they enjoyed a placid content that nothing seemed to disturb. Now we
and our ponies climbed, separately of course, a steep cone of
ashes like that on the top of Vesuvius, only longer; it was strewn
with fresh pumice and erupted matter. I was glad at the top to
remount my chestnut, who, though bad in bogs, was distinguished

on the hills. We were now in a confused scene of hills and valleys, rocks tilted all ways, and lava currents and ashes flung over them, the scene of grand volcanic action. There is something like it on Vesuvius, but on a smaller scale, for there the volcano seems an accident in a fair habitable country, like a forge in a village ; but here Nature is triumphant,—few eyes have seen these furnaces, no touch of man's hand has ever been felt. There was not a scrap of verdure, hills and valleys alike were reddish-brown or black; but streaks of red occurred, and yellow stones were strewn about. The contrast was wonderful between the unity of the colouring and the mad diversity of form; between the shapes which were molten and twisted, and the matter which was hard still stone.

We halted in an ashy valley, where further riding was impossible, for we were on the edge of the field of new lava, everywhere cloven and broken up, and of a reddish hue. Across the valley was a finely shaped mountain-range, the extinct volcano of Kratatinkr, and a series of new low volcanic cones still smoking and streaked with yellow and red incrustations. The lavabed was about twenty feet deep at the edge—the gentlemen reported it as deeper further on. But I did not go far, as, though it was very rough and distorted, it was also so brittle as to be hard climbing, so I preferred making a sketch of the wild place. It was now about 10 P.M. They said we had ridden twenty-eight miles.

We had to return, and how we found our way over the lavavalleys I hardly know; but in due time we got back to the cream brothers, who had valsed amicably a few hundred yards on their way home, with the double motion of a planet on its axis and in its orbit. As no water was near, we rode on in the darkness, trusting much to the ponies, till in about an hour we reached grass and heard running water. Here, therefore, we put up the tent, I holding the little lamp to the pegs, to help the men to drive them in, for it was quite dark. The little tent had a cheery effect, shining golden-brown in the night when the lamp was hooked on the pole. The cold meat was unpacked, and a good brew of hot tea, for which we had brought cream, was made over the spirit-lamp. Life needs no more. Why do people live in houses all the summer time? Why do they go to big hotels for pleasure? Why have we made life so cumbrous, and our wants so many and intractable? Mr Watts, who knew the Icelanders well and liked them much, remarks that contentment is the curse of Iceland. So the Bedouin, the dweller in tents *par excellence*, needs little, cares for little, has few ambitions, and much true peace. He, too, is content with the content that bars all progress; so let us, who belong to the race which marches in the van, shake off this unnatural calm that belongs to the solitudes of nature, and go back to our crowds and struggles, to society and its joys, such as bitter mournful pictures, and craving weary

Tent by Hecla.

music of the future—to science, and politics, and competitive examinations.

A lovely morning shows us how pretty is our camping-ground. Hecla's northern shoulder, and the adjacent hills, are decked in soft pink and violet, as if one did not know what grim wastes they really were. The poor *bondé* is very sleepy, as he has had to watch the ponies all night. We eat up our provisions, every scrap of them, and have a pleasant canter of four hours back to Storuvellir, where the kind family welcome us warmly.

All thoughts of ascending Hecla next morning were set at rest by the clouds on its summit. So saying farewell to our American friend, who was bound for the coast, we rode off for Kirkjubae, fording a pretty deep river, the Laxá, and cantering once more over meadow-land. But at my desire we made a circuit which brought us again over ashes and cinders. What destruction fire has worked here!—frost is nowhere in the battle. In the year 1302, one of the most fertile districts in this country, Skard, was overwhelmed by lava and cinders. Might not an old homestead—a northern Pompeii with MS. in it—be discovered by explorers? The difficulty would be to know where to excavate; for there is nothing like a volcano for destroying landmarks, as I thought in my heart while riding with apparently undoubting faith to see the spot where Gunnar fought one of his hardest battles. There was the broken bank of Knáferholar, where thirty men lay in wait for three. And we rode as Gunnar did to the Ness, by Rang river; and Haldor was in his element, showing the stones they piled after the fight, where one brother of Gunnar's was slain to fourteen men on the other side,—one of whom said at last, "Let us fly now; we have not to do with men but with fiends."—*Vide* 'Njal's Saga.' The mountain Thrihyrning (Three-corner) rises here, edged by Eastern Rangá; and further on, near a pretty little lake, stands a good farm, where they asked us to come in. We sat with the old *bondé* in a wainscoted room painted bright blue, while the daughters of the house brought delicious coffee. Haldor, I may mention, as it has all ended well, was suspected of having lost his heart somewhere in this farm,ˣ and looked anxious and wistful in consequence. He asked leave to stay here over the next day—Sunday—which we ourselves had settled to spend at Kirkjubae.

They showed us the church, where there was a fine medieval salver and a beautiful cup, said to have been forged by the elves, but probably brought from the far south by some roving Viking or Skald long ago. There was a new handsome cope of embroidered crimson satin, and also an altar-cloth richly worked in gold, both presented by the old *bondé*, who was evidently something of a ritualist. No one would venture to use this pretty little church as a bedroom, I should hope. Happily it is out of the track of

ˣ *has since married the girl.*

tourists. I have known them make quite a grievance of not being permitted to sleep in a church, after having made various irreverent, if very mild jokes, about the trifling incongruities arising out of a practice which comes as a matter of course to the natives.

But they do respect their churches; and now that some money is coming into the country, we often find improvements, and even costly decorations, taken in hand by parishes, or, as in this case, by individuals.

Leaving Haldor, whose courtship we believe prospered apace, we rode on about eight miles to Kirkjubae, the house of the priest of the parish. His other church lies about equidistant in an opposite direction; so Sira Isleif Gislason has a good deal of riding, and rides good horses too. No doubt our wanderings would be much more entertaining if I could tell more about the home life of the hospitable houses where we were received; but though there is little one can say without indiscretion, all the east country knows how Sira Isleif is a good musician, with a charming tenor voice. The evening was cheered with part-singing of Icelandic, Swedish, and Danish songs, to which Thorgrimur contributed a deep bass, and a small boy a silvery treble. Music lies deep in the Icelanders, and the misfortunes of two hundred years have not stamped it out, though the howls of old bodies in churches would sometimes make one think so. The art is reviving. Beautiful voices are common, perhaps from the purity of the air, and the people have the Teutonic gift of harmony, and easily learn part-singing.

On Sunday it rained as usual. I had an early gallop on a fine strong chestnut pony, with a hook-shaped blaze, hence called Krokur, which I bought for my own riding, as, though not pretty, he was indefatigable, and a perfect kelpie in the water. Then we all rode eight miles to church through two swollen rivers. The little wooden church was already surrounded by people, many of whom came from afar; others were arriving on horseback, delivering their ponies outside the churchyard wall to some boys, who, helped by the noisy dogs, kept them from running off home.

Neighbourly greetings and kisses were exchanged. The women often carried children on their knees as they sat in their Spanish saddles. Some of the lassies rode astride; but with short stirrups, and a fold of cloth in front, they managed quite nicely. The young men showed their ponies' mettle as they dashed up; and the whole scene was lively and neighbourly. The church was crowded in spite of the weather; the singing was very fair, and Sira Isleif gave an interesting sermon.

We raced back with eight or ten of the congregation, who rode through the swirling Rangá, and came our way. Sira Isleif rode on in the opposite direction to christen a child, and got home late in the drenching rain.

When it rained hard on the Monday, we were told it was a clearing shower. It was much to be hoped that this was the case; but we rode our day's journey for all that in the rain, through the once fertile district of Fljotslid, halting at a poor farm, Hlidarende, because Gunnar lived there 900 years ago. I could only catch glimpses of the wide view from it through driving vapours and rain. When in the evening we reached the farm of Barkkarstadr, I felt rather chilled and weary with wet (for which Icelandic has one word, *vásmödr*), and very thankful to get under cover. They were kind people at the farm. I had set my heart on going next day up a mysterious valley called Thorsmark, of which people told wonders. But "no," said the farmer's wife, Fru Ingebjorg; "on that wild journey you shall not fare to-morrow. Stop here two nights, and I will lend you a fine pony, and you shall visit the falls where Bjarni Thorarensen saw the fairies, and Njal's upland farm." So it was arranged. She lent me a handsome young grey, and we went over the flat lands, skirting the abrupt line of cliffs which border all the wide valley below, called the Land isles, in distinction to the Westmann isles, just visible out at sea—the sea itself being about twenty-five miles distant. The cliff is like a wall broken into occasional rifts. Down these several remarkably pretty waterfalls come foaming; and winding hollow ways run between the rocks, leading to dry caverns tasselled with ferns. One, to which I scram-

bled up twelve feet of perpendicular rock, was curtained inside
with a delicate fern like maiden-hair—a fit retreat for the elves.
Haldor, who was merely a rough working man, told old legends
so well, that we fell to talking over fiction in general. He had read
several of Scott's novels in Danish, and liked them much, but
was especially fascinated by Bulwer Lytton's 'The Last of the
Barons,' and, I think, 'Harold.' "These were the books to give
one something to think of on a winter night," he said. In the
evening I found at the farm a copy of Bjarni Thorarensen's
poems; he who saw the fairies, and who lived some fifty years
ago at Hlidarende. Fru Ingebjorg, seeing how much I liked
the book, gave it to me. His occasional verses and short songs
are often charming. One which I translated as rather appropriate
is entitled "Written in dejection by the Sea"—

> "The skerry away in the fjord,
> So deep in the sea's unrest,
> In silence endures for ever
> The foam that beats on its breast.
>
> Mean is the man who is weaker
> Than senseless rock in the strife,
> And yields to the clash of the billows,
> The countering currents of life."

CHAPTER XVI.

MARKARFLJOT RIVER—THORSMARK—FLOODS AND FORDS.

IF you make up a hot fire, and put on a kettle of water, and then bank up the fire so as to conceal all but the smoke; if you then pile ice on the lid of the kettle, and add a pipe to drain it downwards, you will produce a condition of what chemists call unstable equilibrium—in short, there will soon be a great splutter of some sort. Keep piling on the ice, and do not let the fire go down, and the whole will fairly represent the condition of the southern mountain-system of Iceland just now. You hardly can tell whether ice, or boiling water, or ashes, or molten metallic substances, or some, or all together, will be the next destructive agent or agents liberated.

Sometimes, as when Breidamark glacier overwhelmed Svinadal, the internal heat causes whole glaciers to precipitate themselves into the valleys; as if the ice melting below slipped in a mass off the lid of the kettle. Sometimes there is an eruption of boiling water only, often preceded by the disappearance of a glacier river. This happens, I suppose, when the ice on the lid of the kettle melts into the kettle instead of dripping into the pipe. The pipe dries up, and the kettle hurls off its lid, and boils over. All sorts of things, indeed, may happen so as to make it a nice stirring sort of country for a picnic on a summer's day. But we were bent on a picnic up the formerly mentioned valley of Thorsmark. Once twelve good farms had flourished there; but the land had been all wasted for centuries by a succession of volcanic

and icy devastations. Now there are no inhabitants, and scarcely
any one had seen it. An English painter had written enthusi-
astically about its wonders; and so had an Icelandic poet, who,
while owning that the waters "stormed on either hand, and that
neither horse nor rider would survive a stumble in the terrible
fords which were like waterfalls," yet counselled his countrymen
by all means to go there, especially if out of spirits. Its
entrance, as seen from Barkkarstadr, looked alluring. The blue
mountains seemed wilder as they ran inland until they reached
a climax of frosted silver glacier; and two dark-blue cliffs stood
like a gateway, leaving between them a narrow way by which
the wild Krossà flung itself into Markarfljot.

An Icelandic river could not be symbolised by a nymph reclining by a water-urn, sending a gentle streamlet down to widen
and broaden into a smooth river, carrying ships down to cities
on its shores. Rather we may imagine one of the frost-giants
crouching in a glacier-cavern, and hurling rocks and ice and
débris down the furious turbid waves that burst from the mountains already a destructive full-grown river.

The rivers which drain the glacier-system to the south are
especially short, broad, and furious. They are sometimes as broad
as they are long,—mere outlets, flowing over changing quicksands
two or three miles in breadth. And there is not a frost-ogre in
all the land who despatches a wilder, wickeder river to the sea
than the one who presides over Markarfljot.

This great river has sorely injured the once fertile strath over
which our way led. Volcanoes and glacier-floods have caused it
to make a track about three miles across, down which it runs
in many changing channels. It is very capricious; sometimes
it may be waded, and sometimes it is a serious and even impassable barrier between the south and east country. In the Njal
Saga it is told how Gunnar, when he was exiled, rode over this
country towards the sea with his brother. His horse stumbled
and fell, and as he rose he looked back on the valley. "Fair," he
said, "the corn grows on the river-banks; the meadows are cut,
the whole country is ready for harvest; here will I end my days."

His enemies took care that these days should not be many. This was 900 years ago, but of that verdure there is still left here and there an island of green grass and some patches of wild rye. The soil is very good, and the warm sun might still ripen grain here, I believe, but for this terrible river, which has strewn woods and fields with its wreck of sand and boulders, aided by its tributaries, well named Cross river, Thwart river, and Wrong river—*Krossâ, Thvérâ,* and *Rangâ.*

Besides the ordinary causes of *spates,* these glacier-rivers have another peculiar to themselves called the *Jökull hlaup,* or glacier-leap. As far as I could ascertain, this is caused by an accumulation of water somewhere on a glacier-surface. When it accumulates beyond a certain point it overflows, or, it may be, rushes through a glacier-arch deep in the bed of the river, causing a furious short inundation. In a short broad glacier-stream of two to six miles long the traveller may be surprised by this glacier-leap in mid-stream, converting in a moment a fordable river into a furious cataract hurling down ice-fragments and boulders. In some rivers these inundations are periodical, in others they seem to depend on the weather, but they must be taken into account by the traveller.

Sinister reports of the condition of Markarfljot had reached us— the mild rains had swelled the water; but a farmer in the neighbourhood, to whom the river was but a familiar tricky spirit, came early, pronounced it all safe, and himself undertook to pilot us through the fords of the day—for the fords are always changing. When we came to the river, it seemed as if we had miles to ride before reaching the other side of that network of white wavy currents. Jón the farmer directed the lads how to take the water with the loose ponies; and in they went, I following with Jón by my side. He talked with a kindly patronage of the river, as Undine talked of uncle Kühleborn; and he told me a story, interspersed with poetry, in mid-stream, while I glanced anxiously at the men shouting to the struggling swimming herd of ponies in front, and the whirling white water that eddied round the neck of my little steed. We crossed the river in seven branches, landing on spits of sand or gravel islets; and it took us three-quarters of an hour before we had, without accident, gained the side of Eyjarfjall Jökull. Here we sent on a lad with the loose ponies to a farm beyond, and we two ladies, with Thorgrimur and Haldor, turned up the water-side towards Thorsmark. The scene was beautiful as we cantered by the river over bog-myrtle and blaeberries, and such low luxuriance, towards the mountain gates and silver peaks beyond. On the left hand, as we rose, the desolation wrought by Markarfljot became a network of glittering water, enlivening the dark land. Away below stretched the great flat, edged by the low foam of the bright sea, only broken by one volcanic rocky crag called Dimon.

To the right was Eyjarfjall Jökull, crested with ice, and as we advanced the cliffs closed in to the left till we were riding in a narrow valley, which would have been fertile but for the restless river. The place was really extraordinary; there were only rocks and glaciers to the right, and yet grassy nooks and lawns, sprinkled with birch-trees, opened between the basalt cliffs to the left. The Krossà seemed to have a wicked personality of its own: now it foamed against the rocks to the right, now it flung *débris* on the green slopes to the left,—the valley was not wide enough for its caprices; sometimes it broke into many channels, and then again rushed into one. We forded and forded again to win our way up the valley. The glaciers now almost reached it, each pouring its tributary torrent into the river. We turned for a little way up one branch of it, a cleft between two black walls of basalt which almost met overhead, a complete picture of mountain gloom, saddened still further by the one living thing we saw all day—a lamb with a broken leg dying by the stream. Haldor gave it a kindly *coup de grace*, and we heard the scream of the gathering eagles. Morris in his story of Sigurd the Volsung describes such a landscape as this with both graphic power and scientific accuracy. I remembered the lines as I went :—

" Day long they fared through the mountains, and that highway's fashioner
   Forsooth was a fearful craftsman, and his hands the water were,

And the heaped-up ice was his mattock, and the fireblast was his man,
And never a whit he heeded though his walls were waste and wan,
And the guest-halls of that wayside great heaps of the ashes spent.
But, each as a man alone, through the sun-bright day they went."

We stopped for dinner on a pretty sheltered lawn where a little brook flowed gently. It was not at all cold in spite of the masses of glacier over the way; too mild indeed, for the mountains were pulling down their mist-caps, and then the rain began small and thick.

There were water-worn boulders below, but the rocks seemed chiefly igneous; there was lava too, and the bright blue of glacier spires and fissures contrasted strongly with the black crags. The ice was splitting and cracking with a sound like great guns, and falling in large pieces into some of the white torrents which streamed from its lower edges. Never did I see such a *débâcle;* decidedly it was time to return. We had forded the river seven or eight times that morning, and once we scrambled over a point of rock, making the ponies swim round; and now the water was higher than ever. We climbed on foot up the heights to the left to turn some of these fords; and what it was to walk up-hill in deep cinders, clad in a wet macintosh, through heavy rain, can only be imagined by those who have done it. All looked now ugly and dreary; and difficult as it had been to get into the scrape, it was evidently going to be more difficult to get out of it. I felt like that old woman of Servia who paid five marks to go to the merry-making, but offered twenty to get away from it. For two hours we kept on high ground, and then we had to come down to the main ford. There was the white water tearing down in several channels. Some were easy enough to pass, but we tried the main stream in several places in vain. The men's ponies wrestled in the waves at different points and were beaten back, and they shouted to each other *úfaer* (impassable). But we were bound to get through; for the only alternative would have been to pass the night in a damp cave without food or wraps, till the cold had diminished the rush of water from the glaciers. As I watched these attempts for half an

L

hour, I observed that the middle of the stream was pushed up by the velocity of the current, so as to be decidedly higher than the sides, as it rushed and roared past us, rolling and grinding stones and lumps of ice. Thorgrimur at length placed Krokur between his pony and Haldor's, and said, "We will try, and turn if we cannot do it." And the three ponies did it, though with a great struggle; they seemed doubled up by the force of the current, and Thorgrimur was almost under the waves, which were

> "All crested with tawny foam,
> Like the mane of a chestnut steed."

Then I watched with much interest my companion crossing between the men, and admired the pluck of both riders and ponies.

Thorgrimur looking for a Ford.

We had one other bad ford, and it was darkening before we cleared the domains of the Krossà. A loose pony joined us: he was streaming wet, evidently just out of a river, and had not even a halter on. Rather an anxious circumstance, as he looked as though he might have lost trappings and rider in the river, like "Chiquita the Beauty." But we heard afterwards he had been lent by a farmer to help a party over the river, and then had been sent home to his farm by himself. Presently he turned another way, and we saw him no more. At 11 P.M. we had escaped from the valley, and rode through the rainy darkness to a farm, which we reached at midnight—four dripping vagrants on weary horses.

However, the *bondé* roused up directly, but the womankind and the lights only appeared half an hour later, and till then we sat in the darkness with only a dim window-square visible. The quaint thing was that all this time our guide and the *bondé* kept up a conversation, in which I joined to the best of my powers on the *pluie et le beau temps*, as if it were a morning call; as if we were not sitting in the dark, and ridiculously hungry, muddy, and sleepy. At last a slight supper came, and lights, which of course at this season are rarely required; and then, as our mattresses were not here, I took my courage with both hands, went into the little guest-room, and plunged into the bed. Something rattled, and I hunted it out: it proved to be a plate of fish under the *duvet*. I dared not ponder on what more there might have been, and soon lost all anxieties in sleep.

We were glad to welcome a fine morning, and to ride away betimes. The weather was improving at last, and the country was very attractive.

A strip of fertile flat land two or three miles wide runs between a range of steep crags and the sea. A waterfall we passed to-day, Seljandsfoss, looked especially pretty—it comes down in one sheet of unbroken silver 300 feet; and on this sunny day two rainbows played in the foam that rose high above the pool below. We climbed up behind the cascade, which falls a good way in front of the cliffs, and would no doubt be illuminated and surrounded by *cafés* if it were in Switzerland. We lunched at the parsonage of Holt, in the midst of grassy bogs that look as if some draining would convert them into first-rate pasture; the people were busied in trying to save and dry some very wet hay. Here we met with a cheery farmer, Thorwaldur, who asked us to his house, Nuperkot, and rode with us thither in the evening. Behind it on one side the crags rise in a fine precipice, and on the other they open towards the mountains of the interior, letting in a view of glaciers, waterfalls, and lower green hills,

over which the *bondé's* ponies wander. He owns about fifty, some
of them very handsome. Twelve cows came in to be milked,

Nupeskel farm.

and I went with the workwomen into the dairy, which was unique.
A clear swift stream ran round it inside, and went out under a
bridge at the door,—most handy for washing the dishes, and
keeping everything pleasantly cool.

Next day I walked up to some folds, and saw a good many of the young ponies which range the hills in the summer time. Even in the winter only a few are kept up at the farm. Square open folds of high turf-walls with one entrance, are constructed for their shelter in bad weather. There they keep each other warm, and are fed when necessary; they would be too hot with a roof over them. The finest riding-ponies only are kept near the house in winter, and have hay, and even corn. In summer all alike feed on the rich grass. The winter sheep-houses are roofed in, but are as usual empty in the summer time. Only the ewes whose lambs are weaned come home to the fold to be milked every evening, and are sent to the nearer grazings under charge of shepherds; the rest of the sheep are far on the hills, where an occasional hut or *selar-hus* gives them shelter in bad weather.

In the afternoon the *bondé* lent us excellent ponies. One was a great favourite—twenty-five years had not quenched its spirit: mine was young, and went like a bird, speeding over rock and shingle as if they were grass. His paces were deliciously smooth, his mouth and manners excellent. Thorgrimur was so pleased with a colt he rode that he asked me to change; but the "Four winter" had no mouth at all, and ran away with me, and I could only rein him in when he led the company. This was now numerous,—among others Thorwaldur came with us, and two young men, twin brothers, who had spent the night at the farm; one was travelling our way eastward, and the other came to see him across the next river. The only difference between them was that one was a priest and the other a doctor, so to new acquaintances they were difficult to distinguish apart. We stopped for luncheon on the grassy bank of the river, and had a merry picnic.

Jokulsà-i-lon has a very short but violent course of six miles. It rushes full grown out of the neighbouring glacier, and this day was rather wild, rolling big stones with an ominous grind beneath its milky waves. It is in some unholy alliance with volcanic forces, for its waters smell strong of sulphurets—hence its other name *Fullisá* or fetid river. There was something uncanny about this river from the earliest times. Landnama book says, Lodmundr, called the Old, first took the land to the west of it; he was much addicted to sorcery, indeed a sort of "half troll." He had as neighbour on the other side of the river, another wizard called Thrasi. "One morning Thrasi saw a great rush of water (glacier-leap); he turned the water by his spells towards Solheima, Lodmundr's abode. A thrall saw this, and told Lodmundr how the sea was falling from the north over the land towards them. Lodmundr was then blind. He bade the thrall guide him to the bucket of water that he called the sea. When he came, he said, 'I do not consider this to be sea.' He bade them lead him into the water, and planted his staff in; a ring was on the staff, and Lodmundr held it with both hands, and bit on the ring. Then the water began to fall towards Thrasi's land." Thus each diverted the water from himself, till they met by a chasm, and agreed that the river might run through it the shortest way to the sea. It is now called Jokulsà, and divides the southern from the eastern quarter of the land.

After our meal we remounted, my companion on Thorwaldur's strongest pony, while I adhered to my amphibious Krokur. Our Haldor dashed into the river, and when he had got over to the opposite shallows, he returned to pilot the twin, who in mid-stream allowed his pony's head to be turned for a moment down the stream, thus giving us, especially his brother, an anxious minute, till, guided by Haldor, he struggled round and got out on the other side, apparently rather wet.

In a bad ford the only duty of the rider is to keep the horse's head up-stream, otherwise the less he is meddled with the better. Haldor came back for us — but now my companion objected to cross, and Haldor owned that the river was rising fast, so although I was anxious to reach our night quarters on the other side, where all was prepared for us, I could not but yield. So we all rode five miles back to Skogar, a very clean parsonage, where we passed the night.

Sira Kjartan the old priest here was quite deaf to every voice

but that of a little grandson with a piping treble ; but he loves
talk, so the small interpreter was kept busy. The parsonage
is situated among grassy hillocks near a burn with little falls
and secluded pools.   I went to sketch a noble waterfall, Skogar-
foss, whose roar sounded like a sustained chord on the pedals of
an organ, behind all the farm noises, and the shrill shouts of the
boys and women who screamed against it, on the chance that
Sira Kjartan might hear what they said.   Has this waterfall,

perhaps, deafened Sira Kjartan by its never-ceasing din?   The
approach to the falls is striking, for they are invisible, till on
fording the river you come round the face of a high crag and see
them close before you, and from the best point of view.

Haldor, who had ridden down to Fullisá, came back and
reported that the glacier-river had fallen as usual in the night,
and was now easy fording ; but it seemed as though the spells

of the old wizards haunted the river still; for while I, like the
X blind wizard, considered it a mere bucket of water, Miss Cathcart took the other view, that it was more like the sea, and
declined to put it between us and Reykjavik.   I certainly regretted turning back at such an interesting point, as the
weather was now brilliant, and seemed to be settled; but it
must be owned that there was something to be said for her
point of view.   So Sira Kjartan rode with us back to Nuperkot,
where we dined with the hospitable Thorwaldur, and again he
lent me the fiery little pony, from which I was loath to part.   We
visited some caverns beyond, like great sea-caves, which no
doubt they once were, as this country shows marks of upheaval,
and the sea rolled up to the cliffs over the broad grass-lands
of our day.   One of these caves was long the retreat of an
ancient Viking or "half troll" named Hrutr.   There is a dry
large upper cavern draped with ferns, where at last his enemies
surprised and slew him; and a range of lower caves, now used
as barns for hay, and winter stables.   They were more like
castle buildings than natural rock,—the isolated cliffs rose in
such straight walls from the grassy valley, where hay-making
was now going on briskly.   We stopped for the night at the
parsonage of Holt.   Supper was served in a little room which
formed the end of the *badstofa* — the loft in the roof, which is
the usual family sleeping-place in a *bœ*.   It was reached by a
ladder, and there was a bed between each of the upright posts
supporting the rafters.   The men's portion is divided from the
women's room by a door; and at one end a little room for the
master and mistress is often partitioned off.   On the cross-beams
are shelves for books, &c.; and the clothes are kept in chests.
In this house all was clean.   After supper we sat on the beds,
which are all covered with gaily coloured worsted quilts, and
used as chairs by day, while Thorgrimur read aloud from Njala.
The women paused in their work to listen, the men drew near
from the other end of the room, all intent on the old story written
in the ancient Norse language forgotten in Norway, but the living
Icelandic still.

*We ought to have crossed - even the day
before it was easier than several fords we had ridden.
Thorgrimur's brother had all prepared for us at Dyrholar*

CHAPTER XVII.

OVER MARKARFLJOT—NJAL'S COUNTRY—FLOA—EYRABAKKI—
TO REYKJAVIK.

NEXT day being Sunday, a large congregation rode in and crowded the church. The parson, Sira Sveinbjorn, who seems very popular, gave us after service a good dinner, and himself, with several other people, escorted us on our way to Bergthorshvol, on the other side of Markarfljot. Haldor had gone on early with the baggage-ponies, and if he found the water impassable, he was to be by the river-side to tell us, but the men thought that two dry days would have put the river into a better humour. Besides, near the mouth where we meant to cross, the current would be less heavy; but I heard the Icelandic word for quicksands mentioned.

Even fine ponies usually stand quite still when they do stand in Iceland, but I had noticed one pawing and prancing by the churchyard gate, which the owner Thorwaldur, who the year after travelled with Miss Menzies and me, offered to lend me. It was a fiery little thing, and, excited by the loose ponies, carried me like a swallow—in just such short swift flights. It was useful, as our two best ponies, which had been bought in this neighbourhood, had laid their heads together, and finding we were going the wrong way for them, set off homewards; and there was a great deal of spying with the field-glass and running and riding before they were found and driven back. They were mistaken, as both have found excellent homes in this country, and are petted favourites now.

We rode in a merry troop over the flats till we reached the river, and then the rest of the party said farewell to us after having shown us the first ford. Here, in the gathering twilight, caused partly by a sea-mist coming up, rolled Markarfljot wider than ever, but with a far quieter current, down to the neighbouring sea. The foam-belt, where the waves met the river, was visible. A philanthropist who lived hard by and knew the river, offered to pilot us through, and would take no remuneration, and again there was talk about quicksands. He told us Haldor had passed in the morning, but mentioned that as the fords were variable from shifting sands, he would drive in our loose ponies first, to watch the way they got out. We had five, all unburdened, our own "second horses," and the two deserters.

"Now, Thorgrimur, no paragraph for the newspapers," I said; "we are sober people, who expect to get through," — and he explained that all precautions meant safety, not danger.

We crossed the river in three branches; the third is some miles beyond the others, and is called Áfall. It was now dim twilight, and a scene of utter dreariness. We were on a little island bank of shingle, into which our ponies subsided gradually; before us rolled the broad turbid stream, its further bank almost lost in the grey gloom, only the sea-birds, tossing and shrieking, showed white against the misty colours. Our loose ponies were plunging about or swimming in the current, till they all came aground on a sandbank, and stood there planted, a melancholy row in shallow water. Then the river-guide showed his pluck: urging in his pony, half fording half swimming, he drove them determinately forward—and one here and one there, some with a great struggle, they all got out on the other side.

The men observed which ponies had made the best landing, and thither we rode, cautiously feeling our way through a deep ford. We had a great scramble close to the bank, as our ponies' hind-legs sank in bad sands. It did not come quite so far as dismounting in the river, for which disagreeable possibility I

Fording Markarfljot.

hold myself ready; but still we were pretty wet when we arrived at Bergthorshvol, which is close to Áfall, at half-past ten. Haldor had preceded us; and we found a kind young *prestur* and his wife had got supper ready, and delicious down beds.

I left mine early to go out on the dewy *tun* on a beautiful summer morning. It is the historical background that gives such interest to travel in this pastoral land; peaceful and simple as all was here, the association was with fierce passions, and heroic virtues, and noble endurance. For here was the dwelling of Njal, the hero of the grandest saga—a remarkable character indeed in these fierce times—a man who never bore a weapon, and yet was respected by all. There can be no doubt about the locality; the long knoll is the only rise in the plain, which stretches from the sea to the hills, thirty miles to the north. Eastward, at about the same distance, the ice-crested mountains extend to the sea. Close by the knoll one branch of Markarfljot runs sulkily among its shifting sands. Seawards rise the West-mann Islands—about twenty purple cliffs set in silver: and all was silence this summer morning except the bleating of sheep, the barking of dogs, and the cries of the sea-birds.

The description of the burning of the homestead here, A.D. 1010, is terribly graphic. I seemed now to see the hundred burners surrounding it in the windy autumn night, to let no fighting man escape, though they called on the women to come out and save their lives; for they believed themselves to be no murderers but lawful avengers. "Go thou out, housewife," says Flosi, their chief; "far be it from me to let thee burn within." But Njal's wife was worthy of him. "Young I was when I was given to Njal," she says, "and always promised that one fate should befall us both." So the old pair lay down quietly in their bed, with the little grandson, Kári's son, between them, who refused to leave them; and there they were found under heaps of ashes, but untouched by fire, in the morning.

When the roof had crashed in, and the ring of burners had backed a little from the fire-flakes on the wind, and the spears still flung by the dying men within, Kári, Njal's son-in-law, asked Skarphedinn, Njal's poetical unlucky son, to make an effort to escape by running up a beam, which had fallen from the gable but still rested on the wall. " Run up here, and I after you, and we may both get off, for this way lies all the smoke. But Skarphedinn said he would follow. Then Kári took a flaming bench in his hand, ran up the fallen beam, and flung the bench down from the roof and it fell among those outside, who ran back. Kári's clothes and hair were all in a blaze, he flung himself down and ran low with the smoke." (Poor Kári first introduced sailing on the poop of his war-ship, " clad in scarlet, with much hair like silk flowing under his golden helmet.") " The nearest man said, ' Did not a man leap down?' ' No such thing,' said another; 'they are casting firebrands at us.' Kári ran down to a bog, still to be seen a furlong off below the knoll, cast himself down in it and slaked the fire, then running in the smoke reached a little hollow, still called Kári's hollow, and rested himself, and as soon as he was breathed he sped away till he met a friend. Flosi and his men stayed by the ruins, when still ' the flames leapt up occasionally and then fell low,' till the morning was well advanced, when a horseman came up who said, ' You have wrought a strong deed here.' ' Men may call it both a strong and an ill deed,' answered Flosi; and then they told over the slain, and among them Kari Solmundarson. Said Geirmund the new-comer, ' You call him dead that I have chatted with this morning. Kári had met my neighbour Bardr, who gave him a horse; and his hair and clothes were burned off him.' ' Had he any weapon?' said Flosi. ' He had his sword, Life-luller,' said Geirmund, ' and both its edges were blackened, and Bardr said it must have been softened in the fire; but he answered that he would harden it in the blood of the sons of Sigfus and the other burners.' Flosi said, ' You have told us news that shows we shall have no peace more, for that man has escaped as avenger who is most like Gunnar of Lithend in all things.' " [1]

Kári avenged his kindred, but when justice was done, he and Flosi became reconciled. This is the true spirit of the North.

[1] See Burnt Njal (Dasent's translation), chap. i. p. 29.

There is not the Eastern tendency to indiscriminate massacre. We find even amid the fury of battle and revenge some self-restraint—respect for women, and respect for law. Njal's sons were outlaws at this time.

Nothing could be more peaceful than the scene before us; the little girls sat on the bank by the river, singing part-songs prettily, and the snow-buntings twittered in reply, while I thought out a ballad about Flosi and Kári, in which this scene blended with recollections of the storm encountered three years ago on the now calm grey sea about the Westmann Islands.

THE END OF THE FEUD.

A TRUE STORY OF ICELAND.

A.D. 1017.

An autumn gale and a darkening night,
O'er mountainous waves the foam flies white ;
Swift are clouds in a windy sky—
The ship is battered and tempest-tossed,
And ever she drifts on the Iceland coast ;
List to the sea-gull's hungry cry.

The white waves break on the mariners' dread,
The terrible island, Ingolf's Head ;
Cruel is death on our native shore—
And straight above on the upland fells
Our mortal enemy, Flosi, dwells.
Cruel are foes that were friends before.

Kári looks at the sea and the land,
"For good or for ill is the end at hand ; "
Waves will laugh at the mariner's skill—
The ship is shattered and melts away,
The crew come forth from the stinging spray.
The sea may spare what the foe may spill.

"Many a time have I thought to slay
Him we shall meet at home to-day ; "
Fierce are the storms that men can raise.
"Sworn to revenge and not to spare,
Dreamt of my home in a fiery glare."
When will it die—that bitterest blaze?

"Well may ye deem my sword is good,
Softened in flame and hardened in blood ! "
Ashes are black where once was home—

"Life for life has this conquering brand
Counted my dead out of Flosi's band."
Ever shall murderers meet their doom.

"The feud is fought to the bitter end,
And yet we may meet as friend meets friend;"
The homeless winds are abroad alone.
"And yet he may only thank the wave
That spares his foe for a bloodier grave."
'Tis quiet below the sculptured stone.

"We fear no foe nor any fate,
Let us then knock at Flosi's gate;"
Hark to the wind on the upland fell—
"We are worn-out men and the night is blind,
We'll prove the mettle of Flosi's mind."
Hark to the dash of the thunderous swell.

Flosi came to the wind-shook door,
"What voice is that in the tempest's roar?"
Oh fires within are bright and warm—
"Who stands so dark against the snow?"
"Kári it is, thy deadliest foe."
Hold fast the doors against the storm.

"Thou com'st unarmed, a shipwrecked guest,
Kári, avenger, come thou blest."[1]
Cruelest storms at last will cease—
"Revenge is past, and love shall live;
Ah, doubt not, but the dead forgive."
Under the grass mounds all is peace.

From Bergthorshvol our day's ride was to Odde, which from the most ancient times has been a well-known place. The first author who *wrote* books in the country, Sæmund the historian, lived here. He is supposed to have compiled the 'Elder Edda.' Here Snorri Sturlason the historian was brought up by Jon Loptson, also a man of mark. Mackenzie found a good house here, and a handsome church, in 1811, when Iceland was at its lowest ebb. We were a large party, and had a charming evening, entertained by the kindly and merry old Dean, Sira ~~Gud-~~ ✗ ~~mundr.~~ This house had what is rare, a regular dining-room and drawing-room; and my little bedroom, all to myself, was most

[1] "Come thou blest" is the Icelander's welcome when guests come to his house.

✗ *Asmundur Jonson—*
died since.

comfortable. So large and fine a house represents a good deal of expenditure, both to build and to keep it up, in this treeless, roadless land.

Next day the Dean rode with us to show us the way over Western Rangá. He lent me a nice pony, but so fat that, after much balancing, round came the saddle and I with it to the ground; the only form of accident I have ever met with in Iceland. The journey seemed nearly as much by water as by land, for after Rangá came endless fording of a little river which seemed not to know its own mind as to its course; I lost count of the fords after the fourteenth. Then we had to cross the great Thjorsá. This we did in a ferry-boat, having a row of a quarter of an hour to a spit of gravel near the western shore. The ponies swam and landed here, and we remounted and forded the rest of the stream. The ponies rolled in the black sand to dry themselves, and it may be imagined what figures they were when they had thus groomed themselves entirely to their own satisfaction.

After Odde the country was less pretty. There were still far-off hills to the right, Hecla among them; but the path lay

over old lava, mostly crumbled small into black earth or black sands edging the neighbouring sea. Towards evening we reached Litla Hrauni, the house of the old *Syssel-man* or county magistrate, our guide's father. Here again we were expected and entertained as guests, and there was every comfort for weary travellers. The kind people would not let us go next day, but we visited the station of Eyrabakki, called on the merchant there, whose daughters gave us good music, and played whist in the evening, spending altogether a most civilised day. The following day the weather relapsed into its former evil ways. We rode to Reykjavik in ten hours, plodding on all day in a sort of shower-bath. Nothing remarkable was visible but the Olfus river, and when we came to it we could just perceive it was rather wetter than anything else. It looked like an arm of the sea, for there was not much current, but low sea-waves. That dim rainy day it looked miles across; by the map it is about two English miles. I pitied the ponies, for some of them showed great reluctance to swim out to sea, and were rather exhausted on first landing. Not so the amphibious Krokur, nor the malingering cream brothers, who, as usual, had to be towed behind our boat.

The weather had now spent its fury, and cleared up thoroughly; all our damp possessions were spread out to dry in the sun, and I basked in it myself. Some pleasant days went by in hospitable Reykjavik,—and then Miss Cathcart sailed for Scotland; but it illustrates the odd attractiveness of Iceland, that, undeterred by the wretched weather we had encountered, she returned there again another and a sunnier season.

As I was now alone, I asked Sigrida, a young Icelandic friend, Thorgrimur's sister, to ride with me west, to the scenes of the Egil Saga.

CHAPTER XVIII.

THE last excursion had no doubt been very interesting, but it was sometimes a strain on one's endurance, as it was to outcast volcanic regions, over wild rivers that have wasted the land, and through much bad weather. The next was a thorough contrast, for it was through the dales of the west, the softest part of the country. Day succeeded day of unclouded loveliness, evening twilight brightening into morning dawn. The way was chiefly through green pastoral valleys, and I generally stopped at the farms and shared the life of the people. It was as if one had stepped out of the restrictions of modern life into a simple Arcadia. I took no tent this time, and only one baggage-pony, letting the relays carry some light wraps. Sigrida, a merry girl with a sweet soprano voice, rode along carolling like a bird, often driving the loose ponies, like Enid in the poem; while her brother ranged about with his gun after wild ducks and game, and I kept up the communications, having many a solitary ramble across country; for I found that I had now become experienced in finding tracks, crossing bogs, choosing fords, and all the incidents of Icelandic riding.

The brother and sister were popular people, and so warmly welcomed wherever we came, that our journey seemed to be always, if a picnic by day, a little *festa* in the evening. There was no getting the kindly hosts to receive any money,—whether rich or poor themselves, they made us welcome to their best.

Of course I lived with them and behaved as a guest, and also we often brought game or soup to help out the dinner.

The first day we rode over the Pass of Eysja to Rennyvellir. I had been there twice before, but never in such magnificent weather, which elicited fresh exclamations of delight at every turn. There is no use attempting descriptions. It suffices to say that the great bog formerly mentioned on our first return from Geysir, is now much more passable, turf and stone causeways having been built across the worst parts. The bachelor parson had been succeeded at Rennyvellir by a married pair, who had greatly improved the house; and two comfortable beds were made up in the guest-room for Sigrida and me.

Next day we rode straight over the barrier of hills—a steep scramble—down to the edge of the lovely Hvalfjord, fording half a mile of sea, as formerly described, and arriving in the evening with plenty of game at the parsonage of Saurbæ. It is a bow-shot from the fjord, which here opens to the sea, into which the mountain Akranes runs in a promontory. Towards the head of the fjord the mountains are piled up, looking like a grander Scotland, but for the snow-hill stained with evening red which peers above the rest. The parsonage-house, where several grown-up sons and daughters lived, besides working people, was pretty full; but as Sigrida and I sauntered on the meadow we saw another party of travellers ride up—three men and two women. The young lady, who rode a very handsome pony, I was surprised to see, as only the previous Sunday we had ridden together at Reykjavik, when she said she meant to go abroad. Here she was, looking rosy and pretty, riding with her since then betrothed bridegroom—his sister, a young man, and a friend making up the party. It had all been settled since we met, and instead of staying at home to receive congratulations, she had started off with her betrothed to visit her relations in the north. Her mother had started with them, but by this time they had dropped the mother, and I can imagine no more enjoyable expedition than this summer ride in the

"Happy hours of golden prime,
The affluence of love and time."

But now the house was brimming over. The bride-elect and I shared the little room, with a big bed off the guest-room, which is found in many houses. It is timber-lined, but the turf-walls are about eight feet thick. Half the thickness of the wall forms a table in the window, on the other side a dog often sleeps as in a cosy kennel, and talks to you in the morning. Often this window will not open; but it is easy to take it out altogether, as my companion and I did the following morning; and the guest-room being full of men, we got out thus and down to a ravine where the stream falls in a little cascade into a beautiful pool for a bath. The bride was a fair sight when her abundant hair of ruddy gold was shaken down in the sunshine. She was an old friend, being the imperturbable damsel who had shared our bad voyage in '75. We had a most lively breakfast together, then rode off on our several ways. My way was among birch and willow growth, still to the north-west, flat land with abrupt hills rising from it. There were flights of golden plover, but the birds were packing, and shy,—stalking was needed to get a shot at them. We stopped for coffee at a new well-built house with gold wall-papers! beside a new church, with a dash of architecture about it. Iceland is progressing.

In the afternoon we gained Hofn, a farm on the edge of the Borgarfjord. The farmer was a very handsome man, six feet three, and grandly proportioned. It was sad to hear that drink had got hold of him. He has since died in the prime of life. He sent a man to drive our ponies round the fjord to the first ford— a long night-journey—while he undertook to put us straight across to Borg, some two miles over the water.

We shoved off in a rickety boat. The water spurted up through the holes so violently that I thought the plugs were out. Not at all. And the *bondé*, who steered, when I asked how long she would float without baling, said, as a matter of course, " Oh, twenty minutes! " Luckily we had always one man baling, generally three, and also the weather was perfect. Still the boat became very wet, while the *bondé* talked incessantly, and cared not for the water lashing about his feet. Leaky boats are as common in Iceland as in Norway, where there is not the same want of wood as an excuse. A Norwegian will put off in anything that will keep afloat by means of constant baling. With a birch-bush for a sail, a dipper, and an oar, he will shove across deep arms of the sea; and this is the more hazardous, as neither in Norway nor Iceland are the people generally able to swim. In old days it was considered an almost necessary accomplishment.

These old days seemed very present as we sailed up this beautiful fjord, which is minutely described in the Landnámabók and the Egil's Saga. These first settlers, who came in A.D. 878, headed by Skallagrim, Egil's father, were terrible fellows. Skallagrim was a first-rate smith, but apt to split his anvil; a fierce combatant, who, even when wrestling in sport, when his blood was up killed his son's companion, the young champion of the district, and nearly killed his own son,—would have done so but for the intervention of Egil's foster-mother Bráka, "a woman strong as a man, and mighty in spells." But even on her he turned when she interfered, and she fled to the fjord pursued by him, took to the water and swam for life, while he hurled a rock after her that struck her between the shoulders, and she sank to rise no more, and ever since the sea-reach has been named Brákarsund. Skallagrim inherited some of the "evening fierceness" of his awful father, Kveldúlfr, who became at nightfall wolfish in mind, if not a were-wolf outright.

He was, however, a poet, and some of the very earliest *Visa*, or short songs improvised for different events, are believed to have been really composed by him. He was fond of his sons too, this ravening old sea-wolf. One of them, Thorolfur, was handsome and *débonnaire*, and became a liegeman of Harald Fair-hair; the other, Grimur, called afterwards Skalla, or bald Grimur, was strong, surly, and ugly like himself. Owing to a complicated quarrel, very curious, but too long to tell, Thorolfur was slain by some of the king's men in a fight. The fury of old Kveldúlfr was terrible. The following song has been handed down as composed by him. In translating it I have preserved the alliteration, single and double, on alternate lines :—

> " Thorolf, war-thunderer
> Thou on the island,
> Far from us found thy death,
> Few were thine years then.
> I by Thor's conqueror
> Kept from the camp-crowd,
> Cannot avenge thee so
> Swift as beseems me."

Defying old age—" Thor's conqueror "—he met two young sons of Harald with their retainers by sea. The Berserker fury seized him, and he assaulted and killed them all save two, swept the ships from stem to stern, and then sang this song of triumph, which he forced the two survivors to learn by heart to sing to King Harald. It is said to be the first Northern song in rhyme, perhaps the better to impress it on the minds of the two unhappy prisoners; and it has in it something of the scream of a triumphant eagle :—

> " Vengeance for Hersir sing,
> We're even with the king ;
> Wolf and earne come and go
> O'er Yngling's sons laid low.
> Shrill whistled sword-stroke free
> O'er Hallvard by the sea ;
> And the grey eagle tore
> Snarfari by the shore."

The weakness which was said to follow the " Berserker rage " seized the old man, and he never recovered, but died on the voyage out to Iceland, which he made in another ship at the same time as his son Grimur.

Kveldúlfr is buried on yonder point; for when dying he requested that the *kist* in which his body was put might be thrown overboard, "for I think that I shall reach Iceland yet before you; and where I drift up, there make your abode." Accordingly he was found below the point and buried, as were the family after him, on the windy height.

The description of the country in the brief Icelandic of the twelfth, and also of the present century, might well serve for it still : *Var thar myrlendi mikit ok skógar vidir, ok langt i milli fjalls ok fjorù, selveidar gnógar, ok fiskifang mikit.* "There were

great morasses and woods, and a good space between the hills
and the foreshore; plenty of seal-hunting, and excellent fishing:" though but remnants of the birch-woods remain under the
hills.

Skallagrim guided his ship's boat into the mouth of a little
stream, and set up on the hillside above it the dwelling still
called Borg. We, too, landed there, and went up to Borg, now a
peaceful parsonage, close to a little church of turf, so old and
small that it seems as if it could not much longer expect to be

distinguished from the churchyard. Beside it lies a grey stone,
graven with almost illegible Runes, which have, however, been
deciphered as follows: "Here lies the brave Kjartan, slain by
treachery." The last part of the inscription is doubtful; but all
tradition confirms the Laxdale Saga in the assertion that here
Kjartan, the lover of Gudrun, was buried. He was laid there
when the church was still decked in white in honour of its consecration. Turf churches do not last long, so probably there has
been a succession of them since the original building, and the
shabby little chapel before us has not even the merit of being
venerable.

The Dean was at Borg on a visit to the priest; and the following day being a Sacrament Sunday, the little church was packed to overflowing. I sat among several women in full costume. The old ones wore dark cloth or velvet bodices, set with silver clasps, and laced with silver chains. They had stiff black collars round their necks, embroidered in gold or silver, and short Zouave jackets, also embroidered, and high black head-dresses, rather like an ancient Greek helmet. An average old woman becomes quite an imposing personage when thus accoutred.

The priest's handsome young daughters wore the dress in a modernised form. The embroidered jacket was fitted to the figure, and was finished off by a silver belt. The head-dress was the white helmet or *faldr*, ornamented by a sort of circlet on the brow, and softened by an ample white lace veil.

CHAPTER XIX.

EGIL AT BORGARFJORD.

BEFORE the service was half over, I left the church overpowered by the heat, and observed that some of the shrewder members of the congregation were sitting on the 'turf by the open windows, and thus attending the service most comfortably. I wandered up the hillside, gained the shadow of a rock, sketched, and read in the Egil's Saga, which was written about 1170, till I was quite lost to the present. The thymy cushion on which I lounged was deliciously fragrant; the insects hummed drowsily in the warm air; and perhaps I slept, as certainly Sigrida did, who went out to look for me, and was found fast asleep nestled among the rocks in the opposite direction. It was no wonder, for the weather was indeed hot.

I had, however, read that day a great deal of the saga which had been our first Icelandic reading-book in former years. Vigfusson says:[1] "It is a complete embodiment of the aristocratic spirit of the great Norse families in the early middle ages; the hatred of royal encroachments, above all of personal subordination or feudal innovations, which drove so many men from the continent to the islands, is well shown therein." The character of Egil, its chief hero, is well brought out. "Steadfast in love and hate, cool and yet sometimes passionate to madness, crafty and reckless, grasping and generous, he passes through a checkered life as poet and pirate chief; . . . the henchman of

[1] See Vigfusson's Sturlunga Saga, Prolegomena, 47, 48.

King Athelstan of England, and hereditary foe of King Erick of Norway; now an honoured guest at court, now a helpless prisoner, now a powerful leader, as fits the typical Northman of our traditions."

Some of the episodes woven into the history are very curious and interesting, and have every claim to be true, down to the smallest details. The author says he only records his facts after consultation with old and wise men; and it is curious to observe how he owns now and then that some point is uncertain, and gives the different versions with his own opinion. I shall give here an abridged translation of a few chapters of the Egil Saga, which throw much light on the position of the women of the north in the early middle ages.

The date is about 908, the chief hero, Egil, is a boy of ten, here at Borg. In Norway Harald Fair-hair had brought all the country under his power, and many of the great chiefs who would not submit to his rule had turned sea-kings, or settled in Iceland, Faroe, Shetland, or the Hebrides.

He was now in the prime of life and the height of fortune; his eldest son Erick was a boy of twelve. In England Athelstan reigned, a great king, but much harassed by Danes and Northmen. In France Hrolf or Rollo had seized Neustria or Normandy. Elsewhere in the confusion following the break-up of Charlemagne's empire, no nation was pre-eminent on land, but the Northmen were masters of the seas.

At this time, Brynjolf the son of Bjorn was a rich man who lived at Aurland, a district still known by that name near the upper waters of the Sognefjord in Norway.

Those who have sailed up one of the higher reaches of that grand fjord where sea-waves break on precipices which rarely give space for any dwelling on the shore, may remember the broad green valley of Aurland which contrasts so pleasantly with the barren rocks around.

The valley is traversed by a swift river, which some miles above flings itself down the mountain in one of the finest falls in Norway. There is still a group of wooden houses called

Aurland, and probably since the days of Brynjolf little has been changed. We can easily imagine his long low wooden hall, the main-door porch at one end, the women's door at the other. Within it is all one room : the heavy rafters above are black with the smoke of the fire which in cold weather blazed all the way down the centre of the hall. Across one end was the high seat and the cross bench where the ladies sat, and the chief men on special occasions ; but more often the men all sat at the evening carousal on long benches opposite to each other on each side of the fire, and handed each other the mead and ale across the blaze. Down the sides were wooden partitions, and beds within enclosed by movable shutters. Outside a separate building was called the *dyngeye* or bower, where the women wove and worked. Store-rooms, stables, byres, and sheep-cots surrounded the great hall, forming part of the *tun* or town, as we still say in speaking of a Scotch farm.

Hersir Brynjolf had at this time two grown-up sons, Bjorn and Thord. "Bjorn was a very travelled man, sometimes on Viking cruises, sometimes on merchant voyages. He was a very able man. It happened one summer that Bjorn was in the North-fjord, attending a crowded feast. There he saw a fair May who struck his fancy much. He asked of what family she was, and it was told him that she was the sister of Hersir Thorir, Hroald's son, that her name was Thora, and she was surnamed Lace-hand. Bjorn courted her and asked her in marriage. And Thorir consented to his suit, and said that so it should be. That same autumn Bjorn collected some followers, and sailed with a swift cutter fully manned north to the fjord district."

We know the beautiful voyage that he would make out of the Sognefjord and between the grand island mountains and the mainland, till, where there was an opening seawards, and, as the Norsemen say, the eye of the sea looks in on the land, he would turn in to the lovely Northfjord, and probably go up to what is now called Eide, as there the district Earl, which Thorir was, usually lived. It must have been a great disappointment to the expectant bridegroom to find that Thorir was not at home. His promised bride, was however, very glad to see him. And now they made a great mistake which brought lawsuits and bloodshed down on two generations. Considering that they were affianced with Thorir's full consent, and that no one could tell when a Viking would return from a cruise, if he ever did, it does not seem at first sight so fatal an error as it proved, that Bjorn, who had already earned the nickname of Holdfast, showed himself worthy of it by persuading Thora to sail off with him and let their wedding be celebrated at his father's house at Aurland. When he brought her home it was winter, and he wished the marriage to take place. But the Saga goes on. " Brynjolf liked this ill, and thought it shameful, considering the family friendship between himself and Thorir. 'It will be long before you hold your wedding with Thora in my house without her brother's leave,' he said; 'but she shall be here in all honour as though she were my daughter and your sister.' And so was all in that household as Brynjolf commanded, whether Bjorn liked it well or ill. Brynjolf sent men to Thorir to offer him peace and compensation for the journey his son had made. Thorir bade Bjorn send home Thora, saying otherwise there would be no peace. But Bjorn would by no means allow her to be sent away, not even though Brynjolf ordered it.

" So the winter passed ; and when spring began, Brynjolf and Bjorn one day talked over their arrangements. Brynjolf asked what he wished further. Bjorn said that he wished to go abroad : 'It would best suit me if you would give me a long ship and a crew, and let me go off on a Viking expedition.' Said Brynjolf, 'It is not to be expected that I should give you a war-ship and strong body of fighting men, as I do not know but that you might come back upon me and take me by surprise : already our home is quite disturbed by you. A merchant-ship I might give you, with wares ; with that you might go south to Dublin—that is now the most profitable voyage ; and I will give you a good following.' Bjorn answered that he must take up that which Brynjolf desired. So a good merchant-ship was got ready and manned. Bjorn made all preparations for the journey, but was

not early ready. But when all was right, and the wind suited,
he got into a boat with twelve men, rowed in to Aurland, went
up to the dwelling, and to his mother's bower. She sat within,
and many women with her. Bjorn said that Thora should go
with him, and led her away, and his mother bade that no woman
should be so bold as to warn the men of it in the hall; she said
that Brynjolf might make a bad business of it if he knew, and it
would bring about much discord between father and son. Thora's
clothes and jewels were all already packed and ready to be
carried off by hand, and Bjorn took all with him. They went
in the night out to the ship, spread sail, went down the Sognefjord, and then out to sea. But they had a bad wind, and made
great leeway, and long they tossed on the sea; but their hearts
grew the cheerier the further they got from Norway. One day,
while sailing from the east to Shetland in stormy weather, the
ship struck land on Mosey. They bore out the cargo, and went
up to the castle near, and carried thither all their goods, drew
the ship ashore, and repaired the damage."

And here Bjorn and Thora may be said to sail into sight.
Mosey or Mousa island, still uninhabited, lies off the Shetland
coast, and gives a little shelter to the channel between it and
the mainland in a westerly gale, though the dangerous Sun-
borough Roost may make it but a treacherous refuge. However,
there is a sandy creek between the cliffs where a ship could be
safely beached, and there still stands the "burgh," the most entire
Pictish fort in Shetland or perhaps anywhere—a grim, squat, small,
round tower, the staircase and the little cells of rooms constructed
in the thickness of the wall, the centre court open to the sky;
most dreary, but in these old days impregnable. No doubt
Bjorn covered in the centre space with the ship's tents, and made
all as snug as he could for his bride. We can imagine the fair
maiden worn and sea-weary, yet peaceful when she felt herself
safe within these thick walls; we know she had her gowns and
jewels with her, and no doubt she made the dim rough burgh
beautiful to Bjorn, as they lived there with their crew, the wild
winter sea dividing them from all the rest of the world. If

Bjorn carved a Rune inside, it may yet be found. The Vikings have left many such tokens of their presence in the recently excavated Mæs-Howe in Orkney. One Rune tells how "Ingeborg the Fair" rested there after long wanderings; another tells of some one "in search of the fairest of women." One man tells of his shipwreck, another blames the captain for negligent loss of their ship — a regular court-martial verdict. The good Orkneyan stone has preserved for us the very touch of the hands so far away in the past. But in Iceland, scarcely a Rune survives—the unkindly lavas and basalts give us no records of the old times.

The Saga continues: "A little before winter a ship came to Shetland from the south from Orkney. They brought tidings that a war-ship had come in autumn to the islands. On board were messengers from Harald the king, with the errand to Earl Sigurd, that the king desired that Bjorn Brynjolfson should be slain wherever he could be taken; and the like orders had been sent through the southern isles (Soder) all the way to Dublin. Bjorn heard all this, and also that he was outlawed in Norway. But when he got to Shetland he married Thora, and they stayed the winter in Moseyjarburg. And in spring, when the sea began to grow calm, they sailed out to sea. They had a storm-wind, and were but a short time at sea: they drove from the south to Iceland. Then the wind changed, and they bore west by the coast, and so out to sea. And when they got a wind back again they sailed up to the land. There was no one on board who had been to Iceland. They sailed into an awfully[1] big fjord, and bore along its western strand. They saw that landward was only one fairway and no harbour. They went athwart east by the land and round back up the fjord till it was all shut in by skerries and breakers, then they brought up under a cape. An island lay outside, and a deep sound between: they anchored there. A creek went up west of the headland, and some way above it stood a great dwelling. Bjorn got into a boat with some of his men; he told his followers to beware how

---

[1] "Awful" is evidently classical slang.

they talked of the cause of the journey, as they stood in danger about it. So they rowed to the dwelling-place, and met men with whom they spoke, asking first to what land they had come. The men said it was called Borgarfjord, and the house that they saw belonged to Skallagrim *bondé*. Now Bjorn knew all about him, so he went to meet him, and they talked together. Bjorn named himself and his father, and Skallagrim was well acquainted with Brynjolf, and offered Bjorn all that he needed. Bjorn took that gratefully. Then Skallagrim asked what people of note were in the ship. Bjorn said that there was Thora, Hroald's daughter, sister of Hersir Thorir. Skallagrim was very glad, and said that all that she could want or he could give was at the disposal of Thora the sister of Thorir his foster-brother; and he invited them both and all their crew to come and stay with him. Bjorn thanked him heartily, so they brought their cargo up to the *tun* at Borg, and the ship was drawn up into a creek, which may yet be seen. And it is still called Bjorn's Meadow, where Bjorn set up his booths; and they all stayed with Skallagrim. He had never fewer people staying with him than sixty fighting men.

" But in the autumn a ship came to Iceland from Norway, and the gossip came over that Bjorn had run away with Thora without the consent of her family. When Skallagrim was aware of it, he asked Bjorn how it was that his marriage was without the relations' consent. 'I never expected,' he said, 'that from the son of Brynjolf I should not hear the truth.' Bjorn answered, 'I told you the truth, Grimr, and you should not blame me though I may not have answered further than you questioned me; but now this is to be owned that it is true what thou hast heard, that this marriage was not made with the consent of Thorir her brother.' Then said Skallagrim in great anger, 'And how wert thou so foolhardy as to come to me in that case; or was the warm friendship between him and me unknown to thee?' Said Bjorn, 'I knew that ye were in brotherhood and warm friendship, and for that reason I sought you at home as I was brought by the sea to this country, and I knew that I should

not succeed in escaping from thee. Now it lies in thy power
what my fate shall be, but I expect all good from thee as I am
thy guest at home.' Then came forward Thorolf, Skallagrim's
son (a little boy), and entreated his father not to blame Bjorn for
it, although he had received him. And many others put in a
word; and so it came to pass that Grimr was satisfied, and said
that Thorolf should have his way—'So receive Bjorn, and look
after him as thou wouldst to the best fellow going.'" Thora
had a child in the summer, a daughter; she was sprinkled with
water, and called Asgerd. Bera, Skallagrim's wife, adopted her.
The following year, through the intervention of Skallagrim, Bjorn
and Thora were reconciled to all their relations. They sailed to
Norway, leaving their little daughter behind them. A meeting
was held by the Sognefjord at which Thorir delivered over to
his sister all the property to which she was entitled, and gave
her his full friendship. Old Brynjolf was also present, and they
all held a reconciliation festival, and Bjorn and his wife returned
to Aurland.

This would seem to have ended the whole trouble. Not at
all. Seventeen years have passed away; many other events
are told in the Saga, till once more we return to the Iceland farm
of Borg. Thorolf, who had lately returned from the wars at sea
and in Norway, told his father one day that he wished to sail out
again in summer.

"Said Skallagrim: 'The saying goes, "Happy is he who leads
the harvest-cart at home." Thou hast wandered abroad much,
but take now rather as much property as thou thinkest may make
thee a man of substance here.' Thorolf answered that he wished
to go but one journey, but that was on a necessary errand.
'When I return another time I may settle, but Asgerd thy foster-
daughter must first go out with me to visit her father. He asked
me to bring her when I came from the east.'"

The voyage was therefore undertaken, Thorolf's wild younger
brother Egil forcing his company upon them for his first flight
from home. On reaching Sognefjord, they found that Brynjolf
had lately died, his son Thord had inherited Aurland, and Bjorn

had another rich estate. Thorolf brought Asgerd, now a fair and wise maiden, to her father, and there was great joy at their meeting. He then went off to the Northfjord to visit Hersir Thorir. There should be no mistake this time about the wooing of Thorir's relations, and Thorolf asked *his* consent in form to his marriage with Asgerd his niece. That obtained, he returned to the Sognefjord and asked Bjorn's consent to his daughter's marriage, which he willingly granted.

Thorolf seems to have been much in love with the young lady who was brought up in his home, and the wedding was held to be magnificent. Thorir and his son Arinbjorn, the finest character in the Saga, came south to the Sognefjord for it; no one was left at home save Egil, who contrived to get into considerable mischief in consequence.

Thorolf brought his bride back to their friend Arinbjorn's home, who soon succeeded his father as lord of the Fjord district. But no peaceful return to Iceland was in Thorolf's mind. Every summer, leaving his wife in Norway, he went off on a Viking cruise with Egil, and three years after his marriage he fell in England in the battle of Brunaburgh, fighting on the side of King Athelstan. Egil—who, to do him justice, felt his brother's death deeply, though much consoled by two chests of silver given him as compensation by the king—insisted on returning to Norway to take the bad news to Asgerd, now the mother of two little daughters. "She was very sad, but yet glad to hear all."

"As autumn went on," says the Saga, "Egil became very sad, drank little, and sat with his head drooped in his cloak. Arinbjorn asked at last what ailed him. 'Now though thou hast had a great scathe in losing thy brother, it is manly to fight well against it. Man lives after man. Or what hurts thee now? Let me hear.'"

Egil replies by two songs, as a Skald in love was bound to do, and at last shyly breaks to Arinbjorn that he was desperately in love with his friend's cousin, Asgerd, his sister-in-law. Asgerd was, by Arinbjorn's advice, sounded; she advised that her father Bjorn should be consulted. Egil and Arinbjorn went to the

N

Sognefjord, obtained his consent, and the following year Egil
and Asgerd were married, and sailed back to Borgarfjord after
an absence of five years. Great deference seems to have been
shown to the ladies and their families in all these marriages, and
no trouble spared to make them honourable. But it was all
needed, as the next part of this family history shows.

"Four years went by at Borg, and then news came from Norway that Bjorn Holdfast had died, and that Bergonundur, who
had married his other child, a daughter by a second wife, a man
in high favour with Erick the king, had seized Bjorn's whole
property, both land and loose money, in right of his wife. So the
following year Egil and Asgerd sailed to Norway, and came to
Arinbjorn's house on the Northfjord. There the friends consulted,
and considered the case was so clear that Bjorn's property should
be divided between his two daughters, that King Erick would
not venture to refuse to give a lawful verdict, even against his
friend. Egil therefore travelled to Bergonundur's property, and
there demanded his wife's legal half of the property, 'for they
ought to share alike, though Asgerd is of much higher lineage
than Gunnhild thy wife.' Onundur replied very sharply, 'Thou
art an awfully daring fellow, Egil! thou the king's outlaw, thou
comest to his land and wishest to attack his friends. Dost thou
suppose thou shalt meddle with my affairs, and make such de-
mands for thy wife, when all the world knows she is thrall-born
on the mother's side?' Onundur became quite abusive, and Egil,
seeing he would not give way, summoned him to defend his case
at law at the Gula Thing. 'Yes,' answered Onundur, 'I shall
come to the Gula Thing, and make it my business that thou
shouldst not go unscathed away.' Egil said he would come to
the Thing all the same. When he told Arinbjorn what had
happened, Arinbjorn was very angry that his father's sister
should be called a slave."

Then follows a stirring description of the Gula Thing, where
the king presided and heard the case on each side, surrounded
by armed retainers. Fortunately Arinbjorn had provided ships
enough, all ready to sail, to carry Egil and himself and all their

followers beyond the fury of the king, when the Thing came to a stormy end. Egil, indignant at hearing his wife's mother, Thora Lace-hand, stigmatised as a captive won in war, and her daughter therefore declared illegitimate after the complete family reconciliation which followed her marriage with Bjorn, left the Thing, after hurling the following challenge to the king and to all concerned :—

"I call thee to witness, Arinbjorn, and thee Thordr, and all these men who hear my words, landsmen and lawmen, and all the people, that I forbid in all these lands that Bjorn Brynjolfson owned, settlement and work, and all uses whatever! I forbid them to thee, Bergonundur, and to all other men, countrymen or foreigners, well-born or low-born ; and whoever touches them I lay under the penalties of breach of the laws, wrath of the gods, and breach of the truce !"

It would take too long to tell all the stirring events that followed ; enough to say that Egil, before he quitted Norway in his single ship, slew Bergonundur and his friends on an island, and ran down the ship of one of the king's sons at sea. The property he never wholly recovered ; but Arinbjorn, who was as open-handed as Egil was the reverse, begged Egil to take from him the value of his Norwegian lands in money, as he could not get justice for his friend in Norway. Egil did so ; but the feuds which rose around the case were never healed, and all because Bjorn Holdfast so many years ago did not wait the return of the brother of his affianced wife from the war cruise before he celebrated his marriage.

CHAPTER XX.

STAFHOLT—REYKHOLT—SNORRI STURLASON AND HIS FATE—GILSBAKKI
—PASS OF OK—BENIGHTED.

IN the cool of the Sunday evening the old *profastur* lent me a good pony, and we all rode off together to his parsonage of Stafholt, across the Hvitá.

Here is a large new timber church standing on a height above the river, commanding a wide view of the hill-ranges all round. Many acres of level sward bear excellent hay crops. The little hillocks having been all carefully levelled with the spade, and the land well drained, its productiveness is immensely increased. Indeed some more labour bestowed on the land at home would probably make emigration unnecessary to any great extent If a plough were driven through some of the uneven grass-lands, and a few drains constructed, the hay crops would be twice as heavy, and more sheep and cattle could be kept through the winter.

Next day we parted with, I think, mutual regret from the pleasant family at Stafholt, and rode to the valley of Lundr. The owner of a very small house courteously asked us in to take coffee. The rooms were so small that only two people could sit in each: as to the kitchen, I believe it held the coffee-pot, and the hostess made the coffee, crouching in the passage outside. Yet there was another guest, the priest of the parish, an old acquaintance in his lay days, now a rather fast priest, especially on horseback; but he and Thorgrimur had to sit in the opposite room to ours. We might have been in opposite cells in a Roman catacomb, the whole place being hollowed in the earth, and yet the inhabitants looked healthy. It is whispered that they eat horse-flesh, and nothing is better for the complexion.

The *prestr* insisted on our coming home with him, and he pitched a comfortable tent for Sigrida and me near his house, filled it with fragrant hay, and made it pleasant quarters for a lovely summer night. We were close to a deep circular hollow, which is all that remains of a heathen sacrificial temple. I looked out of the tent the last thing at night on the still valley and the surrounding hills, and could just discern the churchyard wall below us, and then a misty whiteness, that elevated itself to a preternatural height above the wall, with a most eerie effect in this haunted place. But after hovering there for a minute, down came, with a palpable plump on the ground, a white pony which had been poaching on the long grass of the church-yard.

There was a good garden here where common vegetables grew freely, and even rye was in the ear. It had grown rather stalky, but seemed promising enough to encourage the planting of quick-ripening grain. We were hospitably pressed to stay another day, and all rode out to fish near a waterfall in the upper waters of the Grimsà. The priest mounted me on a fine pony, sent to his care as being too fiery for Reykjavik : it bucked so high when held in, that I thought it best—having no third pommel—to let it go and choose its own way over the rough boggy country, which it did with great intelligence, only it mistook our route, —and when it discovered that the rest of the party, far behind, were deflecting in another direction, it dashed across country in a most reckless style to rejoin them. Constant solitary wanderings give these ponies extraordinary dexterity in getting over rough ground : most English horses would not have dared to put one foot before another in some places where this little Icelander went on without a moment's hesitation, and at a good round pace. He broke through the river at no particular ford ; but happily it was low,—too low for fishing. We saw many fish but got few ; the weather was also too sunny ; and where was the rain? Did it ever rain here? and was that never-ending rain still falling in Rangàvallasysslu?

The following day our host mounted me again on his gay pony, and guided us straight over the hills to the north, to the parallel valley of Reykholt, a route which I recommend to no one. We went through desperate bogs. My pony went like a bird, but the rest got into great difficulties. The worst morasses are not generally in the valleys, where there is some drainage into the rivers, but on the wide table-lands, where the wet accumulates hopelessly and dangerously, and only the great sagacity of the ponies makes it possible to get across them.

By evening we had reached familiar quarters—the Dean's residence at Reykholt. It is a good house in its way. There are several wainscoted rooms, and through the shapeless entrance-cavern you enter the inner kitchen-cave, which is clean and tidy, and the fire there actually sits in a grate! Outside the women were washing in water drawn from the old stone-bath formerly described. I sat on the steps and flirted careful fingers into the scalding water, and wondered about Snorri Sturlason. A little way off some pretty fountains leapt in silver spray into the clear air, hills edged the broad dark-green valley, and above them quiet sunset clouds stretched in long lines of changing fading gold and crimson. There was an indescribable remote far-off feeling over all. Oh what a cold far corner of the world for the home of that richly endowed, stirring, strong, restless man! When we think of him living in the twelfth century in this lonely farmhouse, with little access even to the learning the times afforded, and no means of culture beyond what a few voyages to Norway could give, we can perhaps better realise what wonderful individual force there was among the old Scandinavians, and how that ability and power gave them the supremacy they won over whole populations, even when few in number and widely scattered in other countries.

Snorri Sturlason's histories contrast wonderfully with the meagre and dry contemporary chronicles of the rest of Europe. Not till we get to Froissart, 1390, do we find in the South any-

thing of the liveliness and graphic power of the Norse chroni-
clers; but Froissart writes like a naive intelligent child when
compared to Snorri, who has all his vivacity, besides a grasp of
the subject in hand, a caustic humour, and a clear-sighted political judgment, which must give him rank among the very best
historians of every age and country. That his work is also a
masterpiece in style may be much owing to the genius of the
language, which was already in his day thoroughly developed
and an excellent literary medium. And the men of his own
house murdered him here—cut him off in his strong maturity
before his day's work was ended! There are some deeds that
never can be forgiven—deeds that, whatever their justification in
the minds of the perpetrators, have rendered the world poorer and
worse for ever. Snorri was no doubt anxious to bring Iceland
under Norwegian rule, a project fiercely resisted by the descendants of the men who flung off the yoke of feudalism. But under
the circumstances Snorri was probably right, and perished in a
good cause. The once law-abiding Icelanders had allowed their
government to be overridden by a small fierce oligarchy; and
not long after Snorri's death the people were utterly wearied of
confusion, and his counsels prevailed. Iceland became subject
to Norway, and all its fervid spirit and eager masculine strength
were quenched for ever. Snorri's assassination had some points
of resemblance to the murder of our King James the First.
Like James he was concealed in a cellar, and for a time it
seemed as if he might escape from the murderers who ransacked
the house. No doubt Snorri's hall was very superior to the turf
farms of modern Iceland. We read a description of Flugumyri,
a similar house, in the contemporary 'Sturlunga Saga.'

Flugumyri was the home of Earl Gisur, Snorri's son-in-law and
murderer. Retribution, coming with no halting step, fell on him
five years later. His sons and wife were burnt inside their house,
on the wedding night of one of these sons, by the avengers of
Snorri. He himself had a narrow escape. The old miscreant
hid himself in a cask of whey, and though the burners prodded
it with their lances, he managed to ward off serious wounds, and

was not discovered, and lived not only to avenge his family, but to retire respectably to a monastery to end his days. There must have been very mixed society in these monasteries. Besides the true devotees, and the peaceful scholars who needed the protection of the Church, there were the worn-out old pirates, scarred and horny-handed, wise only in the craft of fighting and the seas, and such men as Earl Gisur, who only escaped from the reward of their evil deeds by the influence of powerful friends.

Besides the lives that were lost at the burning of Flugumyri, great wealth for Iceland was destroyed in the house, which is thus described: "All the house was much ornamented with carvings; the entrance hall was wainscoted, and the halls and inner rooms were all tapestried; and much plate and jewellery was there, some of which was saved by people who took refuge in the church, a sanctuary always respected." It is evident from many such records that Iceland was a wealthier country in the middle ages than it is now.

Next day Sigrida and I frolicked down the valley on horseback, and through the river to a rock in the centre, where a boiling spring rises and falls about five feet in the air with measured pulsation. Here I hoped to find a convenient foot-bath, but we could not manage it comfortably; one foot was always scalded and the other ice-cold. In the afternoon we pursued our journey northwards, escorted by the Dean, till we reached the Hvitá. Here we spent an hour and a half before we could attract the attention of the farm-people on the other side who undertake to manage the ferry. Vain were our shouts, and the more touching appeal of the catch, "A boat, a boat unto the ferry;" while owing to the clear atmosphere, we could see the farm-people making hay on the hillsides with tantalising unconcern, till at last we succeeded in rousing a man, who brought over a very rickety boat for us, while our ponies swam the heavy current. Gilsbakki parsonage, where we stopped, is finely situated on the edge of the great valley of lava, which here stretches westward by the course of the Hvitá from the central mountain-system. It is black and contorted, but so old

that low willow and birch and blaeberries grow luxuriantly in
the crevices. Erick's Jökull rises near, and a fine range of icy
mountains trends away to the north-east; and the wind blows
fresh from the desert land, on the verge of which stand the
little turf-chapel and adjacent farm-buildings. On each side is
a deep ravine, where foaming torrents, almost unseen in the
clefts, rush down to the Hvitâ. The old priest here, who is a
great character, and his third wife—undistinguishable from his
pretty daughters—bade us welcome. He is a dexterous carver,
and presented me with a very prettily ornamented wooden box
of his own workmanship.

This evening we did an extraordinary thing. We went out
walking to visit some falls four miles off across the lava. As
a rule, no one walks who can ride. There are no roads or dry
paths; and you are pretty sure, wherever you go, to come soon to
a swamp, or a bridgeless stream, or a ravine. We did find streams
this evening, and Sigrida and I had to be carried over them;
but otherwise the walk was delightful—all over lava, which
gives good footing; while it is so *accidenté*, as the French say—
so boiled and contorted into peaks and caverns, as to be most
interesting; beautified, too, by birchwood, saxifrages, rock-cis-
tus, and above all, blaeberries of the largest size in quantities—
plenty to eat in clusters, and plenty to gather for preserves.

We reached at length the edge of Hvitâ, here a rapid moun-
tain-stream foaming down a rocky channel, and we came to
some fine falls where the river dashes between cliffs that almost
meet above it. Once there was a bridge, which ought to be
restored; for the Hvitâ is a formidable and wholly bridgeless
barrier between the north-west and south-west of the country.

Close by there was a more curious fall of clear water, with
no milky glacier tinge; it formed a good-sized river, and had
no course at all, for it just slipped out of the edge of the lava-
cliff and fell into the roaring Hvitâ below. Whence came that
hidden river? The great field of lava hereabouts has, as we
know, in cooling, left huge caverns like bubbles in its solid mass,
such as ice-lined Surtshellir a few miles off. In other caverns

spring-water perhaps accumulates till it is purified from all the glacier sediment, and wanders in hidden ways till it gushes out into the open channel, worn by the great glacier-draining river Hvitá.

The stars were burning brilliantly when we returned, and the Northern Lights flashed across the window of the little room where I passed the night. "A lovely morning," said the pretty girl who brought in my coffee. All smiled upon our start, but this proved to be a rough day's travel.

In the first place, our hostess prepared such an extensive breakfast that we did not get off till eleven o'clock. It was very welcome, for one small soup-tin and a few mouthfuls of bread and ham were all the provisions we had left, and the gun or ammunition had gone wrong; but it detained us too long. I had now to return towards Reykjavik, and I settled to go for a change by the Pass of Ok, which Thorgrimur had never crossed, but where he had no doubt he would find his way. But it was a very long way to Thingvellir, whither we were bound. We had to ride through a rather serious ford over Hvitá. The water was very rapid and icy cold, and it was impossible to keep one's feet out of it. Wet feet matter little when one is safe over on the other side in the drying sunshine. It was worse that my pony, which went in sound, came out dead lame, perhaps struck by some rolling stone in the water. We had already one lame pony, so I had to ride Krokur all the rest of the way.

We crossed a great bog and passed a handsome farm, which was quite turned inside out. All the furniture and rubbish it had contained was out airing in the hot sunshine—a regular bit of summer work for the dwellers in damp turf-houses. We passed some happy lassies, who had a little tent pitched out in the wilds, and ponies near, and who were going to live for a while on the hills, to collect Iceland moss. And then there was the usual solitude. Generally there was no track, as this route was not frequented; but we plodded on, guided by the glacier-hill of Ok, which we kept on our left—a flattened dome of snow reposing on a base of dark igneous rock. The scenery was monotonous, but on so fine a day it had some desolate beauty. Thorgrimur shot in vain at various birds; for his gun hung fire, going off quite as an afterthought, long after the trigger had clicked and the birds had flown. It was pleasant, on the whole, to see the graceful crested plovers wheel away unharmed; but yet I began to feel distinctly hungry, and to remember the meagre fare at Thingvellir, still so many miles away. For it took us six hours to cross the pass, and then we stopped by a solitary lake, Utavatn, and finished the scrap of provisions. The day had now clouded over, and the wonderful weather seemed changing at last.

Some wild ducks disported themselves on the lake before our hungry eyes. Sigrida and I drove them within shot of Thorgrimur. Alas! with the same results; the gun snapped and hung fire, and we lost the plump birds, which dashed off, as it seemed to me, with screams of laughter to the other end of the lake. Happily we were now on the usual track for Thingvellir, as it grew very dark and mists closed around us. When we came to Sandklettervatn, a weird lake which in the summer withdraws to one corner of its wide winter bed, we could not, as formerly, gallop over its sands, owing to our lame ponies. We tied white handkerchiefs on our arms to see each other, and plodded on through the narrow rocky ravine which follows, and up the stony way called Troll-hals or Troll-pass, where we roused the echoes and perhaps chased away the Trolls by singing the German chorale, "Stille Nacht," in three parts. Those, if any, who heard it through the silent darkness might well have thought the.elves were out; for there is nothing better than constant open air and a little starvation for the voice, and my guide and his sister had, besides, excellent voices.

When we reached the lava of Thingvellir it was black night, and the riding grew very difficult. We could not see each other at all, and were guided only by the voice, and the neighing of the wise ponies. Still Krokur picked his way with unerring sagacity over holes and clefts and crevices. But the loose ponies were now so difficult to manage that we agreed to turn off the lava to the right and wait for day, at a farm where the guide said there was no accommodation, except indeed hay; but we were hungry and sleepy enough to long to stop anywhere. It was 11 P.M., and we had been twelve hours on our way.

We stumbled into a *tun*, and rapped at a door which only came up to my shoulder, and at a tiny window in the roof, all in vain for some time; till at last the little door opened, and a crumpled-up old woman appeared holding a dim lamp above her head. Her nose and chin nearly met. Her whole appearance justified the most sinister suspicions as to cleanliness, but yet she bade us welcome with the unvarying patience of the country, and took us into a miserable little room, where a dirty plank before the window formed a table, and of further furniture there was only a dusky trough-like bed. I cooked with the spirit-lamp the last tin of soup—little enough for three hungry people, but wonderfully reviving—and then Sigrida and I begged to be shown to the haystack, for we could not sleep on the musty tumble of old clothes, hats, and rubbish which did duty as a bed. We climbed over a turf-wall and nestled down by the stack under loosened hay; and thinking how pleasant, after all, must be the life of a tramp, I was soon asleep in the fragrant bed. There are drawbacks to tramp-life, however, and I was wakened after some hours by rain falling heavily on my face. Rousing the unwilling Sigrida, we felt our way to an outhouse or two, which proved to be locked; and at last, as the rain was furious, we battered at the door and window of the little house. It took full ten minutes to wake the sound sleepers within. It was past four, and we sat till dawn on the haunted bed in our damp waterproofs, in a justifiable state of alarm as to its population. I tell this as almost my only experience of the squalor and dirt and vermin that loom so large in the journals of some travellers in Iceland.

But here at last is grey rainy dawn. Quick, benevolent witch, with some coffee! saddle the ponies, and let us be off for Thingvellir, even though it be through slashing rain. We left the lame pony behind us and rode thither fast, where I first made a thorough and most necessary toilet, and then joined some other guests at breakfast. One of them, Sigurdr Vigfusson, a brother of the author of the 'Icelandic Reader,' proved to be a delightful companion. He recited old poems and told old tales so well, that the wet day was quite charmed away; and in the evening we played at whist till old Sira Simon, the parson, inexorably turned the men out into the church, while beds were made up in the house for the ladies.

The parsons are all addressed as Sira or Sir, and the Christian name, as in Shakespeare; but every one else, in good Icelandic, is called by the Christian name only, and it sounds racy and friendly.

Some families boast of a long descent, but the pedigrees want the usual requisite of a surname, so they are rather like beads without a string. Vigfus Jonson's son is Sigurdr Vigfusson; his son may be Vigfus Sigurdson; and a woman calls herself her father's daughter: so the surname changes in every generation. But the country is so small that it is said the people contrive not to lose count of their ancestors.

CHAPTER XXI.

THINGVELLIR IN FORMER DAYS — THE TALK OF THE MAIDENS — SOLITUDES—BESSERSTAD—DOGS—KRISUVIK—HOME AGAIN.

NEXT day, Sunday, the weather was again beautiful, and some men rode over to church; but Sira Simon ruled that there were not enough to form a congregation, so there was no service.

All that day I had a general impression that we were still in the eleventh or twelfth century. We wandered over the ancient historical sites under the guidance of Sigurdr Vigfusson, who really gave one the idea that he was an *eptir gangur* (after-walker, or French, *revenant*), so conversant did he seem with the ways and histories of the heroes of the days of old. He pointed out the sites of the booths of all the various districts when they came to the *althing*,—now they are grassy mounds, with stone foundations. He described the battle in the Njal case as though he had been present, and warmed into eloquence as he pointed out the site where his ancestors had stood when they swayed with burning words the hearts of the people. The *althing* was not in old days a representative body; it consisted of all the freemen who cared to attend. And of course the power of an eloquent speaker was much enhanced when there were no constituents to fear behind the members; they might be swayed by what they heard. Eloquence is thrown away upon pledged representatives.

I have visited Thingvellir four times, spending ten days there in all—so charming a place is it in the fine weather we have generally enjoyed there. It was the centre of national life, the spot where the heart of Iceland beat; and though no ancient buildings remain, the strange natural features of the country, after all, form a more unchanging memorial of the time when that life was strong. All the land hereabouts is old lava, split into two tremendous rents about two miles long and ten miles apart from each other—the Allmannagja on the Reykjavik side, and the Hrabnagja or Raven's Rift to the north.

There are numberless splits between, from the great double chasm which isolates the Hill of Laws, to little cracks of a yard long, but often very deep, which occur in all parts of the valley. The place was well chosen for the annual parliament, the meeting where all the national affairs were discussed, the laws made and promulgated, the lawsuits pleaded, and the judgments given. In the ravines there was good shelter for the temporary booths of the people, and there were pretty rock-girt lawns for the different open-air meetings. There was excellent pasture all round for the horses, and plenty of fish in the lake to vary the food. Now all is solitude; but how easy it is for the fancy to people it with the former inhabitants that have left such detailed histories behind them! Let us try to realise the scene as it presented itself to them.

The *althing* has assembled, say about the end of the tenth century; all along the hillsides the stone walls of the booths have been freshly piled up, and their roofs tented over. Beyond the waterfall, where the Great Rift diminishes to a narrow chasm carpeted with velvet grass, the chiefs are deliberating in council. Old men, who have long laid aside their weapons for the fishing-net and sheep-crook, clad in blue *wadmal*, with broad felt hats and long grey beards; young rovers, who are wont to scour the seas, the fair hair bound with a golden fillet, the sword, perhaps a Damascus blade from Constantinople, in a decorated southern baldric; youths, who have not yet seen the world, hanging on the words of their elders or challenging each other to wrestle,— such a throng as that are making up alliances, consulting and promising support in the great discussion that is perhaps coming on, or the lawsuit which is dividing the sympathies of the people.

Down the central meadow wander men and women together; for the ladies have come to watch the debates and the games, and the girls are brought there by their parents, perhaps to meet the youths, for marriages are commonly made up here. There, with gold threads wrought into his fair hair, clad in shining armour and scarlet cloth, walks perhaps Gunnar Halmundsson, his halbert, made of some southern wood inlaid with gold, resting on his shoulder. "Tall of growth, and a strong man; best skilled in arms of all men; handsome of feature and fair-skinned; his nose straight, and a little turned up at the end; blue-eyed, and bright-eyed, and ruddy-cheeked,—the most courteous of men was he, of sturdy frame and strong will, bountiful and gentle, a fast friend, but hard to please in making them." "Bountiful and gentle"—this, be it observed, is the other view of the Norse sea-rover; perhaps on those English shores where he has left grey ashes and desolation behind him, the gracious follower of Thor is differently described. Who walks beside him?—the lovely widow Hallgerda. Thirty-five years old, five years older than Gunnar, and of no such spotless reputation, she is yet of all women the most fascinating, "clad in her red kirtle, and a scarlet cloak trimmed with needlework. Her hair came down to her girdle, and was both fair and full." Choose some other wife Gunnar, or sail away again on the Viking path and forget her. No; he has read his fate already in these lovely "thief's eyes," as her uncle called them: and Gunnar is doomed to fall, after fifteen years of married life, through her means, and for want of her help.

Pass a score or so of years, and we find the great lawsuit about the burning of innocent Njal is on before the *althing*. Skilful advocates are engaged on both sides, not openly for fees —for, curiously enough, it was considered criminal to accept them —but for the sake of justice, and a little to show off skill in the law. Sigurd pointed out to us the very rock where the lawyer Eyolf was sitting when a friend felt through his sleeve the golden bracelet he had received as a retainer, and prophesied so evil a gift would be his death, as indeed it was. The suit about Njal was a glaring case of assault and murder, sworn to by plenty of witnesses, and without a loophole for a mistake in the indictment, which set forth how Flosi "rushed upon Helgi Njalson, and gave him a brain-wound, a body-wound, or a marrow-wound," reiterating the words in the very style of our English legal forms. However, the counsel for the defence has contrived to bring his guilty client off by a quibble. By deftly changing the position of his client towards a certain county court, he has enabled him to plead that the suit has been brought before a wrong court, and that the case therefore must fall to the ground. Kári, the avenger, the sole male survivor of the burning, cannot

Flosi's Leap.

stand that. He and his friends seize their weapons, and all up the Great Rift and to the Hill of Laws the fight rages.

The narrow ridge of the Hill of Laws is an awkward place for fighting, and the spot is pointed out where Flosi, the defendant, when hard pressed, leapt across the chasm to the opposite side. The sketch shows the point where the opposite rocks jut out to

o

within ten feet of each other; and the leap looks sufficiently possible to give some adventurous people a morbid longing to try it.

Here, however, it should be said, that Gudbrandr Vigfusson,
a great authority, considers that it is a mistake which has iden-
tified the ridge between the river-chasms with the ancient Hill
of Laws. There, he considers, stood the fortified booths, described
as being east across the river, and having the Rift on three
sides; and the name of Flosi, who was in his day chief of the

Waterfall in Allmannagja.

Easterlings, who inhabited these booths, has thus become associated with the spot. The real Hill of Laws is to be found, he
believes, on the lower edge of the Great Rift (Allmannagja), and
the people collected below it on the grass, in the space between
the rocks and the river which crosses to the east. He supports
this view by many reasons too long to discuss here. If he should
be right, the accompanying sketch is taken from the edge of the

eighteen.

real Hill of Laws, not far from where the river crosses the long narrow valley.

Let us imagine a quieter scene by this river about a hundred years later. It is not the time of the *althing*, but the two daughters of the rich *bondé* who owns the land here are washing their linen just where the river breaks out of the chasm; and no prettier place could be chosen for lassies to wash and chat. The Sturlunga Saga tells how both were called Thora, and gives their conversation.

" I wonder, sister, how long it will be before any man comes to woo us; and what thinkest thou lies before us ?" said Thora the elder to Thora the younger.

" I think little about it," said the younger Thora, "as I am very well pleased with things as they are."

" True," said the other, "it is honourable enough to be here with father and mother ; but it is not very merry here, or delightful for all that."

" That is certain," said the younger ; "but it is not certain that thou wouldst like any change better."

" Now that may be," said the elder ; "but let us get some fun out of it, and try our powers of prophecy. Tell me what man you would choose should ask you in marriage ; for I do not suppose we shall sit all our days at home unwedded."

" I care not to enter into that," said the other ; "for all that is fated beforehand, and therefore it is of no use to take thought, or chatter at all about it."

" Certainly," said the elder, "it is doomed by fate how I am to be disposed of. And yet I wish all the same that thou wouldst say what thou forebodest may lie before us, or whom thou wouldst choose to marry."

" I counsel," said the younger, "that we let this conversation drop; for, 'away goes the word when it slips from the mouth.'"

" I don't care," said the elder Thora, "though a tale should come of it. But I shall tell thee first whom I would choose, if thou wilt afterwards tell me."

" Thou art the first of us," said the younger, "and shalt speak first, as thou wilt not let this idle talk fall."

"I wish, then," said the elder, "that Jón Sigmundarson should ride thither and ask my hand, and that I should be given to him."

Answered the younger: "Truly thou hast not let him pass who is to thy mind the best match (*i.e.*, for a man—*karl-kostr*) going, because thou sawest it would be hard for me to choose afterwards. But what I wish would happen is a harder thing, and more unlikely. I wish that Jóra, the bishop's daughter, should die, and that Thorwaldr Gizurson should come hither and ask my hand."

"Let us cease this talk," said the elder Thora, "and say nothing about it."

A scrap of the chatter of girls of six hundred years ago, but very like the modern gossip to which the ever-changing but unaltered river still murmurs its accompaniment in the green valley of Thingvellir.

The spring after the talk of the two Thoras, it is told how the very suitors they had named, Thorwaldr Gizurson having lost his wife Jóra, came together to Thingvellir. They both paid the sisters great attention, but which was chosen by each did not appear. The girls, who apparently had the power of choice, agreed to cast a kind of lot about it, as both preferred Thorwaldr —though, again, the younger declared that it mattered little what they did, for all was foreordained. The lot was certainly arranged by the elder Thora in her own favour ; but yet it turned out that the prize fell to the younger, who married Thorwaldr, the man she had chosen in their talk by the river, while Jón fell to the lot of her sister.

Thorwaldr and the younger Thora were the parents of that evil Earl Gisur, who was son-in-law to Snorri Sturlason, and who saw the end of the independence of Iceland. It was such as he who wrecked the land, till at last the country was, by this very Earl Gisur among others, delivered over to Hakon, King of Norway, in 1260.

This Hakon, who was the leading character of the last scene in the history of Independent Iceland—quite one of the moderns— we had formerly associated with a dim antiquity in Scottish history. It was he who was defeated by the Scots at Largs, and who died afterwards at Kirkwall before he could retrieve the disaster, which the Norse authorities consider was much more owing to the storms which wrecked the vessels than to the armies of the Scots. Sturla, the Icelander who was present, gives a graphic account of the last illness of this "savage Norseman" of our historians. "As he lay ill, he required his attendants to read to him Latin books; then, as he grew worse and it troubled him to follow, he asked for Norse books night and day, —first, the 'Lives of the Saints;' then, when they were finished, the lives of the kings his ancestors, from Halfdan the Black. On they read through the long chronicles whenever he was awake, and not engaged in business or Church services. One day his sickness so increased that his voice was gone, and yet he listened while they read the last, 'Sverri's Life;' and near midnight, just as they finished the saga, God called the king out of this world's life, to the great grief of all present, and multitudes who heard the tidings afterwards." "His death was thought the greatest loss in all the Northern lands," says the Sturlunga Saga; but probably this does not include Scotland, which then succeeded in shaking off the yoke of the Northmen.

Though shorn of its importance and honour, the *althing* still met here year after year, even down to the evil days when every liberty had been taken from the unhappy land, whose Danish tyrants seem to have been almost as great a misfortune as the volcanic eruptions and terrible epidemics which reduced Iceland to the lowest extremity about the beginning of the present century. Then only, as if there was no use in any further struggle, the last flicker of the old spirit went out, and the *althing* at Thingvellir was discontinued. Nor has Thingvellir shared in the modern resuscitation of Iceland. It may certainly be more convenient to the people of our day, whom Sir W. Scott would perhaps call, as he did his countrymen, the "dwindled sons of little men," to hold their parliament under cover—the rather, as they now require a session of two months to settle their affairs, which would be a long time for elderly legislators to camp out. So they have built within the last year a good Parliament House in Reykjavik, and Thingvellir is left to its solitude and its memories.

Thingvellir parish boasts of being about the healthiest in the whole record of statistics, the death-rate being at the rate of three and a half per thousand. Of course, as there are not nearly a thousand people in this favoured parish, perhaps not a hundred, the rate may take about a year to amount to half a death. And the clear air, with the feeling of life and vigour it inspires—let us add, the absence of all luxuries and all cares—cause us quite to believe in this salubrity. Then the place is beautiful, with the restrained loveliness of the North, which, if less striking at first, is more lasting and less deceptive than the glow of the further south.

We had now no provisions of our own, but we went out fishing on the lake ; and the way those delicious pink trout were spoiled in the cooking exasperates me still. "Ancor," as Dante says, "il modo m'offende." They were all we had, and they were all parboiled at once, and served cold ; or further flabbily boiled, and flavoured with fetid smoke. The old *prestr* has died since my last visit, and I hear his successor has made much-needed improvements in the arrangements for the numerous visitors to Thingvellir. It is much to be hoped that night quarters should be provided for them elsewhere than in the church. To an Icelander on a journey it comes as a matter of course to spend the night under the church roof if no other is available. He gives as little trouble as possible, and no feeling of disrespect is involved in the custom. It is otherwise as regards a crowd of foreign tourists. Some of them are perhaps delighted to find themselves the heroes and heroines of so wonderful an adventure as sleeping "out of their beds," and turn the whole affair into an inane and indecorous joke, annoying to their hosts, and still more so to their countrymen, who have to entreat that the manners of Great Britain may not be judged by these.[1]

We rode back to Reykjavik after a light breakfast, stopping, a little *out* of the way back, at a hospitable farm called Grof for coffee and cake. And thus ended this enjoyable expedition, just in time, as we had no provisions left, and two ponies were *hors de combat.*

There used to be a wonderful fascination about my solitary rides, whether in the neighbourhood of Reykjavik, or on this journey when I had lost sight of my companions. One could so realise solitude, though I always knew in what direction to find people, and I was never really lost. It was perhaps a little like the old days in Rome, when we were deep in the catacomb of St Calixtus, and used to run down one or two passages away from our party, then blow out our tapers and try to realise what it would be to be lost there, and then the relief of seeing the faint twinkle of a distant light appearing down some branching corridor. Alone in Iceland you are alone indeed, and the homeless undisturbed wilderness gives something of its awful calm to the spirit. It was like listening to noble music, yet perplexed and

---

[1] My fears as to the result of that sort of conduct have been verified. Since writing the above, the following paragraph has appeared in a last September number of the 'Edinburgh Courant' newspaper :—

"The tourists report that inconvenience is experienced from an order issued by the Bishop of Iceland forbidding the use of churches as sleeping-places for travellers. This, in a sparsely-peopled country, where only one guest-chamber could be set apart in the dwellings of the farmers, was a great boon when any considerable number of natives or tourists travelled together, and its withdrawal is much deplored. The cause of this order is not far to seek, in the manner in which some persons conduct themselves in such places, and are not ashamed to put in print. One tourist describes something like deliberate desecration by a party, . . . which has brought matters to a climax and compelled the order ; . . . while there is no doubt the good bishop regrets the necessity put on him by . . . the few, to cause the many to suffer." It is much to be hoped this prohibition will be withdrawn. Tourists will in many places be ill off indeed without the shelter hitherto afforded by the churches ; and I cannot think so bad a case as that referred to, which was also in my mind when I wrote the above paragraph, is likely to occur again. The people alluded to were probably unaware of the degree to which they shocked the feelings of the natives ; and unquestionably even their conduct is more truly described by what I have said above, than attributable to any deliberate bad motive.

difficult to follow. I have always believed in some link between the impressions made by scenery and by music—the one suggests the other. If the Italian landscape is like Mozart, infinitely varied, sometimes grand and sometimes gay, but always above all things lovely, and with an evident loveliness; and if in Switzerland the sublimity and sweetness correspond in art to Beethoven, —then we may take Iceland as the type in nature of the music of the moderns—say Schumann, at his oddest and wildest; smaller in some ways, and more subjective, needing more from the observer, and yet with a suggestive wistful beauty of its own, with something of weird sublimity about it, and also quaint dissonances. It may be that in landscape, as in music, much is now admired of which the beauty is recondite and subtle, a reaction from the vulgarising of more obvious loveliness—such as is in music ground on barrel-organs, or in landscapes daubed on coalboxes. There is a little *wanderlied* by Rheinberger that used often to run in my head from beginning to end, as a perfect accompaniment to the tramp of our ponies over the waste lands. Besides the rhythm, the music suggests something adventurous, mysterious, and with a touch about it of gloom.

Once when riding alone, like one of the knights or ladies in the 'Morte d'Arthur,' "over waste lands and morasses, following no path but such as strange adventure led me," I saw, on the opposite side of a wide cleft or *gil*, a solitary girl on foot. A great torrent was foaming noisily below in the *gil*, deadening all sound except the clear *sæl* (or hail) which she called across the water to me: behind her lay wastes of purple-black lava-rock, rising in jagged points against the eternal snows of a long mountain-range. A lake lay near, reflecting great stones and rushes in its quiet grey water, but all that stirred was the brawling river which rushed between us. I put the solitary girl, to the best of my power, in a framework of Icelandic scenery and its sentiment as it appears to me. And here she is: for whatever errand she was after, she would probably not object to being behymed in any way, so much are the people here still addicted to verse-making upon all occasions.

Suggested, however, while Rubinstein was playing Chopin.

A BALLAD OF THE IDEAL.

"Thou art like those mortals who have picked up in the woods and
carried to their lips some pieces of the reed-pipe thrown away by the god
Pan. Then they enter into the wilderness, follow the course of the streams,
bury themselves in the heart of the mountains, restless and haunted by an
unknown purpose."—*Maurice de Guérin.*

Why do you wander, fair Karin,
   So far upon the hill,
Where waste lands high meet empty sky,
   Where winds have their will?

Why do you bide there, fair Karin?
   'Tis not to tend the sheep;
They love not to go where the shrinking snow
   Gleams in the crannies deep.

'Tis not to watch the herds, Karin;
   They never care to stray
Where the ice clings still to the heart of the hill,
   All through the summer day.

'Tis not for the horses' sake, Karin;
   They glance and gallop back,
Where hills ablaze in former days
   Have burnt the lands black.

'Tis not for the riders' sake, Karin;
   They shun the shore of the lake,
Where the sad wind moans o'er standing stones,
   And the dead men wake,

Who wandered far in their lives, Karin,
   Yet missed the way and the light—
The way they seek, with wailing shriek,
   Night after night.

Leave them the haunted lake, Karin,
   The phantom summer snow,
And the icy spires, and the ancient fires,
   All they have now.

Come to the warm green vale, Karin,
   Come to the merry throng,
Where the burr of the wheel and the dancer's heel
   Beat time to song.

"Ah, leave me lone on the hill, maidens!
   No sorrow has marred my fate;
Yet by those waves, near the place of graves,
   Long I must wait.

" The winds slept high on the crags, maidens,
    The dead slept low in the ground,
When I was aware that all the air
    Broke into glorious sound.

" And was it an angel from heaven above ?
    Or one of the elfin race ?
Did a long lost friend for a moment bend
    From some blissful place ?

" I know not yet ; but this I know,
    That most I love to be
Where the sunbeams glow on the mountain snow,
    Where all came to me.

" There is little joy in the vale, maidens,
    And little rest by the hearth,
When loveliness our life can bless
    Not of the earth.

" But when I come to the lower land,
    I shall have learned a song ;
The vale shall hear, and the end shall be near—
    I need not linger long.

" And when I come to the world again,
    I shall a secret know,
So sweet to tell that it ends all well
    To whisper it and go."

Of all modes of travelling the pleasantest is travelling on horseback. Let those who do not agree with this proposition avoid
Iceland. Even some people who enjoy luxurious riding on good
horses, with good houses to return to, get wearied with the daily
journey on horseback, sometimes with tired horses, and cannot
put up with the chances of weather, the exposure to sun and
shower—the former generally the most trying—and last, not
least, the flies. I have enjoyed riding-tours in the Pyrenees and
Syria, as well as in Iceland, and these remarks apply to them all.
Every one must admire the Pyrenees, which are only less magnificent than the Alps and more romantic. Be it mentioned that
the flies in the forests and the fleas in the inns are awful in
numbers and malevolence, and the traveller has not the resource
of a clean tent.

Iceland and Syria have some points of resemblance; and one can easily imagine that the traveller might admire neither. The scenery is really sometimes very similar, perhaps owing to the volcanic quality in both. As you ride over the steep, yellow, rocky hills near Mar Saba, to the grand view of the mountains of Moab, beyond the bleak flat which edges the northern end of the bright blue Dead Sea, it might be a fine coast-scene in Iceland, and that Dead Sea the head of the fjord. And the dreary stony hills near Damascus recall the ugly views in the interior of the volcanic land in the north like nothing else that I have seen. Camp-life in Syria is doubtless as luxurious as it can be made,—and in Iceland you are reduced to a life of rough contrivances, but it all comes equal. In Syria fevers and poisons lurk about the land, and many of the people who cross your path are thorough robbers: comfort and protection are needed. But here the climate brings health and spirits, and every passer-by is your friend.

On my return to Reykjavik I was invited by Dr and Mrs Tomsen to dine and sleep at Besserstad, eight miles off. Dr Grimur Tomsen has retired from political life to his hay-fields, but still keeps up an interest in courts and camps. He is the delightful host of an old grey stone house, which stands on meadow-land edged by dark lava, close by the sea, commanding a fine view of the mountain promontory which runs out seawards till the blue hills melt in the distance, Snæfell Jökull rising beyond—an aerial peak suspended above the sea-line. Close by the house stands an old Gothic church of dark-grey stone; and within there are some curious knightly monuments of former governors of Iceland.

At Besserstad I was presented with my Icelandic dog Kàri. He was pure white, with the exception of his black cheeks and nose and pricked black ears, which stood up like two sharp points of rock out of a snow-drift. Indeed in snow he became almost invisible. A sweeter nature than Kàri never ran upon four legs: nothing would make him bite or fight; he was friends with the whole world—except, indeed, pigs and donkeys. There are none in Iceland; and he looked upon them with the utmost disgust, and could scarcely be induced to pass them. I never know a dog who understood language so well, or who tried so hard to talk. As these attempts were not always very agreeable, and as he shrieked with delight at the prospect of a game of ball, or a walk into town, &c., there were many words that we tried to conceal by spelling them; but in two or three days Kàri would learn the *alias* of anything that concerned him, and excite himself as before. Of course he learnt plenty of tricks, such as picking pockets at a sign with the utmost delicacy, returning the property afterwards

Kàri

with apologetic grace: he was, in short, the blithest and kindest of companions, evidently inheriting the qualities of many canine generations with intense human fellowships.

The dogs are important creatures in this land of sheep-farming, and, besides the shepherding, they are also of great use in managing and driving the ponies; the well-bred ones are very gentle and intelligent, but shy unless encouraged, and terribly noisy, barking as they run, and shrieking at the smallest hurt. They are small-sized Esquimaux in breed, and when pure bred are very handsome. There are the long-haired and short-haired varieties, but even the latter have fine thick coats. They are mostly black or white, or fawn, in colour: they are very fleet and hardy, and most companionable creatures.

The following day I joined a Scottish lady at Hafnarfjord, who was staying there with her brother for a few weeks, and with Thorgrimur we rode thence to the sulphur-mines now being worked at Krisuvik. Over the wild hills and along the shores of the subsiding lake of Klefjarvatn, and among the architectural-looking crags of basalt above it, our way lay, till we reached the little iron house by the solfatara, where the gentlemen had decked out a table of planks upon barrels in the shade, and cooked up an excellent dinner. All was oddly beautiful; the cinder-mountains round glowed like jasper, the fresh-water lake in the crater-like basin below was as blue as the Dead Sea in Palestine, and like it had a sulphuric flavour, only of the mildest. The yellow sulphur-fumes rolled up into the bluest of skies, the bog below was as intense a green, and the sea-line to the south was all a crystal glitter. The day ended with a glorious sunset, which flooded everything it touched with red and golden light, and I wondered over the variety of the hues of blue and purple that were needed for the intense shadows that broadened and deepened till the night had come, and the stars shone out with the marvellous glitter of the far north in September. We rode back a merry party, to Hafnarfjord, which we reached after dark. A Danish merchant gave me hospitality; and next morning I breakfasted with the kind couple in a pretty room, the windows being gay with roses and carnations, through which showed the blue waters of the fjord. And then we returned to Reykjavik, —Krokur being rather tired at last. He had carried me in four days a hundred and thirty miles, which, even allowing for a day's rest, was hard work for one pony. Riding him was simply a personal increase of power; he never lagged nor pulled nor pranced, went calmly up and down horrible places, by night as by day, and showed really high courage in bad rivers, where some of his companions were scared. I could not bear to leave him behind me; so a few days later, with him and Kàri the dog, I embarked on board the pony steamer, and had a pleasant voyage home after a most enjoyable journey.

CHAPTER XXII.

FARÖES—TO AKUREYREI—STEINSTADR—OVER OXNADAL HEATH—MIK-
LADÆ AND ITS GHOST—SORCERERS—HIDDEN TREASURES—THE
SPECTRE LOVER.

" WHAT is the wondrous form
    Far in the North,
Round her the circling storm
    Whirls the snow forth?
Maiden with veil of snow
Swathed round her icy brow,
All her heart fire below,
    Far in the North.

What is the glorious song,
    Valiant and sweet,
Loved of the loyal throng,
    Reared at her feet?
Maiden with veil of snow,
Why dost thou haunt me so—
Longing thy song to know,
    Valiant and sweet?

Sæmund and Snorri, these
    Seers of the past,
Send down the centuries
    Words that shall last.
Now in the ages grey,
Long themselves passed away,
Still they fire heart and lay—
    Seers of the past.

Iceland, thou island maid
    Loved of my heart,
Fire-gemmed and snow-arrayed,
    Stern as thou art.

Dread as thy beauty's pride,
I fain thy knight would ride,
Sworn thine whate'er betide,
    Loved of my heart."
        —*Imitated from Bjarni Thorarensen.*

So sang Bjarni Thorarensen, and so thought we when, after
a wet spring in Italy, the accounts of the beautiful weather in
the North lured us once more over the sea to the dear old island,
delighted to return together to our playground of four years ago.

The pleasantest way to Iceland is undoubtedly by the Faröe
Islands. We reached them in the early August of 1879 on our
way to Akureyrei on the north coast of Iceland, on this my third
visit to the country. As we approached their grand cliffs, after
two rainy days at sea, the weather cleared up and the sea subsided. Our course lay this time to the east of the main island,
Stromö. We sailed along a narrow stretch of sea bounded on
either side by long mountain-lines, rising in straight precipices
many hundred feet above the white foam at their base. The
most northerly point—Myling—is a perpendicular crag 2500 feet
high. There was no visible trace of habitation, or indeed of life,
except the multitudes of sea-birds whirling and fluttering like
drifting snow across the dark-red rocks. We steered right on to
where the sunset was barred by purple cliffs, which seemed the
end of all things, but a narrow channel opened as we drew near
it, through which the tide was rushing between two huge cliffs,
and we dashed with the tide through this portal of the northern
seas. This passage gave the sense of remoteness to Iceland that
one used to feel in a story when the great gates clanged behind
the exploring hero.

Iceland, which this year enjoyed all the good weather denied
us in the south, was wrapped in a fog-mantle from the cold sea
air outside ; so two days later we were feeling our way along the
east coast through a mist which did not allow us to see the ship's
bows. Suddenly this fog lifted, and showed us the piled trap-rocks
of Mula Syslu, gaunt precipices, almost overhanging the steamer.
They quite differed in appearance from the recent lava-formations

of the south-west, and resembled the coast-mountains of the wilder parts of Norway, only with the ocean breaking on them unchecked by the circle of islands, which makes that coast so dangerous from the outer sea, and so sheltered within the "Skerry-guard."

The weather was splendid when we crossed the Arctic circle and turned westward, well to the north of the mountain-coast, where the deep blues and purples of the lower hills contrasted finely with the delicate tints of the snows above; the solidity and intensity, as well as the purity of the colouring, were delicious. The wide sea-plain gave its own rippling interpretation of the still brighter sky that stretched in endless variations of

cloud-fleck and clear expanse, blue and green and crimson, away to the far north, where the sun shone still, glowing and brilliant. It grew late, but never dark. Night was nowhere, though the colours deepened in hue as they lost in brilliancy. We steered up the Eyjafjord close to the mountains, which generally rose in barren precipices straight out of the sea. But here and there a stream or river flung itself down from the upper snows in a series of shining cascades. And each of the little rivers brought its own softening touches into the wild landscape; for near them grass grew, and the lowly green-turfed farms nestled beside them, and the cows and ponies, and the haymakers descending from the mountain-pastures could be seen. Below, where the river was seen to form a little creek, the boats were moored, by which each of the lonely farms keeps up its communication with the neighbours on the fjord, itself so far withdrawn from the outer busy world of men. This coast gives the principle of the whole settlement of Iceland. It is nothing but a great mountain-desert, inhabited only along the river-sides, and the fjords which so deeply indent the coast into which those rivers run.

We passengers lingered on deck, enchanted with the scenery. The whole voyage of five days had indeed been pleasant, and we were so few in number that the Camoens was like a private yacht, and we had all become very friendly. Among other agreeable people were three young Italian gentlemen who had meant to go from Scotland to Ireland, and had at first misread our steamer's destination. "Iceland, not Ireland; well, why not go to Iceland?" they said, " which perhaps no Italian had visited since Christopher Columbus." They were delighted with the scene before them, making some comparisons to various choice views in Italy, disparaging to the latter, which I shall not note down, as they may have been the effects of a passing enthusiasm.

It was midnight when the anchor-chains rattled down off Akureyrei, a little straggling village far up the narrowing fjord. There were still fantastic effects of light, though, now that August had begun, the sun was for a little while below the horizon. One hill turned blood-red, another was a cold yellow; the moon rose and added her glitter to the rest, but her light did not count for much.

> "The moon was shining sulkily,
>   Because she thought the sun
> Had got no business to be there
>   After the day was done."

Boats put off from the shore, and people arrived; among others, our old friend Thorgrimur Gudmundsen leapt on board. He had come with a party from Reykjavik to meet us, with fourteen

P

ponies; so we two, at least, had our journey arranged. The passengers who had not already made arrangements had many difficulties, but most of them were able to secure the guides and horses required. The next morning we said farewell with some regret to agreeable companions, and the good ship Camoens, and her cheery captain, Robertson. We landed in the ship's boat, splashed by a sudden violent squall, which made us fear lest the long summer we had been told of was flying away on the wings of the wild wind; but happily it fell towards evening.

Akureyrei is certainly not worthy of its lovely situation. It consists of two or three dozen wooden houses, pitch-black outside, dotted irregularly about a black rocky shore; a bit of tramway for coal-carts, some ugly streets, and a good church. Everywhere there is the untidiness and crookedness of out-of-door arrangements in Iceland; even in Scotland and Italy things are rather more "squared up" and trim. But in neither of these countries would we have been likely to find any one like kind Frù Ranveig, who received us in her neat little house,—not for old acquaintance' sake, for we were strangers, but because we were strangers known to some of her friends. A good supper and good beds were provided; and we had a champagne breakfast next day, because it was a birthday, or some such inadequate reason. And then with pride and joy we mustered our ponies. Fourteen sounds many for two ladies, who travel with wonderfully little personal baggage, though of course my small tent, and our wraps and mattresses and some provisions, formed part of our outfit. But each of the four riders had two ponies, and there was a baggage relay; for luxurious travel in Iceland means many ponies and few people. We cantered off in the warm sunshine, a merry cavalcade, we two ladies—with Thorgrimur and his sub. Thorwaldur, a good-looking young fellow with some dash about him, in attendance—away from the little township and the people, out into freedom and mountain spaces. Presently we left the bright sea-coast and turned inland, passing near Modrüvellir, where a solid stone house recalls the former importance of the place, once the dwelling of Gudmundur the Powerful, a great chief who owned the land hereabouts early in the eleventh century. The Ljösvetninga Saga, or history of the men of Lightwater, tells in quaint detail of his doings and those of his descendants.

The only king who ever trod the soil of Iceland till the Danish king's visit, in 1874, was here for some years as the guest of this Gudmundur. He was Raeric, one of the petty kings of Norway, conquered by Olaf the Saint. He was very bold and stirring, so Olaf put out his eyes, but kept him as his cousin, in high honour, about his person. Poor caged blinded eagle! Sometimes, says the saga, he was very sad, and then, again, so merry that he would drink them all under the benches; but always he pondered on his wrongs. Several times he attempted the life of his kinsman Olaf. The last time, as they sat together in church on Ascension-day, the blind king felt Olaf's shoulder, to find out if he wore armour. "You wear gay clothes to-day, kinsman," he said; and when St Olaf explained how he did so in honour of the feast of the Ascension, "I cannot understand much about your white Christ," answered Raeric, and plunged his dagger deep into his cousin's rich mantle-folds, which happily turned the point. Olaf then ordered an Icelander, with whom he had won a most quaint wager, to take Raeric to Greenland, or at least Iceland, which was done; and at last poor Raeric enjoyed much peace there, in Modrüvellir. There is now here a new high school for students in the north, which has lately been established under Mr Jon Hjaltalin, formerly sub-librarian in the Edinburgh Advocates' Library, an accomplished scholar and a good friend to the British, in whose country he has passed many years.

This part of northern Iceland shows no signs of volcanic action; it reminded me of Ross and Sutherland on a larger scale, without heather, but with more grass, and occasional glaciers. Our way led through valleys and over grass—most pleasant riding; so we did what is said to be thirty-five miles easily, and stopped at the farm of Steinstadr, or Stone Stead, so called probably because the hills opposite were crested by rock-pinnacles of the most curious shapes, rising above a glacier. A pyramid, blunted at the top, stood by a slender spire; through the glass we could realise their huge proportions, which made us long to explore the recesses of these extraordinary mountains.

We were expected at the farm, and found both the guest-room and a little bedroom in the roof, reached by a steep ladder, newly washed and still damp. It made one feel rheumatic to look at the moist floors viewed as beds. However, extra washing is such a rare drawback hereabouts, that I risked spreading my War Office valise on the damp wood under the open window, to do honour to the excellent intentions of our hosts. In the morning there rose out of the floor a lovely apparition, the tasselled head of a pretty girl; as she glided upwards a fragrance filled the air, and the tray emerged with the hot reviving coffee.

Peaceful and Arcadian was the Oxna valley through which our way led; cattle and ponies wandered by the little river in fine pasture. We rested in a charming spot where the pastures rise to the foot of the crags which are crested with snows; to the right the mountains sank a little, forming a *col*, which we had to cross. On mounting it we found all was loose shale and rock; only the vivid mosses seemed to flourish, tossed about like bits of green velvet over the black wastes of stone. Having crossed the *col*, we reached, in the afternoon, another pastoral valley, where we had coffee on the grass near a farm, surrounded by the inhabitants, who were greatly interested in our ways. Feminine travellers are rather a rarity; besides, now we were in company with greater rarities still—our fellow-passengers, the young Italian gentlemen who had camped by the farm where we had slept, and ridden with us most of the day. They were high-bred gentlemen, and the inhabitants had never probably seen anything like those slender dark-haired representatives of the graceful old Latin civilisation. They had asked us when we were on board the steamer if there were good hotels in Iceland, and if English or French was generally understood; now they knew a little more. They had hired a tent, and we had helped them to secure the one guide at Akureyrei who knew a little English, which one of the Italians spoke a little also ; and there is nothing like contrast. We had doubted whether these young fellows from the garden of the world would care for the stern barren North ; but they were delighted with everything, and charmed the people wherever they went. Here our routes diverged, as we still kept near the northern coast, and they turned southwards, where they found good sport and much to amuse them, as they told us on the voyage home.

Here their guide's dog deserted them for us, encouraged per- haps by the notice I took of him. Not that the dog was really his,—he was merely a stray one which had joined their party at Akureyrei, and which now devoted himself to me.

Mori ! they may call you *búrakki*—that is, a dog which wanders from farm to farm—or *flakka*, a dog which roves independently ; but allowing that you had a passion for travel, did we not all share it? were you not faithful to us as long as we travelled ? Certainly when our journey was ended our faithful hound dis- appeared, probably joining some later excursion ; for when all travelling was over for the season he returned to Thorgrimur for good. We called him Mori from his brown colour ; doubtless he has many other names. He was of a yellow-brown hue, exactly matching the usual tint of the earth, and the same all over, even to his eyes. He was almost invisible when running by our side, but not the less was he our good genius. He managed the ponies with wonderful intelligence, saving men and horses half the labour of driving. " Mori, thetta " (*i.e.*, Mori, after that one) was all that was now needed generally, instead of the rush of the driver after any one of the ponies which so often wandered east or west of the right way. His yellow eye, his trembling pricked ear, was on them all., He worked harder than any one, dropped asleep coiled under his own bushy tail when we halted, but in the evening became our affectionate companion, and guarded the tent, invariably picking out the best bed for himself. He guided

us home if ever we wandered away on foot, shared all our fortunes, and was our joy.

Evening had fallen when, after forty miles of riding, we reached
the parsonage of Miklabæ, near the Hjerads river, where we put
up our tent, and lingered over our evening coffee listening to
strange stories till far into the night.

It is sometimes said the old beliefs have quite faded away in
modern Iceland, and no doubt the people are shyly afraid lest
foreigners should laugh at them as superstitious; but when
time and place are suitable, such as while riding after dark,
or in a lonely chapel at midnight, one may still hear something of the old folk-lore. Indeed I have been asked by a
clergyman not to encourage the people to tell stories, which
made them afraid to look over their shoulders in the long
winter nights.

There is a gloomy ghost-story connected with Miklabæ which
illustrates one of the darkest of the Northern superstitions. There
is no doubt of the truth of the main outlines of the story, which
came before the magistrates at the time it occurred; but probably the details have been coloured to suit the old belief of the
power of the dead over the living.

Sira Oddur Gislason, a namesake of our modern friend, was
the parish priest here in the year 1781. A girl named Solveig
was in love with him, but he did not return her love, so in
despair she gave herself a fatal wound in the neck, and died
imploring him with her latest breath to let her rest in consecrated ground, and not as a suicide outside the churchyard, and
without a funeral service—in one word, *dysjardr*. She threatened
him that otherwise he should himself never lie in hallowed
ground. Sira Oddur referred the matter to the bishop, who
ordered that she should only have the burial of a suicide; and
now, according to the popular belief, in cases of people who died
for love or were not properly buried, she was likely to "walk."
It was said that Sira Oddur from henceforth never dared to ride
alone after dark—he always required a companion—and told how

Solveig haunted him on lonely roads after nightfall. One afternoon he rode off to his annex chapel some miles away, and when he
was ready to return to Miklabæ he asked a friend to ride with him
that evening to his own *tun* wall: this he did, and there they
parted, Sira Oddur being now within call of his own people.
Those at Miklabæ told how they were roused late that night by
strange noises, knocking, and cries, and sounds as if some one
were climbing on to the house-roof. They were frightened, and
did not at once open the door, and when at last they took heart
and went out, all was silent. They found Sira Oddur's pony by
the *tun* wall, his whip on the grass, his gloves thrust under the
saddle-bow, but from that time to this there has never been a
trace of Sira Oddur, nor the smallest clue to his fate. Of course
there were additions to this so far reliable story, telling how
Solveig appeared to several people, and even bit one in the neck
with the fatal vampire-bite, which was believed to cause death,
and infect the victim with the vampire nature; but these were
the stories of frightened farm-servants.

People "did not lie quiet" or "walked after," according to the
euphemism used in Iceland, not always because they had led evil
lives, but also as the result of certain modes of death, or for want
of proper burial. Revenge was supposed to keep other dead
people stirring who were sometimes vindictive enough to threaten
to haunt an enemy, and then kill themselves to execute the
threat. The body, besides, was supposed to have a kind of life
independent of the soul, which might be quite away in some
good or evil place, even while horrible apparitions of the dead
person were haunting the upper air. It was believed that potent
sorcerers could wake the dead body by infusing the vitality be-
longing to some evil familiar spirit, and send it out to torment
an enemy or terrify the neighbourhood. *Sitja uti ok vekja tröll*—
to sit outside and waken trolls was a recognised work of wizards.
On the other hand, a living man might leave his body in a deep
sleep, while his soul roamed about in possession of the body of
some other creature—such as a wolf, an eagle, or a bear—return-

ing to its proper habitation after a time, wearied with its wanderings in other forms.

Iceland was celebrated for its sorceries and its potent magicians: one round whose name many stories have clustered was Sæmund the Wise, the compiler of the 'Edda.' Two of the more recent wizards were, strangely enough, clergymen: Sira Halfdan Narfason of Skagafjord, in the sixteenth century; and Sira Eirikur Magnusson of Vogsoar, in the south, in the seventeenth century. The wildest tales are told of them both; and they also had the distinction of being virtuous sorcerers, who only used their supernatural powers for good—as, for instance, in this story of an "awakened" body. One night some one knocked at Sira Halfdan's door, and the girl who opened it saw a strange-looking man clad in dripping oilskin, who asked with a stifled voice for the parson. He looked out, and at once knew what he had to deal with,—that this was only a body possessed by the familiar of a rival magician to do him a mischief. He lighted up the inner room in every corner, and then bade the stranger enter, desired him to answer with strong conjurations, and asked, "Where and when were you drowned?" "Yesterday at Grundvik, in the south," said the body. "Did you come here willingly?" "No, by hard compulsion." "Where is your soul?" "I think it is in a good place." "It is time for you to rest," said Sira Halfdan; and the body fell back lifeless as he spoke, and was properly buried by the parson, while he conjured the familiar into something else, and returned it to the sender.

Another popular superstition, which it is not good to recall alone in a church at night, is that on certain festivals a midnight mass is held in the churches attended by all the dead folk buried in the churchyard. Some long-dead parson preaches to them, and the ceremony is called the *kirkjugardrinn risi*—*i.e.*, the rising of the churchyard.

A story is told about such a congregation, which at least is not without a moral for troublesome servants. A priest had an old housekeeper who was greatly plagued by the ill-behaviour

of Gudmundur, one of the farm-servants, and she threatened to
haunt him after her death. She died, and not long afterwards
he perished out on the mountains, but his body was found and
decently interred. However, it did not rest quietly—it was soon
dug up again ; and it became evident that this occurred wherever
it was buried, till at last the bones were gathered in a sack and
laid behind the church-door. Soon after the spectre of Gudmundur appeared to one of the servants, who was a brave girl ; it
entreated her to go to the church at midnight on All-souls' Day,
" there you will see many people, and among them an old woman
with a red hood : say to her, ' Woman with the red hood, forgive
the skeleton that lies behind the church-door.' " So she went to
the church at the time appointed with a companion, and the
windows were all lighted up : that was enough for her friend,
who stayed behind, while the girl looked in at the window and
saw within a shadowy crowd, all unknown to her, and among
the rest an old woman with a red hood. She gave her message,
and the old woman bowed and said " Yes ;" and the bones of
Gudmundur were buried and never disturbed again.

Those who have loved money too well in their lifetime, or
have hidden it away, are said to be restless after death, and
may be seen wearily counting it all night long, chained to the
spot by the effects of former greed.

There are many legends about hidden treasures, remarkable as
associated with so poor a country ; but the legends tell how, first
the Vikings, and then the monks, were wont to bury their money
to hide it from their enemies. Such treasures are guarded sometimes by a haunting spirit, but more often by such magic fire as
Odin cast round the Sleeping Beauty, Brynhild. The saying
goes that at Helga Fell, near Borgarfjord, much treasure might
be found on the site of the old cloister ; but on any attempt to
excavate, magic flames seem to burst out in the neighbouring
church, and the workmen are forced to stop. A few years ago,
however, the local priest caused some Danes to dig among the
old foundations, as he could not persuade any Icelanders to do

so. Nothing remarkable was found, so the Icelanders are satisfied the right spot where the treasure still rests has not been found.

A man told me how, a few years ago, when he was on his way to a farm on the west coast, he and his companions saw from the ridge of a hill they surmounted in the evening twilight, a fire, as they thought, at the farm. It blazed so high that they rode as hard as they could across the intervening valley, in hopes of being in time to give help. But when they crested the next hill, all was dark, and when they reached the farm, no one knew anything of the fire; but one of the household was out fishing, and they heard afterwards how, that very night, he was lost at sea. This corpse-light, or spectral fire foretelling death, was a well-known old Norse belief, as in the case of Roslin Chapel, which blazes with a magic flame

> "When fate is nigh
> The lordly line of high St Clair."

There is still a lingering belief that the spirits of unbaptised children haunt the neighbourhood of their unconsecrated graves, and "to shriek like an out-buried child" has passed into a saying. We stayed in a house in the south which about twenty years ago was much disturbed by some invisible agency, which announced itself to be the ghost of an unchristened and murdered child. It was the house of a magistrate, and a man accused of child-murder was at the time closely confined in one room pending his trial, and this disturbance came with him, and ceased when he was condemned to the galleys, and taken away to Denmark.

The thing took rather the form of spirit-rapping—a superstition hitherto unknown in Iceland. Something rapped on the walls, tossed about the furniture, and talked in the air, asserting that it was a *second* unchristened child, murdered by "Olaf," the criminal in the house. Whatever it was, it annoyed the family not a little, and baffled all the wise men of the district, who made

every investigation they could think of—removing the servants
and the boys, and carefully watching Olaf, who was fettered,
I believe,—at any rate closely confined in his prison. Nothing
was found out, but the disturbance lasted from Christmas 1857
till the end of the May following, when Olaf was removed.

Many local names in Iceland refer to the Trolls or the Elves.
The trolls were the demons of the old mythology, malignant
and gigantic beings, who wandered in the waste places. Some
men were partly of their lineage, and were formidable though
generally rather stupid creatures, called half-trolls. The elves
were soulless elemental spirits, neither good nor bad, but dangerous if provoked, and better spoken of by some periphrasis, as the
good folk or the darlings, than called by their names. They were
fond of music, and loved the brave musicians who would dare to
play to their dancing ; and numberless pretty stories are told of
the poets and songsters, to whom they imparted some of their
gifts. The modern poet Bjarni Thorarensen, early in the present
century, disappeared for three days when he was only three years
old, and is supposed to have been then carried off by the elves,
who gave him the gift of poetry. The saying goes that "the
elves love the fiddle and the angels love the *langspiel*," or Icelandic zither, an instrument which is now seldom to be met with.

Many stories are still current about prophetic dreams and the
warnings of second sight ; and I heard one authentic tale of the
apparition of a person at the point of death from one of the three
men who believed they saw the spectre. But these stories are
not so peculiarly Icelandic in character as to be worth repeating,
so I shall end these few words about the chief popular superstitions with a story which was told us by our former guide,
apropos of the difficulty of pronouncing the word Gudrun, and
which, though it has already been translated, is so characteristic
as to be worth retelling.

There was once a young man who had promised his affianced
bride that he would come to fetch her with him to church for the
midnight service on Christmas Eve. He duly set off on the way,

but he had to ride over a swollen ford, where his horse lost its
footing, and a wave dashed over the rider, carrying with it a
block of ice, which hit him on the back of the neck and gave him
a fatal wound.   The maiden waited long for her lover: at last
in the dark night a horseman came to the door and silently
lifted her behind him on the saddle, and rode with her towards
the church.   On the way he turned round to her and said these
words, after the Norse fashion, in the form of a scrap of verse:—

> " The moon glides and the dead rides;
>   Seest thou the fleck, the wound on my neck,
>   Garoun, Garoun ? "

The maiden's name was Gudrun (or God's wisdom), but spectres
cannot pronounce the holy name, hence the mispronunciation.
The maiden was terrified, but they rode on till they came to the
churchyard lich-gate.   Here the rider drew rein and said—

> " Wait thou here Garoun, Garoun,
>   While I flit Faxi, Faxi,[1]
>   East from the tun."

When Gudrun heard these words she fell to the ground senseless,
but in falling she caught the bell-rope which hung from the
church-bells under the lich-gate, as is usual in Iceland.   The
bells all rang, the spectre vanished, the congregation poured
out of the church.   They recovered her and heard her story, and
searched the river; here they found the body of her lover with
the wound in his neck.   When first I heard this story, I asked if
the horse Faxi was also a spectre; my informant thought not,
and that probably our very old wall-eyed pony was the horse.
" The morals of this story are," he continued, " first, you must
learn thoroughly to pronounce the difficult word Gudrun, or you
may be taken for something evil; secondly, that if even evil
things are not bad enough to ride over *tuns*, far more ought we
to flit all the ponies carefully east or west from churchyard or
tun."

[1] The name of the horse.

Professor Maurer, while attributing to this story an independent origin from that of the German "Leonore" legend, says that it shows how the popular beliefs of the same race are cast in the same moulds while differing so greatly in local colouring and details; and in Iceland the folk-lore is the more remarkable as being still alive,—not yet, as in Germany, obliterated by the crowded uniformity of modern life.

CHAPTER XXIII.

WE camped two nights at Miklabæ, spending the evenings at the parsonage, where building was going on. The houses stand on a grassy hillside, which rises behind into cliffs and a great wedge-shaped mountain. A wide glacier-river, Hjeradsvatn, rolls through the grassy flats below, and on the other side fine mountains enclose the valley, range behind range growing blue in the distance. A good hay crop is already stored and turfed round the parsonage; but the people are still making *out-hay* down in the marshes near the river. Sira Jacob, the parson, is a personable man, with a fine family, chiefly grown up, and is a great horse-fancier. After dinner, in this far land, which some people call uncivilised, we sat by the harmonium while the pastor's son played—and well—from masses, operas, and chorales. The girls and he then sang together in parts, which they read with ease. All had pretty voices, but the young man's was a quite remarkable tenor. He was only twenty, and we thought he might do well to go abroad to cultivate music as a profession, —if, indeed, some of the richness and brightness of his voice would not be lost away from the pure home air. The lad was also handsome, with chiselled features like a cameo, and a tumbling mass of light-brown hair. His sisters were quite pretty,—a touch more of animation and of kindliness to their own good looks would have made them really beautiful. There was a pretty little boy besides, whose voice was like a high clarion. Many Swedish and Icelandic part-songs were given with much effect—Thorgrimur contributing his fine bass—till it was high time for us ladies to nestle down on our cork mattresses,—made fragrant and soft with hay,—in the cosy tent. Sunday dawned cloudless and lovely: we sent off Thorwaldur and the baggage early to announce our late arrival at a friendly farm, and stayed for the church service.

Now the church people come riding in,—some down the mountain-side, many along the slight track called the road; others come up the grassy valley where the land swells in little mounds, as if it were the churchyard of a vast former population. Some men are dashing through the great river, from the next parish. As they collect they break into four groups: the men; the women, who have their own talk; the ponies, who seem also to exchange ideas; and the dogs, which, in a *hunda-thing* or dog-meeting, play, growl, bark, do all but talk to each other—nay, judging by their wise faces, they have no lack of conversation too. The church is crowded; the little altar well vested; the priest wears a handsome cope; but nothing else is ornate. The building is but a shabby barn, and too small for the congregation. The men who sing sit near the altar, in what is the chancel on a small scale. Then comes the mass of the women; the non-singing men sitting generally behind, or even at the windows. I expected good music here, knowing what sweet voices the home house could furnish; but no. There appeared an ancient spectacled *vor sanger*, or precentor, who evidently would brook no new-fangled ways. He led the drawling song as the "many-wintered crow leads the clanging rookery home," and we felt he would lead it to his life's end. If he ever had a voice, it had departed long ago.

A layman begins the service with the Lord's Prayer. Follows a short, "dry" communion office, called the Mass, intoned in plain song, just as in an old parish church in France or Italy; but the gospel for the day is read again, without intoning, from the pulpit before the sermon. The priest disrobes and remains in his black gown and ruff, before entering the pulpit; and after a sort of bidding prayer and the gospel, follows the sermon,—in this case an interesting one, most attentively listened to. The service ends as it began, with the Lord's Prayer, repeated by a layman. Six hymns were sung by the people during the service—that is, by the men in the choir. The women seldom join in, however well they may sing. The theory of the service is that there are three divisions: the priest; the choir, who make the responses; and the congregation, who may join in the hymns. The authorised hymn-book seems to be the representative of Icelandic theology; a short communion office, and the epistles and gospels for the year of the Latin and English Churches are often bound up with it. Litany, canticles, and even creeds seem to have dropped out of their service, but all are found in a metrical form among the hymns, to be used at the discretion of the minister. Some fine airs—German and Swedish chorales, and others said to be genuine Icelandic—are appropriated to different hymns; but the singing in old-fashioned parishes is often appalling. The younger ministers have, however, generally been taught some music by a very musical professor, Mr Svein-bjornsen, who gave all the youth who passed through the college in his time some instruction in the divine art. And such instruction falls on good ground, for the people evidently have the Teutonic ear for harmony, and very often remarkably good voices. Men are beginning to take real interest and pride in the singing; and through it, no doubt, church-going is acquiring a fresh interest. We thought the people liked going to church as a matter of course and use and wont in the country, and do go, through great difficulties; but I cannot say I saw any great signs of that emotional religion of which Henderson speaks. The Church is certainly Erastian, and the people seem to me phlegmatic. In Reykjavik the church is not well attended. There is no dissent, and theological questions have not the important place they hold in Scotland. The most burning one we heard of was who should repair the church at Reykjavik, which was getting ruinous. The people of Reykjavik said all the island should help, as it is called the cathedral, and therefore belongs to all. But all Iceland replied that it was the parish church of Reykjavik (and certainly they have no other), and that the townspeople were bound to repair it. Meanwhile it was not repaired at all, and remains in all the simplicity of dilapidated ugliness. It possesses one treasure only, a font decorated with a beautiful bas-relief by the sculptor Thorwaldsen, who presented it to his fatherland. The other cathedral church of Skalholt, which was unfortunately burnt at the time of the Reformation, must have been a fine building. Even in Iceland its destruction made a sensation, and the saying still runs—

> "I talk for ever, the old wife says,
> I've been a chatterer all my days ;
> But even I stood still in amaze
> When Skalholt Church went up in a blaze."

The people accepted Christianity when reasonably convinced of its superiority, and also of the strength of the "military mission" of St Olaf, but without much enthusiasm, and with a careful proviso that they might be baptised in the hot springs in cold weather. In the same way the Reformation was imposed on the country by the Danes with little but political excitement. The Reformers, indeed, cut off the head of the gallant Bishop, Jón Arason, who, like the old Vikings, said that he greatly preferred to die the death of his patron, St John the Baptist, to a cow-death indoors ; but even he seems to have been more of a political than an ecclesiastical victim.

There is only one bishopric now. Till 1801 there had been two sees, but the Danes at that date economised expenses by destroying one. There are nineteen *profasts* or rural deans, and 171 parishes. All the livings are in the gift of the Crown, practically appointed by the bishop, whose recommendation is necessary and all-powerful. The priests derive their income chiefly from glebe lands annexed to each church ; there are, besides, some small tithes and very small incomes derived from part of the confiscated Church revenues. Some church farms are large and good, and enable the incumbents to live as thriving farmers. The

Q

obvious drawback is, that farming may well absorb the *prestr's* chief energy, and he becomes more occupied about horses, sheep, and cattle, than about his parishioners. Some priests are much helped by a clever wife, son, or manager. Some, it must be owned, are very secular indeed, happy if they do not fall into the national vice of drinking, to which the long cold rides over their large parishes act as an incentive. Then, of course, they lower the standard all round them, for they have a powerful influence for good or for evil. The priest is often the chief local authority in secular matters as well as spiritual; he sees the newspapers, and can tell his people the news of the outer world; he can tell the prices and markets which regulate their business; he understands Danish and Latin; he is sure to have at least a few books; and he is often a learned and accomplished man.

The land is divided into nineteen counties, each county having one dean and one *sysselman* or magistrate, appointed by the Crown. These men are socially in the best position in Iceland, are generally cultivated people, have good houses, and are comfortably well off. Below each *sysselman* are several *hreppstjror* or parish authorities, appointed from among the neighbouring farmers. To our ideas the authorities are too invariably nominees: more freedom of election would give more vigour and spirit to the people. However, the Icelanders are a very law-respecting nation; crime is rare, and what little there is, has generally something to do, directly or indirectly, with brandy. But drunkenness is not so bad as in Norway or Scotland—though it infects people higher in the social scale than is the case with us now, in modern times. Happily the women do not drink, so the men are responsible for almost all the alcohol consumed in the year—viz., something less than two gallons per head per annum for the whole population. But with the exception of a few veteran and known topers, including, alas! some clergymen, it is rarely that a man is drunk on duty; it is at supper that the drinking begins, or when friends start on a journey, or at a wedding or funeral feast. The higher classes now drink French and Spanish wines, as there is direct trade with these countries, which import largely the stock-fish of Iceland. The corn-brandy comes from Denmark ; and for that among other reasons, the more the old Danish trade monopoly is broken up, the better for the island.

The worst point about the drink is that the standard of public opinion is so low on the subject, drinking habits are thought too little of even by the clergy. Much has been done to improve Norway by stringent laws about the sale of liquor, which have been carried by the peasants themselves ; and perhaps in Iceland, too, it will be found advisable to legislate in that direction. It is now not easy for even a respectable stranger to buy spirits in Norway, and rather difficult to get drunk. It can, however, still be managed, and handsomely too, as we once had an opportunity of seeing.

My friend and I one day two years ago drew up our *carrioles* at a hill-station in the wild mountain district that lies between the Storfjord and the Northfjord, the abode of a people whose language still approaches the Icelandic spoken by their stirring forefathers—the *firdi fylki*, fjord people. A fine-looking man reeled across the road to receive us with the remark, " I am drunk."

" So I see," was all that I could answer; and then he explained, rather incoherently, that he and every one else in the district had been all night at a wedding,—indeed we gathered that this was the third day of the feast. Leaving a little girl to unharness and do all the groom's work expected from the Norse lassies, we followed the jovial station-master and his wife, who was sober, to a farm a quarter of a mile off, through meadows crowded with horses of all sorts, and corresponding vehicles. There were various buildings of weather-stained wood, the largest being a great long low room—a barn, perhaps, but probably not unlike the halls of ancient days—with its blackened cross-beams and rows of small windows. Two long narrow tables ran down the hall, their ends almost lost in the dusky shadows ; a short table ran crosswise at the head, as, of old, the place of honour, and of most of the women. At one end of this cross-bench were the bride and bridegroom, decorated, stolid, and abstracted, as if they had sat there for long, and had to sit there still much longer.

Numerous old women, of position, doubtless, sat also on the cross-bench,—black-hooded, like crows, according to the costume of the district.   Far in the Rembrandt-like shadows of the dark-brown interior, a man was standing up singing something very long, to a tune which, as it had no beginning, threatened to have no end.   May Wagner never find it and weave it into an "endless melody:" it recalled his style, and reminded one of his operas. The rest of the company all sat, and a great silence prevailed. No small-talk, no frivolous whispers, took off from the solemnity of the scene, which was picturesque in its way,—for some women were well dressed, and some of the older men wore red caps, which gave a little positive colour to the browns and blacks which prevailed.   Room was made for us next the bride and bridegroom, and we were kindly supplied with food.   Great wooden bowls contained messes strange to our eyes : the guests took their portions on rimless wooden platters ; so things were apt to slip off. There were a few finely-shaped silver spoons, which, as well as the knives, seemed mostly private property.   There was a lull in the eating when we were there ; but drink circulated briskly, quaffed in a curious variety of vessels—teacups, glasses, horns, and even some silver tankards of fine old plate.   And what drink ! I sipped a little to the health of the married pair : it was so strong that it almost choked me, and tasted like something meant to clean furniture.   I am afraid that it is doing the society no injustice to say that none of the men whom we observed looked quite sober,—and many were decidedly tipsy; but no one seemed concerned,—neither the men, who were very civil, but somewhat incapable—nor the women, who, as a matter of course, did their work.

The bride chatted in a friendly way: she wore a great crown of artificial flowers, not becoming to a *sonsy* but weather-beaten face.   When we rose to take leave, and Miss Menzies presented her with a leather *aumônière* she wore, the company shook off their stolid appearance,—they all started up and drank to us with shouts of applause.   There were no *carrioles;* but a woman and a girl harnessed ponies to two tax-carts, and I drove my

friend away in one, they preceding us in the other, and announc-
ing right and left along the road the gift made to the bride.

This might have been a feast of chiefs in the days of the sagas :
all the difference would probably have been that the guests would
have worn richer clothing, and more weapons than the handsome
knife, which is still part of the everyday costume of the Norwegian
peasant.

The women of Scandinavia certainly have the advantage over
the men of being free from three drawbacks to which their lords
are often subject : they do not drink, they do not chew tobacco,
and they do not fidget. Some old dames may indulge in a harm-
less pinch of snuff—and I have seen girls smoking in Norway—
and that is all very well ; but chewing, with its attendant nasti-
ness, is only too prevalent among the men. It shows perhaps
ultra-fastidiousness to notice the habit of fidgeting, that is the
natural result of having to stay indoors in cold weather in chilly
rooms. Of course the more fortunate women have their work to
keep them warm and stirring ; but the men habitually pace up
and down the rooms like polar bears, which no one could object
to ; or some of them go through a serious of home gymnastics,
such as swaying to and fro on their chairs, which sets every
nerve on edge. They often swing their feet continuously when
riding ; this looks ill, but is catching, and certainly keeps the
feet warm. There are some *bondés* and parsons far from neighbours who let themselves drop into idle habits that would not be
tolerated in a society of equals. But they are exceptional, and
would not have been alluded to by me, had I not seen them
mentioned in books as typical Icelanders.

In appearance the Icelander is generally thoroughly intelligent-
looking, whether handsome or the reverse. He often has the
breadth of face and frame characteristic of seafaring people, and
something of the awkward gait of a sailor ashore ; no one on the
island is drilled, except a man here and there who has served in
the Danish army, and in these specimens one can see what fine
men they often are when "set up." At Reykjavik the average
of good looks is not high ; but up the country handsome men and

women are often to be met with of the fair Norse type—regular features, abundant hair, and pure fair complexions with shell-pink tints. The red on the cheeks and chin is apt in after-life to become too vivid from the fierceness of the climate. One day, when we had waded through a bog up to a very dirty little farm, it was startling to see in the dim smoky room a lovely girl, her pretty features and exquisite complexion set off by the loose golden hair, which shone round her like a halo. The smoky neutral tints behind her seemed just what a painter would dash in as background to a study of the head of an angel. I am sorry to say the beautiful young Astrida is now dead—

> " Rose elle a vécu la vie d'une rose
> L'espece d'un matin ; "

so I do not give the address of the dirty background.

The old costume, with its high white helmet and softening veil, is most becoming to the wearer, as we had occasion to observe once at a wedding, where those women who wore it quite cut out the followers of modern fashions. If the ladies of Iceland only knew how much it enhanced their good looks, which they sometimes imperil by wearing southern fashions which can hardly be fresh, they would never leave off wearing it. And yet, perhaps not. Women do not aim so much at beauty and becomingness in dress, as at being like other people ; and the spirit of the age is against national costume everywhere, and in favour of a dull uniformity all the world over.

CHAPTER XXIV.

To return to our travels. We had a merry dinner with the priest and his family, and about four o'clock two of his beautiful ponies were led prancing to the door for me and our guide, and we started off. I kept close to Sira Jacob, as we had to ride the Hjeradsvatn, a formidable glacier-river which had drowned its last man only a month before. Our loose ponies were soon swimming, but guided by the priest, I got through dry-footed on his excellent pony. That was a pony! just a bit of life and fire beneath one, skimming over hummock and rock as if each little foot were winged. All that afternoon we rode through fine mountain country, not volcanic, but noble both in form and colour. We skirted a lonely lake, where we met many people returning from church—mothers, carrying children on their knees as they sat sideways on their saddles; lassies, with tasselled heads, evidently the nucleus of attraction to brown-coated swains, who scrambled their ponies along edges and bad bits to keep alongside of the ladies. Towards evening we descended into a sweet dale, called the black valley, from no apparent reason, and there, to our vexation, beheld our ponies feeding. So our intended hosts for the night would have no warning of our late arrival.

In the valley is a little church and a little house, which we entered, followed by seven queer-looking small inhabitants, who, all in a row, male and female, stared at us with a heavy stare of 7-body power. One shaggy old gentleman, in the genial stage of drink, wants to embrace us all. It is the custom—no personal attention to us—and he succeeds with Thorgrimur. Miss Menzies and I escaped into the meadows till the ponies had rested, and we started again along a narrow path overhanging the Blandá, a milky glacier-river, pretty broad and very swift. Night comes on and finds us still scrambling along by the river, choosing out such path as our instinct, or rather our ponies, select. Two shadows join us—all that we can discern is that they are well mounted—one male, one female. Over the slightly marked track we rattle pretty quickly, now plunging through bits of bog, now running against hollow banks all unseen, and over all sorts of bad places only fit for such ponies as these, till at midnight our roving band strikes a turf-wall. Our little troop is collected and respectably driven to the door of a large farmhouse, where all are asleep but the dogs, who dash out and challenge us. But soon follows a pretty lady in a smart dressing-gown, and a maid behind her. Cordially delighted to receive us benighted wanderers, she serves us with warm milk and biscuits : she makes up two down-beds, and we sink to sleep blissfully in a flower-scented room.

We were most pleasantly entertained here next day—the mistress of the house being an old friend. She spoke scholarly English, and there was a good collection of books. This house, though it had thick turf-walls, had none of the cavernous rounded look within that is almost always seen in the south. The passages and rooms were squarely cut out in the brown turf, which was rich in colour, and really made an effective background to the good-looking folk who lived there.

The house of ~~Bakkastadr~~ stood just under a great hill, which sheltered it to the north, and which was all dotted with sheep. Green meadows swept down to the great Blandá—the river—and beyond many softly tinted hills faded into sky. It was a picture of quiet pastoral beauty, and one had to remember how all this ground was like iron with frost half the year—and how, for a week together, there was black night—not to believe one had found a true Arcadia.

Holtstadr.

Our host and hostess, and others, escorted us on our way, for we needed a guide to show us the ford over the deep river. The milky waves were very cold, and the water was too deep to ride dry-footed. Over this ford rode Halfred, the dangerous poet, 900 years ago, defying Gris, his rival, and flinging a fatal spear across the river. It is a peaceful land now. What more could the young wife want, I thought, who ambled her pony beside us? They may be poor in actual specie, but there are cows, and sheep, and horses, wide lands, and a cosy, well-stocked house; no superiors, perfect social as well as political freedom. Mrs Grundy may hold a humble court at Reykjavik, but up the country that formidable old lady is as weak as Pagan in the 'Pilgrim's Progress.'

We had a picnic dinner on a bank of blaeberries, and feasted on them for dessert; and several part-songs were sung, for there were voices among us of the four registers : and then the bride, with her husband and cousin, rode away—*farvel* they sang, and we pursued our way in the opposite direction. Low clouds had been lying about on the ground all day, though the sky was so clear above, and now we suddenly found ourselves in one of these clouds, deep in a bewildering bright mist. Thinner above, for we were still dimly aware that the sky was blue—it was so thick all round that the companion alongside was a blue shadow, and vanished half-a-dozen paces off in the whiteness. Such mists are not uncommon hereabouts, especially when, as now, a cold air-current from the vast regions of polar ice first touches land that for months had been warmed day and night by the sun of summer. Such a mist I have encountered in fine weather on the High Alps, perhaps from similar causes ; but there is generally, at least, the landmark of the slope of a hill: here there was nothing at all but the circle of ground round the pony's feet, and one moved in oppressive isolation, always seeing an edge or end of everything straight in front. How our guide found his way I cannot tell, but he did unerringly, for suddenly we came up against a wall. Black gables loomed close above our heads, and there was a dim glare as of fire, when a door opened, and out ran, with a merry greeting, Sigrida, my companion of last year. With her appeared an elder sister, Margarita, and her husband, Sira Paul. How pleasant it was to come in from the dim damp clouds outside to warmth and food, and the most cordial welcome from all, including some children! All were delighted to see their brother and uncle, who was hailed with acclamations by the name of Toggi; for it is the fate of people who rejoice in sonorous names like Thorgrimur and Sigrida, to be known to their friends by such abbreviations as Toggi and Sigga. We had a merry evening, caring little for the mist which clung so close to the windows, and left us to imagine the beautiful view over the Hunafloa, of which our hosts told us.

Early the following morning, when I got up to gather mushrooms on the dewy *tun*, this mist was all being folded up and put away; and in truth, it seemed as if the colouring thus revealed was so bright and precious, that it needed being covered at night like silks and velvets. For the first time in Iceland I got my mushrooms cooked by Sigrida, who declined, however, as did the other women, to eat them, though the men all considered them excellent, and declared they would eat them from henceforth, whatever their wives might say. The day was glorious—the glass at 70°—but a crisp air prevented it from being oppressive. We started on our journey, a large party—our host and his wife, with two or three other friends, convoying us on our way. Mori was missing. In his enthusiasm for work he had joined the shepherd in the early morning, and was known to be far away. We sent after him, however, and then cantered down the sunny strath, a sweet combination of grass-valley, with a glittering sea-inlet, narrowing towards the mountains in front. Behind us rose far-away mountains across the great sea-reach of Huna-fjord. But oh, it was hot! and when we plunged into the inlet and rode for half a mile through shallow clear sea, how we envied our ponies! It was quite refreshing to get our feet wet as we splashed through. I have seldom seen a hotter man and horse than here overtook us with Mori on the saddle-bow. And in Iceland you are cast away on a hot day with no chance of a shadow unless you are near rocks. Here is a cool blue shade at last, cast by a good new stone church, the best, perhaps, in the country. Thingeyri, a place much mentioned in the sagas, once the seat of a monastery, lately entirely rebuilt at the cost of one farmer. There are handsome old fittings within—a fine reredos of alabaster and marble, apparently fifteenth-century work, and obviously Italian. Some old family portraits adorn the organ-loft, among them the picture of the man who, in the seventeenth century, had presented the elaborately carved wooden pulpit, still in the church, as well as some older and very good brass ornaments.

The large party canters on till we all take possession of the house of a meek saddler, who hurriedly and anxiously deals out coffee and new milk to us; and I hope our society repaid him, for nothing else did. We were now in the pretty valley of Vatzdale : a succession of low volcanic mounds of former days, but now all a velvet green, diversified the way; while a lake or a river divided us from the parallel mountain-range. We were riding dreamily along in the sleepy afternoon sunshine, when suddenly we saw the people in front at a standstill. They hushed us as we came up, and pointed out, poised in the marsh at a distance, a fine eagle. Thorgrimur, gun in hand, was dis-mounting to creep up within shot. I asked for hat-feathers; and we all kept ourselves and the ponies still in expectation of the fatal shot—when suddenly the eagle walked quietly away ! he had on trousers, too—and was a little boy ! The clear atmosphere, bringing a very distant object apparently near, had deceived us all, but the first movement enlightened us, and just in time. And yet, what did that lonely urchin in that solitude ? Was he *hamrammr*, or skin changeable, like his ancestors ? Could he sweep at will over the hills in eagle-form ? Thorgrimur got no benefit from these classical doubts ; often was he implored to spare the eagles when we sighted small boys. In vain that day the wild ducks and plovers hung on his saddle. He was a sure shot, but so much the worse with that sanguine imagination.

When we had ridden many hours, and the sunset had burned

out, we came to a *bœ*. Hospitality is good, and I did not know
before meeting the mistress of this house that it was possible to
find too much; but she possessed an enthusiasm of hospitality
that surpassed all reasonable limits. Her husband was from
home, but her nine children swarmed all over the little house.
It was old and rotten, and past all cleaning, and they meant to
build another; meanwhile she welcomed us as if they had. We
were seven people, and meant to go further, but she refused to
let us go on. Finally we divided our party, Miss Menzies,
Sigrida, and I remained behind with the baggage-ponies as there
was good pasture, and the others rode on to the next suitable resting-place. I did suggest looking at the room which was offered
us for the night; but no, it was not ready: we were evidently not
expected to pry into mysteries, but to sit quiet in the guest-room,
squeezed between a table, a bed, and an overflowing book-case.
It was dusk when we insisted on seeing our room, now ready,
and stumbled along the dark passage into a dismal den with a
tiny shut window. Two troughs, black with a grimy old age,
contained white *duvets* brimming over their dusky edges. If the
eyes were amazed, the nose was horrified; and the prospect of
a large small population being left behind, although many of the
nine children had been just turned out, was certain. Meanwhile,
in trotted, with an air of being in his own room, a large sheep.
He sniffled at the beds, considering evidently how to get in; and
was delightfully tame, but apparently used to respect, standing
square in the passage, and giving way to no one. He settled the
question for us. We returned to a well-spread supper-table, but
told our hostess that we must go on. Sigrida, indeed, stayed,
in deference to her feelings; for her distress at our not liking
her room was only softened by the ample justice we did to her
supper. Nearly the worst thing was, that we could not simply
ride on by ourselves—we had to take the nine loose ponies, as
we were pretty sure to be dependent on our own wraps for the
night, and food for the morning; and besides, the attendant
squire, who brought them up after supper, had had even a more

jovial supper than we had, and had never calculated on being roused up at ten at night. Though exceedingly civil and anxious to please, he had no ideas, and could not pull a strap tight. However, we rode off in the dim starlight, for there was no moon, ascertaining from Sigrida the name of the farm where her brother meant to stop, and parting with our hostess, who had tears in her eyes at our non-acceptance of her well-meant hospitality. We had not gone far when down fell a pack. After considerable delay in hoisting it up, we went a little further, and down came another. When all this had happened *da capo*, perceiving that the loose ponies were dispersing right and left, after supper, and getting lost in the darkness, we saw it was best for Miss Menzies to stay with the man and fallen packs, while I collected the other ponies before they strayed further, and drove them on. At last I got the group of eight safe in front: there was just light enough to count them, and to be dimly aware of the river, up which I knew the way must be—though, as usual, the track was too slight, and indeed too optional, to be seen ; and it is all like riding across country, happily without fences. It was delightful travelling, as many ladies who are wearied with journeys by steam and in crowds will admit, to be trotting along unknown ground under the wonderful starry sky of these high latitudes, keeping eight loose ponies together in front—quite alone, and uncertain even about distance and destination. At last against the night-sky, dark rounded masses like houses show, and I consider how to dispose of the loose ponies before reaching the *tun ;* for it is a dire offence to drive loose beasts on to the *tun*—either you must leave them without, or tie them head to tail. However, I turned them all into a flat space, where they fell to grazing, and let my pony grope up among the turf-walls which enclose *tun* and churchyard, till we reached a house. A lassie was passing to the byre, and stared at me, stiff with surprise. " Be you blest ; have you guests to-night? " " Come you blessed, we have." " Is one called Thorgrimur ? "

To this she says " Yes," and fetches him out, together with

Miss Menzies had to ride behind the man and lead his pony ; otherwise he would not have advanced a step.

every one else—quite a crowd—to hear my story. But no one,
I am bound to say, thought much of the ram grievance.   "Now,
that was only the home-walker"—*i.e.*, the tame sheep, who often
helps to manage the others—they remark.   However, every one
bustles about ; some to meet Miss Menzies—some to fetch up our
wraps, which are soon shaken down in a large airy church, very
preferable to the ram's room.

CHAPTER XXV.

VATZDALE is a fair valley, and the old Vatzdale Saga tells all about its early history: how the splendid young sea-king Ingmundr, who flourished in Norway in the ninth century, after many wars and wanderings settled with his friends and followers in this grassy solitude. He had often declared, that wherever he wandered, Norway should remain his home; but the motto of the story is,—None can avoid his fate. Three Finnish witches prophesied that in Iceland he should settle finally; and so he did. They even described the spot where he should build his temple. At the farm of Hof you can trace the site still—a wide round hollow; below runs the river where Ingmundr, then called the Old, lost his life. He was treacherously wounded by a scamp to whom he had promised protection, and who quarrelled with his sons at the fishing. But the brave old man told no one, but wrapped his cloak round him, and went home and sat down alone on his high seat. He sent a messenger warning the murderer to fly from the fury of his sons, and not till some hours later did his sons discover he had died there—upright and alone. The saga tells of several generations who lived in these farms, which still bear the old names. The grandson of Ingmundr, Ingolf, was "the handsomest man in all the Northern lands." Here is a song about him, made by a little girl 800 years ago :—

" All the pretty maidens
Wish to dance with Ingolf;
All the grown-up damsels.
Woe's me, I'm too little !
' I too,' said the Carline,
' I will go with Ingolf
While a tooth is left me,
While I've strength to hobble.' "

"An autumn feast was once held at Grimstunga," says the saga of the farm now before us, "and a playing at the ball. Ingolf came to the game, and many men with him from the dale. The weather was fine, and the women sat out and watched the game. Valgerd, Ottar's fair daughter, sat on the hill-slope, and other women with her. Ingolf was in the game, and his ball flew far up and among the girls. Valgerd took the ball and hid it under her cloak, and bade him find it who had cast it. Ingolf came up and found it, and bade the rest go on with the game; but he played no more himself: he sat down by Valgerd, and talked to her all the rest of the day."

Then begins the old true-love story that did not go smoothly. Ingolf flirted with Valgerd without proposing to her, and her father sold his land and went south. More troubles followed : manslayings, and a forced marriage with another man for Valgerd ; for she was at last deserted for newer fancies by the attractive Ingolf, who, though a great champion and a kindly man, was very inconstant in his numerous love-affairs. When dying of a wound he had received in a fight with outlaws, he characteristically desired that he might not be buried in the mound with the rest of his family, but close by the river pathway, that the maidens of Vatzdale might remember him as they passed to and fro.

Valgerd was the sister of the wild youth Halfred, called the troublesome Skald, a far-famed man, the favourite Skald of Olaf Tryggvasson, King of Norway. From Halfred's poems, many of which are still extant, is taken most of the latter part of the history of that chief hero of the North — "Halfred the Skald, wrinkled, and grey, and bald :" Longfellow wrongly describes the warrior, then in the flush of early youth, who never lived to be old, as he died about the age of forty, "never enjoying life

again," after his master King Olaf fell in battle. The saga describes him as "tall, strong, and manly-looking, and somewhat
swarthy, his nose rather ugly, his hair brown, and setting him
off well." He was born in 968, and brought up in this very farm
of Haukagil, where now to-day our tent is pitched, close beside
a little burn which springs in a waterfall down the rocks behind
the house, from the dreary desert above of Grimstungaheide.

The central waste land begins here, and there are no more
habitations for nearly seventy miles. In the frousy farm, on a
book-shelf in the box-bed, I found the Life of Halfred, and sat
reading it in the tent, whose looped-up door opened on a scene
probably unchanged since Halfred saw it eight centuries ago.
There were the hills, pink-tinted in the waning light, the undulating dark-green foreground; the swift river that gave stir to
the landscape; the neighbouring farm, with its pointed gables
and surrounding out-buildings, its sounds of barking dogs and
cattle going homewards—its name, and probably its fashion, the
same as it was in the tenth century. It seemed easy here to
conjure up from the shadows of the past the memory of a man
who, with little to guide him but inborn genius, did good work
in his day.

He had first to leave Iceland on account of an unlucky love-
affair. Kolfina, the fair damsel at Knjuki down the river, a girl
"fond of dress and display," loved him; but her father chose for
her a rich suitor called Griss, a man who had served the Greek
Emperor at Constantinople, but was now "rather elderly, short-
sighted, and blear-eyed." Long-sighted enough, though, to see
when he went a-wooing that some one was there before him,
and kissing Kolfina at the bower-door, too. This was the young
Halfred, who shouts out, "Thou shalt have me for a foe, Griss,
if thou wilt try to make this match;" and who rides off from the
scoldings of the elders with this verse, still preserved—

> " Rage of the heath-dweller, trough-filler, beer-swiller,
>   Count I no more
> Than the old farm-dog's yelp
>   At the farm-door,

R

more than 60

> Howling at parting guest,—who cares for his behest?
> My song shall praise her best,
>   Her I adore."

Halfred is a marked character, poetical and irritable, gay and
unruly—always ready with a song in feast or fray, in battle or
storm at sea.   However uncertain in temper, he was, nevertheless, most constant in his affections.   The fair and wealthy lady he
married, and whose death, it is said, he much lamented, never
drove from his mind the remembrance of Kolfina, his first and
last love.   And though King Olaf succeeded with great difficulty
in converting him to Christianity, he could not break him off a
lingering fidelity to the old gods of Valhalla, whose names, the
king observed, occurred much too often in his verses.   And all
the last years of his life were spent in collecting information
about that well-loved King Olaf, his ideal hero.   Thus he furnished some of the materials for the 'Saga of Olaf Tryggvasson,'
one of the best of Snorri Sturlason's lives of the kings.   In the
compilation called the 'Heimskringla,' this life appears in an
abridged form, some of the most interesting incidents and characteristic touches being left out ; but the unabridged saga was
the one always current in Iceland, as Olaf Tryggvasson was
more highly esteemed there than in Norway, where the popu-
larity of Olaf the Saint, his successor, rather dimmed his fame.

I shall insert here a translation from Snorri Sturlason's 'Saga
of Olaf Tryggvasson' (written *circa* 1230), not from the abridged
edition, which was translated by Laing, but, with permission, from
an extract of that saga given by Vigfusson in the 'Small Icelandic Reader,' Clarendon Press Series.   It gives an account of
the efforts of Halfred to ascertain the fate of King Olaf after he
lost the great sea-fight against Earl Erick Hakonson and the
Swedish king.

"There were always two opinions as to whether King Olaf
survived the battle.   Those men that came out of the battle all
agreed that he had not fallen on board the Serpent ; yet, however that may have been, says Halfred, Olaf Tryggvasson never
came back to the kingdom of Norway.   Halfred says, that though

it would be some alleviation of the sorrow of the friends of Olaf who were most grieved at the loss of such a chieftain, if he were in life, even if he were deprived of kingdom and country; and though intelligent men, who were in the battle, witnessed each what he saw last of Olaf the king, no one could ascertain with full certainty whether the king had survived or not.

"Kolbjorn the Marshal had defended the prow during the day of battle with other forecastle-men. He was accoutred in weapons and clothes exactly in the same way as the king; and he had so attired himself because he thought if that should be needed that now was, to afford some shelter to Olaf the king. And when the slaughter of Olaf's men became at its worst in the forecastle, he went up to the poop to the king. It was not easy to know which was which, because Kolbjorn was one of the tallest and handsomest of men. There was such a hurtling storm of weapons on the quarter-deck, that the shields of Olaf and Kolbjorn were fringed with darts. And as the earl's men pressed up on the quarter-deck, there seemed to them that so bright a light came over the king that they could not look at it; and when the light was gone, they saw nowhere Olaf the king.

"There were many accounts of what had happened.[1] Snorri Sturlason says, that when King Olaf saw that most of his men had fallen, and that Earl Erick and many men rushed aft upon the quarter-deck, Olaf and Kolbjorn the Marshal both leapt overboard, each on his own side; and some of the earl's men were lying out in small boats, and killing those who leaped into the sea. And when the king himself had leaped overboard, those in the boats wished to take him prisoner and bring him to the earl, and he drew his shield over him and dived down. But Kolbjorn the Marshal drew his shield under him to defend himself from the spears that were aimed by those in the boats that lay under the ship, and he fell so into the sea that his shield got under him, and thus he could not dive before he was made prisoner.

"What follows is taken from the words of Kolbjorn the Marshal himself—that when he came up to the poop, and the king was

---

[1] The compiler, who apparently preferred this account.

shooting at Earl Erick, Kolbjorn saw what other men had seen
before, that blood ran from under his sleeve of mail. And a
little after, he thought he saw the flash of the king as he leaped
overboard, in his armour and all the accoutrements he had worn
through the day; and he drew over him his shield when his
enemies tried to take him. And just at that moment Kolbjorn
looked at his antagonists, and saw that so many had come up
upon the Serpent that you might say the ship was full of them.
Kolbjorn said afterwards that a little fright came over him just
then. He turned to that side of the ship where Olaf the king
had been before; and as he did not see the king, he left his shield
behind him, and leaped overboard. And as he came down into
the sea, there was under him a beautiful shield, that he thought
he recognised as the shield the king had borne that day. And
as Kolbjorn came on the shield, he was aware that a man swam
skilfully under the shield; and that man let go the shield when
he felt the weight on it. Next Kolbjorn was taken prisoner, and
dragged up into a boat. They supposed him to be the king.
He was then led before Earl Erick; and when the earl was aware
that it was Kolbjorn, and not the king, he gave Kolbjorn quarter.
And this is the story of Einar Thambarskelfir, that when Earl
Erick charged up from the forecastle to the poop of the Serpent,
Einar saw that drops of blood ran down King Olaf's cheek from
under his helmet. And as Einar wished to find out how the
king would act when the earl should win up to him, there came
on Einar's ear so heavy a blow from a stone that he fell senseless. And when he revived and rose up, he saw nowhere the
king.

"Thus says the Icelander Skuli Thorsteinson, Egil's son, of
Borg, that he saw Olaf the king standing on the quarter-deck of
the Serpent, when he, Skuli, charged aft the ship with Erick the
earl. And he said he stooped down to drag a man's corpse from
before the feet of the earl, and when he raised himself up, the
king had disappeared. And a little later, when the shout of
victory arose, several of the men who fought against Olaf saw
that a man clad in scarlet swam to the Wendish cutter, which it

was believed belonged to the men of Astrid the princess, wife of Earl Sigvald. And these men in the ship came to meet him, and dragged him up into the ship, and they rowed away their hardest. And ever after there was a rumour among the people that these men had carried off King Olaf alive with them, though various men spoke against it. On the whole, Halfred says that to him ⋅ it seemed more likely that the king had not escaped with life because of the great odds against him. . . . Afterwards, when there were rumours of Olaf being in foreign lands, all doubt disappeared in the minds of many that he had escaped. But Halfred was bound to make his record according to what he was told at the time. As he witnesses himself, and laments that he was not there to fight on the side of Olaf the king."

It had been prophesied that the four greatest treasures in Norway should be lost this year. The passing away of King Olaf having been told, the narrator, after giving some more details of the battle, goes on to tell us the fate of the other three most precious things,—Thyri, the queen; Orminn Langa, the king's ship; and Vigi, the king's dog.

"When the slaughter was ended on board Orminn Langa, and the ship was ransacked and rid of the corpses of dead men, Thyri, the queen, was led up from under the hatchways. She was overcome with sorrow, and wept sorely. When Earl Erick saw that, he went to her, and said, with much concern, 'Here there have been heavy tidings in the fall of many noble men. We have wrought much woe,—not to thee alone, queen, but to all the people in Norway, though it falls most near to thee, as was to be expected. Now, though work that is done cannot be undone, yet I would fain atone as much as I can. If I have any power in Norway, I shall give you your rights in the land everywhere to the best of my power, and your honour in all things.'

"The queen answered: 'Your words are spoken with the manliness and kindliness that you have often shown were yours; and willingly would I live if I could, and thank you for your goodwill to me, but so sore a grief has smitten my heart that I have no hope left of prolonging my life.' And it was as she said; she could neither eat nor drink for grief. She asked Bishop Sigurd what was the least allowance of food that was permitted by God to be taken to preserve life (*i.e.*, to avoid the guilt of suicide); and she then tasted what he named as the least possible; and, with these marks of obedience, Queen Thyri died after nine days.

"Earl Erick Hakonson took possession of Orminn Langa, the ship, after the victory, with much ship property in her. The earl manned the vessel afresh carefully with a first-rate crew, and steered it himself. But although the Orminn Langa was strongly manned with gallant fellows, they just brought her as awkwardly as might be from the west into the bay, but she would never trim or answer her helm at all. Then Earl Erick caused Orminn Langa to be broken up. Some men say that he let her be burned.

"Einar Thambarskelfir and other men, to whom Earl Erick had given quarter after the battle, went north to Norway with the earl. Vigi, King Olaf's dog, had lain in the forecastle of Orminn Langa all the day of the battle, and all the time afterwards. But when the earl came east to the bay with the ship, Einar came to where the dog lay before he went ashore, and said, 'Masterless are we two now, Vigi.' At these words the dog sprang up growling, and gave a loud bay, as if his very heart was touched. He ran ashore with Einar, and went up to a mound. There he lay down, and would eat food from no man, although he guarded the food brought him from other dogs, animals, and birds. Tears welled out of his eyes and ran down his cheeks: thus he mourned for his liege lord, and lay there till he died. And so, in piteous wise, the Northmen lost the four most precious things in the country, as the blind yeoman of Mostr had foretold."

Ten years after this battle (A.D. 1014), Halfred, after a life of adventure, lies dying on board a wind-tossed, half-wrecked ship, from an injury received by a falling yard-arm, and chants these lines, which I quote, as I feel sure many will sympathise with this less-known aspect of life on board an ancient Viking ship :—

" Down on my heart and side
Crashes the weather-worn spar ;

> Scarce ever so heavy a wave
> Has swept o'er a boat before.
> Wet am I, wave-washed and worn,
> And shattered at heart and breast;
> And the sea is aboard our craft,
> And nowhere the skald can rest."

He still recurs to his old love away in Iceland, and adds :—

> " The binder of her wimpled brow
> Will shade these lovely eyes, I know,
> With white hands soft and tender.
> The rain-storm flood will have its way
> When she has heard how dead I lay,
> Though once I did offend her.
> When overboard the warriors cast
> Her skald, her love,—of all the past,
> The love she will remember."

So I laid down this story, which afterwards I translated. We have it, probably, just as it was first written, in the reign of our Henry III., before the English language was born, though the old Norse of the narrative is essentially the spoken language of Iceland to this day. It is of real historical value, for the Skalds were not merely like modern poets ; they were the press, they were public opinion, they were the "special correspondents" in wars, and they were the orators, chanting themselves the verses which they were expected to improvise at a moment's notice ; so they represented both the literature and the politics of their day.

264

CHAPTER XXVI.

OVER GRIMSTUNGAHEIDE TO KALMUNSTUNGA—VARMALEIK—
BENIGHTED—MOSSFELL.

THE weather had grown strange, a warm wind blew with violence, and below the clear sky a great black cloud seemed to lie on the southern horizon. " The dust on Grimstungaheide," explained Thorgrimur; after the long drought the wind had raised it, and would make it difficult, if not impossible, to cross. A dust-storm is much dreaded. But fortune, as usual, befriended us : dark clouds gathered, and a short but sharp thunderstorm, with torrents of rain, broke overhead—a most rare occurrence in summer, though the volcanic regions of Iceland are not unfrequently vexed with lightning in winter. Some of the children at the farm had never seen it before, and were terrified. The night fell in drizzling rain, so we were resigned to give up our long journey next day, and were much surprised, if not injured, by being roused early and told the weather would do. Why, was not apparent; and when the mind is made up to rest through a wet day, it is rather trying to start before eight, as we did, in mist and drizzle. However, Thorgrimur was weather-wise as usual; for no sooner had we gained the table-land immediately above the valley than the mists and rain went off, and it proved to be a fine day. The sands too were well watered, firm, and excellent for riding.

We passed near Thorhallstead, the scene of one of the most terrible of ghost-stories; and well in keeping with it is its lonely situation on the edge of the desert land. Thorhall, a farmer there in the eleventh century, could keep no herdsmen for the haunt-ings ; at last he got Glam, a stranger, to take the place, " great of growth, uncouth, his eyes grey and glaring, his hair wolf-grey."[1] He proved to be "a loather of church song, foul-tem-pered, and surly," and on Yule Eve, a strict fast-day, called for meat. The housewife gave some on compulsion, and he "fared out growling and grumbling."

" Now the weather was such that mirk was over all, and the snow-flakes drave down, and great din there was, and still all grew much the worse as the day slipped by. Men heard the shepherd through the early morning, but less as the day wore ; then it took to snowing, and by evening there was a great storm ; then men went to church, and thus time drew on to nightfall, and Glam came not home ; then folk held talk, as to whether search should not be made for him, but because of the snowstorm and pitch-darkness that came to nought.

" Further on, on Yule Day, men fared out to the search, and found the sheep scattered wide about in fens beaten down by the storm, or strayed up into the mountains. Thereafter they came to a great beaten place high up in the valley, and they thought it was as if strong wrestling had gone on there, for all about the stones had been torn up, and the earth withal. Now they looked closely and saw where Glam lay—as blue as Hela, and as great as a neat. Huge loathing took them at the sight of him, and they shuddered in their souls at him, yet they strove to bring him to church, but could only get him as far as a certain gil-edge a little below." They had at last to bury him where he lay ; but he did not lie quiet. He became, as he was killed by a vampire, a hideous vampire himself, and all went from bad to worse for two years, till Grettir the Strong heard of the haunt-ings and resolved to confront the fiend. In vain his friends tried to dissuade him. Grettir says gallantly, " Woe is before one's own door when it is inside one's neighbour's." All Vatzdale was becoming haunted when Grettir rode up to Thorhallstead to

[1] 'Grettir the Strong.' Translated by Magnusson and Morris.

destroy Glam's hideous half life. The way the story is now worked up to a climax is truly thrilling—when the "door cracks" and "Glam stretches in his monstrous head, and then rises high in the roof, lays his arm on the tie-beam, and glares inward over the place." Grettir conquered, but for ever after was afraid in the dark—a terrible doom for a hero. People do not believe in those sort of things now, but they feel them still; and in these solitudes I have met with brave enough folk who were certainly rather like Grettir, afraid in the dark. Some of us have come out on the other side, and wish the dark would only show something the daylight may conceal. Grettir the Strong was an historical character, but his history is decorated by some legends which were a sort of common property in the north. Beowulf, the hero of the Anglo-Saxon poem, has a similar struggle with a vampire; and certainly the author of the Grettir Saga, supposed to be Sturla in the thirteenth century, had read the Saxon Beowulf, or possibly a lost Norse original.

It is a sign of the growing prosperity of Iceland that we rode for the first eight miles along an excellent bridle-road, now in the course of making across this, one of the four ways from the north to the south of the island. There was a river at first, and grass here and there; but all this ceased when we crested the great trackless table-land above. The day, though fine and with occasional sunshine, was not brilliant, and only superlative weather could mitigate the dreariness of the wide prospect. The land trended away slightly downwards in front, but rose again high into the horizon in distant mountain-tops, grey or white with snow, confusedly blended among clouds and mingling with the sky. All the vast space between was a waste of stone, pale sandy browns melting into dim grey, wildly riven and broken, as though the central fires had cracked and crumbled and over-thrown great mountains, and left all in cold ruin. Not a touch of verdure far or near; all was chaotic and disorderly, empty, huge, and desolate. Twenty or thirty miles away some lakes could be seen, glimmering points of light in the greyness; otherwise everything was like everything else. This is called the people's way or highway, but I would defy any one set down here suddenly to pick out any trace of a road. There was no salient feature, and no landmarks but an occasional little cairn, hardly to be distinguished from the natural stone-piles, and these far-off snow-mountains. How these wastes can be crossed in thick or bad weather, I cannot imagine ; but indeed they are then not safe. The whole centre of Iceland is this kind of uninhabited land—stones, or sand, or lava, or glacier ; much of it is actually unexplored to this day. To the west it is crossed by travellers at its narrowest point, 'Holtvordsheide, which we had crossed in 1875. Then comes this Grimstungaheide, next Storisandr, or the Great Sands, and 200 miles to the east Sprengissandr crosses it at its worst and wildest, leaving huge unknown regions between. These tracks are all the conquest man has made of central Iceland. The idea of its extent gives a deeper impressiveness to the wild chaotic landscape, which cannot be better described than by Morris when describing Sigurd's ride in quest of the Valkyr Brynhilda, of whom the legend tells that she dwelt in Iceland :—

" So on we rode to the ' southward,' and huge were the mountains grown,
And the floor of heaven was mingled with that tossing world of stone;
And we rode till the day was forgotten, and the sun was waxen low,
And we tarried not though he perished, and the world grew dark below.
Then we rode a mighty desert, a glimmering place, and wide,
And into a narrow pass, high-walled on either side,
By the blackness of the mountains, and barred aback and in face,
By the empty night of the shadow,—a windless, silent place."

We met no one all day, and saw no living thing except a few swans. No wonder the imagination has conjured up the idea of trolls and half-trolls, and generations of outlaws inhabiting undiscovered valleys among the untrodden hills. The outlaws were once real enough ; and no doubt the terror they caused has never quite died away. Here, in old days, we peaceful travellers might very likely have met some shaggy wild man who was an outlaw in all the land, perhaps with a handsome price on his head, who would, no doubt, expect us to give him food and clothing. It is certainly an improvement that such people are not now turned out loose to take their chance,—though, perhaps, determined sportsmen, who lament the want of big game in Iceland, might have found hunting them most exciting sport, especially as they were generally "many men's bane" before they were killed.

We had ridden thirty miles before we reached the first of the lakes—Arnavatn—the largest of a number, probably fifty or more, that are hereabouts strewn over the map,—called fish-waters, and in olden days the great resort of outlaws and runaways. By this lake Grettir lived, says the story, for two years with another outlaw, a treacherous villain, always watching to betray him; but Grettir discovered his falseness in time, and drowned him in the lake.

Hereabouts a bishop and all his train once perished in the snow. What mattered all these grim tales to us? There was a bank with grass and low shrubs by the lake. Here we nestled while the hungry ponies attacked the grass, and we made splendid tea. We had with us a bottle of cream; and we opened a tinned fowl and ham, and had a picnic, to be marked with a white stone, say a diamond. The air was delicious; the place had a sweetness about it by force of contrast which made us propose camping here, but our guide feared wind was coming again; and after a delicious halt of an hour and a half we rode on again. The country grows more picturesque as you approach the southern volcanic hills. Ericks Jökull rears its crags in isolated gloom from the reddish black of the lava-field; the cold ice above takes an evening glow; other dark or snowy hills light up with sunny reflections long after the sun himself has disappeared behind the purple banks to the west, and many little lakes reflect the yellow sky. We got on the lava at dusk, over which the ponies picked their way daintily; but when we reached grass they strayed on all sides, and needed constant driving. Mori had been twice kicked and was tired out, so he rode on the saddle-bows for the last five miles. At a little after eleven we reached the first habitation, the well-remembered farm of Kalmanstunga, and with some trouble roused the inmates. It is an inn as regards bills, but not as regards the guests being masters of the situation or expected to give orders. We had some coffee, and slept as best we might in various uncomfortable places— mine being my mattress poised on the rounded lid of a chest in an empty but musty room numerously peopled by fleas. We were much more refreshed by a wash in the stream and a walk towards the beautiful Geitlands' Jökull than by the night's rest. Blessings on the pure air and cold water, which make us as good as new again after a ride of more than sixty-five miles the previous day, often over rough ways. We were the first foreign

ladies who had ever crossed Iceland from north to south, as far as is known. I cannot say that we felt tired after breakfast, though this day we only rode six miles to Gilsbakki, where we camped under the lee of the house of our old friend Sira Jon. The dreaded wind had come, and we were glad not to be out on the *heide*, though it was pleasant walking in sheltered places in the ravines and under the sunny banks of picturesque Gilsbakki. Here lived the poet Gunlang Ormstunga (serpent's tongue), whose love for Helga the fair, granddaughter of Egil Skalagrim,

and its unhappy end, is the subject of a charming history of love
and war, which shows the wild Northmen in their tenderest
aspect. Helga married another man, for her family would not
allow her to wait long enough for her own true love. She was
a true wife to an honourable man; but she did not live long.
" One day she was very ill, and sat on the hearth leaning against
her husband's knees. 'Bring me,' she said, 'the cloak which
Gunlang gave me;' then she took it in her arms, looked at it
long, and so died."

The 23d of August dawned sunshiny, as usual, but perceptibly
cooler. We rode off betimes, over ground which I knew already,
skirting the river in search of wild ducks and plovers, of which
Thorgrimur always shot enough this year for us to have plentiful
dinners of game. We camped out at Varmaleik, which is beautifully situated just at the foot of the mountains which edge the
wide marsh-lands of Borgarsyslu. These marshes, clothed with
good grass, are the nurseries of an excellent breed of ponies;
they are the best. of guides through bogs, in after-life, and
deserve implicit trust.

The following day, after a long ride over grass in the sunshine,
we pitched the tent by a burn-side near the mouth of the pretty
Hvalfjord. One porch, as usual, was laced up and pointed to
windward, the other opened on to the sunset over the sea. The
brass hooks on a strap which formed our wardrobe were buckled
to the centre pole; the railway lamp was suspended across. Sigrida, who was skilled in cookery, served the wild ducks with
correct sauce. Miss Menzies and I played a farewell game of
piquet. We often played at piquet, but it became monotonous,
as she always won: occasionally we played chess with Thorgrimur, in which there was also no variety, as he always won very
soon. This was our last night in the tent, which I regretted,
though my companions were apt to be sarcastic about its size
and dryness; still almost everybody admired this tent. To-day,
as I sat at the door, a meditative native, after a long fixed gaze,
remarked to me—

" A pretty tent; do you always live in it ?"

" No ; we have houses at home."

" Ha ! Are you gathering moss ? "

" Oh no ! Quite the contrary, rolling stones," I mentally added. " So ! "—a pause. " Have you anything to sell ? " Could he really take us for tinkers ? " Nothing." " What is the use of it, then ? "

What indeed ? *Cui bono*, is life worth living, even in a patent small marquee-tent ? I would talk no more with that embodied ' Contemporary Review' for fear of being disillusioned.

We were often thought rather a show, and there used to be an evident struggle in our visitors' minds between good manners and curiosity. Once long before, but I did not mention it at the time for fear our visitor might have been some friend's grand-father's third cousin, I found a very old, plain, hairy, and dirty man sitting by Miss Menzies on my own air-cushion, smiling, saying, " Pretty tent," and rocking his body to and fro. They say this trick is an hereditary trait in Iceland, derived from weaving ancestors ; but this seems unlikely, or we should see trades going on in dumb-show everywhere—an awkward sur-vival in the case of recently ennobled tailors and coopers. I satirised my friend's taste in guests, and she burst out indig-nantly, " He is a dreadful old man, so dirty that I can't abide him, and so deaf that he hears nothing ; and I can't get him to stir, and the more I say the more he smiles ; and I dare not leave him here or I know he will finger everything."

I opened a box at the door, feigning great interest in its con-tents, which fetched the old fellow, who came to see what was inside it, and then we got between him and the entrance, and shook everything thoroughly out that he had touched.

To return to our journey. Next day we had arranged to start early, and four ponies had run away—Borgarfjord ponies, now near their native place. This is one of the troubles of travelling here. The ponies, which are turned out to feed themselves after their day's work, graze so much more freely when not hobbled, that we generally allowed all but one or two old sinners of our party to go loose. Now and then there was some delay in finding them, and this day we sat long forlorn on the house-top of the nearest farm, sweeping the country with the field-glass, before the truants were found. So we did not start on our long journey till 1 o'clock. I was riding far in front, and quite alone between the hills and the narrow waters of the Hvalfjord, for I knew my way all about this country, when I came upon the little farm of Hrafnarburg where Ulfshilda Bjarnardotir lived. Here we had camped two stormy nights four years ago, and she knew me at the first glance, and received me with an enthusiasm perhaps partly due to the fact that they had only once had visitors since, partly, I flatter myself, because I could now chat in Icelandic.

This day we passed through a paradise of birds, only disturbed by fishing-eagles. One of them—no boy this time—swept across the fjord, pounced on an eider-duck, and bore it off; but as it was tearing it up, Thorgrimur shot it through the neck, and it fell dead with the half-devoured duck between beak and claw. A noble old bird, a white-tailed sea-eagle, fully six feet across the spread wings; it now ornaments the entrance-hall at home.

The evening had fallen grey and misty, and it was early dark, when Miss Menzies pointedly inquired what o'clock it was; and when, by means of a fusee, we had discovered it was 10 P.M., she remarked that we had breakfasted at 10 that morning. Instantly we all knew that we were furiously hungry, but a halt was not to be thought of: biscuits to put in our pockets, and nibble as we rode, were served out, and we plodded on through the darkness, now turning up the steep track over Eysja, which I had already crossed three times. The men and ponies in front disappeared; next, my own dark pony's ears vanished; and Mori, a moving shadow with a bark, turned now and then to fetch me up. The two riders behind me were also invisible in the darkness, and the mist became rain. All idea of picking the way was gone, and yet we trotted gently forward along blind tracks, which we knew overhung a precipice, trusting all to the ponies' instinct.

Down on the other side of the mountain, where we had now

and then to ford a little river, it grew more and more puzzling. The men had hard work counting the loose ponies, sometimes going after a stray one, and trying to find tracks *out* of the river. At last we were quite lost; we ladies kept the nine loose ponies together while the men quartered round like dogs out shooting, on foot, and feeling for the track with their hands. We got it at last, strange to say, in the thick blackness of the rainy night. Shouting and whistling to each other, and groping cautiously across the rough land, we at last hit upon something square and straight, the turf *tun* wall at Mossfell. ˋI shall think more highly of the powers of horses henceforth, for the darkness was more like that of a dark room than night in the open air. It was one in the morning now; but as usual, sure of a welcome, our guide climbed up to a bedroom window and shouted "salutation and blessing" to some model inhabitants, who, instead of saying the reverse to him, got up and dressed, we meanwhile unsaddling and standing helplessly by our ponies in the rain, which poured off our hats and waterproofs in torrents. A lantern at last glimmers through the wet atmosphere, and a man and a girl appear with refreshments. Our men carry the boxes into the chapel, and then subside. Thorwaldur is snoring in one pew, his face on his arms. Thorgrimur, who, besides all the rest, has carried a gun instead of a whip during our twelve hours' journey, lies on his back in another pew, and is asleep in a moment. I have still energy enough to cook soup, and to serve it out in hot platefuls with biscuits to my companions. That, and a little hot milk, are dinner and supper both, for no one has spirit enough to cook the game; and then Miss Menzies and I are left by the rest to our slumbers. Sigrida leaves the church last, lured by the promise of a down-bed in the house. We hear her stumbling nervously over the graves, and at last imploring me in her pathetic soprano to show a light from the church-door, as she cannot find the gate. Sigrida is not so brave in a churchyard at night as in other places, and is alarmed at missing the entrance of this old burial-place, where the mighty Egil has reposed now for nearly 900 years, and all the generations of Mossfell since. When at last she suc-

S

ceeded in groping up to the house, she found her brother had got into the guest-room before her, had just succeeded in getting his boots off, and had fallen sound asleep on the promised down-bed. However, her shake-down on the floor, and our cork pallets, were quite luxurious enough to insure a good night's rest to such tired travellers.

Rain next morning. We were so spoilt by continual fine weather that we felt quite unhinged. We crossed to the parson-age-house to breakfast with the young priest and his wife—the bride who had received me here the previous year. Here, at Mossfell, lived during his latter days,

> "After a great life, with eyes waxing dim,
> Egil, the mighty son of Skallagrim."

His last recorded action has suggested some possibilities that have made many a passer-by glance curiously at the neighbouring stream's bed and waterfall. The old man had two chests of silver money given him by our English king Athelstan. To these he clung with a grasping greed which grudged them to his heirs. When his son-in-law and daughter, the master and mistress of the house, were absent at the *althing*, he mounted his horse for the last time, and, blind as he was, accompanied by two thralls, he set off with his chests of silver. He returned with neither thralls nor silver, and took to his bed from that day. No trace of the men or money was ever found: some thought the thralls escaped with the silver, but it was hardly likely that could remain hid. The old heathen hinted that he had employed them to hide his treasure, and then slain them ; and spoke mysteriously of hiding-places in the bog and the waterfall. Near the latter some silver coins of Athelstan have, they say, been found. There is a chance for seekers after hid treasure! Seriously, Iceland is not half enough excavated. I feel sure examination of some of the mounds and older homesteads might well reward the antiquary. Strong oaken and metal chests can still be seen in some houses—one of those might be found underground, and con-tain who knows what—perhaps a MS. of a lost saga. The rain soon cleared off, and we rode in four hours to Reykjavik, which bewildered us by its crowd and bustle. All things are comparative, and we had been in great solitudes; but there was really the unprecedented number of some twenty-five English tourists waiting for the steamer. So after two days spent with our Reykjavik friends, we started again for the east, to utilise the interval before the steamer should arrive.

Reykjavik is, indeed, less Icelandic than any other part of the country; there is a strong Danish element, and more class distinction. There you may see the amphibious-looking people common to most ports, haunting the shore with the awkward look of seals on land; sometimes put down in the eager traveller's notebook as typical Icelanders, which is rather as if we should be judged by the loafers on the pier at Oban or the Broomielaw. They say men in cities tend to become wolves; and there is a distinct species which follows the tourist crowd as the dog-fish follows the mackerel. This wolf rages in Switzerland, it haunts our Highlands, and is not unknown in the seaports of Norway, though it has not yet penetrated far inland. Reykjavik is not a city, and I do not think it yet possesses a developed wolf; but there is a prick of an ear, a gleam of a fang, just appearing now, which hints of what may yet be when tourists come to be regarded as mere prey, and not as honoured guests. Something of the sort is inevitable; yet I believe that a strong nature and good education will still keep the genuine Icelanders independent, and generous, and fair.

CHAPTER XXVII.

EXCURSION TO REYKJADAL AND EYRABAKKI.

THE way to the half-way hut on the road to Eyrabakki is much improved; a capital raised path leads over the rough land, soft, yet firm, and perfect for riding. It ends in a circular valley, evidently the subsided crater of some old volcano. There is grass below, but the hills which rise on every side are of dark shingle, scathed and ashen—indeed the whole range is a reminder of ancient fires.

In the middle of the valley stands a little hut of two rooms and a loft. It passes for an inn, and owes its distinction to being many miles from any other house. It is inhabited by a family whose *forte* is not innkeeping, but silversmithing; and it is further and thickly inhabited by others not in the census. Here we partook of some doubtful coffee, sitting on the table with our feet on the bench to avoid touching the floor; and we also purchased some tasteful modern silver-work, just finished by the landlord. Beyond the hut we turned to the left up a picturesque hillside, issuing on a high table-land, paved with enormous slabs tilted at various angles, as if a giant's hall pavement had been broken up by an earthquake. The day was beautiful, and so was the view over the crest of the high land (called Hellisheida). We sighted the wide plain below, sea-edged, bounded in front by the distant, majestic Eyjafjal Jökull, its snows tinged with evening red; round from it swept the blue hill-range Thrihydnynja, Hecla, and others, till they joined the range on which we were, the nearest being Ingolf's fjall, where Ingolf, the earliest Norse settler was buried. The Niebelungen story tells that the fire-prison of Brynhild was in Iceland; and the scenery here suggests the wild tramp of Wagner's "Ride of the Valkyrs," and the rocky desert where the armed maiden was left [1] to sleep till the coming of the hero. Then we descended into Reykjadal—an uncommon sort of valley, as well as we could make out in the bewildering moonlight. Hot springs smoked about, and some of the ponies got into literal hot water, to their great irritation; there was also a cold stream, which we rode in to avoid the formidable bog, which at last we had to cross. Our destination, Arnabæli, a mound above the marshes, seemed close by, rising dark against the light sky long before we reached it after nine o'clock. A good house with a church near the broad silvery Olfus river, where we were kindly received by the family of Sira Isleif Gislason, who last year had received me at his former parish of Kirkjubae. After supper we adjourned to the moonlit church, where there was an excellent harmonium, on which Miss Menzies performed till far into the night, to the great delight of the family. Many harmoniums have been imported since my first visit to the country, and considering the difficulty of transport, their presence testifies to a great love for music. We saw one at Reykjavik that had been constructed by an Icelander, with no knowledge of the trade except what could be acquired by examining the instruments imported. We stayed next with our kind friends at Litla-hrauni, Thorgrimur's parents, who had invited us to revisit them. This flat land between the rivers Olfusá and Hvitá is called the Floa ; and a most romantic early history—the Floamanna Saga—exists, telling us of its heroes, and especially of the Greenland discovery voyages which

---

[1] Since this was in the press, we have seen with some indignation how Wagner, in his "Niebelungen Ring" Operas, has infused a passionate, immoral element, not found in the original, into the old Norse fable of the "Curse of the Gold." The giants appear also in these queer operas as if they were injured beings outwitted by the craft of the Asa, instead of merely personified natural forces, especially bad weather, which it is the object of all the useful arts to subdue or circumvent.

set out from its port. It is a cheerful place in fine weather, with the distant mountain-barrier circling the district north, east, and west, and the sea glittering to the south; but in bad weather wonderfully dreary, when the hills are all lost in mist, and a foaming broad line of surf breaks upon the low black lava-rocks and wind-tormented sand-dunes and grasses. So it was on Sunday, when from the church-windows we saw how the sea flashed under the wind, which moaned and shrieked over the flats, and strewed the graves with sea-weed and tangle—the graves where yarrow grew so strong and thick that they seemed beds of white flowers. There were twenty-five new graves this season, a large number of deaths for the population: this exceptionally dry season has not been a healthy one.

We returned to Reykjavik on a wild day of September, and found the Olfus river in a great commotion. From the ferry farm came a man and a powerful lass, and the boat was shoved down into the water. The rain increased, and a wild squall lashed up a yellow foam all over the river. A seal came up, and gazed at us fixedly as if he were the demon of the storm, and was watching to prevent our passage. Thorgrimur carried us into the boat when it was afloat, and there we sat in the lashing rain with our feet in the water. Meanwhile the seven ponies, which were thoroughly and naturally disinclined to encounter the wind, rain, and waves in their faces swimming, were all roped round the head, Thorgrimur hauling four ropes, the strong lass three: they took their seats at the stern, and tried to lug the ponies in, while two men rowed. We got under way; but when the ponies came to deep water, they all backed and fought till they dragged us fairly aground,—one old grey, the ringleader, rearing in the water and splashing us from head to foot, as though everything were not wet enough already. They tangled their ropes and got mixed up, so that we could not tell which heads owned which legs; two got under the boat, while the wind blew and the foam flew fiercer and fiercer in our teeth; and all the while the seal looked on. He was more than canny, like the seal, who was a *fetch*, that swam round Thorkel's spell-sunk ship in Laxdale. At last, by aid of my hunting-whip, the ponies were started, and away we went, hauling the seven heads with rolling eyeballs and snorting nostrils behind us. When more than midway, we cast most of them loose to find their own way over. The seal, or whatever ruled the squall, had now done its worst, for on the other side the weather moderated; a little later, as we rose up the mountain-side, off rolled the clouds and the waterproofs, out came the sunshine and dried and warmed us, and made the hill-pass beautiful.

Iceland was looking its best on the day fixed for our departure, making us almost long to miss the steamer as we rode home from breakfasting with the Tomsens at Besserstad. The brown land with such dreary possibilities about it, now varied from topaz-hues in the sunshine, through clear umbers and red madders, to the intense purple-black of the fantastic lava, which, again, was decked with white and yellow lichens like gold and silver embroidery. So the sun works as goldsmith and decorator on the rough material of the barren North, for he has his will in that clear pure air. All too soon we sailed out of the calm atmosphere and blue sea into the grey water and cloudy south-easterly weather, fated to endure a rough passage of six days.

And next morning, from the steamer, we watched the wild grey sea fretted into foam, under a dark-grey sky—only far to the north a low line of bright green sky was still to be seen, and beneath it glittered points of intense light,—it was something like a jewelled necklace hung on a dark curtain; and it was our last sight of Iceland, and her mountain-peaks, and clear autumnal sky.

In this little story of our summer wanderings I have tried to say, like Herjolfr, the fair witness in 'Landnama,' "the whole truth, good and bad, about the land," but only so far as I saw it myself, or had good opportunities of forming an opinion. So there is not much said about geology, of which I know too little for my observations to be of value. For the same reason I have avoided the subject of the deep-sea fishing—a matter of great importance to the inhabitants. The newspapers are full of it. A cod is stamped on the current coin, and formerly three codfish figured on a most unwarlike ensign.

But the historical and romantic aspect of the country, which is chiefly dwelt on here, is well symbolised by the other national flag, which bears a white Icelandic falcon on a blue field—the princely bird which was almost priceless in former days, and is itself a type of the trained power, mettle, and energy of the "hardy Norsemen."

In some sort we may look upon ourselves as their representatives in the modern world; we have inherited, with a strain of their race, their spirit of enterprise and their love of the sea. Everything relating to them has therefore a special interest for us; and when we inquire into their history we find that Iceland holds the key to the knowledge we desire to gain. As her natural features are unique, so her place in the eyes of students of the past and lovers of romance is exceptional and full of significance. And my hope is that these sketches of travel, though they only aim at bringing the aspect of the country and the life of the people before the eyes of my readers, may help them to realise the causes which give to this lonely island of the North her peculiar attractiveness and charm.

INDEX.

Agriculture, 111   Gudmundur Dyrafiord Saga, 89

ERRATA.

Page 57, line 8, *for* " Mattias Jochmundsen " *read* " Matthias Jochumsson."

  " 117, line 11, *for* " 230 " *read* " 2300."

  " 146, line 24, *for* " Huni " *read* " Hruni."

  " 157, line 9, *for* " molten metallic substances " *read* " molten lavas."

Eruptions, Geysir, 25, 144.
Eyrabakki, 176, 277.

Faröe Islands, 5, 223.
Fishing, 291.
Floamanna Saga, 40, 277.
Fullisá, 165.
Funeral, 32.

Geysir, 23, 143.
Gilsbakki, 75, 200, 269.
Gisli Surson's Saga, 40, 88.
Grettir the Strong, 40, 264.
Grimstunga, 264.

Landnamabok, 41.
Land tenure, udal, 35.
Language, 1, 56, 119.
Laxdale Saga, 39, 96.
Literature, early, 36.
—— modern, 55.

Magistrates, 242.
Markarfljot, 158, 170.
Miklabæ, 230.
Mossfell, 59, 273.

New craters, 151.
Njal Saga, 138, 153, 155, 172, 208.

importance to the inhabitants. The newspapers are full of it. A cod is stamped on the current coin, and formerly three codfish figured on a most unwarlike ensign.

But the historical and romantic aspect of the country, which is chiefly dwelt on here, is well symbolised by the other national flag, which bears a white Icelandic falcon on a blue field—the princely bird which was almost priceless in former days, and is itself a type of the trained power, mettle, and energy of the "hardy Norsemen."

In some sort we may look upon ourselves as their representatives in the modern world; we have inherited, with a strain of

INDEX.

Agriculture, 111.
Akureyrei, 225.
Althing, ancient, 207.
—— modern, 109.
And the Wealthy, 44, 96.
Aurora Borealis, 127, 134.

Besserstad, 219.
Bishops, Gudmundur, 53.
—— and priests, 241.
Blandá, 248.
Boiling bogs, 131.
Borg, 183.
Breidafjord, 88.

Celtic element in literature, 45.
Church service, 154, 239.

Danish government, 106.
Dogs, 219, 229.
Drink, 242.

Edda, 47.
Education, 120.
Egil's Saga, 39, 80, 181, 185, 274.
Eruptions, Geysir, 25, 144.
Eyrabakki, 176, 277.

Faröe Islands, 5, 223.
Fishing, 291.
Floamanna Saga, 40, 277.
Fullisá, 165.
Funeral, 32.

Geysir, 23, 143.
Gilsbakki, 75, 200, 269.
Gisli Surson's Saga, 40, 88.
Grettir the Strong, 40, 264.
Grimstunga, 264.

Gudmundur Dyrafjord Saga, 89.
—— the Powerful, 227.
Gunlang Saga, 269.
Gunnar Halmundson, 153, 155, 158, 208.

Hakon, king, 212.
Halfred the Skald, 249, 256, 262.
Hardar Saga, 64.
Hecla, 149, 276.
Hints to travellers, 135.
Holtvördsheide, 85.
Housekeeping, 114.
Hrutafjord, 87.
Hunafjord, 252.
Hvalfjord, 60, 179, 270.
Hvammfjord, 96.
Hvitá, Eastern, 145.
—— Western, 81, 102, 200, 202.

Kari Solmundson, 9, 172, 209.
Kirkuvogr, 129.
Krisuvik, 122.
Kvenna-brekka pass, 99.

Landnámabók, 41.
Land tenure, udal, 35.
Language, 1, 56, 119.
Laxdale Saga, 39, 96.
Literature, early, 36.
—— modern, 55.

Magistrates, 242.
Markarfljot, 158, 170.
Miklabæ, 230.
Mossfell, 59, 273.

New craters, 151.
Njal Saga, 138, 153, 155, 172, 208.

Nordtunga, 76.
Nuperkot, 163, 168.

Oddé, 175.
Olfusvatn, 177, 278.

Ponies, 16, 136.

Rennyvellir, 32, 179.
Reykholt, 67, 198.
Reykjadal, 277.
Reykjanes, 10, 131.
Reykjavik, aspect, 11.
—— hospitalities, 114.
—— tourists at, 275.

Sagas, 38.
—— women of, 49.
—— morality of, 38, 50.

Sea-fight, King Olaf's last, 258.
Skalds, 37, 263.
Snorri Sturlason, 48, 69, 198.
Society, 116.
Sorcerers, 66, 231.
Sulphur-mines, 124, 221.

Thingvellir, 22, 29, 103, 206.
Thjorsà, 147, 176.
Thorsmark, 160.

Ulfljotsvatn, 140.

Vampires, 65, 98, 231, 265.
Vatzdale Saga, 40, 255.
—— valley, 251.
Volcanoes, 117, 149.

Westmann Islands, 10, 172.

THE END.

PRINTED BY WILLIAM BLACKWOOD AND SONS.

WILLIAM BLACKWOOD & SONS'

NEW LIST.

DICK'S WANDERING. By JULIAN STURGIS, Author of
'Little Comedies,' 'An Accomplished Gentleman,' 'John-a-Dreams.'
3 vols. post 8vo, 25s. 6d.

"Mr Sturgis has kept us interested and amused, and has constantly awakened a
sweet smile by his descriptions of people and the casual good things which fall from
his pen."—*Saturday Review.*
"A novel of genuine humour, power, and interest."—*Daily Telegraph.*

TRAITS AND TRAVESTIES; SOCIAL AND POLITICAL. By
LAURENCE OLIPHANT, Author of 'Piccadilly,' 'The Land of Khemi,'
'The Land of Gilead,' &c. Post 8vo, 10s. 6d.

"He has the gift, not common in this country, of the *esprit Gaulois;* he aims his
strokes at follies and abuses without any semblance of effort. His wit is at once keen
and light-hearted......Not only, however, are Mr Oliphant's stories new and delightful, but the turn of thought which they suggest, and which he follows up without in
the least riding it to death, is specially unexpected and humorous."—*Saturday Review.*

TRASEADEN HALL. "WHEN GEORGE THE THIRD WAS
KING." By MAJOR-GENERAL W. G. HAMLEY, Author of 'Guilty or
not Guilty,' 'The House of Lys.' 3 vols. post 8vo, 25s. 6d.

"An admirable novel. There is spirit in the style and culture in the matter; the
themes are as fresh as the thoughts are bright......We may repeat that we have rarely
met with a book by a veteran writer so full of freshness and unflagging animation; it
is much more than a mere novel of the season, and it deserves a place on the book-
shelves among standard fiction."—*Saturday Review.*

"'Traseaden Hall' is in all respects an admirable novel—it is animated and humorous, soldierly and scholarly."—*The Times.*

"'Traseaden Hall' is the best novel General Hamley has written, and is one of the
best novels of the time."—*Academy.*

NEW AND CHEAPER EDITION.

A LADY'S CRUISE IN A FRENCH MAN-OF-WAR.
By C. F. GORDON CUMMING, Author of 'At Home in Fiji,' &c.
Complete in One Vol., post 8vo, with Map and numerous Illustrations.
12s. 6d.

"Told with spirit and liveliness, interspersed with fascinating descriptions of gor-
geous scenery."—*Spectator.*

"We are transported, by a series of vivid pictures of easy lives and glorious scenery,
to the clustering islands of the Southern Pacific......The brightness that made Miss
Gordon Cumming a universally welcome guest is reflected in every one of her chapters;
and her style is as fresh and clear as it is simple and unaffected."—*Saturday Review.*

"Another delightful book."—*Athenæum.*

"It reads more like a romance than a plain true tale......The whole book is not only
interesting and instructive, but, at the same time, most delightful reading."—*Illus-
trated London News.*

"'A Lady's Cruise' is one of those books that is not only readable, but highly instructive. It is historic, romantic, artistic, picturesque, and fascinating."—*Christian Union.*

www.ingramcontent.com/pod-product-compliance
Lightning Source LLC
Chambersburg PA
CBHW021037030726
47496CB00006B/1575